# THE DIVINE AFFLICTION

# ALSO BY ROBERT M. FLEISHER

# THE DIVINE AFFLICTION

## ROBERT M. FLEISHER

PRIMARY PRESS

First published by Black Rose Writing 2018
First Primary Press edition 2024



PUBLISHED BY PRIMARY PRESS
a division of Primary Productions LLC
www.primary-productions.com
New York, New York

Library of Congress Control Number: 2024950520
ISBN: 978-0-9828441-9-9

Second edition, November 2024
Printed in the U.S.A.

*I offer a special thank you to my family and friends for sharing their good hearts with me during our time on earth. The love, strength and wisdom derived from our times together are the meaning of life, which we all seek but often have difficulty finding.*

*A special thank you to my loving son Andrew for all of his guidance and inspiration and for showing me what it means to be a talented writer. To my amazing daughter Alison and her husband Marc for giving me grandchildren and unconditional love. For my sister Barbara and her husband Marvin who've read each of my manuscripts prior to publication. For my brother Steven whose adventure offers great story ideas and his wife Sue who always does a fine first edit. To the loves of my life who have sustained my body and mind and spirit. And to Lynn.*

# THE DIVINE AFFLICTION

*Vocatvs atque non*
*Vocatvs Deus aderit*

—Ancient Spartan Proverb

# A SPEECH TO PARLIAMENT • 1995

*Bovine Spongiform Encephalopathy* (BSE), commonly known as *Mad-Cow Disease*, is an infectious and incurable disease that destroys the brain and nervous system of cattle. The destructive agent is neither bacteria nor a virus, and it breaks all the rules of biology, as we understand them.

The first confirmed case of BSE occurred in Hampshire, early 1985. By now, we have identified it in 150,000 cattle and more than half of all British herds. The disease has been epidemic in British cattle for ten years. It is now time that all herds must be destroyed. This shall wreak havoc on the cattle industry of our Great Britain.

Spongiform encephalopathies are not unique to cattle. We find forms of the disease in other species, including humans, where it goes by the name Creutzfeldt Jakob Disease.

The incubation period can be more than twenty-five years, which means that, once infected, the disease remains dormant and undetected during that time. The ailment bores holes into the brain and nervous system. When established, it causes dementia and death.

Prior to the terminal phase of the disease, behaviors tend to be erratic and unpredictable. The symptoms can be mistaken for other common mental illnesses such as psychosis, schizophrenia and Alzheimer's disease. However, on autopsy, the brains of Creutzfeldt Jakob Disease victims are sponge-like and full of tiny holes, thus the name spongiform.

There is no treatment.

The auditorium remained unnervingly silent.

# CHAPTER
# ONE



A cold granite tombstone offered relief against Eve's bare skin. Stagnant heat of late summer's night produced an abundance of sweat that drenched her bare body. Jason pulled her hips tight to his and she panted with every thrust. Her nails broke flesh on his back, and he groaned with pleasure. It seemed that nothing could stop their connection, nothing until the grinding sound of a diesel engine stole their fleeting visit to paradise.

"What's wrong now?" he asked, oblivious to the source of her distraction.

"You don't hear that? The lights..." she stopped mid-sentence pulling away to gather her clothing.

The sound of gravel rustling under heavy load announced an unmarked tanker passing through the south gate of the still cemetery. Headlights bounced off grave markers, offering momentary animation to otherwise stationary structures. After several turns, the tanker stopped. Lights and engine went silent against the voice of a thousand night crawlers.

From fifty yards away, the couple observed the driver, cloaked in steamy shadow, tending delivery through a hose fitted into the ground.

"Lets' leave," Eve begged.

"Hold it. This is kind a weird. Just hold on."

After fifteen minutes, an eternity for the impatience of youth, the tanker left the site.

"What was that all about?" she said, as she hurried to finish buttoning her blouse.

"Don't know, but I'd want to get a closer look."

"For what?"

"Follow me. There's no one around."

As they moved toward the delivery site with caution, Eve tripped on a grave marker buried at ground level. Jason caught her before she fell to the turf.

"This is creepy. Let's go," she pleaded.

"Quiet. We're almost there."

Though they used caution in approaching the delivery pad, no one saw Eve and Jason again. No one knew this young couple rendezvoused at the cemetery. The search revolved around all of their usual haunts. After an intensive investigation, authorities concluded that runaway status might better explain their mysterious disappearance.

# CHAPTER
# TWO

A THUD ROCKED THE UNDERCARRIAGE OF THE BLACK SEDAN. THE sound of bones crushed beneath the right rear tire followed this intrusion.

"Oh God!" exclaimed Derrick Daniels as he jolted out of his daydream. He hit the brake, and the car screeched to a halt.

"What the hell was that?"

He stared into the rearview mirror. His chest tightened, and a nauseous feeling surfaced.

*Thank God, it wasn't a person or someone's pet. It looks like a possum or muskrat. Big, ugly looking beast. I better check for damage.*

Stepping from the car, he saw blood splatter and glandular tissue on the rear panel. He gagged at the sight, almost losing his morning coffee. There was no body damage. It seemed obvious that the animal ran into the road, got caught under the tire, thrown into the wheel well, and returned to the asphalt, where crushing weight extinguished the life force. Derrick started walking toward the dead animal but changed his mind. He returned to his car.

Shaken, though relieved he had not killed someone's pet, Derrick continued east on Byberry Road alongside the Clear Valley Cemetery. His irrational fear of being anywhere near a graveyard no longer bred high anxiety now that he passed one on his way to work.

Something peculiar drew his attention. It was more roadkill, though not the occasional flattened animal dressing all country roads. Instead, an abundance of critters lay dead along this stretch of highway. At least one animal for every hundred yards traveled. He observed clusters of two, three and even four flattened furry creatures of various species.

*What could possess these animals to run into oncoming traffic? There are more and more of them each year, and it starts in the fall.*

The hot days of summer faded from the landscape for at least a month. Now, a chill in the air hosted early morning travelers. For several weeks, colorful leaves treated those so inclined to notice their seasonal migration from painted trees onto the roads below.

The fascinations of nature held Derrick's attention, but not enough to interfere with the concentration needed to navigate his routine course. He had driven these roads since he moved to the easy-living suburbs. Derrick's thoughts continued to wander in the way that required an effort to remember if the last few traffic signals were green as he casually drove through them.

Derrick noticed seagulls nesting upon the fence of an old country house. The oddity of seeing gulls in the country forced him to rise above deliberations so deeply buried within as to be obscure and beyond recall. A gust of wind that, perhaps, carried the scent of a predator caused the birds to stir. Wings beating, away they flew in a formation rivaling the best that men of aviation could offer.

*That's odd. Seagulls and the nearest ocean is eighty miles away. They never made it south? I wonder if they can handle the winter. I guess they'll know soon enough. The wildlife seems restless. Something's up. I wonder what it's all about.*

The sights and sounds of the city displaced the solitude of the country as Derrick worked his way to the expressway and then onto the streets of Philadelphia. His level of attention rose, along with his blood pressure, while dodging the pedestrians who roamed industriously without much concern for their own safety.

"Card, please."

The sharply spoken words pulled Derrick away from another short daydream. The look of confusion on his face invited a second plea from the armed security guard who waited for him to produce his pass before lifting the gate to the garage of the Federal Building.

"Sir, I need your card for clearance."

Responding mechanically, Derrick produced his security card for a swipe through the automated reader. He rounded many turns on his way to the top of the parking garage. He parked his second-hand, five-year-old BMW in a reserved space and walked to the elevator.

After a short ride, Derrick stepped onto his floor, where the hall-ways matched the marble façade of the building's exterior. Ornate carvings preserved in the architecture adorned every view if the eye should wander from floor to ceiling. Polished ornamental brass door handles and kick plates dressed each entrance. Government exuded big business with limitless budgets.

"Good morning, Mr. Daniels," greeted a young receptionist who had the melodic tone and fanciful expression of a fawning groupie. She offered a look of deep admiration to all the seemingly impor-tant people she welcomed. For Derrick, she felt more.

She blushed whenever Derrick approached, confident he knew he was the object of her fantasies. He was, after all, the most attrac-tive man in the building. Broad shoulders on a six-foot two-inch frame displayed strength in an otherwise refined appearance. He had no jutting jaw or sunken eyes to match his powerful build. Instead, he had features neatly sculpted into a perfection of size and symmetry. Long lashes accentuated his vivid green eyes.

Derrick graduated from Temple University Law School at the top of his class. Not much of a student in college, he did not have the high grades or personal introductions required to enter the elite law schools. However, once matriculated, he learned the workings of the legal profession. Derrick realized the lawyers who ran the world were more often a product of the prestigious schools they attended and their own class rank upon graduation. With that knowledge, the serious student emerged, but too late for recruitment by the best firms. He felt sorry he had not worked harder in college. The last thing he wanted was to be associated with Temple Law School, whose biggest donor made his fortune in the personal-injury field.

Derrick decided he would defend big business from the constant assault by everyone who loved to enjoy the fruits of a first-world economy while bashing it all the way to the bank after a successful lawsuit.

It disgusted Derrick to see so much abuse of the legal system. He wanted to make a difference. His lawyer friends joked he would drive a Honda while they lived lives of opulence. They were on the "right side," they argued. As much as they tried to convince him to change his mind, he knew he could do well as a corporate defense attorney and sleep at night.

On his walk to the end of the long hallway, Derrick passed many cubicles forming a warren of activity and chatter in the center space of the large complex. He entered his cramped office, one of the few lining the periphery of the building, providing privacy and solitude for the more important constituents. He removed his coat and noticed a thick envelope propped against the phone on his otherwise tidy desk. With the immediacy of retrieving an important possession, Derrick opened the packet. Inside he found a plane ticket to Colombia attached to a scarcely legible copy of an itinerary.

*Oh, Hell. I knew it would come to this. They want to send me to Bogotá to coordinate the prosecution of the drug cartel with a bunch of corrupt Colombian lawyers in that God-forsaken country. Just the way I like to travel—on the government budget complete with cheap rooms and food that goes right through me while risking my life in some rat hole.*

The thought of travel to foreign lands set off memories of how the Jamaicans brutalized Hailey. As a legal scholar with impeccable credentials, Hailey seemed an unlikely target for such treatment. However, when he returned from an official prosecutorial mission on the island of Jamaica, he was doomed. While his efforts incarcerated several of the top kingpins from the island, those who remained in power resorted to revenge as a natural process for their continued survival.

Abducted on the streets of New York, they tortured Hailey for several days before slitting his throat, according to the forensic report. They dumped his body at a police station in Queens as a warning to the Americans. The brutal treatment and haughty exhibition showed defiance toward the all-powerful American government that had the impudence to infringe upon the sovereignty of their drug trade.

Derrick's hands trembled. He threw the ticket back onto his desk to shed the thoughts of his colleague's agony.

An unnerving screech, followed by a loud crack, sounded from behind where Derrick stood. Startled, he turned to see a bloodied mess smeared on the floor-to-ceiling window. A pair of birds, during an in-flight battle, apparently flew into the glass, splattering their bodies before falling to the street below. The sight and sound, coupled with Derrick's anger, sent numbing chills throughout his body. He grabbed the plane ticket and marched from his office.

Into the hall, he charged defiantly back the way he had come. Each loud and heavy step broadcast a manifestation of his mounting anger. At the double doors guarding the largest of the offices on this floor, he stopped and pounded out the announcement of his arrival as hard as he could without injuring his fist against the massive mahogany entrance. From within, a bellowing voice commanded him to enter.

Inside, mahogany hardwood floors formed a perimeter for the oriental carpet, which would fit better in the offices of a Fortune 500 Company.

"Good morning, Daniels," said Eric Mason, the head of Justice's litigation division. His tone implied, by way of disgust, and without verbalization, "So what the hell can I do for you?"

Mason, a fifty-five-year-old government man, held employment at the Justice Department for thirty years. Having started as a law clerk, he worked his way up to head a division, but never received invitation for membership into the inner sanctum—the elite club of government leaders who affect change in the world. It did not bother him that he had reached a dead-end, because his spirit contained not an ounce of ambition. Throughout his career, he received sufficient pay to live a rather dull, but stress-free life dictated by minimal needs.

A midriff, expanded to near fifty-two inches, held center focus on his neglected, round-shouldered body. Mason occupied his mornings by an odd quest for vanity in maintaining a balding scalp. Painstakingly, he wrapped his few remaining locks of gray hair from left to right in order to cover as much scalp as possible. He had a habit of pursing his lips and licking his teeth, producing uncouth smacking sounds. It always appeared that his paunchy cheeks still held food from a meal never finished.

"Good morning, Mr. Mason," replied Derrick in a curt, but polite manner necessitated by an obligation to maintain his professionalism. "I hate to begin the day with a complaint, but what is this plane ticket doing on my desk?"

"Great idea. Let's not start the day with a complaint," Mason agreed. "You're going. There's nothing to worry about."

"You keep saying there's nothing to worry about, but in Colombia they're taking out at least one prosecutor every month. The remaining, few, local lawyers are the incompetent ones. For Christ's sake, they may even be consorting with the drug lords by now. And these are the people you expect me to work with?"

"Daniels, it's a different world down there. The Third World. Things that go on there just don't fly here in the US."

"Oh really? Two years ago, in Queens – Hailey – slaughtered like a pig," countered Derrick.

Looking up from reading glasses balanced on the tip of his nose, Mason replied with little concern, "The Jamaicans."

"Right. That was here in this world, my world." said Derrick in a disturbed tone of voice.

"Do you remember what happened to the Jamaicans after that incident?" asked Mason.

"Yeah. They self-destructed. They started killing each other like flies," replied Derrick.

"Sort of."

"What do you mean, sort of?" asked Derrick.

"You never heard this from me, and you don't repeat it to anyone. You got that?"

"Okay."

"They never killed each other. It just looked that way. The Agency took them out after they hit Hailey," whispered Mason.

"What happened to due process?" demanded Derrick as he paced the room anxiously.

"It do walk out the door when they mess with us," said Mason mockingly.

Derrick's eyes opened wide, his jaw tightened in response to what Mason revealed.

"That was the end of them," Mason stated firmly.

"There's still a load of Jamaican drug dealers on the streets here. The bosses back on the island, they're still operating," argued Derrick.

"Drug dealers are like maggots. They thrive in the gutter of humanity. But the ones in Jamaica… not the same ones," explained Mason. "This new generation, they got the message loud and clear. Now, they operate the best they can, petty stuff now, but they won't try to tangle with our courts again."

Derrick stepped to Mason's desk and leaned into him.

"You're telling me this to make me feel safe. You tell this story to anyone who comes in here bitching about their safety."

Mason slid back on his chair to open the space between them, regaining his zone of comfort. Derrick had a method of invading personal space in adversarial situations. People found this uncomfortable. To Derrick, it was a way to penetrate a veil of deception.

"No, Daniels. Well, in a way." He paused. "I'm telling you to make you feel safe, but I'm not making it up, if that's what you mean."

"We live in a democracy," said Derrick. Waiting too long for an explanation, he added, "Well?"

"Don't be so naive, Daniels. Do you seriously think we could fight this drug war the way our democracy has evolved? It's bad enough we have to let crooks go by the grace of due process. When they get too much of an upper hand, we revert to fascism, like it or not. That's why you don't have to look behind you every minute of every day here in America. You got that?"

Derrick didn't answer. Instead, he launched another question. "Do the Colombians know this?" He backed away from Mason's desk.

"I honestly can't answer that question. They don't share that information with me. It's another agency. *The* Agency. I get to hear what they want me to, but I'd guess with all of the violence in Colombia, and none of our prosecutors being targets, you have little to worry about. It doesn't concern you. Not one of our prosecutors has been targeted anywhere in the world since the Hailey incident."

"You mean as long as I'm not the next Hailey."

"Come on, Daniels. You know they'd take out Morganstern before you any day. He's a prick, and they'd go for him first. You have nothing to worry about until you hear Morganstern hasn't showed up for work."

"That's consoling," said Derrick sarcastically.

"I'll brief you on your itinerary this afternoon. You're going."

Derrick left the office. Neither man acknowledged the encounter ended, typical behavior for the men and women of the Justice Department. They appeared to know instinctually when it was time to move on. Mason became absorbed in his paper-strewn desk, while Derrick walked along the corridor wading deep in his own thoughts.

"Derrick," a sensual voice called out from the doorway he just passed. The voice jostled him back to the present. He retraced his last few steps to enter the small office. On the walls hung news clippings covering violent crimes from all corners of the country. The desk held piles of articles bulging from manila folders not yet hung nor deemed significant enough for display.

"Hi, Savannah. Looks like they're keeping you busy."

Savannah sported the aura and looks of a model. She was often mistaken for one of the paralegals, all of whom were glamorous. Long, silky black hair framed her flawless face. A tiny nose, almond eyes, and full sensuous lips all oriented flawlessly to produce a celestial visage. She had long slender legs, a tiny waist and the display of more endowment than expected for such a slim body.

Savannah graduated at the top of her class at University of Southern California Law. Because she wanted to be near the action, business law had no appeal to her. If she could not create excitement for herself, she would have to move on. At twenty-eight years of age, she invested her last two years with the Justice Department searching for that excitement.

Growing up in a backward farm town fostered contempt for the mundane. The ugly duckling syndrome marking her early years melding gawky with tall. In her youth, she exhibited exaggerated facial features. No one could predict she would turn out to be so attractive; a real swan. Her utmost wish: to escape the small town that offered an empty future.

Savannah owned the uncommon combination of brains and beauty. Most everyone in the office knew she had an attraction for Derrick. He had no interest. As a workaholic, he had little time for his marriage and no time for play.

"I don't know if it's them or if it's me. I sometimes think if I just kept my mouth shut, they wouldn't find so many wasteful things for me to do," she declared.

"It looks like you're out of your department," said Derrick, thumbing through all of the articles related to violence. "What does this have to do with the terrorism division? Violent behavior is Mercedes' department. She deals with all of the wackos walking around. You're supposed to go after the terrorists in the courts."

"I am, but I told them if something big didn't come my way, I was moving on. I've petitioned for a joint operation with the CIA for the past two years, and they never delivered. After my threat to leave, they came through. It turns out they need my expertise."

"Your expertise?" questioned Derrick. "We're all lawyers. We have the same training."

"We're all just lawyers. That's true, but when I was at Stanford undergrad, I majored in biology, before I decided on law. In the summers, I interned in the government labs at Los Alamos.

"We're going after something big. Something I turned them on to. When they ran the profiles to find an agent for the mission, my name came up as the most qualified over all of the CIA operatives. I was the one with the legal and science backgrounds needed to investigate this case."

"What's the matter with you?" asked Derrick. "Why would you want to risk your life on a covert spy game?"

She stood and walked over to Derrick. A furtive glance to the doorway insured no one was watching. She pressed her body to his and pulled his jacket collar up as if to ready him for a chilly day.

"What risk? Guess who's going to come along to protect me."

Embarrassed, Derrick, too, looked to the doorway, pushed her away and responded with a sense of unease. "What are you talking about?"

"That's right, baby, you and me," she answered seductively. "I guess you haven't seen your flying papers yet. They should be on your desk by now. Well, I don't want to keep the anticipation too high, or you won't be able to perform when we arrive."

Savannah winked at Derrick and strode back to her desk. She sat in a revealing position by design. Derrick had trouble keeping his eyes away from the intended target. She understood the power wielded with sensuality.

"I'm sorry for the suspense," she said. "I thought Mason would have told you by now. The Colombian connection you'll be prosecuting has major ties to the Pakistani drug growers. And . . ."

Derrick interrupted, "Where do you get your information? The Colombians and the Pakistanis hate each other. They're direct competitors for the American market."

"The rules have changed, love," said Savannah confidently. "They joined forces. It's been suspected for a while. Some important meetings are supposed to go down shortly."

"So how is it you, in anti-terrorism, know all of the latest developments, and me, in drug enforcement, I know shit?"

"Did you ever hear of prions?" she asked coyly, while ignoring his question.

"No," he responded impatiently.

"Prions are why we are going to get to be together."

"Stop the riddles."

"Prions, the protein particles that cause a whole slew of diseases. Don't you read *Scientific American*?" she asked.

"As a matter of fact, I don't."

"Well, it's been in *The New York Times*, too. Anyway, prions cause mad cow disease and may be implicated in Alzheimer's disease along with other potential plagues. You had to hear of mad cow disease. Anyway, the weird thing is that these prions aren't even lifeforms, yet they attack their host like an all-consuming beast."

"Well, I am duly impressed with your scientific knowledge for being *just* a lawyer. Oh, I almost forgot. You, the biology major at Stanford, thing."

"Derrick, there are lots of things you don't know about me that I could show you. And maybe, if you're good, I will." She placed her index finger into her blouse and seductively probed her lace bra underneath.

"But that's for later," she said abruptly. "As it turns out, I was interested in prions, so I started to do some research. The leading authority on prions is Mohamed Abdul Alimet."

Having no knowledge of the subject, "Yeah?" was all Derrick could muster to fill the intentional pause in Savannah's story.

"Yeah? Where is your head, Derrick? How many times at lunch have we talked about Alimet?"

She did not wait for an answer. "Like every day, maybe."

"Oh, please, Savannah. We all talk about our own cases, and no one remembers every detail of all the bullshit."

"This guy was the State Science Minister for Libya – defected to Iran. He's brilliant, and ideologically he's on the wrong side."

"So, this guy is poisoning us with prions, and we all get Alzheimer's."

"Close," she said. "We think he has learned how to modify behavior, to control rage."

Derrick scanned the office, looking at the numerous articles related to violence plastered on the walls and it all made sense. "We could use this guy working for us."

"Derrick, my dear, when I said control rage, I meant he can produce it, not stop it. That's why, if our suspicions are correct, we have to stop him, or at least learn how to control the technology. If all the cases of violence and lunacy we read about everyday are related, we are in big trouble. Can't you see it? We may be destroying ourselves, the result of some kind of control they could have over us."

"I never understood chemistry. I threw up when I dissected a frog. How am I supposed to help you?"

"You have to check out the Pakistani drug connection. While you're doing that, I'll be checking out the prions and Alimet. I need you and your trip as the cover. It will be set up to appear as though I'm going with you to Pakistan as a team. From there, I can get over to Iran by some creative travel arrangements. As you can imagine, they don't like Americans coming to Iran through the routine channels. The fact is, they don't like us there at all. Anyway, as a bonus, by sending us together, the Justice Department saves on the flight, hotel and meals. You know, two birds with one stone."

"Well, you have it all wrong," said Derrick boldly. "I'm off to Colombia, not Pakistan. Not that I'm safer there."

"You didn't speak with Mason, did you?" asked Savannah.

"I just left him. I'm off to Colombia."

"Do you have your ticket with you?"

He nodded in the affirmative.

"Let me see your ticket."

Derrick removed the ticket from his suit pocket and tossed it onto her desk confidently. She opened the envelope and read. A smile dressed her face, and she tossed the papers back on the desk.

"It's too bad you missed the small print," she said.

He grabbed the ticket from the desk. "Right here, Colombia, can't you read?"

"Why don't you see whose name is on that itinerary and that ticket?"

Derrick examined the papers closer.

"Jesus Christ! This is Harris' ticket," he said mournfully upon seeing the name of his partner, Harris Morganstern, embedded in the middle of the document.

"I thought you spoke with Mason. Didn't he tell you?"

"He didn't explain shit. He must have thought I was complaining about going to Pakistan. Colombia is bad enough. He's dreaming if he thinks I'm going to Pakistan. Wait. I bet he switched the tickets deliberately, so he'd ease me into this outlandish destination."

"You're coming with me, baby."

"We'll see about that."

"You wouldn't want to protect me?" she asked meekly.

"If I find out you had anything to do with them sending me to Pakistan, you'll need someone to protect you . . . from me," said Derrick.

Ignoring Derrick's rhetorical threat, she bragged, "You'll love traveling with me. I'm great company."

"I just hope you got us separate rooms," cautioned Derrick with sarcasm.

"Do you believe the taxpayers would be happy about that?" countered Savannah.

Derrick had no need to respond. He walked out of her office and headed along the hallway to challenge Mason. This time he didn't knock, as he felt obliged to intrude. Upon opening the heavy door, Derrick saw Mason in the very same position that he left him in just moments before.

"What now," asked the disinterested paper shuffler?

"You're real slick," said Derrick with tempered anger.

"What's that supposed to mean?" Mason asked.

"You never mentioned Pakistan, Iran, the two birds with one stone shit."

"Two birds? I thought you knew. Why the hell else would you have been in here complaining? You got the itinerary. I put it on your desk this morning," explained Mason.

"You gave me Harris' ticket. You did that on purpose, so I'd be eased into the whole travel idea."

"Don't be ridiculous, Daniels. Big deal. I made a mistake. If you read the damn ticket, you would know what's going on. I even told you we would go over the itinerary this afternoon. Just get with it. We need you over there."

"I refuse to go. You'll have to get someone else. Send Harris."

Mason's face turned red. Bulging veins grew rigid upon his neck.

"Harris is going to Columbia as you so duly determined. You know he can't handle anything complex," Mason exclaimed.

"You know all of the legal precedents. There is no one better versed on international law in our department, and you can prosecute like the devil. You're the man for the job. And before you refuse again, this isn't an option if you wish to finish out your term here."

Mason lived with aggravation, but rarely became mad and refrained from making idle threats. The authorities at the top hounded him to get the job done, and he put on the pressure when necessary. Derrick felt the Justice Department needed him more than he needed them, but leaving on bad terms wasn't what he wanted. In the world of legal maneuvering connections were often the most important asset. Derrick could not afford to burn bridges at this point in his nascent career. He knew he had to get this mission behind him. Then he could make his exit from service at a time without controversy.

# CHAPTER
# THREE

The Justice Attorneys took lunch breaks in the government-subsidized dining room just about every day. Camaraderie attracted them, not the institutional food served in a drab cafeteria setting. As busy as they seemed, whatever the caseload, they always enjoyed the mid-day break.

Mercedes Carpenter, already seated at the table, waited for the others to arrive. She specialized in defending the government against suits from the families of government employees killed by co-workers. Twenty years ago, this department did not exist, even as a thought in the minds of anyone associated with government policy. Times changed.

Anyone who knew Mercedes described her as cute because of her ultra-short hairstyle in combination with a button nose. Freckles covered much of her face but concentrated into a pronounced butterfly pattern on each cheek. This further helped to define her cuteness. The staples of her wardrobe consisted of finely tailored pantsuits or dark-skirted business suits. Like her hair, her wardrobe always looked masculine. The suit coats she wore all had darts, not out of necessity, rather because she preferred clothing tailored for women.

Karl Armstrong, who worked in the Anti-dumping division at Justice, dropped his food tray on the table next to Mercedes in disgust, as his unconventional way of starting a conversation. The unexpected clatter startled her.

"I suppose your day isn't going so well," she said politely, while avoiding eye contact. Karl's weak eye drifted about in such a way as to make others feel awkward when they looked into his face. At twenty-nine, he experienced early onset balding, and had not yet resigned to the style of head-shaving that helped others look better than those who leave the threads of remaining hair to flutter about untamed.

"Do you believe they're sending me to Japan for up to three months?" replied Karl in a dejected voice looking for consolation.

"It goes with the territory. You knew that when you signed on," she said.

"Sure. They tell us there's the possibility we may have to travel, but that's never been anything more than a disclaimer. At worst, it's an overnight trip to D.C. That is, until they got me involved in this endless anti-dumping investigation. Try five times to the Orient for me in the last three years. Who do you know who had to travel anywhere farther than D.C.?"

"I guess you haven't heard about Derrick and Savannah?" said Mercedes.

"What? Is she carrying his baby?" he said in jest, sprinkled with a hint of jealousy.

She ignored his cheap remark. "They're leaving next month for Pakistan."

Karl laughed.

"What's so funny?" asked Mercedes.

"She probably set that trip up and told him it's for the Department," he replied with a hardy laugh.

"No, really. They are on separate missions. A lot is happening now. Some of the foreign intelligence gathering is starting to pay off."

Derrick, Harris, and Savannah finished loading their trays with nourishing, bland foods and went to join their associates. Harris started to eat his lunch on his way to the table. He balanced his tray with one hand, while the other wielded a fork to shovel as much food as possible into his mouth.

No one at the Justice Department liked Harris. Derrick tolerated him, by ignoring a multitude of failings. He felt sorry for him. Being his partner for the past two years revealed Harris' weaknesses that accounted for his flawed personality. He saw him as a pathetic, lonely guy with little talent and in need of praise and recognition.

Justice Department co-workers and, surprisingly, his superiors considered Harris a threat. At meetings, he searched for ways to impress senior personnel, even if it meant stepping on the toes of higher-ups within his own division. A poor self-image and a life of shallow relationships and poor choices made him a loathsome soul. The more he tried to get close, the more he offended those around him.

His physical appearance mirrored his personality in an uncanny sort of way. Harris had the appearance of a snake. He was tall, six-foot-three, and rather thin. He stood hunched over from the effects of chronic back problems that resulted in a serpentine-like spine. An elongated face, coupled with a relatively longer nose, provided the expectation that a forked tongue would fly in and out of his mouth at any moment.

Harris maneuvered awkwardly to sit next to Mercedes. She pulled her chair away just a little each time he pushed his chair closer, causing her to feel trapped between him and Karl. Though Harris was married, it was not a happy union. He always tried to flirt with the women from any department in the building.

"Derrick, I hear you are heading out of town, too," said Karl in a manner conveying that misery loves company.

"I am," Derrick replied, "And I'll be on your flight according to the orders I've read. Where's your final destination?"

"Japan," said Karl. "Not that that's so bad. But I could be there up to three months this time."

"Let's not bitch here," said Derrick. "I'm heading for the Third World. Be happy you'll be in civilization."

"Sending Justice Department attorneys to foreign lands is becoming the rage," added Harris, who just found out he was going to Colombia by himself.

Mercedes jumped in to the conversation. "Speaking of rage, there was another rampage killing last evening. It took place in Chicago. A lunatic killed seven co-workers—lined them up and executed them. I'm investigating the sickest cases you could ever imagine."

"I have this theory there's a diabolic force making it happen," said Savannah.

"Right," said Karl with an air of sarcasm, causing the others to laugh.

"No. I'm serious."

"She's been watching too much late-night television on the Sci-Fi channel," said Derrick in jest.

"Make fun all you like, but when I save the world, don't expect me to talk with you nonbelievers."

"Let them laugh," said Mercedes. "They can joke about it all they want, but my office investigates all cases of workplace rage, and I know, for a fact, behavior is out of control. Not just with government employees; I'm getting the details on the most horrid cases throughout the country."

Harris, looking to become part of the conversation chimed in, "We've always had rage in the workplace. They just report it better now, so it seems worse."

"That's just what the government wants us to think," said Savannah. "If the public knew the real statistics, heads would roll. The authorities don't have an explanation, and in time, everyone would be afraid of the person sitting next to them. Panic would break out."

"Oh, come now," said Derrick. "Everyone knows the world has become more violent. There's nothing new under the sun. We've just become immune to violence. We no longer become outraged enough to pressure the politicians to act. Once they shut all of the mental hospitals, the schizophrenics started roaming the streets. The dangerous ones end up in the prison system. They've become our mental hospitals. The suicidal crazies get their moment of fame in homicidal acts before their lights go out. I think it's just a desperate way a bunch of losers say, "Hey, look at me."

"Derrick's right," said Mercedes. "There's definitely more violence, but it's worse than anyone realizes. I see the actual numbers. I am telling you, violence is epidemic. It can't just be explained away as a depraved desire for identity."

"Forget all this talk of insanity," said Karl. "There's nothing to worry about. They have an herbal remedy, a vitamin to keep you from coming down with these types of things."

Savannah's face froze. She thought Karl was onto something.

"What are you referring to?" she asked seriously.

"I'm kidding. I'm joking with you, Savannah. Just forget it."

They all laughed except for Savannah and Mercedes.

"We've become such a culture of violence that no matter how grotesque it gets, we are immune to the reality of it all until it hits close to home. That's why you can joke while the families of the victims mourn," chided Mercedes.

"It's not like that. We have compassion," said Derrick apologetically. "You have to make light of it, or you'll lose your sanity."

Karl wanted to change the subject. "Derrick, are we going to get in a last game of doubles with the guys before we leave?" he asked.

"Are you going to show up?"

"What's that supposed to mean?"

"Last week you forgot about our every Tuesday night game."

"I didn't forget the game. I forgot it was Tuesday."

"I can't see how you can forget what day it is. And besides, it's getting to be a burden to play anymore," said Derrick. "How can a group of intelligent men, not counting you, Karl, continually lose track of the score?"

"Forget the score. How about forgetting who served?" countered Karl as he forced a chuckle.

"It's funny you mention that. My girls seem to have the same trouble when we play at my apartment complex," added Mercedes.

"It's nothing. It's universal, as you get older. You just have too much to process. You forget things," said Harris.

"It's more than that," Savannah responded earnestly. "They know we all use that excuse. Yeah, we have so much more to remember. As we get older we can't retain it all. You don't get it, do you? They have you in the palm of their hands. Your complacency is so entrenched you can't even fight the enemy. They have us right where they want us."

"Who the hell are *they*?" asked Karl holding back laughter.

Frustrated, Savannah hesitated with all eyes on her, and she exclaimed, "You *know* who they are."

The group sat silent, glanced at one another, then looked at Savannah, and in unison, as if rehearsed, said, "Right." They laughed heartily. Savannah lifted her middle finger and brandished it for all to see.

"I thought you and I were headed for Colombia," said Harris, directing his remark to Derrick. "Now, I hear I'm on my own. What's going on?"

"Your guess is as good as mine."

"I thought we were a team," said Harris. His voice expressed concern, a trait generally not in his nature for revelation. "The agency always has us working in pairs to set up the legal proceedings here at home. It has to be ten times harder to develop a case in foreign lands. Even in Colombia, where they are supposed to want us, they aren't going to cooperate. How could they split us up?"

"It's simple," Savannah interjected. "I explained it to Derrick. He has to coordinate the proceedings in the Pakistani courts. There just are not enough staff lawyers to be everywhere. They have to thin out the troops."

"I'll keep you posted on the Internet," said Derrick. "You'll set up your cases utilizing the identical strategies I'll use in Pakistan. I'll supply you with all the documentation. If you run into roadblocks, you'll let me know, and I'll figure out a tactic for you."

While Harris looked to take credit, Derrick remained the talent behind the duo. Harris knew it, as did everyone at the agency. Harris would not fare well in Colombia but for the Internet communications available to him and tethered to Derrick. However, Harris would later brag about successes as if he was the architect of their accomplishments.

Mason arrived to consume his lunch, which included mounds of soft pasta soaked in a rich meat sauce sitting next to a double serving of chocolate cake. He headed over to his feeding ground, where he would isolate himself at the back of the lunchroom. There, he found solace in solitude and in the sports pages of the *Daily News*. He made a point of stopping by the table of his underlings.

"Wait until you see your actual flight plan, folks," said Mason, directing his comment to Karl, Derrick and Savannah.

"How bad can it be?" asked Savannah.

"Well, Karl flies past his destination in Japan to spend two sunny, extraordinarily hot days in Bangkok. Then, he flies backwards to Tokyo.

"You guys," he now directed his comments to Derrick and Savannah by pointing two fingers at them, "are headed out of Bangkok to Bubiyan, a nice little town in Kuwait to be precise. From this lovely land in the sand, you will fly, in a one engine Piper Cub, to Ma-amir, a small border town in sunny Iraq."

"That's when I will have the divine experience of riding a camel into Khosrowabad, a desolate border town in Iran," Savannah volunteered.

"I see you read your itinerary. Just remember, if you get caught, there's a chance we will never see you again," Mason cautioned. "And after waiting for Savannah to return to the world-class accommodations you'll have enjoyed, you, Derrick, will be headed to your final destination in Pakistan. Of course, you do have the option of accompanying Ms. Ambrose into Iran if you feel the opportunity is a once in a lifetime experience you don't want to miss."

"If you ask me, this sounds like a splendid vacation, all at Uncle Sam's expense," Derrick mused.

Mason directed his gaze toward Derrick and concluded by asserting, "You certainly are the Chosen One."

# CHAPTER
# FOUR

An invitation to the gala charity affair arrived months ago. Most involved considered it to be the best gathering of the year, well worth attending. The elite constituents of the business, legal and political communities would gather with the privileged members of society in one room annually.

Derrick had no interest in these affairs and less desire to attend. He knew how important the festivities were for his wife, Adrienne, so he let her plan their social calendar. He went along.

Derrick was Adrienne's ticket to the important people of the city. Without a substantial donation they could not yet afford, their names would not be on the radar screen. Instead, attorneys who headed large law firms invited them to society events. Their firms represented wealthy Americans, as well as even wealthier foreign nationals involved in questionable dealings. They were eager to rub shoulders with Derrick, being an up-and-coming prosecutor in the Philadelphia office of the Justice Department. The politicians and lawyers controlling city government considered contact with anyone from Justice a smart schmooze. Of course, they could not pay for Derrick's admittance, but giving entrance to his wife under the guise of her charitable volunteer work avoided the appearance of impropriety.

Derrick's marriage to Adrienne was the engine that propelled his career. She let style and taste consume her. Adrienne made certain Derrick bought the finest suits and accessories. She pampered her own interests as well. It did not matter that the costs of haute couture strained their budget. He had a stellar future, and she knew it. Adrienne believed the need to save now was an inconsequential burden best left to the proletariat.

Born into a middle-class family, Adrienne had a mother who stressed ascent upon the social ladder more than values. Combined with looks that turned heads and the subtlety of motive, she was able to seduce and then secure her future with Derrick, who was thrilled to have such a lovely wife. His consumption by school, and then work, left him with little time to be concerned about the social amenities offered to those traveling in proper circles. Adrienne fulfilled Derrick's need to have a life beyond career.

Together, they seemed a picture-perfect couple. Adrienne stood tall, almost five-ten. She possessed the stature of a fashion model with long legs and a thin, delicate bone structure. Her body, with slight substance, looked better in clothes than bare. Her petite nose turned up just slightly. Large blue eyes, set apart well beyond that which most would consider normal, instead of looking freakish, presented as a hypnotic attraction. Adrienne's jaw, defined by sharp lines, complemented the outstanding prominence of her bulbous cheekbones. Long, silky, dark hair draped her shoulders. Her stunning appearance attracted stares from men and women alike.

"Hon, can you clip my pearls?"

Derrick, interrupted from the task of completing his bowtie, walked behind Adrienne and held the black South Sea pearls upon her caramel-tanned skin. He secured the clasp. She touched the pearls with all of her fingers as if they afforded some sensual pleasure.

"Aren't they the most beautiful things you've ever seen?"

Derrick leaned over and kissed Adrienne's neck. He pulled down the strapless gown to reveal her petite, firm breasts, and caressed them.

"They are the most beautiful things I've ever seen."

Adrienne grabbed the top edge of her gown, covered herself and adjusted her breasts to fit comfortably within the sequined designer creation.

"Later. They're all yours, but later," she said. "Of course, only if you're a good boy tonight."

"Come on, Adrienne, you know as well as I do, by the time we get home, we'll be too tired. We don't have to be the first ones there." He spun her around and began to kiss her lips. She pushed him away.

"You're ruining my lipstick. What's wrong with you?"

"Okay, Okay, you just better stay awake tonight."

The Four Seasons Hotel hosted the event in the grand ballroom, one of the more elegant quarters in town. At twenty-five-thousand dollars a plate, this affair had no rival and exuded a perverse opulence. In contrast, the homeless roamed the neighboring streets, ignored by the political class who often made empty proclamation of their generosity and good deeds directed toward those less fortunate, though not this evening.

This event allowed the politicians to meet and greet under the guise of charity, while political and professional motives prevailed. Charity and charitable events became the means for the proverbial smoky, backroom, brown paper bag filled with cash payoffs. Best of all, they are not easy to expose. This evening, the judges, being *honored* guests, did not have to pay, nor could they afford the high price of admission. Lawyers, who appeared before them, could do their courting without violating ethics codes, as long as charity was the reason to gather. In a town known for its abundance of plaintiffs' attorneys, this was the must attend event of the year. This market place offered exchange of all sorts of introductions and favors. Contacts for future dealings were available for those willing to pay for and play the game.

Derrick felt somewhere between annoyed and repulsed at the knowledge that right-and-wrong were not the basis of negotiations in many government endeavors. He felt troubled by the adage that *who you know* begot better results than *what you know*. Derrick would never sell his influence, so it amused him to see the sleazy lawyers trying to get close to him throughout the year.

Most lawyers developed methods to keep their name visible. Some made overtures for Derrick to use their vacation homes or boats for personal pleasure. He could expect to get a dozen assorted, unsolicited sporting event and hard to get concert tickets each year. They came in the mail with a private note attached garnering the unspoken suggestion that someday they may come calling. He would return the tickets taped to a form letter, in such a manner that rendered them useless, and remind them that Justice Lawyers could not receive gifts.

When they arrived at the grand event, Adrienne glowed from excitement born in the King's Ball like atmosphere. Formally dressed attendants with top hats and batons welcomed all guests. A chamber quartet and harpist conversed with melody and motif in the central foyer as tuxedoed hotel staff guided everyone toward the clamor of the Grand Ballroom.

"Isn't it just fabulous?" raved Adrienne with a warm gushing spirit that elevated and danced within.

"It's a party. A big party. The way you get excited over these things is a bit sorry."

"A bit sorry? These are all the people you need to meet if you expect to get out of the slave-hole you work in. Justice is a stepping-stone, not an endpoint. You're the one who always told me that."

"Right. But I said that before I saw all of the whoring going on in places like this."

"So, what are you saying?" asked Adrienne with a scowl of consternation.

"I'm just not happy with what I see going on. I'm frustrated. I know there is no money in government service, but there has to be a way to make the big bucks legitimately. I just haven't figured it out yet."

"Over there, look. It's Jim Young," exclaimed Adrienne with childlike enthusiasm.

"Who's Jim Young?" asked Derrick.

"He's the President of City Council. I introduced you to him last year. He's the one who helped our auxiliary get the zoning changed for our new thrift shop. I worked with him. Come on over. I want him to know who you are. He's going to go places. He's the kind of people you need in your contacts."

"You go ahead. I'll join you in a minute. I want to get a drink. Can I get you something?"

"Get me a champagne cocktail. And darling, don't be forever."

Adrienne waltzed across the room to engage Jim Young. As the most glamorous woman at the affair that evening, heads turned as she moved toward her target. For the aspiring President of City Council, attention getters bore golden publicity. Standing alone, not yet noticed, he welcomed Adrienne's approach.

"Adrienne, so nice to see you."

"Mr. Young, it's my pleasure. I'm flattered you remember."

"Works of art and beauty are not to be forgotten, and besides, anyone willing to put themselves out for charity is to be commended. Your effort for the auxiliary is most worthy. And please, call me Jim."

"You are so kind, Jim."

She seductively pushed her breast against Jim's arm and rubbed his shoulder with her hand acknowledging his compliment. Adrienne glowed with delight. Jim Young knew all the proper things to say in any situation. He would become the City's next Mayor, if all were to go well with his upcoming election bid.

"Perhaps we could get to know one another better," Jim said, receptively leaning into her. "Before you leave, I need to have a number where I can reach you. There are times when we could use a hard worker, a foot soldier like you, for the Party. When the Mayor shows up, come on over, so I can introduce you."

"I'd be delighted."

A rather dapper, elderly, silver haired fellow approached with his hand held out to Jim in greeting.

"Mr. Foxman. Great to see you. Adrienne Daniels, meet Mr. Foxman. His firm, Foxman, Brandon, was kind enough to make available your tickets for tonight's event."

"Let's cut the formality. It's Howard. So nice to meet you Adrienne. Is it okay to call you Adrienne?"

Glowing at the offer of informality Adrienne responded with a resounding, "Most certainly."

"The charity toil you do cannot be repaid by a mere one night of celebration. And of course, your husband Derrick is here to celebrate, too?" asked Foxman.

"Yes, yes, he is," she stammered with the exhilaration of meeting yet another powerbroker and not giving thought to why such an important player knew of Derrick by name.

Jim Young and Mr. Foxman excused themselves to greet others. Though now standing alone, Adrienne felt more important at that moment than any time in her life. She knew this evening would be her inauguration into the league of powerful people.

As Derrick made his way back to Adrienne, she moved farther from the crowd that formed around Jim Young. Now, there was no reason to bring in her reluctant mate. She felt empowered to make her own contacts as a political helper among the influential.

"So, when do I get knighted by the King?" asked Derrick, handing Adrienne her cocktail.

"Maybe later. If you're good, I'll get you introduced to the Mayor," she said, enjoying the role of powerbroker. "How does that sound?"

"It sounds like you forgot the original deal."

"What deal?"

"The *making love if I'm good* deal. How short is the memory of a social climber?"

"Oh, yeah, that, too," she said, seductively pressing her breast against Derrick's arm.

For Derrick, the tiresome hours passed ever so slowly. For Adrienne, the same hours, thoroughly cherished, flew by much too fast. She did get the ultimate honor of meeting the Mayor, who to her dismay directed his small talk to Derrick.

They rode home that evening in silence and deep thought. Adrienne fantasized about how everyone wanted to get close to her at the next gala ball. She imagined the Governor requesting an introduction provided by the Mayor, her newfound friend. Derrick envisioned turbaned drug lords killing him in the badlands of Pakistan. Their thoughts and interests stood galaxies apart.

By two in the morning, they drove past the cemetery at the intersection of Byberry Road and Philmont Avenue.

"Look at that," exclaimed Derrick in a whisper as if some outsider might hear him.

"What? Look at what? And why are you whispering?" asked Adrienne, upset by the intrusion upon her dream state.

Derrick pulled his car to the side of the road, about fifty feet before the traffic signal. The road narrowed, making it impossible to gain position out of the traffic lane, but he didn't obstruct passage, and no other cars rode by at this late hour. He wanted to observe without interruption, should a late-night denizen happen by.

"In the cemetery. That truck. Do you see it?"

"I'm not blind, Derrick. There's a truck. So what?"

"It's an oil tanker. There's a guy pumping oil into a cemetery in the middle of the night, and you don't see anything odd with that picture?"

"I'm sorry. You're right," she said in a bored voice. "That is weird. What do you think he's doing there?"

"I have no idea, but it isn't the first time I've seen this."

"What do you mean?"

"You know how I get home late sometimes from the office when we're preparing to go to court. It doesn't seem to matter when it is, one, two, even three AM, I've seen that truck in there. This has to be something crooked. And what are the chances for me to ride by and see this delivery at odd hours, just about any day of the week? It's like they're making deliveries throughout the night, every night."

"Do they have an underground heating oil tank for that building on the property?" she asked.

"Probably, but it would be next to the building. How much heating oil can the grounds keeper need? And even if there was a heating oil tank, why make deliveries when everybody is asleep? It has to be some kind of underground toxic waste dump. Yeah, that has to be it. No one will go digging up a cemetery. It's the perfect place for toxic waste."

"What are you going to do? Shouldn't you call the police?"

"I don't know. I'm sure someone will report it, and they will investigate sooner or later. Anyway, it's late. We still have unfinished business."

Derrick reached over and placed his hand on Adrienne's shoulder affectionately. She exhaled the breath of boredom. He moved his hand lower and nestled it onto her bare breast hoping to elicit arousal.

"Derrick, it's so late. Let's do this tomorrow when I can get into it."

Several tomorrows passed, but the opportunity for a physical encounter rarely materialized. It was always too late, one of them was too tired, or too many things had to get done.

# CHAPTER
# FIVE

Though he did not know what compelled him, the opened door to Mercedes' empty office tempted Derrick to enter. Should she return, his foray would prove embarrassing, but the opportunity presented, and he decided to act. On the screen of her computer, Derrick saw a series of statistics for suicides in the United States over the past twenty years. On her desk, he observed similar pages stamped "classified" over each page. At first glance, the hard copy classified pages looked identical in every respect to the pages on the computer screen. On further examination, he noticed that the numbers were significantly higher. The difference in the rate of increased suicide between the two sets of pages appeared to be astonishing, even for a novice in the field.

"So, you had to see for yourself."

The voice, though familiar, friendly and in reality, expected, caused Derrick to turn in surprise. He confronted Mercedes with a red swell of embarrassment dressing his face: guilty as charged.

"You weren't here, so I thought I'd wait and . . . well, I just sat down and . . ."

"Admit it. You wanted to see what I was talking about at lunch each day."

"I saw your door open and thought I'd stop in to say hi. When I glanced at your screen, here . . ." He paused, hoping his excuse sounded believable.

To ease Derrick's embarrassment, Mercedes spoke for him. "Pretty amazing stuff. We're not supposed to see those classified pages."

Derrick, recovering from his humiliation, chose to remain silent.

"When I said violence is epidemic, I wasn't exaggerating. All of you make light of this, but the numbers are off the charts."

"Why isn't it made public, so someone can do something about it?"

"They're afraid of mass hysteria. It's like suddenly, they say the chance of getting killed by a nutcase isn't as remote as you thought. You'd become a paranoid recluse. That's my guess. They don't explain their motives. They tell me enough to do my job. It's a lot darker than increased numbers of suicides and murders."

"I don't mean to make light of it, but if you look at the kids out there, it's not such a surprise," Derrick offered.

"Not such a surprise?"

"The biggest box office hit this weekend was some sort of hideous massacre movie. The video games encourage ultra-violence. It's everywhere. I can't believe a psychiatric expert hasn't figured out the problem. Are they all blind to cause and effect?"

"It's worse than that, Derrick." Mercedes leaned over his shoulder to retrieve a page from her desk drawer. "Take a look at this."

Mercedes handed Derrick a plain, white, typed sheet of paper that read:

*Irradiate all field rations prior to delivery. Destroy provisions processed before this directive or offer them to the inhabitance of the foreign host.*

"What in the hell is this?" exclaimed Derrick.

"I have no idea."

"You have no idea? Where did you get it?"

"It was attached to the file you're looking at on the screen, and it was stamped *classified*, too."

"How come this copy isn't stamped classified? Didn't you print it out with the other pages?"

"It was a mistake. All of these confidential pages were attached to the unclassified pages, but they were not meant for me."

"Did you try to ask someone?"

"I tried, and the next thing I know, they wiped the file from my computer. No evidence it was ever there."

"So, where did you get the hard copies?"

"In anticipation, in case authorities upstairs wanted to erase them, I printed out all the confidential statistic pages you see here. Just as the last page, the one with that weird message, was ready to print, my screen went blank. Nothing other than the unclassified pages remained. Once the file disappeared, I decided to write that directive from memory."

"Maybe you got it wrong."

"Derrick, my photographic memory got me through law school. Trust me, that's what it said, verbatim. It scares me to think it may have to do with my department. Could you imagine if the food supply is somehow affecting us?"

"What are you going to do now?"

"Not a thing. Savannah is onto this odd theory about something she called prions and how they affect our brains. The only way to destroy prions is by heating them to 800 degrees. Maybe the radiation has something to do with this. I don't know. I'm a lawyer, not a scientist."

# CHAPTER
# SIX

AT THREE AM, THE SUBURBS SURROUNDING PHILADELPHIA RESEMBLE sleeping hamlets from a bygone era. Quiet and inactivity prevail in the listlessness of early morn. In Derrick's neighborhood grand weeping trees and thick foliage cast eerie shadows from light of the full moon onto expansive manicured lawns and stately homes built of stone with carved slate roofs. Though the sky remained darkened, the soon to rise sun began washing away evening stars. Winter landed early and gripped the northeast with a harsh cold spell. The morning air felt bitter, dry, and frigid enough to blister one's throat without much exertion.

Derrick stood by his door waiting for the van. He felt a melancholy, composed in part by the doldrums of the coming winter months and part by the apprehension he experienced before a flight; this flight in particular.

A military transport plane was set to depart from the McGuire Air Force Base at zero-six-hundred hours, taking Derrick, Savannah, and Karl on the initial leg of their long trip. When the driver, a military man, arrived, he loaded Derrick's one large, overstuffed duffle into the back of the generic, army-green, van. He drove off to pick up the others. They traveled east along County Line Road, the same route Derrick journeyed each day.

"You notice all the roadkill?" asked Derrick, as they drove by a large, flattened possum. It sounded like small talk, but he wanted to explore the subject with someone who drives on a regular basis.

"This is a zone, sir," replied the driver emphatically.

"What do you mean by that?" asked Derrick, surprised by the enthusiastic response.

"A zone. I see these all the time. Lots of roadkill, sir, but it seems to be in zones. You know."

"No, I don't know," said Derrick trying to hide his impatience to learn more.

"I can be riding all over, and I see none of this anywhere. Then all of a sudden, there's a shit-load of these critters all over the road. Like here," he said pointing out the window to a cluster of three more casualties of the highway. "This is what I call a zone. This just ain't natural. It's like something spooked the little bastards, and they run into the traffic."

"Where's another one of the zones you're talking about?" asked Derrick.

"Main Line. There gotta be three or four zones out that way. Yardley's got a big one. Then you got the ones over in Jersey, Princeton, Cherry Hill and Haddonfield. That's just the local ones around here. I find them all over, Connecticut, New York, Delaware, plenty in Delaware. Never made much of it."

"Where did you hear the term <u>zones</u>?" asked Derrick.

"Made it up myself."

"Then it's been rather obvious to you, right?"

"Guess so. Never thought too much about it. Just that it's been getting worse over the last few years, I reckon. And something else interesting too."

The silence was extended and intentional, almost as if the driver wanted to be asked. Derrick obliged, "Yeah?"

"These zones. These areas I call zones are always nearby ritzy neighborhoods. You know. Where the rich folks live. Like around these parts here. Never made much of it."

The rest of the ride played out in silence. It offered Derrick time to think about the roadkill and how he was not the only one to notice the abundance. He thought about the truck in the cemetery on a secretive mission arriving several times every night. What could they be dumping? It made sense, the perfect place to hide contaminated waste, toxic chemicals and just about anything required to remain dead, along with the eternal inhabitants silenced in the soil below.

His mind wandered farther. He thought about how his existence had become so work-driven that it regretfully impinged upon his relationship with Adrienne.

Each bump in the road and the chatter of the poorly constructed van kept Derrick from nodding off, yet he bordered close to a dream state. With eyes shut, his mind drifted. He jumped when the sliding door bolted open for Karl to enter.

"Good morning, fella," said Karl with a zest indicating he either had been up much earlier than necessary, or he was a *morning person*.

Derrick yawned and just shook his head to acknowledge he was now awake, but not in the mood for conversation. This gesture did not stop Karl.

"How can you not be up for this, Derrick? You'll never again have this opportunity. And it's on the government, not a penny out of your pocket."

"I thought you didn't want to go. What changed your attitude?" asked Derrick.

"It's called pragmatism. I couldn't get out of it, not that I didn't try. Fate deals the cards. I play the hand. There's a way to get something out of any situation. You'll see," explained Karl.

"You can take this trip and shove it," said Derrick with eyes half-closed. "Did you forget already? I'm going to be riding a camel for the better part of a day in a hell-like desert. This is not what I consider a first-class vacation."

"Where's your sense of adventure?" asked Karl. He paused and thought for a moment, then continued. "Anyway, you're right about not being first-class. I can't believe they won't just stop in Japan and drop me off. They're taking me a million miles out of the way."

"Don't complain," said Derrick. "We're going all the way around the world in the wrong direction."

"You know the government works in mysterious ways. They must have arrangements with certain countries to use certain airports at restricted times. That's the way it could make sense," Karl theorized.

A silence lingered long enough to indicate the end to their conversation. The rattling van produced a dull harmonic that now drew Derrick into a deep sleep. He didn't hear Savannah join them. When he awoke, they were pulling through the gate at the Air Force base.

"If it isn't sleeping beauty," joked Savannah.

"Wow, I was out cold."

"Very true. And you can add that you make for rather bad traveling company," noted Karl. "I sure hope you'll join us for the flight."

"Look, Karl, I know how to do this to avoid getting jet lag. I've been to L.A. a dozen times, and I never feel it. It's all in the catnaps," said Derrick.

"Oh, are you going to be surprised," exclaimed Karl. "You never took a trip like this. You'll think you're tired, you go to sleep and you're up in two hours watching the clock. I'm telling you, this voyage will throw you for a loop. Of course, it won't throw you as bad as a camel."

"Very funny," said Derrick.

"Why the hell do you have to travel that way?" asked Karl, now directing his question to Savannah.

"On a camel? That's the way into Alimet's laboratory. He's living in an obscure village in Iran. The Iranians fund his research. Libya, his country, is too dysfunctional, too unstable and can't risk being tied to the research. Besides, they don't have the facilities and materials needed, so they're in bed with Iran. Alimet's secret research flourishes in the desert."

"Sounds like a scary trip. I guess my stay in Japan is nothing compared to that."

"At last," exclaimed Derrick. "He can see why I'm not excited about this adventure."

Karl offered no further comments and the three travelers settled down for some needed rest.

Air Force transports were not designed to accommodate the genteel public, which would account for such an uncomfortable flight. They served as practical personnel carriers designed to get troops and equipment to all theaters of operation as expeditiously as possible. Derrick had to walk the aisles to alleviate the aches and pains in his lower back and buttocks. Savannah, the most pliant, could sleep for extended periods in just about any position.

Karl, in the manic phase of his sub-clinical bi-polar rhythm, read a book, talked with whichever crewmembers wandered about, or scribbled notes in his diary. He seemed to have endless energy, requiring no more than a few restless naps during the entire thirty-six hours of travel.

# CHAPTER
# SEVEN

The taxi ride from the Bangkok airport to the hotel began at dusk. The vast number of high-rise buildings surprised Derrick and Savannah, who had never been to Bangkok or any part of this world.

"I think you're the lucky one," Savannah said to Karl. "You get to stay here for a few days. What a fabulous city. It's a shame we're leaving tomorrow. We'll never get to toast the town."

"You call this a city," said Karl. "Don't let the bright lights and neon fool you. This is just a Third World shit-hole trying to be a first-class town. They believe the more skyscrapers they have, the more recognition and stature they'll get. Until they clean up the trash in the streets, they're just another cesspool."

Karl had strong opinions about Bangkok supported by his past trips to this land on behalf of his work with the Department of Justice. He was investigating the dumping of Japanese cars into the US market. Every time he traveled to Japan, he had a stopover in Bangkok for a few days. With nothing to do in a strange land, boredom encouraged him to explore the town on each of his trips.

"You guys are the lucky ones. You are the ones in for adventure.

I'd trade with you in a heartbeat to go on the caravan express," Karl said mockingly.

"Oh, come on," said Derrick. "Stop rubbing it in. We're not a crew from National Geographic?"

"If you knew how to live, you'd put the top down and enjoy the ride. You'd make the best of it," replied Karl.

"He's right," added Savannah. "You've got to look at the excitement, the intrigue, the mystery. It's out there waiting to thrill you."

"Lady, my idea of a thrill is an evening in a hot tub, not a ride on a smelly camel through the desert night."

"Oh, don't be such a pessimist," she admonished. "I have a wonderful itinerary for us. You'll see."

Derrick rolled his eyes and gave a glare of profound misgiving to Savannah, the self-ordained travel guide.

The taxicab pulled up to an unassuming entrance of the Rose Guest House. On occasion, government housed workers in some of the better hotels. Not this time. Recent years of critical oversight by Congress resulted in one-star lodging more often than not.

First-rate quarters were on streets juxtaposed to the resident squalor. The Rose Guest House was a step below the destinations of most tourists and situated a hundred yards from the Chao Phraya River.

Tributaries branching from the river's flowing waters fed the canal system that lay beneath the streets. The smells of waste and decay filled the air. Oddly, and devoid of explanation, the foul odors happened in waves, but not the result of air currents in this land without breezes. Young boys stood by the river with lines of hemp fastened to hooks, holding bits of scrap food. They hoped for a catch that would put welcome protein into their families' diets. Even the night heat was unrelenting. The luxury of a shower or a cool air-conditioned room offered relief for the privileged few.

As they exited the cab, a barefoot solicitor approached the travelers and inquired, "Boat ride, Madame? Boat ride, Sirs?"

Though of diminutive stature, the beggar looked scary. His front teeth, to the canines, on both the upper and lower arches were missing. The remaining teeth had a thick layer of porous, green plaque where they joined his reddened gums. A prickly growth of gray whisker stubble shaded his face. Crusts of pigmented skin decorated his weathered face. The scarred, discolored iris of his left eye wandered randomly within its socket without function.

Karl motioned the beggar away using exaggerated hand gestures.

Savannah looked shaken by the appearance of this stranger on the dark, quiet street.

"I don't feel safe here," she said.

"The people are harmless. The boat captains on the river give the beggars a few pennies for bringing them fares. They can look creepy, but if they get out of line, they take them off the streets. And unlike our revolving door jails, wherever they take them, it must be bad. It seems to work, because with all this poverty, there isn't much crime in these Asian countries," explained Karl.

"Let's get you to your rooms. You have a full day tomorrow. Did you forget about the early flight to Kuwait? It may be best to get some sleep, unless of course you're up for kinky sex over at Patpong Alley."

"Don't think you're going to leave me here alone," said Savannah nervously.

"I was asking you, baby. What'd you think? That I was asking Daniels? You and I know he has no interest in adventure. Now, you're a different story. If you say the word, I'll take you on the town and get us a six pack."

Savannah batted her eyelashes flirtatiously and said, "You know I'm a Southern Comfort cocktail lady." She glanced over to Derrick and added, "Besides, I'm taken."

Derrick made his usual disgusted face in response to Savannah's salacious innuendo. He grabbed their suitcases and faced the hotel entrance. Savannah engaged his arm and escorted him into the hotel lobby. Karl followed.

# CHAPTER
# EIGHT

THE MORNING PRODUCED A GLORIOUS CHANGE IN VIEW. PEERING FROM her window, the lazy river caught Savannah's eye. As she gazed the horizon and heavenward, the true magnificence of the ultramodern skyline greeted her with sun rays leaping from the mirrored behemoths. The multicolored, reflective panels, used abundantly in the modern architecture, exhibited an extravagant splendor. No ancient castles, no medieval structures offering old world charm, just shanties of straw and wood in the countryside while pretentious design grew tall in the cities. A mix of green foliage, remnant of the rain forest that thrived in this land years ago, flourished in the gardens below her window.

The hotel restaurant, the designated place to meet for morning coffee, offered a modest buffet for travelers. Everything was basic, devoid of the gourmet embellishments and excess of portion to which American life had grown so accustomed. An abundance of fresh fruit provided the most inviting element of the spread.

Karl fiddled with some sort of electronic contraption that piqued Savannah's interest as she approached the table.

"What's that?" she said, forgetting the social graces afforded by a greeting.

Karl ignored her question. "Good morning. I hope you slept well."

"Like a log," she replied.

"Where's your traveling buddy? I thought you'd come together," said Karl with emphasis on the word "come."

"That's what I'm counting on for the next phase of this trip," she said unabashedly, and acknowledging his vulgarity with a manner of confidence. "So, what's that contraption?"

"Here he comes now," said Karl, motioning toward the vestibule that led into the dining area.

Derrick approached sluggishly, sporting disheveled hair and glassy eyes not yet ready to focus on the day. "What's the phone gizmo?" he asked, also without any morning greet.

"I was just about to explain it to Savannah. This is my new, miniaturized, cosmic communications device. This is the wave of the future. You know how cellular is the big thing? Well, it's not universal. Let's say you guys are in the desert, and you have to get a message to me. The cell phones you've grown accustomed to won't be worth a damn. You see, there aren't compatible cells where you're going. There aren't any cells at all where the two of you are going," said Karl followed by a chuckle.

"So how is your phone going to work?" asked Savannah who never did understand the new technologies.

"It's going to be my savior. You see, instead of relying on a cellular antennae tower, it connects to a satellite networking system through cosmic rays that can keep me connected anywhere in the universe. No more lost signal. No weak areas."

"I read about those phones," said Derrick, "but I thought they were big and bulky devices."

"You read about military satellite phones and they are bulky, but now they've even miniaturized them. Satellite out of range means no connection. This is different. This uses cosmic rays from all over the universe. Look at this thing. It's the size of a pack of gum. I'm just having a little trouble with it right now. This is the prototype I'm testing for Joel Davis."

"Who?" asked Derrick.

"Joel Davis in technology over at Alcohol, Tobacco and Firearms. You know how the guys in ATF are. They are either techno-wizards or gung-ho infantrymen ready to break down doors. Joel is the technicians' technician. You've met him at lunch. He comes over once in a while, to show me the latest stuff those guys are working on. He asked me to field test this phone, knowing I would be out here with you. Here, this is your unit," Karl said as he pulled an identical phone from his pocket. "When you're in the remote, darkest corner of the Arabian continent, give me a call."

"You think this device can work?" asked Derrick skeptically.

"Davis is talented, and he has the pocketbook of the Treasury to work with, so they'll get it right. All you do is press this button when you want to test it. You scroll down, and when you see my name, you press this button and wait. You'll hear me in short order."

"Sounds good, if it works," said Derrick.

"It better work. I have money invested with Davis. He has some of his personally patented circuitry in this contraption from before he came on at ATF. If this works out, he plans on leaving the service of his country for a piece of the action in the private sector, and so do I. I'd like to get out of this shit job and settle down on an island."

"You've been dreaming that dream a long time now, haven't you?" said Derrick. "What's this, the tenth venture you've bet on? If you would save all that money, your dreams would come true. The way you're going, it may never happen."

"My daddy used to tell me, 'If you never take a chance, you'll never taste success.' He was a good old soul but . . . well anyway . . . You may want to spend your entire life doing the dirty work to save the world, but I'm out of here as soon as my ship comes in," said Karl.

"How about if you program in my home number. I'd want to call Adrienne later."

"No problem. First, I put in the country code, just like regular cell phones." Karl pressed several buttons and then looked at Derrick. "Okay, what's your number?"

Once Karl entered Derrick's number, in a matter of seconds, the phone beeped to lock it into the small device.

"I hate to break up this meeting of the techno-nerds, but we have to catch a plane," said Savannah. "Get the check."

The waiter brought the check to Karl, who noticed the bill was grossly incorrect.

"What's the matter?" asked Savannah seeing the look of confusion on Karl's face.

"I'm glad to see you can't get good help anywhere in the world. He overcharged us." Karl looked condescendingly to the server, "Three coffees, not thirty-three, boss."

Visibly upset by his error, the waiter promptly produced a corrected bill.

# CHAPTER
# NINE

KARL WALKED DERRICK AND SAVANNAH TO THE CAB THAT WOULD TAKE them to the airport, and he bid them well. With nothing but time to spend, he strolled along the main street located one block from the river. Row after row of shops filled each block with none much different from the thousands of tacky establishments found in every Third World tourist trap where they live to hawk their wares. Everything sold for prices yet cheaper if one wandered on a bit farther.

Having spent more time than necessary perusing the neighborhood flavors that included a few beers at bars frequented by locals, Karl decided to visit the Weekend Market, an extravaganza for the serious shopper. Less than ten minutes by cab, he immersed himself in the mix of tourists looking for souvenirs and the locals looking for delicacies.

The market, situated in a square, partitioned into hundreds of open stalls with roofs covered by every color of canvas, exhibited a mix of invigorating commerce and abject poverty. Canals, born of the main river, ran beneath the market causing the hideous smell of decaying debris to rise, engaging one's senses in an unwelcome manner.

Intense and incessant, the heat of the day made movement among the buyers and sellers feel dirty. Crowded booths, with their stagnant air, made the high temperatures seem all the more hellish. How the locals could buy the raw meats, putrid looking foodstuffs, and cut-open fruits, all of which were host to the flies feasting upon them, seemed incomprehensible. The air temperature, into the high nineties, meant the chance for a healthful meal at The Weekend Market diminished as the time of day advanced.

The prospect of finding old treasures lost within the piles of junk kept Karl at the market longer than he anticipated. Simple items of little value in these poor countries could command decent prices from collectors back home looking for primitive statues, religious paraphernalia, and odd mementos born at least fifty-years ago. The hunt provided Karl with anticipation of reward for his days otherwise wasted on this repeat holdover.

While dodging his way through the crowded aisles, an old woman sitting on the ground next to her raw meats, the particular cuts of which were unknown to Karl, beckoned, "Some very fine meats for you, sir."

The old woman's appearance, as repulsive as the foods she sold, sported wrinkled skin, and she had three teeth protruding at odd angles from her mouth. Her print dress, like her skin, seemed several sizes too large for her frail body. From her nose ran a clouded watery fluid she wiped onto a filthy piece of cloth.

Karl ignored her, but as he tried to pass, she took hold of his bare leg, just below the hem of his shorts. He jumped from the unexpected intrusion. Losing his balance, he fell to the ground and landed onto pieces of the raw meat covered with gnats and flies that were not about to relinquish their meal.

"You old fool," he hollered, "what the hell do you think you're doing?"

None of the shoppers noticed the incident. With everyone packed together on missions of their own design, with the booming chatter of barkers and buyers, no one had afforded interest or time for concern. Several shoppers stepped over Karl. With much difficulty and embarrassment, he stood and further scolded the old woman.

"How dare you even touch me, you wretched witch."

An old man rushed from nowhere and helped brush away the residue of butchered flesh and imbedded insects that stuck to Karl's legs from the fall.

"Sir, I am so sorry. She never meant you harm."

Karl stared into the face of the old man. He looked like the beggar from the night before. In a land of millions who all looked similar to him, it seemed too peculiar a coincidence, but the distinct appearance and features of the vagrant from the previous night looked identical.

"Allow me to make amends, sir. Permit me to provide your transportation for the entire day, at no cost to you. And I will have my son fashion for you three custom shirts in the fabric of your choice. He is a master, and he will repay the error of his mother, my wife, who has so rudely offended you."

The chance at getting something for nothing intrigued Karl, and after all, he did deserve compensation for his tumble. With an air of righteous indignation, Karl agreed to the deal and the old man directed him to a tuk-tuk, a motorized tricycle that zipped about the city as a cheap means of transportation.

In a Chinese dialect, the old man gave instructions to the driver. He then turned to Karl and said, "You pay the driver nothing. He will take you wherever you wish. He will be your personal attendant all day. First, he will take you to have the measurements for your custom shirts. By evening, they will be delivered to your room at the Rose House."

How odd, thought Karl. This was the old man from the previous night. He knew Karl stayed at the Rose Guest House. What a strange coincidence to meet again in the market place of thousands and find him defending his wife from the tongue-lashing Karl served up to a pathetic old woman trying to sell her wares. In a city this large, this congested, and this dirty, it seemed too much of a coincidence.

# CHAPTER
# TEN

THE TUK-TUK SPED OFF, TRAVELING THROUGH THE STREETS AND squares, dodging the traffic that came from every direction. More than once, Karl conjured up a vision of an accident whereupon he ended up on the roadway. Everyone seemed to drive in this dislocated manner, and he tried his best to remain calm. In no more than ten minutes, they arrived at a small shop at the end of a narrow street away from the maddening pace of the city.

The sign above the shop announced the home of a custom shirt-maker written in Chinese. This hole in the wall differed from the abundance of custom shirt-makers on the main streets and in lobbies of hotels, whose signs felt friendlier to those to whom they catered; the American tourist. The woodcarving above the door, fashioned in the shape of a shirt, confirmed to Karl they arrived at the proper destination.

The driver, who apparently spoke little or no English, grunted and motioned for Karl to enter the shop. Knowing the nature of the poor and uneducated in this country meant communication efforts would be challenging, however he tried the best he could.

"You'll wait here for me, right?" Karl said as he exited the tuk-tuk.

Again, the driver motioned with a backhanded wave for him to enter the building.

"You wait for me. Do you understand?" Now, Karl used animated hands to convey his message. He pointed to the driver, then to himself, and mimicked the motions of steering a car as he spoke. "You wait for me. No drive off. Yes?"

Again, the driver motioned for Karl to enter the building, and he said his first English words as an obedient parrot, "Yes, yes, yes."

"You don't know what the hell I'm saying, do you, asshole? Yes?"

"Yes, yes, yes," mimicked the driver.

Karl moved away from the tuk-tuk toward the building and offered one last charge. "You wait. If you don't, I'll never find the way back to my hotel, you simpleton."

Another repetitive reply, "Yes, yes, yes."

Upon entering the building, Karl noticed the foulest of smells, much like that which he encountered at the Weekend Market. A weathered stairway accompanied him on his journey to the second floor. From where he stood, came the howling scream of a saw. It sounded like woodcutting for a construction project. He climbed the rickety staircase. With each step, the rotted boards spoke of an old, dilapidated building. As he got closer to the sound, he identified that it originated from behind a closed door at the far end of the second-floor landing. Imprinted upon the door closest to him he saw the image of a tailored shirt. He entered.

A middle-aged Asian man looking the part of a tailor sat at a sewing machine situated at the back of the room. The machine purred softly, losing competition with the noise in the hallway. Not looking up from his work, he said, "Good morning. It is so nice to have you stop by for your free shirts.

"So sorry for actions of my mother. She wants to help family still. After all the years of her labors, she remains at work in market. Forceful selling is the way among our people. Her sight fails her. I am sure she did not see you are foreigner, who offends by such devices.

"Come, let me take measurements. Then I make you shirts." He gestured for Karl to approach.

Karl, feeling a level of uneasiness, for reasons unknown, walked over to the sewing machine. The tailor stood and motioned Karl toward the mirror. He directed him to sit in the old wooden chair.

"Hold out your arms, sir," he said, as he removed the tape measure draping his neck. He measured Karl's arm span, followed by each arm individually as they hung by his side. After each measurement, the tailor stepped over to his sewing machine where he jotted his notes.

While measuring Karl's neck, he looped the tape measure in such a fashion that it became a noose and bound his hands to the chair. With extraordinary speed, he restrained Karl in a way he could not move to free himself without choking. Though he could move air into his lungs, it was with great difficulty. The pressure on his throat made him submissive but didn't lead to unconsciousness.

From behind the curtain, at the back of the shop, stepped two middle aged men, and the old man from the market.

"I know it is impossible for you to speak, so do not even try. You may hurt yourself," said the old man. "Allow me welcome you to Thailand, Mr. Armstrong. Let me start by explaining we know why you are here.

"I will have Buree release the tape from your throat, so you can answer some questions."

The tailor cut the tape that bound Karl's neck, and he could breathe unencumbered. He used the free ends of the tape to bind Karl's hands yet tighter. Shocked and disoriented over this unique abduction and unaware of the gravity of the situation, Karl yelled, "What the hell do you think you're doing?"

"Mr. Armstrong, I will be asking the questions, if you will. We know why you are here. What we need to know relates to how much detail your government has discovered. When did you learn of our connection with the Japanese?"

"What?" exclaimed Karl, confused.

The old man nodded to the short, powerfully built fellow standing to Karl's right. From his waist, he removed a short leather belt fastened to a wood spoon. He launched the odd device toward Karl's head. A swishing sound came from behind, and it culminated with a loud snap and a searing burn to his scalp.

"What the hell?" Karl yelled.

"I do not wish to see you punished more than is necessary, but I must insist. I am the one to ask the questions.

"Doctor, will you please ready him, so we can proceed."

The frail-looking man standing to Karl's left side stepped to the sewing machine and from beneath it, produced a metal box that resembled some type of electronic monitor. He walked back to Karl's side and motioned to the stronger man with a simple nod. It seemed apparent these two worked together before and needed minimal verbal communication. The man on the right produced a large knife from a sheath hidden beneath his trousers in the center of his back.

"No, please don't," screamed Karl almost hysterically upon seeing the blade.

"Please, Mr. Armstrong, we are not here to hurt you. We just want information. Now, I do hope you will cooperate." He paused. "And I suspect you will."

With those words of reassurance, the man with the knife sliced into Karl's shirt to expose his bare chest. The man called "doctor" removed several wires from the metal case and placed them strategically upon Karl's naked skin.

Following a moment of adjustments to the wire leads and the dials on the machine, the doctor nodded to the old man.

"Let us begin," he said. "Are you the American Justice Department's chief investigator of automobile dumping?"

"Yes," responded Karl, delivering the one-word answer in a stressed manner. He had an underlying fear that if he gave the wrong answer, the electrical device would somehow shock him.

This apprehension made all his answers seem tentative, arousing even more suspicion from his interrogator.

"Were you sent to Japan on your assignment?"

"Yes, that's where I'm supposed to be as soon as I leave here," said Karl.

"Were you sent here to confirm a link between the Japanese and the Thai governments?"

"You lost me."

The old man looked at the doctor. The doctor looked up, tilted his head to the side and raised his eyebrows expressing uncertainty.

"Does the name NH 45 mean anything to you, Mr. Armstrong?"

"What?" Karl replied. His forbidden query brought an immediate response. The wiping sound and the sharp pain to the back of his head reminded him to pick his words with caution. Karl winced, but remained silent for fear of reprisal.

"Does the name NH 45 mean anything to you, Mr. Armstrong?" yelled the old man, losing his composure for the first time.

"No, nothing. I never heard of anything like that," Karl pleaded.

Again, the old man looked to the doctor who repeated his head tilt of ambiguity.

"Mr. Armstrong, do you, for a minute, believe I don't know why you are here? We have your itinerary. We know you are to stay for two days, and then you depart to Japan. We even know everyone you are going to meet with once you arrive in Japan. What we do not understand is your appearance here in our comfortable metropolis each time you travel to Japan. Why would you travel so much farther to Thailand if your destination is Japan? There is one answer. You have somehow found out. Now, I will ask you again, what does NH 45 mean to you? And please, no more questions, just answers."

"I'm telling you, I don't know what you're talking about. I never heard of NH 45. You have the wrong guy. You need to let me go."

Disregarding Karl's plea, the old man continued.

"Mr. Armstrong, I am going to mention some words that could seem unrelated to one with no knowledge, but if you are holding anything back, the slightest response will be picked up by the good doctor. I shall say a word, you will respond yes, if it has meaning to your visit to Thailand, or no, if it has no relationship. Do you understand?"

"Yes," replied Karl obediently and with a profuse sweat dripping from his forehead. He noticed, for the first time since they bound him, his thumbs remained free enough to touch his waist. He could reach the cosmic phone he planned on testing. Inconspicuously, he pushed at the button on the side, expecting it would connect him to Derrick, who was now in flight. Karl hoped, by chance, that Derrick would hear the interrogation, realize his colleague was in mortal danger and contact the authorities.

"Let us begin," said the old man. "Cyclops."

"No," said Karl.

"JT union."

"No.'

"Nagasaki."

"No."

With each word, the old man eyed the doctor for a sign Karl was lying. With no confirmation, the uncertainty served to make the old man more determined.

"Cyclops," he said loudly above the noise of the saw that came from the room at the end of the hallway. The whining high-pitched sound persisted as a constant in the background. Its tone varied on a regular pace as the saw bit into its chore.

"No," said Karl firmly.

"JT union," yelled the old man.

"No," Karl shouted desperately in return.

# CHAPTER
# ELEVEN

"WHAT'S THAT SOUND?" ASKED SAVANNAH UPON HEARING A SHRILL ring.

Derrick looked for the source of the intrusive noise.

"It sounds muffled. Check your coat pocket," she urged.

Derrick reached into his coat where he felt an unfamiliar object, the miniature phone he received from Karl earlier in the day. When he removed it from his pocket, they noticed a tiny red-light flashing.

"I thought the plan was we call him from the most remote desert location we could find," said Savannah.

Derrick put the device to his ear and listened. After observing Derrick holding the phone for about a minute without speaking, Savannah asked, "Why don't you say hello?"

"Shhh," responded Derrick curtly, as he motioned for her to be silent.

Another minute passed. Savannah, again, felt the need to inquire about the content of the call. "What's going on?"

"Here, you listen. What do you make of this," said Derrick, passing the phone to Savannah.

For another minute she listened intently, at which time Derrick asked, "So, what do you make of it?"

"It's nothing; a bad connection."

"No," said Derrick with a sense of alarm in his voice. "Did you hear it? It sounds like static, but I heard some words. *Cyclops*. I heard the word *Cyclops* two or three times. The shrill sound, that's not static. It's background noise."

Savannah placed the phone to her ear again and listened for another moment.

"You're right. I can hear words, but the noise in the background makes it impossible to get more than a few here and there."

Derrick pulled the phone away from Savannah and listened for yet another moment, after which time, he declared all he could hear were the background noises.

"Did you hear the word *Cyclops*?" asked Derrick.

"No, I heard *split wave*, and I think I heard Karl's last name, *Armstrong*. I don't know if that's what I heard, but it sounded like *Armstrong* and *old lady*. I don't know; it didn't make sense."

Derrick took out his cell phone and opened an electronic note pad.

"Tell me what words you heard."

"I heard *split waves*, definitely and *buying time*," said Savannah. "To be truthful, there was so much noise in the background. I can't swear I heard what I just told you."

Derrick jotted down the words they shared and stared at the paper in deep thought. He looked toward Savannah and said, "Nothing. Not a clue. It doesn't mean anything to me. Here, you take a look."

The notepad listed the words Savannah heard next to those Derrick deciphered. "You know, Cyclops. In Cyclops. Code name. Project. Starving children. Proceed." She stared at the paper and wrote the words in different orders.

"Well?" asked Derrick.

"It's some type of message. It has to be from Karl," Savannah reasoned. "Who else could be on this phone?"

"It could be what's his name? The tech guy, Joel Davis. If he and Karl are testing this thing, they are probably talking to each other," Derrick noted.

"I sure hope they had better reception than us," added Savannah.

"If Karl invested money in this dud, he's gonna be with Treasury a lot longer than he'd like," said Derrick. He paused and thought hard, searching for clarity.

"That's not it. Not at all. I think he called us. I think Karl is in trouble," said Savannah intuitively and with much concern in her voice.

Derrick did not respond, nor did he wish to enter into conspiracy theories with Savannah. Instead, he rose from his seat next to her and spread out on an empty row. All of the rows were empty as they were the only passengers on the flight going to their remote destination. He stared at the small phone that seemed to be calling out for him to take action. Scrolling down the list of contacts, he stopped at Karl's name and pressed the send button. Holding the phone to his ear, it took a minute before he heard an unusual sounding tone that resembled a busy signal. He pressed, "end" and scrolled to Adrienne. It was the perfect time to call. He felt lonely and speaking with her would offer comfort. He heard an odd repetitive sound, but different from the busy signal received when he tried to reach out to Karl. Derrick presumed this sound to be equivalent to the connecting ring of traditional phones, but after a long time, no one answered.

# CHAPTER
# TWELVE

"You do not know the meaning of revenge, Mr. Armstrong? You do not know the hearts of those defiled? You are good. They trained you well. We cannot risk the beauty and the progress of this country. You think they alone could support the incredible growth you see as you fly into this country. They have more than two thousand modern buildings towering over the city. This could not have happened without my people's help and Thailand's complicity."

"You are Thai," said Karl trying for a statement to avoid the striking blow from the strongman, though meant as a question.

"No, I am Japanese. I am here to derail your government's efforts to uncover the dumping. You see, we have arrangements with the Thai government to get our cars into the American market through channels that ordinarily slip past your scrutiny. When we learned you made repeated visits to Thailand before your Japan stop, we suspected you were onto our scheme, or worse, our motive. But it seems either you know nothing, or you have been trained well to control your... how do you call it, doctor?"

"Autonomic," replied the doctor.

"That's it, autonomic functions. Well, we cannot take risks. We must know for sure. There is one way to be certain. Bring him to the back."

The strongman tilted the chair, while underneath, the doctor placed a dolly into position. This allowed them to mobilize Karl, still firmly tethered and unable to offer protest. The old man led them out of the tailor shop and down the hall toward the source of the wailing sound. Karl, confined to the makeshift wheelchair, rolled along behind him. The old man stopped before the door.

"I was hoping it would not come to this, Mr. Armstrong. Are you ready to tell me what you know?"

"God help me. I have no idea what you are talking about."

The old man opened the door and entered. The ghastly sight weighed heavily upon Karl making him swoon. Only seconds away from black out, the thud made by the chair as it slid from the dolly brought Karl back to a staggered consciousness. Along the wall to his left, dozens of human bodies hung from hooks like those seen in a slaughterhouse for cattle. To the right side there were at least eight hampers filled with dogs, rabbits and assorted vermin from the streets. Two workers wearing masks, goggles and white, blood stained uniforms operated the grinding bandsaw. As they butchered the carcasses into smaller, manageable parts, a crew of ten women, similarly dressed, sliced and separated the meat from the bones. Another crew of women wrapped the flesh that resembled the meats Karl saw at the marketplace into packages.

Karl turned chalk white as the blood drained from his face. His mouth hung open in disbelief. The old man recognized the look of horror and fetched water from one of the workbenches. He splashed it onto Karl's face to bring him about. At the wave of his hand, the bandsaw stopped, leaving the room silent, as if he threw a switch that controlled all animation and activity.

"What is this place? What are you going to do to me?" demanded Karl, voice quivering and in a state of shock.

"This is the government's main means of feeding the poor," the old man replied.

"You can't be serious," exclaimed Karl.

"You can't comprehend a thing of this nature. How do you think we keep a city of so many humbled masses in line? There is essentially no crime here. As far as the outside world sees it, our prisons are respectable. They house our petty thieves.

"We have a sanctioned death penalty that is rarely used. The last time in 2009. Not too often, as it would appear to the sniveling critics of world injustice. Other than the few housed on death row for appearances, most of those who commit capital crimes end up here. They pay their debt to society in a rather novel way. You see, they come back to feed the poor.

"Living in a land of wealth and corruption, it's hard to imagine some people must resort to an institutionalized form of cannibalism." The old man paused as if waiting for an answer he knew he would not get. "It is hard to imagine. There is much your kind can't imagine—the way my people suffered at the hands of your bomb. Many resorted to despicable acts of barbarism just to survive."

Tears welled up in the old man's eyes as he spoke.

"When backs are up against the wall, we do things our civilized side suppresses. Perhaps, you will be able to shed light on my questions now that your back is against that wall. So, my good friend, does the sight of this room help you remember more concerning the relationship between the Japanese and the Thai government you forgot to mention?"

The old man motioned to the strongman standing behind the chair holding Karl captive. Alone, and with little effort, he lifted Karl in the chair and placed him upon the conveyor belt four feet from the blade of the saw. The old man nodded his head, and the operator activated the process. As the piercing sound revved to full speed, he cleared the carcasses of several dogs from the table to make room for Karl.

Realizing his life was in immediate danger, Karl reacted.

"Okay," he screamed. "Okay, I was holding back. What do you want to know? NH 45, it's the code name."

Karl's words interested the old man enough for him to motion the operator to silence the bandsaw again. In the eerie calm that spread as the blade ground to a halt, the workers stood quiet at their stations, heads bowed, as they took care to avoid eye contact with anyone. In silence, the stench of blood and raw meat dominated the assault on the senses. Karl tasted the putrid, airborne, particulate matter that settled upon his tongue. His throat, parched and aching, prevented him from swallowing.

"Tell me what you know about Cyclops. I'm more interested in Cyclops."

The real test arrived. Karl had no knowledge of anything that concerned the old man. Cyclops might be another code name, but unable to provide details, death appeared imminent. Thirsting for words to form in his parched mouth he blurted, "Cyclops is the code name of the actual project."

"Tell me more," said the old man.

"That's all I know, I swear."

The old man gave a nod. The operator flicked the switch. The shrill sound of the saw came alive and exhausted Karl's remaining strength. A deep void, borne of the dreaded act at hand, left him shattered. The strongman slid the chair along the conveyer belt until Karl's right foot was positioned perpendicular to, and just inches from, the razor-sharp blue blade.

"We have no more time to waste. Children starving . . . we must feed them. We held up this line long enough. Proceed."

With a second nod of his head, the operator of the saw took hold of Karl's right foot and tied it to the leg of the chair with a short piece of hemp. He repeated the binding on his left foot, so Karl was firmly strapped to the chair. He held Karl's shoulders as the strongman braced the bottom of the chair, and together they guided it toward the blade of the saw. In utter shock and transcending his physical state, Karl felt no pain by the time his ankle made contact with the blade. When his foot, now severed, fell to the ground, he observed another foot lying next to his. Unnoticed before, this had to belong to some other victim who had gone through a similar interrogation, he reasoned.

Once Karl realized he would never survive this ordeal, no matter what he knew, he panicked. He began to scream. His shrill voice could barely be heard, as it competed with the similarly pitched bandsaw. The workers acted as if nothing unusual took place. They understood their station in life. They knew firsthand the penalty for disobedience. Resignation, fear, and secure jobs kept them muted.

"It's not too late Mr. Armstrong. We can take you right over to the hospital and get you patched up, but I need answers. Do you have anything to say?"

Karl, now panting, could not utter a word. He began to sob.

"It looks as though I am wasting my time, Mr. Armstrong. You have no knowledge of the split waves. You were bluffing, buying time. You never heard of NH 45, or Cyclops."

Karl could not speak. With rapid short movements, he timidly shook his head in the affirmative to acknowledge the old man was correct in his statements.

"I am sorry we had to meet, Mr. Armstrong."

He pulled a small recorder from his breast pocket and placed it into his pants. Turning to the doctor he said, "When they are done here, see to it that Mr. Armstrong is brought back to the market. Take him to the old woman. She is expecting him." He nodded to the operator of the saw, his last act before he exited the slaughterhouse.

The workers went about their business with the precision of an active assembly line. Karl twisted his body wildly longing for escape. The chair shook violently from his contortions. The operator needed the strongman and the doctor to steady the conveyer table, lest it topple. Having spent all remaining energy, Karl fell victim to exhaustion. By the time they finished severing his legs, consciousness lapsed into an absolute slumber from the bleed out. He convulsed spasmodically as the medial cut through his body reached the diaphragm. The workers used both hands to maintain control. It appeared they had done this many times before.

No one said a word. They all knew their jobs and communicated with nods that meant whatever was expected. The women took each sectioned body part to a table, where they reduced Karl to eight packages of freshly slaughtered, boneless victual. The strongman gathered the packages. He and the doctor left without saying a word.

# CHAPTER
# THIRTEEN

Derrick tried to reach Adrienne several times using the prototype phone. Each time he failed. Not connecting with Karl and now having no success calling home the device appeared flawed in design. Derrick calculated the time back in the Philadelphia region, and believed Adrienne would be home to answer his call.

He last tried to reach her at six-thirty in the early morning, a time that should have found her nestled under covers and sound asleep. Instead, that particular morning, Adrienne awoke early to be prompt for her meeting with Jim Young and the staff of supporters spearheading his bid for election to Mayor of Philadelphia. She felt such honor to participate on the ground floor of the career of someone important.

On her second day of volunteer work, Jim invited Adrienne to meet him in his office on the twenty-second floor for lunch. To her surprise, and delight, she was the only one present. She suspected he had recognized her zeal and enchantment in serving his cause. For this, she anticipated a special assignment that would ingratiate her further.

When Adrienne entered his office, she found Jim seated behind a huge mahogany desk. The dressings included a solid gold fountain pen, an electronic Rolodex connected to a sophisticated phone intercom and no clutter.

"Have a seat," he beckoned.

Adrienne walked to the chair opposite his desk and sunk into the plush leather, allowing it to embrace her by the wealth and splendor it represented. As she crossed one leg over the other, her dress rode up inadvertently to reveal shapely thighs. Jim's eyes stared a bit too long, but she was oblivious.

"I want you to know how honored I am to be a part of your campaign," she said with the joy of a schoolgirl fawning over a favorite teacher.

"The honor is mine," said the consummate politician. "Having a dedicated team pulling together is what winning is all about. Leaders are nothing more than the figureheads that represent the will of those with a common goal. The team deserves all of the credit. Trust me, I know. And having you on my team is all that matters."

Jim opened a drawer, pulled out a stack of papers and placed them on the desk. "Permit me to explain why I wanted to speak with you, one on one, today. Here is a list of the most powerful citizens in Philadelphia. There is a sheet on each one. When the time comes, you must contact them to pay up. They come through every election like clockwork. Sometimes they need a little prodding, but they give in every time. This information is extremely private, and I can't trust this responsibility to just anyone," he said.

Adrienne felt a burst of excitement knowing Jim trusted her for such a responsible position.

"You can count on me. Anything I can do to help, I'll be there," she said proudly.

"It's so kind of you to say that, but they are words, and words are so often . . . just words."

"No, seriously," she added. "Anything, and anyway I can assist . . . you let me know."

After hiding his ever-present smile, and with a serious expression sweeping over his face, he beckoned, "Come over here."

Almost as if in a trance, Adrienne arose from the chair, walked to the desk and stood next to Jim. He got up and positioned himself behind her. Without touching, he brought his lips close to her right ear and spoke softly.

"If you cannot keep your commitments to me and my team, you must have no hesitation to leave. If you wish to go at any time, feel free to do so. Do you understand?"

With nervousness, Adrienne's voice cracked as she replied, "I understand."

"You made a bold statement when you said, *anything you can do to help.* I said, *these are just words,* and you, again, insisted your pledge is more than just words. Your pledge *is* a covenant. Do you understand what I am saying?"

"Yes."

"I am planning on revealing to you, and only you, information that can never go beyond these doors. Are you willing to accept this responsibility?"

Again, she responded in the affirmative without discussion.

"I cannot stress enough how once you enter into my inner circle, you will have things on me that could ruin my career. As a result, we must have a mutual covenant that prevents any recklessness. Do you understand what I'm saying?"

"I understand," said Adrienne feeling a peculiar combination of pride and apprehension.

Jim gently placed his hands upon Adrienne's neck and soothingly massaged her shoulders. As they wandered along the top of her chest, he pressed his body to hers from the rear. Reflexively, Adrienne reached for his hands and held them tight to halt their progress.

"I thought you understood the covenant we must have to proceed with your responsibilities."

"I know what you said, but, but, I don't know," she stammered. "I love my husband, and . . . and . . ."

"That's why I chose you, because you do love your husband, and you will have just as much to lose if you were to ever turn on me. That's why it must be this way. Do you understand?"

"Yes."

"Do you understand?" he repeated firmly.

"Yes," she said emphatically.

*Do you understand,* served as a hypnotic mantra drawing Adrienne toward the corrupting forces of power and prestige.

The craving for station and wealth corrupted many with stronger convictions than Adrienne. Material desires defiled her character, making it easier to take the leap. Her final answer came when she released her grip from his hands, allowing him to explore secret parts once reserved as her husband's exclusive domain. He massaged her breasts thoroughly, reaching all parts without removing her bra. Guilt ridden and with perverse sense, she enjoyed the seduction.

"Now, I want you to bend over my desk and place your hands flat to hold yourself steady."

Not understanding her compliance, her lack of hesitancy, Adrienne obeyed. She heard the sound of Jim unzipping his pants. Her heart skipped beats and she panted.

"Pull down your skirt and panties."

With a painful reluctance she obeyed, upon his repeating the demand.

"Now place your hands back on my desk."

Adrienne stood in this vulnerable position expecting a penetration that never came. Jim relieved his desires on her exposed skin making certain to avoid insertion. The experience felt cheap and disturbing for Adrienne. For Jim, the act seemed primal. Throughout confirmation of the covenant, tears rolled down Adrienne's cheeks. What little conscience remained fed a spigot of guilt, still she could not walk away.

A dozen sessions, each more perverse, were required to affirm the never-ending covenant before Adrienne was able to assuage her guilt. The favoritism and position Jim's affection afforded Adrienne made the sacrifice worthwhile.

The affair would have negligible effect on her relations with Derrick, because, in her view, the ends justified the means. Besides, this busy married couple relegated sex to weekend encounters as the passion of young love faded from their lives. During the weekdays, Derrick and Adrienne were too tired to perform anyway.

# FOURTEEN

The plane transporting Savannah and Derrick to Bubiyan landed on a tarmac several hundred yards from where commercial aircraft set down. On this airfield, authorities assigned military transports to a designated area, providing terminal space in an old dilapidated two-story building. Upon exiting the aircraft, they experienced strong winds lifting the sands of the surrounding desert limiting visibility.

Military navigator, Lieutenant Will Slattery, and pilot, Captain Victor Henry escorted Derrick and Savannah to the old building. It resembled an Arabian hotel from another era that weathered many storms without much maintenance or restoration. Several coats of paint peeled away from the structure, each commemorating modern histories in an ancient land. Ceiling fans rusted in motionlessness hung from the entrance ceiling. The dim lighting cast an uneasy feel and the emptiness of the structure seemed foreign for those who thrive on activity and life all around.

"Looks like you'll be holed up here for at least sixteen hours," said Captain Henry. "This is a big one. You won't get your next flight out till midnight."

Derrick had the expression of disgust on his face when he asked, "What's a big one?"

The Captain laughed. "You never been here, have you?"

"No, never."

"These storms, they come out of nowhere. Brutal, I say brutal. A pilot's nightmare, especially when we are on tactical missions. The landscape changes just like that." He snapped his fingers. "One minute you're in control. The beauty of the desert from upstairs, it's a sight. Straight ahead, you see sculpted terrain, so distinct you could draw a picture of it with your eyes closed. The next minute, it's on you like white on rice. You're sweating your balls off to keep the ship steady." He paused and turned to Savannah in recognition of his uncouth comment. "Excuse me, ma'am." He turned back toward Derrick to continue. "And when it all clears, you'd think you landed on another planet."

Savannah interrupted, "It sounds rather dangerous for flight, but I'd guess it's no better traveling on the ground."

"Look here, if you have to be traveling in these parts, you take this with you." From his aviator jacket, he extracted an expensive military compass and flipped open the protective cover to reveal the magnetic needle searching northward. "Make certain you know the direction you're heading. You just have to believe in the compass reading and keep heading in the right direction. You will get there just as long as you believe in the compass. Don't ever try to use landmarks or your sense of direction. Around here, it's as if they lifted you up, spun you about and dropped you on Jupiter."

Derrick handed it back to the Captain saying, "I'm sure the government will provide us with a capable guide. You keep this."

"No, I insist," argued the Captain. "These guides ain't worth shit. The first sight of a storm and they'll book it out of there looking for refuge. If you can't keep up, you're a goner. Here, take it. It's my gift to you. I'd hate to see you folks lost in the desert."

Savannah and Derrick looked at each other expressing similar emotions grounded in different sources. For Savannah, the adventurous mission lost its shine with the reality of life-threatening danger. This wake-up call spoke of an assignment that now appeared more menacing than she expected. What started as a forced obligation of employment for Derrick became an insane mission worthy of battle pay.

In the lobby of the building, a rather ethnic Arabian gentleman appeared from the shadows to greet them. Huge bushy eyebrows grew as one across his forehead. A rather large nose eclipsed all other features. He spoke English rather well with a classic Middle Eastern accent. He wore a dark business suit, Italian, rather than the garb of the locals. Stark white socks detracted from an otherwise fashionable statement. Like so many in this land, he no longer possessed a full dentition. At least two spaces created by missing teeth welcomed people when he smiled. A bright red fez with a gold tassel covered his dark black hair that appeared unwashed for a long time.

"Good morning, good morning, my American friends. It is so nice you arrived as you did. If just minutes later, you would have been diverted due to the storm. I beg your patience. Yafti, your guide, has arrived, but the storm delayed your pilot. His will be the flight arriving once the weather clears. They always do clear. Please make yourself comfortable. You can take all the blankets you need." He pointed to a bin. "And rest over there on the floor."

In the corner sat Yafti, a frail young fellow leaning against the wall. He had a blanket propped against his head to protect him from the hard, rough surface of the cinderblock. He appeared to be sleeping, or he had no interest in meeting the principals of his mission at this time. He wore soiled baggy white linen pants and a matching blousy shirt. Sandals protected his feet, blackened by grime from lax hygiene. He covered his head with cloth, wrapped strategically, to shield his neck from the assault of the desert sun and sand.

Derrick and Savannah each grabbed a blanket and staked out a space at the wall whereupon they took refuge. Captain Henry went to the canteen and ordered an imported beer. He seemed comfortable with himself and did not want to, nor did he offer to join the others. Lieutenant Slattery, who said not a word, sat at the opposite end of the lobby and proceeded to devour his paperback novel.

"What do you make of this hellhole?" Derrick asked Savannah. Not interested in an answer, he continued. "There is no way we should be on this mission. They have special agents for this kind of fieldwork. You know . . . the CIA," he stated sarcastically.

Savannah didn't' respond, and at this point, there was little either wanted to discuss. Their silence magnified the intensity of the tempest that roiled around them. They knew they were out of their league and may pay for Savannah's miscalculation of the dangers involved in their assignment.

After several hours, the winds diminished in force. A few minutes before eleven P.M. the buzz of a small engine plane came into focus to awaken the desolate outpost. Intermittent screeching of rubber skidding against the tarmac announced the landing. The harsh sounds derived from a less than expert navigator, a daredevil or someone impaired. However, this small plane was the lone way Derrick and Savannah could get to Ma-amir, Iraq, the next stop on their journey.

Derrick reflexively opened his eyes upon hearing the unsettled sounds of the landing. The rustling of his movement caused Savannah to stir. Looking around, they saw no one in the poorly lit lobby, darkened even more by daylight long gone.

Soon, a stranger tripped over the threshold and almost fell as he entered the building. His solid build, and exaggerated masculine stride, accentuated by shifting of his weight from side to side, did not fit well with the short, five-feet-six-inch stature. A leather bomber jacket with cut-off arms exhibited well-defined muscular development and housed broad shoulders with a massively developed chest, mounted on top of narrow waist and hips. His appearance scribed the blueprint of an aging athlete with swagger, perhaps a gymnast with some trophies to his name. He wore a blue English aviator's cap from a generation past. A medal pinned to the cap, matched the one attached to his jacket. Both the jacket and cap saw action well before the military service of someone forty or so years old. Tinted aviator glasses revealed searching eyes.

"Wow. They gotta fix that ledge, they do," he said in a thick English accent as he recovered from the misstep. "Where's my party? It won't be long before we can take off. You must be Ambrose and Daniels. Where's Yafti? Did I pronounce that right, Yafti? Where the hell is that scoundrel?"

"You must be our pilot," said Savannah.

"Fredricks at your service, Ma'am. I have been charged with your transport and safety. It is my duty to take you from this lovely oasis to the camels awaiting your arrival. Have you seen your guide as of yet?"

As he spoke, a large shadow of a man approached from the darkened canteen that now appeared closed. The shadow contracted into the undersized form of Yafti as he strode into the light.

"Yafti?" Fredricks called out.

"Yes, sire, are we ready to depart?"

"Get the bags onboard. I'll just make a quick stop at the loo, and we'll be on our way."

"I have boarded the luggage, sire."

"A fast one, that Yafti," said Fredricks directing his comment toward Derrick.

Fredricks strolled toward the darkness of the canteen. He knew the layout and went straight to the lavatory. Awkwardly, the others waited for him to return.

Yafti stood in silence facing the floor. It bothered Derrick that Yafti did not attempt to communicate with his clients. Not willing to wait until a calamity, Derrick initiated conversation.

"You'll be guiding us into Iran, right?" he asked.

"Please, sire, I do not wish to offend, but silence is most desired. It is not suitable to speak of travel to that land," he whispered while looking furtively about the empty building.

"There's no one here," said Savannah.

"Madame, if you please, it is not to a safe destination we seek to travel. It would be of interest to the terrorists that Americans are even near to the border towns, let alone entering into Iran. Many seek rewards for this information. It is best that few know our objective. My people choose me for these missions. Your government can trust my family, and they call upon us often. My family name is at risk if I fail. Please, until we are in flight, do not make mention of our destination."

Derrick pulled Savannah aside. "For Christ's sake, we're lawyers. We should turn back now and get the hell out of here."

With Derrick's last word, Fredricks emerged from the shadows and motioned for them to follow.

Fredricks, the principal of a private hire transport company, was the one pilot willing to risk flying near, and sometimes into, Iranian air space. There was just as much chance either friendly or hostile fire would intercept or shoot him out of the sky in this part of the world.

"Okay, mates, bags packed and ready to roll. We have to get out right now, ahead of any other storm that'll be forming."

As sheep, they followed into the heat of night and boarded the small prop plane. The departure felt unsettled, as the tires made screeching sounds, much as when Fredricks arrived. The landing gear acted as a bumper against the runway adding to the drama. Following a moment of tentative flight, they lifted into the air and headed to their destination.

Yafti sat in the back of the plane next to the net binding the luggage in place. Derrick and Savannah placed themselves right behind Fredricks.

"I understand your mission is classified," said Fredricks. "It seems just about everybody headed out this way is on a classified mission."

"You do this flight often?" asked Savannah.

"Three times in the last six months. Not much doing in Bubiyan, so three flights are a pittance. But I do get more offers to take packages into Khosrowabad. Heaven knows what's going on there."

Derrick, now showing interest, interrupted, "What kind of packages?"

"Don't know. I just get offers. I'm not permitted to make those runs. The town is off limits to licensed commercial flights. That's not to say they can't find traffickers to go in. There's always someone willing to take the risk. Whatever it is they deliver there, it's unusual. You have this city that's a speck of dust on a map, and over the last few years, there have been more flight calls than tea in England. It doesn't figure."

"How far will it be from Ma-amir to Khosrowabad?" asked Derrick.

"It's a ten-minute flight. However, from what I hear, you have at least ten hours by camel if the sands remain calm. Yafti, your guide, he's good, but don't wander off," warned Fredricks.

They planned on touchdown at a desolate, eerily dark field in Ma-amir. As they made their approach, the landing field offered minimal light to the blanket of blackened sand. After another grace-less landing, Fredricks left the engine running while he and Yafti unloaded the few bags they took with them. Yafti dragged the bags from the plane.

Fredricks' affable nature changed. He seemed hurried, as if he wanted to takeoff straight away. Derrick felt concerned about the obvious nervousness, but realized it made sense for Fredricks to leave with nothing other than risk offered should he stay. In a matter of ten minutes, Fredricks wished them luck and made way for safer airspace.

# CHAPTER
# FIFTEEN

From a distance, a peasant tending three camels appeared from the darkened landscape. Yafti called out in a strange sound of the wild, promptly mimicked by the herder.

Now in familiar territory, Yafti exhibited a dramatic change in temperament. For the first time since meeting Savannah and Derrick, he took charge. He began by fastening their luggage to the camels. He checked on, and secured, the large, canvas water sacks draped upon the beasts, attached to saddles that had numerous hooks to hold provisions.

After a sketchy speed course on dromedary travel, they headed toward Khosrowabad, leaving the herder behind.

"Yafti," barked Derrick, "it's nearing two in the morning. I don't believe we can make the whole ten hours without a rest."

"Not a problem, sire. Just another kilometer and we will make camp. It was my intention to get away from the airstrip by about an hour's ride. Then we rest till morning. Once refreshed, we continue. I expect we will arrive by early evening tomorrow."

Following the hour of travel, Derrick and Savannah's eyes felt heavy, their bodies ached, and they were ready to fall from the beasts of burden. In the desert, Yafti took care of all remedies. He pitched their tent and made the campsite hospitable.

Savannah's usual cage of confidence, rattled for the first time in her life, had her questioning the wisdom of playing secret agent. She pulled her sleeping bag close to Derrick's and nestled against him. Yafti remained seated near the fire, unprotected. If he slept at all, it was with an uncanny ability to respond to all sounds, as the vigilant guard watched over them.

Yafti greeted his charge before sunrise. He understood the desert well, and travel before dawn was a matter of necessity. By ten AM, Derrick and Savannah learned why their provisions included such an abundance of water. They were encouraged to drink often in order to avoid succumbing to the desert heat. Just before eleven o'clock, they reached a huge natural dune that offered protection from the glowing mid-day sun. They rested in the shade for three hours. The hot sands no longer animated the desert air. When that undulating ripple seen looking into the distance ceased moving, and when the surface cooled from its greatest elevation in temperature, they continued to their destination.

By early evening, the town appeared. It seemed to materialize from the nothingness of the desert. Abject poverty surrounded them in a most literal fashion. Children came begging the moment they arrived. They were between five and twelve years old. Tattered, filthy rags covered their privates, while the rest of their bodies remained bare. Skin aged beyond chronological expectation browned by the sun several shades darker than their race dictated. Sores, in various stages of healing, decorated their bare feet. Yafti scooted the beggars away with some words and exaggerated hand motions.

Derrick and Savannah followed Yafti to a hut designated as their housing. Private dwellings, given up by the locals, substituted for accommodation in this land devoid of hotels or other lodgings found in the developed world. Villagers welcomed renting their shanties for unheard of sums by the foreigners who had been coming as of late. Opening up their homes and taking refuge in desert tents was an easy choice.

"In the morning, I will return," announced Yafti. "We will travel early to the farm compound where you will have the opportunity to observe the one they call *the Sheik*."

"That's Alimet," Savannah said as an aside to Derrick. She turned to Yafti and asked, "Do you know what sort of work he does on the farm?"

Yafti turned around and peered side to side suspiciously. In a whisper he replied, "All that goes on at the farm is forbidden. We are not to speak of it. The government could have one beheaded for inquiring."

"We're here to help," said Derrick, as an offering to get Yafti to confide in him. "Our people who hired you to guide us are on your side. You can speak openly."

"Since they have come to our village, there have been unexplained occurrences. Some of my people are no longer the same. It started with the swallows and sparrows found dead in the streets. At first, we thought poisoning. Later we saw them destroying themselves. Flying into the walls of our temple, our houses. They were mad, if a bird can go mad. Then our goats, which we have but few, went mad with fever. They butted one another to death in a piteous manner. The authorities showed great interest. They collected the birds and the goats and replaced them, so we could continue to have food. Though all very strange, we know not to ask. We thank Allah for the reparations. I must go now. I will return in the morning; shall we say four AM?"

The hut provided the barest of essentials including nowhere to sit comfortably. Derrick and Savannah positioned themselves at a wooden table that lay close to the floor. They ate from government rations provided by the specialists who prepped them on their needs while traveling. Beds made of goatskins and the floor offered uncomfortable repose.

When getting ready to end the day, Savannah turned to Derrick and noted, "Not much on TV tonight. Thought maybe we'd go upstairs and get to sleep early." Though she maintained her sense of humor, the pitiable setting cast its pall over all possibility of carnal delight, either fantasized or real.

"When we get back," said Derrick, "I am going to sew your mouth shut, so you will never again volunteer for an adventure like this. And if you try to involve me in your hair-brained schemes again, I'll get you disbarred and see to it you spend the rest of your life working as a paralegal for a personal injury attorney."

"Good night to you, too," uttered Savannah, as she pulled up a goatskin cover to protect her from the desert's cold night air. They exchanged nothing more that night.

# CHAPTER
# SIXTEEN

THE STARK BEAUTY OF NATURE'S BAREST ECOSYSTEM ELEVATED THE morning trek. A rising sun peeked over the horizon allowing the golden orb to set upon white undulant waves of pristine sand. The landscape, which extended for what seemed to be infinite miles, cast shadows that created gradient shades of earthly colors. For city dwellers that never experienced such a stunning terrain, it was as if exploring another world.

The camels appeared awkward, yet efficient. They traveled well upon the ever-yielding sands, marching without orders. It seemed they knew their destination, but to a discerning eye, Yafti made the subtle adjustments to guide their course.

After hours of trailing through this endless stretch of baked desert, Yafti brought the group to a halt.

"There, there in the distance you can see the compound," announced Yafti.

"Where?" asked Derrick.

"Nothing. I see nothing," said Savannah, straining her eyes.

"It will become clear to you as we get closer," said Yafti as they continued their trek.

At first sighting, their minds played games with them. The

oscillating atmosphere that hovered above the scorched sands made the detection surreal. The silhouette of the compound faded and reappeared repeatedly. As they got closer, perceive depth improved. The point of focus grew in size, and they could see it was real.

Two miles from Alimet's compound, they stopped and waited for their ticket onto the grounds. In a few minutes, a Land Rover appeared from behind a sand hill, driven rather hard with the reckless abandon of youth. That seemed to be the mentality, though not necessarily the chronology of all the adventurers they met so far.

The camels whinnied at the approach and backed away from the aggressive vehicle. Upon closer inspection, what seemed to be a woman stepped out to greet them. She had a Slavic accent but spoke English rather well. With short-cropped hair and bulging leg muscles, it was difficult to ascertain gender. Her voice, however, sounded soft and sensual.

"I am Nicola, your guide onto the grounds of the compound. You will change into the outfits I have provided for you," she commanded with the full confidence of a leader.

Derrick and Savannah disrobed and dressed in the garb of a Russian-Muslim mix, the likes of which they had never seen. It was certain to blend in with the company they would soon encounter.

"If anyone speaks to you, nod, and point to me," Nicola continued. "I will be your tongue for today. Do not speak, or you may lose yours.

"You are here under the pretense of attending a lecture by the renowned Sheik Mohamed Abdul Alimet. He is conducting experiments with prions, as you know. He shares his work with those who support him and his fellow citizens. They invited the two of you as representatives from Vilnius, a small town in my country, where covert studies in human behavior happen. Here, take your badges. You will wear them at all times.

"You are doctors of psychiatry, and your interests are in the effects on behavior associated with the prion folded proteins. They will not ask you questions, and the principals at the lab do not speak your language, so they should not interact with you.

"Throughout, I will be speaking to you in a Russian dialect known by few. It is to appear that I am your interpreter. In reality, you will understand all that is going on. You see, the universal language is English in areas of science. The diverse groups that come here to study all have the common language of English by which they communicate.

"You will also hear numerous Arabian tongues. Just ignore them. I will be your guide. When I need to communicate with you, I will naturally use English in a whisper, interspersed with the Russian so they will not catch on.

"Your guide will wait here for our return." Yafti nodded in affirmation. "Then, are we ready?"

On the ride to the farm, Nicola explained she had been an agent with the KGB before the breakup of the Soviet Union. The end of the Cold War saw newly independent agents traveling to where interested parties appreciated and rewarded their skills. She had ties to rogue Arab nations that provided much-needed information and links to the West. For years, American intelligence used the skills of these unemployed agents with great results. They could penetrate where the Americans earlier failed.

The distant perimeter of the compound had, essentially, no security. Behind the main building, a farm flourished in the middle of the desert, complete with a silo that held imported grain. Sheep and goats roamed a fenced in area. Uniformed guards armed with automatic weapons stood vigilant in front of the main building.

Nicola led Derrick and Savannah to the entrance where the guards checked their credentials with names on the admissions list and let them enter. A servant ushered them to a small auditorium where twenty others milled about. The guests included a multitude of nationalities, but mostly represented by Arab and Asian men.

A voice over the speaker system instructed, in English, for the participants to take their seats, and in moments, the lights dimmed, except for the podium. In strolled the Sheik. He wore a long lab coat covering much of his short body. The traditional keffiyeh crowned his head. A thick, untamed gray beard dominated his face. Leathery, wrinkled skin, from years of exposure to the damaging rays of the sun, made him appear older than his actual age.

Standing in front of a large blackboard, and without introduction, he began his lecture as if continuing from where he might have finished previously.

"As noted, the most recent lifeform to be studied, the prion, once dismissed as an oddity, an impossibility, is now under intensive investigation. Here at the desert laboratory, I have taken my research to extraordinary levels. While the world searches, I have discovered. How naive of the scientific community to think these proteinaceous forms are few in number. In a world where there are ten thousand new insect species discovered each year, and it is believed there are millions yet undiscovered, how can it not humble the scientific mind to fathom the vast number of lifeforms that have invaded our bodies in the past, are there now, or will take up residence in the future?

"It is the soul infected in Western cultures that now tries to invade our people. The spread of behaviors beyond the dictates of all civilizations festers upon their shores. They have wealth and freedoms used to pervert the values of humanity.

"Alas, my research has found an answer for which you come. The lifeforms that don't actually live can be harvested for the good of Allah."

Alimet's dissertation remained nonspecific in regard to what Savannah wanted. He made numerous references of his desire to rid the world of disease, but it was not clear just what disease beguiled him. The confusion of his words lent an interpretation that, for him, disease could be blasphemous behavior. Nothing specific tied the Sheik, or his supporters, to any biological attack on the United States. The lecture ended, and the guests remained to speak with the Sheik's lab associates. He left the hall as abruptly as he arrived.

Nicola led Savannah and Derrick out of the compound.

"We traveled a long way for nothing," said Savannah. "I want to take a closer look at the penned animals."

Trained and living for stealth and adventure, it did not pose a problem for Nicola to accommodate. As they approached the fenced-in yard, upon first glance, the animals looked like any others. To the perceptive observer, they had an odd gait, stiff and shaky in their movements.

Several of the animals wandered over to a channel that led them into a small building. One particular sheep walked in and out of the building repeatedly. With each step, it paused to regain balance, and several times the creature fell to its knees.

Crawling under the fence, Derrick, Savannah, and Nicola made entrance into the building following the path of the animals. Inside they discovered a well-equipped laboratory fitted with the most elaborate modern apparatus available at all cost. On a lab bench, Savannah located a notebook. With great interest and greater anticipation, she opened the prize expecting to find meaningful answers to her mission. She saw Arabic writing, and with disappointment she turned to Nicola.

Nicola understood what Savannah wanted and tucked the notebook into her pocket. Before they could turn to leave, the lock on door at the far end of the building clicked. Nicola placed the notebook back upon the table.

"Get down," ordered Nicola, shielding her charge before she took refuge herself.

In walked the Sheik with two assistants. He shouted commands, and the aides scurried to assemble two hypodermic syringes. They used great care in measuring out the exact amount of each reagent. From behind huge, floor-to-ceiling refrigeration units, Savannah, Derrick and Nicola watched and listened.

The lab assistant rang a bell, and in wandered two sheep, the shaky one they observed earlier and another that was milling around the entrance. Each assistant restrained an animal and proceeded to inject. They spoke in an Arabic tongue that held no meaning to Derrick or Savannah, but Nicola listened intently.

The first sheep experienced tremors as the injection took effect. Within minutes, the animal became restless, hard to handle, and agitated beyond the expected behavior of such a normally docile species. High-pitched squealing sounds came from the beast. Its rear legs kicked repeatedly in an attempt to strike the assistant.

The other sheep had the opposite reaction to the injection. It appeared to have difficulty standing and as a result leaned against the leg of the assistant. He steadied the animal and backed off, leaving it to confront the more aggressive counterpart.

When released, the restless sheep attacked the passive animal. The assault was relentless and without provocation. The meek animal made no effort in defense. Following collapse upon the ground, the result of the first salvo, the docile animal let the assailant have its way until, obvious to all, it died.

After subduing the violent animal with expected difficulty, the assistants injected it with another solution that drain its life force. The Sheik and the assistants applauded as if they had succeeded in their mission. They lifted the animals to separate operating tables and opened their skulls. They removed their brains and placed them into bottles containing a nutrient broth. They conversed for a few minutes and then left the laboratory.

# CHAPTER
# SEVENTEEN

For Derrick and Savannah, the visual display defined the Sheik's work as hostile. Nicola tugged at the elbows of the stunned observers to get them to make their exit.

"We must leave now," she commanded. "Any moment, maintenance crews will get here to dispose of the animals. We have no time to lose."

She checked to make certain the yard remained empty and guided them out of the compound. No one spoke a word until they reached the safety of the Land Rover and began their ride back to meet Yafti.

"What are they searching for?" asked Derrick, breaking the silence. "I'd think they have bad intentions from what we saw back there. What did they say in the lab?"

"The Sheik somehow found a relationship between the prions and rage behavior. He predicts he will have mastered the control of the prions in a matter of months. It seems he will use his method to attack the Americans," explained Nicola.

"He said that?" asked Savannah excitedly, hoping to have real evidence to support her suspicions.

"Well, not really," said Nicola. "That's my interpretation, but what he actually said was they would finally win against the American devils."

"It can't be better than that," exclaimed Savannah.

"We saw rage, but that doesn't mean the experiments are not for other purposes," explained Nicola. "For example, at the lecture, he stated his team is in a race to find a cure for Alzheimer's disease. He said he suspects that prions are the cause of the dreaded memory loss. So, when he said, 'we will win against the American devils,' it may be that he boasts of the race to the cure. What we saw as rage could have been the dissolution of a brain lesion from the injection. Pain and rage can appear one and the same. Things are not always what they appear to be."

"I don't care what you say, you won't convince me they aren't evil men with evil intentions," said Savannah. "If I could get hold of that book in the lab, I bet it would explain it all."

Nicola stopped the Range Rover abruptly.

"Authorize me to go back, and it will be yours."

"Let's go," said Savannah eagerly as Derrick cringed, having had enough sleuthing for a lifetime.

"Hold on," cautioned Nicola. "First, I go back alone, and you stay here."

"I'm okay with that," said Derrick.

"Second, this will cost your government an additional five thousand, US."

"Deal," said Savannah.

"Here's the key to the Land Rover. There's extra water and food in the back. I'll return in no more than two hours. That will give me time if they are cleaning the site from the experiment we witnessed or conducting other experiments. In no case are you to leave this location."

"What if someone sees us out here?" asked Derrick.

"Trust me, no one will find you here. I know the compound. I know where and when they travel. You are safe here. Trust me."

Nicola hiked off to retrieve the notebook. Derrick and Savannah waited apprehensively as the heat of the day came upon them. The shade offered by the roof of the vehicle did little to dampen the stifling atmosphere. They could not use the air conditioning of the Land Rover, as gas was a commodity revered in the desert. Leaving the doors open and remaining inactive helped conserve energy.

Not long after Nicola left, the hot sun diminished as a dark haze drifted in from nowhere. The air currents, a welcome relief initially, grew into gusts that announced the beginning of a sand storm. The look of panic on Savannah's face swelled, as did the intensity of the storm. They shut the windows and doors of the vehicle and remained silent, locked within the tinderbox. Neither of them wanted to face the reality they confronted. Rather than words, they exchanged worried glances as the onslaught of the sand pelted the windows. Soon, the wind's intensity caused the vehicle to sway violently, evoking concern from Savannah.

"Can this thing turn over?" she asked.

"This thing weighs a ton. It's not going anywhere," said Derrick, trying to be confident in his answer, though the sobering truth was that he didn't know.

The howling winds escalated. The grating sound of sand scraped against their protective barrier. Every few moments, they flinched with fear when an unseen, foreign object, indigenous to the desert, struck the vehicle with a cracking sound.

"There's no way she could survive this on foot," said Derrick. "When she said she'd be back in two hours, she never gave us an alternate plan, like what to do if she doesn't get back at all."

"Derrick, she knows what she's doing. That's her job. And besides, what can we do?"

Derrick had no answer. Rather, he glanced at Savannah with a look trending toward disgust.

"That's why she said we had extra food and water. I guess that was the contingency plan," added Savannah.

The two hours passed eternal. They kept checking their watches with the hope time would move along faster than it seemed. After four hours, the sky cleared as if a supernatural force lifted the haze. The sun now beat down hotter than ever, jettisoning its radiance from the zenith of the heavens. There was still no sign of Nicola, and desperation showed in their agitated mannerisms.

"I can't take it anymore," said Derrick. "Waiting here is not the solution. She could be a hundred yards away, half-dead, and we'd never know it. What's worse, if she doesn't return, where the hell are we? If we go back to the desert Hilton, we are going to die in the desert Hilton. If we go back to that compound ..." He paused, "You know . . . they kill spies in this country. For Christ's sake, they kill anyone who doesn't agree with them in this country."

"So, what do you propose?" asked Savannah.

"We've got to search for her. We do it intelligently. We have the compass."

"The one we almost turned down?"

"Yeah, that one, smart ass. We drive due west for one-quarter mile, then turn it around and go east to get us back to this spot. That's the way we can do it. We'll repeat it going north, south, and east until we find her."

"You're out of your mind. If we are off by a degree, we could be lost forever. Don't forget, if she can't find us, she goes back to that hellhole and gets a ride home. She has all the legitimate credentials to be there. We're the ones who can't show up there and have no way of getting back. I hate to say it, but we are screwed unless she gets back. She said stay put, and that's what we have to do."

Derrick opened the door and stepped out of the vehicle.

"You've got to be out of your mind. Stay put," begged Savannah.

"I just have this feeling she's yards away, buried in the tons of sand that shifted in the last few hours."

"Please, stay put."

"Don't worry. I'm just testing my theory. I'll stay in sight."

Derrick wandered in each direction, playing with his compass. He tried to figure out the accuracy of retracing his steps by marking the sand, walking a hundred yards and then returning by the guidance of the compass needle. Each time, he was off by several meters. In one case, he couldn't find his marking at all. The folly of his idea became apparent.

At his last effort, while he was eighty yards from the vehicle, still in sight of Savannah, a faint voice came from her direction. He turned to view her. She waved excitedly to get his attention. "She's back," he thought.

With renewed energy, Derrick ran to the Land Rover. As he approached, he saw Nicola lying upon the ground with her head resting on Savannah's lap. He retrieved a pouch of fresh water and allowed the incoherent patient to drink.

"What happened?" asked Derrick frantically.

"I don't know. She stumbled to me while I was watching you. But, it wasn't the storm."

"How do you know?" asked Derrick.

Savannah pulled opened Nicola's blouse to reveal a puncture wound below her bare breast.

"She was clutching her wound. She said one of the assistants caught her in the lab. Before she could fight him off, he lunged at her with the injector they used on the sheep. She had trouble telling me what happened."

Derrick listened to Nicola babbling. She made no sense. The words were now out of order and had no continuity of thought. He slapped her face gently, and inquired, "What happened?" With no response, he slapped harder, grabbed the collar of her open shirt and shook her.

"What the hell are you doing? You'll hurt her," shouted Savannah.

"If we don't get her back to us, we're never getting out of this alive. Do you understand what's at stake?" shouted Derrick.

Without further protest, Derrick continued his questioning. Nicola seemed lucid as she expressed momentary visions of clarity, but they were short lived, and she reverted to non-sequiturs.

"You've got to help us," he shouted.

"All that's good. I know the good. Take back, so I can go," said Nicola in a tone void of emotion.

"You're good, you're good," he shouted. "You're the best."

Her pupils dilated, and she replied, "Yes, I'm good. I said that, didn't I? I said that."

"Yes, yes, you are good, you're the best. Tell me what happened," Derrick pleaded.

"He caught me by surprise. I got it, but he caught me. I did get it."

Nicola clutched at the leg pocket on her cargo shorts. She pulled out two pages of the notebook she stole from the lab.

"I got it. Five thousand, US. Five thousand, US. I got it."

For all of the damning desert heat, Nicola exhibited no signs of sweating anywhere on her body, yet her mouth was wet causing an excess of saliva to froth at the corners. Derrick feared he didn't have much time to get the information he needed. By now, her breath appeared shallow and labored.

"Get us back," he shouted. His loud voice pulled her away from the drifting state where her eyelids became heavy and hard to keep open. "You're good. You can do it. Get us back. What's our heading?"

Again, she clutched at her pocket and produced illegible directions. Her body displayed spasmodic twitches every few seconds. Her words became distorted by an inability to swallow the abundance of saliva that now flowed from her mouth. She coughed, sputtered, and with great effort spewed out, "North by northwest, three-hundred thirty-seven degrees."

"Are you sure?" shouted Derrick, his loud pleading again pulling her back from wherever her mind traveled.

"I'm good. I'm good," was all she could say. She kept repeating the two words for another thirty seconds. With one final spasm, her back arched, causing the sound of cracking vertebrae. Nicola went limp and fell lifeless. Savannah pushed Nicola's body from her lap, as if cursed, and stood with hands held to her face to hide her horror.

"I can't believe how totally fucked we are now," said Derrick, who never used foul language as long as Savannah had known him. "We're going to die out here, I'm telling you. You weren't satisfied with what we saw back there. You needed the lab book," he shouted. "And what did you get, two pages of Arabic scribble?"

Savannah, who never cried in front of anyone, felt her shield of self-assurance crumble. Derrick's verbal assault caused her pain, and the drastic situation they confronted worsened the matter. The stark reality they may well die in a foreign land and in a terrible manner weighed heavy. Selfishly, her personal ambition placed them in jeopardy. A profound feeling of guilt overwhelmed her innermost susceptibilities, and the emotion manifest as uncontrolled weeping.

"God, I'm sorry, Savannah," said Derrick tenderly.

He pulled her close to embrace and comfort her. His kindness fed her guilt even more. As tears rolled over her cheeks, he wiped them away with his hands, and kissed her forehead. At that moment, she wanted to kiss him passionately. She knew his kiss was for consolation. If she did not initiate the kiss of passion, it was not going to come from him. As much as she wanted him, she could not bring herself to defile his character as she jeopardized his body. Soon, she gained her composure and turned away to conceal her shame.

"I'm the one who's sorry," she said. "I brought you here, and I had no right."

"No, you're wrong. We came here to crack a case. When I joined Justice, I didn't expect this, but I joined out of a responsibility to do the proper thing. Just because I do it in a court, I can't deny my duty even if it means my own safety. For Christ's sake, look at all of the soldiers who've given their lives, so we can live free. It's people like that, and like you, who get the job done. I admire you for that. Now, let's stop wallowing in self-pity just because things look bad. Let's use our ingenuity to get out of this infernal hell."

From his pocket, Derrick pulled out his compass. "What was the reading she gave us?"

# CHAPTER
# EIGHTEEN

Derrick and Savannah buried Nicola in a shallow grave. Without a guide, the beauty of the desert turned into an endless landscape of sameness. For city folks, the task of navigating in a barren land devoid of landmarks was daunting.

"Can you read a compass?" Savannah asked.

"How hard can it be? You just let the needle float and that's north. Line up the north on the compass to that point, and now we can pick any degree and follow the course."

It sounded easy, but Derrick was not certain. He would try to use common sense, logic and the little he remembered from days long past as a scout.

After engaging the clutch and shifting into gear, the grinding sound of a novice manual transmission operator was evident.

"Do you know what you're doing?" asked Savannah.

"Can you do better?" Derrick responded.

Savannah kept quiet, realizing her doubt of Derrick's ability and her lack of constructive help in matters of desert travel were not going to improve their lot.

Once Derrick got comfortable with the shifting action of the Land Rover, they moved ahead in a timid but direct manner. As one horizon melted into the next, their destination seemed to have no end.

Derrick stopped the Land Rover and turned off the engine.

"What's wrong?" asked Savannah.

"Don't you hear that?"

In the starkest of settings, a muted ram's horn sounded in the distance. Straining to see, far to the right horizon, four tiny dots appeared in the sand.

"It's coming from over there," shouted Savannah.

Derrick started the Land Rover and drove with confidence toward the distant figures. As they got closer, the image of Yafti and the three waiting camels came into focus.

Yafti waited out the storm with the ease of a desert dweller. He had no fears for himself, but the bad weather had him worried for his patrons. To his surprise, the loss of Nicola made their return even more miraculous.

They agreed Yafti could have the Land Rover for his use, as long as he first made inquiry to see if Nicola had family who would be entitled to her property. He drove them back to the village, and they prepared for the next leg of their mission, Pakistan. Yafti waited outside the hut while Derrick and Savannah freshened themselves and readied for travel.

In the privacy of the cramped quarters, Savannah asked Derrick, "Do you think I should ask Yafti to translate the pages Nicola brought back from the lab?"

Derrick responded with suspicion. "Can we trust anyone here? If it's too revealing, it may become a liability for us. For all we know, these people could be trying to set us up. They find us with these papers, and we become an enemy of the state."

The element of curiosity played upon Savannah's thoughts. She knew her unit would translate the pages when she arrived back in the States. To wait was the safe choice, as suggested by Derrick, but she fell prey to inquisitiveness and called Yafti into their quarters.

"Yafti, we need your help with translating this page, if you can," said Savannah. She decided to show one page at first. If there seemed to be a risk, she would hold back the other. If it was innocuous, she could always produce the rest of the material.

"I would be honored to assist, Ma'am." He held the paper abnormally close to his face, indicating impaired vision. This was common for the desert inhabitants, whose retinas often scarred permanently by overexposure to ultraviolet light that reflected off the sands.

Yafti's willingness to accept the task suggested he had some schooling beyond the vast majority of the local population.

"It says, *with the correct balance of protein subsets,* then there are notations that have no meaning to me, but it continues, *the composition of behavior can be controlled over a vast range. The elements vary from comatose to unyielding rage. These findings are consistent with the results found in our studies of memory loss, which precedes the comatose state. The animal studies nearly completed, we have already begun human trials, utilizing the villagers.*"

He spoke each word as if it had no relationship with the one that came before or after the other one. The pace of his articulation mimicked a child reading aloud, words never before encountered.

Savannah pulled the paper away from Yafti, fearing he might understand the contents. Should he realize the implications to his people, a panic could result, jeopardizing his entire community.

"Pardon, Ma'am. I thought I was doing rather well. Perhaps a bit choppy, but clear," lamented Yafti.

It was evident from his reaction and concern over his reading he had no understanding of the content of the material. She decided to let him continue.

"You did just fine, Yafti. Continue."

"*Once the dispersion of the protein substrate is completed, we will watch as our enemies destroy themselves. Nothing could be so better conceived than this miracle of biochemistry. Where we could not dream to prevail over our adversaries on the field of battle, we have found the answer. May Allah rule over all.*

"Now I see more of the formulas I cannot understand, and then there is a section from the Koran. Shall I continue?"

"No, that's okay," said Derrick, not convinced Yafti didn't understand the content. He found it inconceivable how Yafti had reasonable command of the two languages without the capacity to comprehend what he just read. If Yafti did know what was going on, the risk remained that he could notify government authorities supporting the Sheik. This, in turn, could result in Derrick and Savannah landing in prison and prevent them from getting the information back to America so authorities could build a defense against the evil plot.

In disagreement, Savannah protested with a whisper as she pulled Derrick aside. "What's the matter with you? This is earth-shattering, and you stop him?"

"Let's not push our luck. If he catches on, and if his allegiance is to the fundamentalist faction, he won't let us get leave here alive. If he warns his people, and the Sheik's forces interrogate him, he'll tell how we, the evil Americans, are onto them. Let's hope he's not just acting dumb. Now, pack up, and let's get the hell out of here. We still have to get home, and we can't waste time."

The long trek through the desert, back to Ma-amir, offered Yafti ample opportunity to eliminate Derrick and Savannah if he had such intentions. The return trip, like most return trips, seemed shorter than the original journey. When they arrived at the airfield, Yafti ushered them onto the waiting twin-engine plane.

The pilot was, again, an Englishman. Savannah and Derrick didn't wish to divulge their discovery to yet another stranger in their travels. They sat anxiously and said nothing until it was clear this pilot had no interest in them or their lives. He occupied himself by singing to tunes played loud enough through his headphones as to be carelessly annoying.

Derrick began by stating, "It's probably not what it looks like," referring to the pages from the lab book.

"It stated how they can't prevail over their enemies on the field of battle," argued Savannah. "It said they will, *watch as we destroy ourselves*. The rage, the control over behavior, it all adds up."

"Savannah, we're lawyers. We trained to look at things under the microscope, to analyze things to death. You're making assumptions that could be false."

"How can you say that?" she challenged.

"That Yafti, can you vouch for his motives? He may have been a plant to feed us false information. We don't know. Or when he read, *not being able to prevail over adversaries on the field of battle,* that could be a metaphor for disease. Perhaps, infection…bugs, that's the enemy that might be destroying themselves. Disease just may be the adversary they couldn't meet on the field of battle."

"I didn't look at it that way," said Savannah, with her enthusiasm deflated.

They decided Derrick would attend his meeting in Pakistan, rather than rush home with their discovery. If they were wrong about the Sheik's conspiracy, abandoning the long-awaited conference in Pakistan would be a disaster. They didn't wish to find themselves chasing fertile imagination while real problems escaped intervention. Mason, and all of their superiors, would never allow them to hear the end of it.

They decided not to risk the security of the United States by wiring or transmitting their findings by radio. They would wait. They would reevaluate the contents of the lab book while they waited. This would give them time to analyze the merit of their suspicions while letting the emotion of the moment pass.

# CHAPTER
# NINETEEN

The extreme travel robbed physical and mental sap from the weary couple. Their bodies ached, their spirits strained, and they looked like they aged because of the grime and stresses not yet washed away. In Pakistan, they had their first opportunity to shower. Though the facilities were primitive, it didn't diminish the long-awaited pleasure of indulgences too long deprived.

With little time to rest, a guide accompanied Derrick and Savannah to a restaurant located at the dead-end of the street, a block from their hotel. He indicated that he would return for them once they finished dinner. As the lone patrons, they felt vulnerable. A musty smell attacked their senses, making it easy to imagine the food was not the freshest.

Expressing arrogance and displeasure with the foreign guests who invaded his life at an hour too late for dining, the waiter brought them their warmed-over fare. The few employees waited impatiently, for their interest was to leave for the night. In spite of the poor service and second-rate meal, it was a feast for Savannah and Derrick, who had eaten government rations exclusively to avoid dysentery from the foods available in the desert villages.

Derrick placed a morsel on his fork. Before he ate, he offered a prayer. "While this looks disgusting, I thank you, Lord, for my daily whatever, and for bringing us out of the land of wherever."

Savannah laughed and said, "Amen." Derrick devoured his food to settle the hunger pangs gnawing at his gut, an unfamiliar sensation. Savannah looked troubled. Her hunger would have to wait. She wanted to resolve her "save the world" concerns before she could fulfill her bodily needs. Second thoughts about what they should do surfaced.

"Maybe we should report back to Justice and forget your meeting. I mean, let's get on the next commercial flight out of here and go home. If we follow through on the arrangements set up for our return, we still have to go back to Japan and meet Karl to see if he's ready to come back with us. Then it'll take three more days to get home. I don't think something this important should wait another second."

Derrick continued his feeding, and between chews, he spoke. "The notebook said they were ready for human trials, right?" Savannah nodded. "Human trials can take years. This might be an evil plot. This might be bad news alright but is it an emergency?" he asked rhetorically, and then answered himself, "No way."

"This isn't the free world. Human testing doesn't take years in these countries," countered Savannah. "When they need to see how this works on humans, they can go to the prisons and inject the petty thieves. They can go into that poor village and pick up their subjects at will. You heard what Yafti said. Some of his people aren't the same . . . the birds killing themselves. The testing has started. Don't you see it? Can you ever forget what that poison did to Nicola?"

"We don't know what the hell they put in her, or how much. I'm sure that in the heat of battle they gave her whatever was laying around, maybe the same injection that killed the sheep. As far as Yafti's people not being *the same*, that's not much to go on. I think you could make that argument for some residents in just about any city back home.

"I don't want to come here ever again. I must go to this meeting now, or they'll send me back once they punch holes in our story."

Derrick's logic won out over Savannah's emotional plea. They finished dinner avoiding further discussion of the imagined plot, deciding suspicions blown out of proportion should not guide their decisions.

Their escort returned and joined them for dessert. He would accompany them to a meeting with the top Pakistani officials involved in drug enforcement and interdiction.

Riding along streets that felt ever more secluded, they stopped at a building in a squalid part of town. They didn't expect such a meeting place but understood the need for secrecy. When dealing with officials concerning illicit drug trade, governments want to remain as low profile as possible. The drug lords wield much power in nations where political stability remains fragile. Government forces endure constant fear of retribution enacted against them for trying to eradicate the cartels. Regimes of the developing nations strove to win the American dollars earmarked for busting the drug trade. American support, in many cases, helped to maintain effective interdiction reigning over anarchy. The clandestine location for high level discussions made perfect sense.

Two guards posted at the entrance wielded automatic weapons. After admittance, another pair of guards escorted Derrick and Savannah to the tenth floor, where several men occupied a table in a sterile, vacant space.

"Mr. Daniels, we were expecting you, but advised you would be traveling alone." The raspy voice came from a man sitting behind a bright light that made it impossible to see his face. The sole revelation about his appearance came from his silhouette on display when he turned to either side. He had a huge chin protruding beneath an inset maxilla.

"Yes, yes," stammered Derrick, looking for an excuse. "I was supposed to be traveling alone, but plans changed, and people decided my assistant should come along. I expect in our business the chiefs want to keep us honest. I'm sorry if this places any burden on you."

"It's I who am sorry, Mr. Daniels. We cannot be too careful. The drug dealers are immensely popular in our country. They promise dreams to the poor, dreams that shatter lives. The reason we requested a top-level representative meeting with us relates to the marriage of feuding factions that have now altered the balance in our drug war."

"Just recently my superiors informed me of the connection between your country and the Colombians. How did this happen?" asked Derrick.

"Your government has been so diligent and thorough in their intervention that the Colombians have incurred major losses. Your DEA confiscated an enormous number of shipments worldwide. They destroyed entire crops, ruining several seasons of toil. The Colombians had no other choice but to reroute their trafficking operations."

"Why Pakistan? They hate you. Pakistani drug dealers are their biggest competitor," noted Derrick.

"When two enemies have a common threat, they will become friends by necessity. Worse is the level of violence the Colombians brought with them. While we fear for our lives, they have no fear. They go after our prosecutors, as they do in Colombia. That is why we need your help. In the past, my people would not support such an outrage, but now the people are on their side. You see, they give my people jobs and make them dependent upon their success. We are a poor nation. It doesn't take much to own these people."

"How can we help?" asked Derrick.

"We need economic aid from your country, so we can feed the poor and lift them from poverty…"

Derrick interrupted, "That isn't my area. I can't get money for your people."

"We know. That has already been set up through diplomatic channels. The money will start to flow. What we need from you is a plan for prosecuting the drug lords and the locals who have embraced them. We wish to go through the World Court, the same tribunals set up to prosecute war criminals. This is the way to fight these people on every front. For your country, you will finally win the war on drugs. It has been elusive for much too long."

"It may be too ambitious," Derrick countered.

"My friend, nothing is too ambitious when *our* survival is at stake," said the cloaked messenger, emphasizing that he spoke of America's survival as well his own.

"Drug abuse in our country has been around a long time. Elevating the problem to that of survival is a bit of an exaggeration," said Derrick.

Without responding, the man in the shadows snapped his fingers. The two guards that stood at the entrance clicked the heels of their boots and opened the door. The loud sound startled Derrick and Savannah. When they turned in response to the activity, they saw a bloodied man held up by two other guards.

"Bring him in," he commanded.

They seated the prisoner in a chair placed at the center of the room. He could not hold his head erect but tried hard to see who was present. The bright light radiating from the desk in front of the room scorched his eyes, blood red from blows to his face. He sat fragile and frightened. With elbows locked in a fetal position, his hands trembled excessively as a manifestation of his dread. Each time he tried to lift his head, gravity, pain and weakness pulled his gaze back to the floor, an obvious indication his neck had been badly injured. Slow and uncoordinated movements lent the appearance of being drugged.

"Perhaps our prisoner will convince you that the seriousness of your problem back home is more than you realize. This is Alexander Durante, the mastermind behind the Colombia drug cartels. You don't get to see associates of this high ranking. They are insulated, kept safe in the compounds built to protect the drug lords."

"How did you get him?" asked Derrick.

"This was our lucky find, Mr. Daniels. Isn't providence the

courier of life? The sun, how do you say . . . shined upon us? While the drug lords don't risk revealing themselves, they had no choice if they were to develop a union with our people. We watched for the past year as the small-time traffickers set up the deals, but these soldiers didn't have authority to close a covenant. They sent Mr. Durante to finalize arrangements for syndication. We decided to make an effort toward intervention when, by circumstance, we picked him up. As it turned out, he gave himself away."

"What do you mean?" asked Savannah, intrigued by the story.

"He panicked. He started asking for a deal. Fear of our prisons motivated him. At first, it made little sense. The men who travel in these circles are hardened. They live and die by the sword. This one, he was different. We came upon the true mastermind of the business end of their operations. Mr. Durante acts as the accountant and the lawyer of the major Colombian cartel. He settles all of their dealings. Though he possesses great intelligence and entrepreneurial ability, he has little tolerance for valor. He started telling us this incredible story that was beyond belief."

"It looks as though you beat it out of him," said Derrick in a prying manner.

"Mr. Daniels, one can never be too careful. How could we tell if his story was a fabrication? We had to test his story, and I can assure you, he made up nothing."

He turned the bright light onto Mr. Durante's face causing the feeble creature to shudder. He turned away. "No more. Please, no more," he shouted.

"Tell them what you have told us, my friend," commanded the man in the shadows.

Durante lifted his head cocked to the left, straining to keep it up just enough to see his inquisitor.

"Please, sir, water," he begged.

"Tell your story, and you shall have some cool, refreshing water. Now, talk."

"We have targeted the population of the United States. Our goal is to take over . . . to take over . . . to take over," he repeated almost as if he was in a trance.

"Take over?" asked Derrick.

"Tell him," shouted the man from the shadows. "Tell him, or you get more." He slapped his hand to the desk, making a loud snapping sound that made Durante jump reflexively and tremble ever more.

"The drugs, they are treated. I told you they are treated. You cannot mention you heard this from me. They will kill me. I need your protection. Please . . . please help me," Durante pleaded.

The frail fellow could no longer endure the severe treatment at the hands of the Pakistanis. His head fell for one last time. The limp form lay still. All of the tremors and trembling stopped. The man from the shadows snapped his fingers. The guard grabbed Durante by the ear and pulled his body upright. He jabbed his thumb into Durante's neck and pressed hard above where the jugular vein lies. With no response, it was obvious to all that the prisoner died.

"So sad, Mr. Daniels. I was hoping you could hear it, how do you say, from the horse's mouth? The Colombian drug cartels feel the one force that can stop them from world domination is America. In their own country, they win the hearts of the people by providing them with jobs and money. They have their minds by making them slaves to their wares. Yes, the one thing stopping them is a strong power with international capabilities that gives financial and tactical support fighting the drug wars in the fields. Right now, America is so fit and determined to meet the challenge. They want you and your people out of the way. You see they have begun contaminating the drug supply sent to your country."

"We've known about paraquat for years," responded Derrick. "For Christ's sake, we were the ones who first used those herbicides to destroy the marijuana plants everywhere they were grown. Worse case, some users get cancer twenty years down the road."

"It's not herbicides you have to worry about, Mr. Daniels. They are out to destroy your people. He told us how they have adulterated the drugs coming to your shores. Strong behavior modifiers, mood-altering agents, these are the things you must respond to for your survival."

"Did he give you details?" asked Savannah.

"His story was somewhat cryptic. We tried to put the pieces together. What we have surmised is the adulterated drugs have an effect on three areas of concern—moral behavior, anomie, and suicide."

Somewhat embarrassed, Savannah whispered to Derrick, "What's anomie?"

"Anarchy, lawless behavior or something like that, shhh," he whispered in reply, trying to absorb every word.

"There has been a cultural revolution in your country, if you will, over the last thirty years or so. Drugs that were once not acceptable have become, how do you say, recreational? Even the euphemism to describe it shows the extent of the change. Recreational, ha." He paused to laugh. "Drugs are now so mainstream they have become a vehicle which they can use to control."

"You're wrong," protested Derrick. "It can't be. Durante was bluffing for his life. You said so yourself. He wanted to make a deal. He made up a story with the hope you would let him go. Recreational drugs do all the things you described to some extent. They always have. This is no revelation."

The man in the shadows leaned forward, lifting a bit more of his face from the shroud of darkness. His position now revealed deeply set eyes with large black pupils, lying upon a blood-red glaze where the whites reside.

"That is the beauty of their plot. You won't see it coming, sir," he said in a solemn manner. "It is the frequency and magnitude of the aberrant behaviors that they alter. You are . . . how do you say . . . blind-sided?"

"I believe this is a massive speculation," said Savannah, not convinced any more than Derrick.

"We thought the same. We have a program here that allows us to extract the truth from anyone. *Anyone,*" he repeated with emphasis.

"I'll want to contact my partner," said Derrick. "He's in Colombia. I'll have him do some investigating and see what I can find out to validate your story. In the meantime, we will work with you to split up this partnership. Even if there is no merit in this Durante's claims, we have to clean up here and in Colombia. It seems that every time we put a cork in the bottle, they find a way to get the flow going again."

"We wish to use the courts to defeat them, that is why we seek your counsel," the shadowed voice exclaimed. "We know there are no other people like you Americans, who have so cleverly used the courts to have their way. In addition, if we resort to the lawless ways of our foes, it is perceived as immoral by your government, and we risk losing our aid. I request, no word of the methods of extraction used on Durante to your superiors, if you will. Getting the job done under the auspices of the courts is best."

# CHAPTER
# TWENTY

DERRICK AND SAVANNAH HAD AN UNEVENTFUL FLIGHT TO JAPAN. THE cab drive to the hotel immersed their senses in modern society the type of which they missed for too long. An unexpected welcome party greeted them upon their arrival. At the check-in desk, a clerk acted as if they were dignitaries. The bellman picked their bags, and a concierge, summoned from his post escorted the travelers to their rooms. Little conversation took place as none of the hotel's lower level personnel mastered English skills.

Their suites were adjacent to one another on the fifteenth floor. The concierge needed a special access key to stop the elevator on this level, a floor dedicated for special guests.

Escorted to Savannah's room first, they entered a palatial suite in both size and grandeur, with decorative appointments of exceptional grade and authenticity. For the otherwise sedate Japanese, this extravagant decor seemed out of character. Fine marble dressed the tables, counters and floors. Ornate gilded woods carved in the tradition of fine European artisans formed the structural components of splendid tables placed against each wall and at the sides of every plush chair. Tang Dynasty sancai ceramic wares colored with rare period specific glazes discreetly donned every flat surface along with Jomon vessels, blending old with new and East with West.

The bellman placed Savannah's minimal luggage onto a suitcase valet sitting in the entrance of a large closet. Once situated, they went to Derrick's room, identical to the one they just left. Because three other suites made up the entire floor, the guests had relative privacy and seclusion.

After dismissing the concierge and bellman, who both refused to accept gratuity, Derrick and Savannah entered the sitting room positioned next to the bedroom. For a few moments they found no need to converse. The splendor of the moment required appreciation before discussion. Derrick broke the silence.

"I don't believe I've seen a room this elegant, at least nothing I ever stayed in. Maybe they think we're someone else."

"They may not be very good at English, but what's the chance another Ambrose and Daniels were scheduled to check in today with adjoining suites?" asked Savannah. "I just don't get it. Justice never puts anyone up like this; well, maybe the Attorney General, but not the rest of us. As great as this is, there's something wrong. Something creepy about this place and the way we're being treated."

On the desk next to Savannah sat an envelope of fine linen stock. In an elegant calligraphic hand, *Derrick Daniels* was printed upon its facing. She rubbed the raised golden letters with her fingers.

"What's that?" asked Derrick.

"It's for you." She handed Derrick the envelope, and he opened it inquisitively.

"They sure know how to treat a guy around here," he said. "This is my personal invitation to a massage and spa treatment. You probably have one, too, back in your room. I bet Mason set this up, so we won't quit when we get back to the States."

"There's no way he'd think of that," said Savannah. "I say we find Karl and get the next flight out of here."

"I think we have to be rational about all of this," said Derrick.

"I'm going to get Karl, now. After we tell him what's going on, we'll make arrangements to leave."

Savannah went to her room while Derrick headed to the front desk. Much activity greeted him at the lobby where a maintenance crew wheeled huge metal planks into position next to all of the windows.

"Can I help you, Mr. Daniels?" asked the agent who registered Derrick earlier.

"I wanted to know Mr. Karl Armstrong's room number."

Without looking into the computer register, he responded.

"Mr. Armstrong not checked in."

"That's impossible," said Derrick with more surprise than command in his voice. "He was supposed to be here days ago. He had meetings. Are you sure? Maybe you can look him up on that screen."

"So sorry. I know all guests, and he not here. Mr. Karl arrival date set for past Tuesday, but he never register. There was no cancellation also. Is there something else I can do for you, Mr. Daniel?"

"Yeah, I want to be on the next flight out of here. Can you arrange that for me?"

"Again, so sorry. There is no flight out of Japan for very least twenty-four hour, Mr. Daniel."

"How's that possible?" asked Derrick.

"There is monsoon approaching. As you see, we prepare for high winds to come." He pointed to the workers fastening shields upon the glass windows. "Storm in gulf at present. Once warning signal sounds, airport must close. You should try relax. You are in no danger here. Our building, very worthy. However, I do suggest you keep drapes in room closed. There will be announcement."

Everything the clerk mentioned seemed reasonable, but an uncomfortable knot in Derrick's gut grew tighter the more he looked around. He discounted the feeling as born of stress and tension from the extensive travel in foreign lands, the possibility of terroristic activities they came upon, and their near-death experience in the desert.

Using his room key to gain entrance onto the fifteenth floor, Derrick returned to the peculiar isolation of the sterile corridor. He walked along the hall to join Savannah in her quarters.

"Where's Karl?"

"I don't know. According to the clerk, he didn't check in."

"But that's impossible. He had important meetings set up. There's no way he could miss them."

"Tell me about it."

"We have to get out of here," Savannah said with urgency.

"You can forget about getting out of here early."

"What?"

"There's a monsoon on the way. They're busy shielding all of the plate windows in the lobby right now. We can't get out for at least twenty-four hours."

"Something bad happened to Karl. Where's that paper?" asked Savannah.

"What paper?"

"The one with the strange words we put together on the plane. Remember the cosmic phone call?"

Derrick searched his pockets and found the crumpled notepaper. He looked it over for a moment with lines of confusion bending his brow and then handed it to Savannah.

"Split waves. What are split waves?" she asked.

"Maybe it concerns the ocean or the tides," he guessed.

"And Cyclops, that's a one-eyed mythical creature. What could that have to do with waves and an old lady and starving children? This makes no sense, but I'm telling you, Derrick, this is all about why Karl isn't here. Something happened to him. I know it. It's my intuition," said Savannah.

"Nonsense. If it'll make you feel better, I'll call Mason now and see why Karl's been delayed."

"Wait. E-mail Harris and see if there is anything to that drug-spiking story?"

"Fine, I'll do that," said Derrick. He leaned over the table and picked up a gilded linen envelope, identical to the one in his room. "I see you received an invitation, too. Let's take them up on the spa," he suggested. "It makes sense to take advantage of the situation. There is not much else to do. You make the appointment, and I'll make the calls."

Derrick utilized the hotel communications network to send an e-mail to Harris in Colombia. Having access to encrypted government routers, there was no need for concern using the hotel computer.

The message read: *Harris, need your help researching Alexander Durante, an operative who is supposed to be high up in the organization. See if your contacts know the name, and to what level he is involved, if any. We will go after the cartels via international treaty agreements. Get me the names of all Colombian prosecutors with experience in the International World Court. We will use them to conduct a coordinated effort at prosecuting from their end. There is a definite connection between the Pakistani and Colombian organizations. I would never believe it if I didn't hear it from the top prosecutor in Pakistan. We will be back ahead of you. E-mail your findings ASAP. Daniels.*

Derrick placed an international call to the Philadelphia office of the Justice Department in order to allay Savannah's fears about Karl. Because of the ten-hour time differential, the offices back home had closed, and all of the numbers he tried went unanswered.

Deep thought about past events, and the current concern for Karl, found Derrick in a trance-like bearing as he returned to Savannah's room. "What did you find out?" she asked nervously.

"I sent the message to Harris, and now we wait for a reply. That can take days with the investigating he needs to do. He'll e-mail me, but we can go over the details next week when he gets home."

"What about Karl? What did Mason have to say?"

"Savannah, it's one AM there. They are not a twenty-four-seven operation at our level. We'll have to wait until nighttime here, and then I'll try again."

An unexpected knock at the door startled Savannah in her state of heightened alert.

"Are you expecting someone?" asked Derrick.

"That should be the spa people. They said they'd pick us up."

Upon opening the door, a petite Japanese woman dressed in traditional garb greeted them. She bowed and said, "I take you to Nirvana."

"I could use some of that just about now," whispered Derrick.

"Follow please," said the diminutive escort.

They did not have far to go. The spa comprised two of the three remaining quarters on their floor. Savannah and Derrick separated, each entering a different room. Their respective attendants instructed them to undress and shower in the privacy of their personal small bathroom. They wrapped themselves in thick Turkish robes before exiting into a large common space where their respective attendants waited.

Four stunningly beautiful young Asian women, having features more western than oriental, attended to each of them. They exhibited an odd combination of sensuousness and a shyness more born of respect than modesty. Loosely fitted garb, revealing their naked bodies every time they bowed or bent over, left modesty behind. With limited language skills, they motioned directions for Derrick and Savannah to follow. As two attendants held up large towels to shield the nakedness of their guests, they instructed them to remove their robes. Just out of sight from one another, the attendants guided their guests to their personal hot tubs. The water, colored a soothing shade of purple, had a delightful, almost intoxicating aroma from lavish bubbles coating the surface. Stepping into the tub, their senses welcomed a bath of perfect temperature.

"This is the life," Derrick stated loudly so Savanah could hear him above the hum of the whirlpool jets.

One of the lovely young women placed her finger to Derrick's lips indicating silence was the preferred way at the spa. He complied.

The attendants added several oils of various hues and pleasing aromas to the waters of each tub. The warmth of the water, accompanied by the gentle effervescence of bubbles skating upon their skin, allowed the guests to reach a state of relaxation capable of vacating the most troublesome thoughts and fears.

After Derrick and Savannah enjoyed the calm for a few more moments, a resonating gong echoed throughout the spa. Responding to the signal, in unison, the young women removed their kimonos and stood at attention exhibiting an unexpected vision of nakedness. Each one appeared chosen for specifications by design, specially selected for duties of geisha. With the sound of a second gong, they entered the hot tubs with natural sponges in hand and positioned themselves next to their assigned guest.

While the modesty of Western culture holds a strong influence, the aura of the spa and the anonymity of being in a foreign land voided Derrick and Savannah's resistance, allowing them to experience the full companion treatment.

The attendants scrubbed every inch of their bodies, providing a thorough cleansing. One attendant sponged along Savannah's inner thigh. As the touch became threatening, Savannah pushed her hand away in protest. Another assured her this was the natural way of cleansing. Savannah relinquished her resistance and let the attendant complete her task.

Derrick experienced the same methodical treatment. He, too, found embarrassment and attempted to halt the activity. One of the attendants noticed his abrupt movement, took his hand in hers and rubbed it soothingly to gain nonverbal approval.

Upon experiencing fifteen minutes of pleasure, a third resonating gong silenced the whirlpools. The attendants helped Derrick and Savannah from their respective baths, dried them and brought them to twin massage tables. Face down, they laid naked, except for the towels covering below their waists. They waited peacefully for the next part of this unexpected experience.

An attendant briskly rubbed each appendage and kneaded the muscles resulting in an overwhelming sensory input. A thousand nerves harvested pleasure from body to mind in a way that joined the two realms in harmony.

While at the edge of complete tranquility for Derrick and Savannah, a door at the rear of the spa opened, and out came a figure dressed in a priestly robe, wearing a mask that hid the gender of the cloaked individual. The mask had the features of a woman but did not match the tall and broad-shouldered stature of the shrouded character.

In her hands, she held two vials containing a dark cyan-colored liquid. She walked over to the massage tables and placed the vials into a rack on the attendant's table. There she donned rubber gloves, uncapped one of the vials and poured the contents onto Savannah's scalp. The coldness of the thick fluid made her squirm a bit until distracted by the sensation of several other warm white lotions poured simultaneously onto her back, arms and legs.

The attendants worked the white lotions into her skin, and Savannah's every muscle became limp from the soothing experience. The cold, thick, blue lotion ran onto her temples. Before it could drip into her eyes, Savannah attempted to raise her arms to wipe away the excess solution. With great force, each attendant pulled her flat onto the table. The violation startled Savannah, and she attempted to sit.

Savannah glanced toward Derrick and saw the masked woman pouring the cold liquid upon his head. As Savannah tried to call out to Derrick, one of the women stuffed a gag into her mouth. The drone of the whirlpool jets drowned out whatever sounds escaped her lips. Another woman massaged the blue fluid around Savannah's temples as the same process befell Derrick. She struggled to free herself from the tethers attached to keep her still. Derrick, upon seeing Savannah struggle, tried to offer aid, but found himself restrained as well.

The application of the cyan serum and the overwhelming struggle against the physical restraint, allowed fatigue and drug to sedate their bodies, causing them to fall limp. A drug-induced fog drifted over their conscious thoughts, producing a dreamlike state. The masked woman announced commands in Japanese, and the obedient team, in unison, removed the tethers from Derrick and Savannah's limbs. Their arms hung heavy and still. The masked woman clapped her hands twice, and the entire group cleared the spa.

# CHAPTER
# TWENTY-ONE

Time stood still for Derrick and Savannah. A collection of memories tied to their journey danced just below conscious thought. They remained deeply bound in a slow dream. After remaining alone in the spa for, but moments, seven Japanese men wearing business suits entered through the door at the rear of the room. They approached the unsuspecting couple.

"You are sure they cannot attack or flee?" asked the tallest of the men present.

"I am certain of this. The drug is exceedingly potent when administered to the temporal lobes of the brain through the skin. The plexus of veins in the scalp are abundant. They absorb the active ingredient in sufficient quantity to get the desired result without risk and without trace. When we tried to inject the drug, it deactivated by the time it reached the brain. It must be administered in this manner," explained the leader of the group.

"Why not use the traditional interrogation?" asked the tallest of the group. "It is most effective."

"We cannot afford to eliminate too many of their operatives. It would raise suspicion and ruin our purpose. If these two don't know of our plans, they must return to their people and have no memory of this questioning."

"But what assurance do you have this will work?" asked the tall man.

"There are some dose-related flaws, but the amnesia effect of the drug is complete. They will not remember this experience other than as one of pleasure. Let us proceed.

"Mr. Daniels, what would you wish to do right now?"

Derrick, lying face down, mumbled, "The truck."

The leader lifted Derrick's head like a dead weight and ordered him into a sitting position. He complied, albeit slowly.

"I repeat, what would you wish to do right now?"

Derrick's head rocked left to right, and he repeated, "The truck. I'd like to know about the truck."

"This is nonsense," snarled the tall man impatiently.

"To us, it is nonsense, but to him, it is what is on his mind. It does not matter what it is. We will use his desire to get him to answer our questions. Observe.

"Where is Mr. Armstrong, your traveling partner?"

"I don't know," replied Derrick.

"You must tell me where he is, or I cannot tell you about the truck. You do want to know about the truck, Mr. Daniels?"

"Yes, yes, I must know about the truck."

"Then tell me, where is Mr. Armstrong?"

"I don't know where he is. He disappeared," replied Derrick.

"You see," said the leader, "he doesn't know what happened to his colleague. We know that, and if he did, he would have wanted to tell us all. It is impossible to resist when we hold for ransom a principal desire. Now, I will ask things we do not know, about which he may have knowledge.

"Mr. Daniels, where is your colleague, Mr. Morganstern?"

"In Colombia. In Colombia researching for me."

"That was very good, Mr. Daniels." He paused, and then continued his inquiry.

"Mr. Daniels, what is Cyclops?"

"The mythical beast with one eye."

"No, Mr. Daniels. What else does the Cyclops represent?"

"I don't know. I don't know," responded Derrick with an air of consternation on his face. His eyes remained closed.

"You want to learn about the truck, do you not, Mr. Daniels?"

"Oh, yes, I do want to know about the truck," said Derrick deliriously, his head hanging down.

"Then you must tell me about Cyclops."

"I don't know. The phone, it told me."

"What phone?" demanded the inquisitor.

"I'll call Karl on the phone and ask him."

"What is Cyclops?" the inquisitor shouted louder.

"The truck. Tell me about the truck," said Derrick reverting back to his desire.

The tall man showed impatience in his posture. "The ways of the traditional questioning were fast, effective and final. This is nonsense," he stated firmly.

"I tell you, this is a better way," insisted the younger man. "I'm sure, he knows nothing about Cyclops. Let me proceed.

"Mr. Daniels, NH 45. What does that mean to you?"

The code name did not register, and Derrick sat still, not saying a word.

"Mr. Daniels, the truck, do you remember the truck?"

Derrick sat motionless with his mouth forming words that never materialized.

"He knows nothing, and his internal circuits do not know how to respond. Let me try the woman now. She may know more. The brains of women have different chemistry than that of men. They dwell more on the emotion, which involves the serotonin pathways. They respond better to this drug."

The leader went to Savannah and eased her to a sitting position. Her head hung to her chest, and her eyes remained closed. Her resplendent, naked beauty garnered an audible wooing from all men present. The leader turned to them with a look of disdain.

"Gentlemen, we are here first to accomplish our goal."

The others quieted down.

"Miss Ambrose, can you hear me?"

Savannah's head perked at the mention of her name, and with eyes still closed, she responded with a simple, "Yes."

"Miss Ambrose, what would you wish to do right now?"

"I want to make love to Derrick."

The men laughed modestly, somewhat surprised at the answer. Though they appreciated sex as much, if not more than most cultures, to them the process was more cerebral. In their way of life, business was the first order. To desire sex over more important matters amused them.

"I can see to it you have your way with Mr. Daniels, but first you must tell me about Cyclops."

The word set off a response in Savannah, both physical and spoken. She lifted her head, opened her eyes and began to announce the words written on the paper from the mysterious call they had received in the plane.

"Split waves, buying time, Armstrong, old lady, you know Cyclops, code name, project, starving children, proceed."

The men started to speak amongst themselves in a manner of great urgency. After a moment, they became silent, and the tall man spoke.

"They know something. You must find out what they know," he demanded.

"Miss Ambrose, split waves. Tell me about split waves."

Savannah could not respond. She sat silent with her eyes closed in a trance-like state.

"Miss Ambrose, you must tell me about the split waves, and then you can be with Mr. Daniels."

Savannah began caressing herself, but she did not say a word.

"She knows nothing," exclaimed the interrogator. "She speaks as a parrot. She knows nothing. The words she heard somewhere, but they have no meaning to her. They have no idea about the Thai connection or our plot. They have no knowledge of where, why or how. We have nothing to worry about."

"That is not good enough," shouted the tall man. "All of our efforts are at risk. All the years of planning will be lost. Our pride and honor are in jeopardy."

One of the other men who had not yet contributed to the discussions interrupted. "The words are from the dialogue of the interrogation that took place in Bangkok. I have the transcript. It came this morning. They somehow heard or read what was being said."

"How is that possible?" asked the tall man.

"I do not know. Perhaps their State Department kept Armstrong under radio surveillance, but I, too, am convinced they don't grasp the content."

"I say we get rid of them," said the tall man.

"No, it is too risky," countered the leader. "They will have a serious investigation if all of their agents go missing. We cannot chance it. If they do not know what any of this means, and we eliminated Armstrong, who also had no knowledge, we can assume the Americans are in the dark about our plans. If they know, then we cannot stop their efforts to halt our mission. There is no argument to favor their elimination."

The tall man thought for a moment and nodded in agreement.

"Miss. Ambrose, you can go to Mr. Daniels and make love as requested," said the leader. "Gentlemen, for your enjoyment, we can watch the power of this controlling drug."

Eagerly, Savannah stepped off the table and walked to Derrick, whose head still hung down with eyes closed. She pressed her naked body against his and began kissing his neck with eager lips. Her hands caressed his cheeks and floated over his strong shoulders. Derrick displayed no response. The arms of slumber embraced him in seated pose. As the expected show did not materialize, the leader grabbed Derrick by his hair, and lifted his head.

"Open your eyes, Mr. Daniels."

Derrick responded robotically.

"Mr. Daniels, can you see this beautiful woman craves a union with you?"

Derrick gazed with a blank face but did not respond.

"Mr. Daniels, I want you to have your way with this woman," commanded the leader. "What is the matter with you, Mr. Daniels?"

"I can't. I'm married. I can't," stammered Derrick.

The leader turned to his associates, "You see, while the drug is very potent, it cannot make one violate certain core beliefs."

He turned back to Savannah who continued trying her best to stimulate Derrick without success. "Come here, my dear. Mr. Daniels wants to have you, but you must step over to your table." He positioned her face down at the end of the massage table with her feet spread out upon the ground.

"Gentlemen, if you so desire, now is the time to have your way with her. She is ready for all to enjoy."

The multiple acts appeared vengeful by way of contorted faces, grunts and groans unlike most carnal encounters. These men wanted more than a physical release. They pursued retribution.

# CHAPTER
# TWENTY-TWO

THE HOTEL LANDED ON THE US GOVERNMENT-APPROVED LIST, THOUGH residing near the bottom and held hardly habitable status. Located in a remote Columbian outpost made it an expectedly meager accommodation.

Harris Morganstern spent the night with a prostitute. A bone-dry mouth filled with a foul taste brought him to consciousness and forced his eyes open. With tongue glued to palate, he looked around to locate the bottle of whisky that sat on the table next to his bed. He swished, forced a gargle that bellowed deep within his throat and swallowed. This, he reasoned, would eradicate all parasites that invaded his body from unseemly activities performed the previous night.

Disarray met his gaze once his eyes focused. The few pieces of wicker furniture stood scattered haphazardly. Bed linens lay on the floor. Food, the leftovers of which were in boxes strewn about, stained the cheap hemp curtains.

Harris couldn't remember much of the previous night. A hollow measure of loneliness remained to feed his feelings of depression and remorse. For years, he tried to fill an inexplicable void with a voracious sexual appetite. Once engaged, he would perform risky acts knowing they could cause him harm. The behavior he couldn't control at the height of a lustful encounter often produced a morning-after spent shrouded in guilt.

He felt an ache in his groin confirmed by pressing near his gland. Upon closer inspection, his face contorted with scorn and turned red with anger. When frustrated, annoyed or angered, Harris had the habit of speaking aloud.

"Goddamn whore! Little slut, near sucked my dick off."

He looked about and shook his head in disbelief.

"I can't fucking believe the mess she left."

His anger turned to desperation as he darted about the room.

"Where the hell is my computer? That little cunt stole my fucking laptop. She'll get twenty bucks for it, and I'm shit out of luck. I'll fix her good tonight, little whore. I'll find her and fuck her good."

Derrick's e-mail concerning the information he discovered at his meeting in Pakistan arrived the day before the computer theft. Harris penned the information he needed to begin his investigation on a scrap of paper. Now, he searched desperately to locate the paper lying on the floor. Harris set up an important meeting with his contact at the prosecutor's office in Sevilla. The bureau in Cali, where most of the drug activity flourished, was the site of numerous murders acted out against their prosecutors. The State Department in coordination with the Department of Justice selected residences and meeting sites based on the amount of criminal activity. Sevilla seemed far enough away to be considered safe.

An unexpected knock at the door startled Harris. He scrambled back to the bed, lifted the mattress and pulled out a pistol. He approached the door with the weapon hidden behind his back. While he could not travel on a plane with a gun, he never had a problem buying a small caliber pistol on the streets for his personal protection. He could discard it when he left town. This provided him with a fifty-dollar insurance policy, cheap enough for the omnipotence it offered, even though it was against company policy.

Standing to the side of the door, he called out using his limited Spanish, "Hableme."

"Señor Morganstern?" inquired the voice from the hall.

"Yes."

"I am here to take you to Señor Coronado in Sevilla."

Harris opened the door with great caution. Before him, a young peasant boy stood barefoot upon the filthy floor. Harris looked at the boy's feet, and with an air of sarcasm asked, "Are we going to walk there?"

"No, Señor. My brother, he has the truck down on the street."

"Tell him I need fifteen minutes. Tell him I'll be down when I'm damn ready." Harris eyed his cheap travel watch. "I told them not to get me till ten. You're two fucking hours early. You tell him that."

Harris shut the door and went to relieve a full aching bladder. The task had become more difficult with age following too much alcohol and vigorous sexual activity. Once the weakened stream faded, it took much effort to squeeze out the last drops of morning dew.

Harris gazed into the faded mirror whose defective silver coat revealed a distorted grotesque image staring back at him. He decided shaving would be an intrusion upon his sensitivities. A quick shower in cold water, not by choice, helped to revive his sensibilities. He wore his hot climate traveling outfit. Khaki safari pants and a khaki linen shirt made up his preferred ensemble. He placed his pistol into his waistband and concealed it by allowing his shirt to hang loose. To protect his pale skin from the strong South American sun, he wore a rather tattered straw Stetson. He took this lucky hat along on all trips out of the country.

Once on the street, Harris approached his waiting transportation.

"In the back, gaucho," commanded the driver of the pickup truck. His voice spoke a profound disdain for Harris and all of the Americans who came to his country wielding their power and influence.

"That little shit sits in the back, cowboy. Uncle Sam's paying for this service, and I expect some." Harris paused to give a sardonic smile. "Without the attitude." He delivered his words with an air of superiority that justified the young man's contempt.

Knowing Harris pulled the weight, he motioned for his young brother to obey Harris' command.

The ride to the courthouse felt slow and uncomfortable from the unpaved and rutted roads. Dust floated behind the truck, but just enough got into the cab to further parch Harris' sore throat. When they arrived, they dropped him at the entrance of the modest building. The truck sped away, spinning wheels, to send a cloud of dry dirt into Harris' face.

Two guards stood at the entrance holding automatic weapons. Extra security had become a necessity in this land since the government began making concerted efforts to destroy the drug trade.

Harris arrived to interview an undercover officer who infiltrated the powerful cartel. Though not high up in the organization, this agent gained access to meetings that required his skill with recording devices. The chieftains had all of their meetings recorded, perhaps, their way of assuring contracts and agreements remained quantified and enforced without having traceable written records. They electronically disguised voices to avoid evidence for prosecution. The modern leaders of the drug cartels had become cautious and sophisticated in their operations.

"Good morning, Mr. Morganstern, I am glad to see you arrived and haven't any bullet holes," was the greeting offered by the affable Carlos Coronado. He lost five prosecutors in the past year, the result of a stepped-up campaign by well-funded and heavily armed drug money rebels. Their goal—halt the activities in the courts designed to end their enterprise.

"Now that you have arrived, I am hoping to hear good news. We have no strategy, and the morale of this office is at its lowest since I took charge five years ago."

"Not to worry. We have a plan that will free your people from the drug lords. We'll use the World Court in a coordinated effort at prosecution," explained Harris.

"Trying to prosecute these people will be impossible. But even if we were to prevail in the courts, punishment of these villains will prove to be elusive, my friend," commented Carlos.

"That's why the World Court strategy works so well. We don't need to bring them into court. We conduct the trials in absentia. Once we get our convictions, the international community will fund and support the operations to gather this scum and lock them away for good. And if they put up a fight, ha, they'll take them out."

"And how do you expect to prosecute without witnesses, without suspects, without prosecutors at the rate they are eliminating us?"

"What about your undercover agent I'm here to interview? They told me he sits in on, and makes audio recordings of, all the drug lord meetings. It takes one break, and we crack the case. He could be our ticket."

Carlos Coronado frowned. "He was to be of great assistance. He revealed the connection between the Pakistan and Colombian factions. However, just late last evening, the rebels, they have him. Usually, they leave the bullet-riddled body as a warning. He must have been very important to the leaders. You see, they took him back to learn what he told us before they torture him. Alas, Senor Morganstern, we have no key witnesses for the prosecution."

Inside Harris felt the dread of defeat, but he knew he had to maintain an outward appearance of strength.

"Don't you worry. We have intelligence all over the world working on this. I have a team that will get the job done. Once I return to America, I'll work out all of the details with my people," said Harris, with his chest out, proud as a peacock. He knew he could bluff his counterpart here in Colombia. He didn't know what to do, but he counted on Derrick to develop a plan. If all went well, Harris understood that upon his return with a solution, they would treat him like royalty. They would regard him as the savior of the weakened government sovereignty.

"I need the name and credentials of your prosecutors who have had experience with the World Court."

"There are two who trained abroad. They have had much experience, but they left this office."

"They left for private practice?" asked Harris.

"They left fearing for their lives. There is no private practice in our country. At least nothing like the golden opportunity your lawyers have in America. Barristers, here in Colombia, live ordinary lives just a step above the poverty level. However, I know, as do all of the educated in our country, until we eliminate the violence and corruption, we cannot thrive. Until we develop our economy, there will be no one to sue. They should gladly join us if there are assurances the prosecution will take place in the World Court, away from our violence. I will get for you their names."

"Great. Now, I need your help," said Harris.

"Anything I can do is your wish answered," replied a humble and grateful Carlos Coronado.

"Does the name Alexander Durante mean anything to you?"

Carlos' look of victory faded from his face. He shook his head in a way that portended more bad news in the substance of their conversation.

"You must mean the Madman of Lima. He came to this country a dozen years ago, a graduate from some of the finest European schools. Supposed to be extremely bright, but his people rejected him when his involvement with the monetary policy of Peru turned out bad. Those in government believe his influence caused a deep recession. After exile, the Cali cartel solicited him for a high-up position. The last I heard, he controls their finances and sets up deals."

"Why the title, Madman?"

"There is word he demands young boys for his pleasure. He is said to be a sadistic man who finds delight in torture. It is through the lawlessness of the people ruling the badlands that he gets his wishes.

"I lost one prosecutor who tried to bring him to justice for the murder of Pedro Lomas, a twelve-year-old, killed by that devil. When it seemed as though the investigation was on track, my lead man was assassinated on the way to work."

"Maybe it was over the drug prosecutions and not the boy," Harris suggested.

"Not at all. He was my best prosecutor. I never put him on drug cases. He worked on domestic issues. The Lomas murder did not relate to the drug wars; it was a crime of sadistic lust. Durante was too important to the Cartel. They had to prevent our prosecution at all costs. The message was clear, and we dropped the charges out of fear.

"He is one to challenge the best of our investigators, when our time comes to prosecute the cartel. He set up all of the trails to hide their wealth and redirect it into legitimate business. It is he who they protect."

"One more thing," said Harris. "I met a little woman last night, and she stole my belongings. What are the chances she'd come back to the bar where I met her?"

"She will not be at the bar from her past night for six days. These women travel from cantina to cantina each night to avoid their johns from the previous night. If you wish, I will send a constable with you to pick her out and we will try to recover your belongings. You had to be at Los Rios when you met her."

"How'd you know that?" asked a surprised Harris.

"In Zarzal, where you are boarding, there is but one establishment to find a drink and a woman, and that is Los Rios. It would be too far and too dangerous for you to travel to the next town to meet this girl. I am correct?"

"You'd make a fine detective, Señor Coronado."

"So, perhaps, you will now allow me to repay you. I will escort you tonight to find this girl in Tulua. The bar there is very nice. As long as you are with me, you will be safe. You can relax once we locate her."

"Thanks, but no thanks. I appreciate the offer, but I have to get home. It wasn't a big deal; just loose change she got. One last request, though. I need to use your Internet connection. My computer's down."

"That is the least I can do for you, Mr. Morganstern."

Señor Coronado took Harris to a backroom housing a rather unsophisticated computer set up.

"This thing gonna work?" asked Harris.

"I can assure you, your message will be delivered."

His e-mail read—*All will be ready down here. There are two experienced prosecutors left. I will have credentials shortly, if they accept the assignment. Regarding the Durante fellow, he's a real player. It turns out he will be a formidable foe. He has a brain. He sets up all of their deals. Harris. P.S. He's a little boy mud packer with a penchant for hurt.*

Not due to leave before noon the next day, Harris had desire and time to find the young girl from the prior night without assistance from the prosecutor's office. He wanted to serve justice to the prostitute in his own way.

In the dark of night, Harris summoned a cab to travel along the same rutted, arid roads seen on his trip to Sevilla. When they arrived in Tulua, he told the driver he would pay forty American dollars if he waited, all night if necessary. It was a good deal for a cabby who could otherwise spend much of his night chasing empty streets.

Rancho, the establishment in this outbound city, was just another small-town watering hole. The American traveler never saw this village. The sense of being a foreigner felt palpable to Harris in this place more than any previous experiences in Colombia.

When he entered the bar, the eyes of the local patrons turned and fixed their gaze upon him. The cold silence stilled time for Harris, who now wondered if he should have taken Señor Coronado's offer to accompany him. The element was rough and intimidating. If not armed, Harris would have turned and left. He stood his ground and scanned the room. The patrons, not feeling threatened by his presence, went back to their small talk, reestablishing the loud chatter. There, in the corner booth, he saw the girl who robbed him the previous night. Alone, she sat smoking a cigarette, in deep thought and oblivious to her surroundings. She didn't notice Harris enter the bar, nor did she see him approach.

"Hey, baby," he said as he took a seat next to her. He pulled in close, so he could grip her arm and squeeze while avoiding anyone noticing.

Alarmed, she tried to pull away, causing her drink to fall to the floor. The activities of the night continued unfettered as they drowned out the shatter of breaking glass.

"Let's not have any trouble," said Harris tightening his grip. "I can get my friend, the constable over here just like that."

Harris forcefully lifted her from the booth. She went along without a struggle, knowing the arm of the law played fierce and heavy upon the peasant population. As he walked toward the exit, the attentive bartender approached with a bat in hand. Harris pulled the pistol from his belt and leveled it at the burly man's gut.

"Back off, macho man," Harris commanded. "You don't want to die for this whore."

Eyes of scorn set upon Harris from the few patrons now alert to his attempted abduction and departure. He turned to position his back toward the door while scanning the crowd with his pistol. Upon exiting, he lifted his reluctant escort by the waist and carried her to the waiting taxi.

In the cab, Harris began roughing up his catch. He kept grabbing her flailing arms and began kissing her aggressively. Embarrassed by the presence of the cabby, she hesitated to perform the acts she engaged in behind closed doors. Harris slid his hand under her dress and lifted her panties. Because his hand remained out of view, she stopped her resistance and let him play. It was not long before he unzipped his pants and forced her face into his lap. This calmed him for the rest of the ride. At his hotel, he paid the cabbie an extra twenty dollars and instructed him to forget about this ride.

When they reached his room, Harris threw the young girl onto the bed.

"So, you think you can play with the big boys? You think you can fuck with the big boys? I'll show you big hard dick, you bitch."

On the bed, the young girl cowered, trying to hide behind a sheet she held close. Harris dropped his pants and removed his rigid penis. It was huge, as promised. On the previous night, the young girl relied upon the booze to please him. She feared that in a sober state, taking him deep inside came with the risk of pain and internal damage.

As he climbed onto the bed to begin his escapade, there was a loud crash. The hinges on the door to his room pulled from their anchors with a fierce cracking sound followed by door and frame slamming onto the floor. In walked four brawny outlaws led by the angry driver of the truck that took Harris to Sevilla earlier in the day.

One of the men had a severely pocked face with, evermore, grotesque scarring from old knife wounds. He extracted a whip hanging on his belt. With the precision of a master, he snapped the leather upon Harris' penis, causing him to tumble to the floor. The pain rendered him breathless. He could not scream, though his mouth hung open without declaration or sound. His eyes widened with a searing terror felt deep through his core.

"Gaucho," called out the leader, "I bet that hurts, does it not, Gaucho?"

Harris could not respond. He held the whip tight, trying to create slack to ease the vice-like grip that placed him at their mercy. The outlaw wielding the whip kept the tension in play as he made the motions of an angler.

"I caught big one. This is the big one," he crowed.

The other outlaws laughed at the sight.

"You come down here and fuck our women. You like? You think you can come down here and fuck our women? We like that?" said the young leader.

He fired off question after question. Neither did he want, nor did he expect a reply.

"You fuck our women, and then you want to hurt them? This

could be my little sister." He paused, and restated. "This could never be my little sister. You know why?"

There was a sterile silence.

"You know why?" demanded the leader.

Nervously, Harris rocked his head in the negative.

"My little sister, she died in a room like this, Gaucho. A man like you, who likes to hurt little girls, that is who took her life. But that's not why I am here. This girl is a slut. She is a common crook. I am here to return your property."

The shortest of the outlaws had a fat face resembling that of a bull. Layers of flabby gut half-covered a hunting knife stuffed into his belt. He produced Harris' laptop from behind his back and held it up for him to see. "You want?" he asked mockingly.

The young leader produced a gun from his waist, raised his hand and pointed the barrel at Harris' face. "In our country, criminals have to pay," he declared.

Eyes shut, Harris waited. Not a sound escaped his lips. He wanted to plead for his life, but words of contrition locked frozen within the depths of his fear. His heart pounded. The agonizing beat syncopated a rhythmic pain within his head. The bullet would surely release him from the misery he had come upon.

There was a blast from the pistol. Harris jumped, but there was no relief. The bandit was just playing with him, he thought, until he heard the thud of the young girl's body fall from the bed onto the floor.

The gunman snapped his fingers, and the whip holding Harris captive dropped to the ground. This offered Harris the initial realization his penis turned blue and felt no sensation, pain or otherwise.

"You want to fuck our women? Go ahead, fuck her now, limp dick."

Harris began sobbing. He fell to the floor next to the body of the dead girl, supplicating himself, hoping for the mercy of his foes. He cried audibly, while repeating, "I'm so sorry. I'm sorry, so sorry."

"It wasn't the girl who got you into trouble, Gaucho. It was the message you received on your computer. Your partner wanted to know about Alexander Durante, yes? He believes there is no one here named Durante. I sent that message from you hours ago."

"It won't work," challenged Harris, somehow holding out hope his original message to Derrick would offer him clemency. "He knows. I sent out my message early today."

"Oh, I almost forgot," stated the bandit, "your good friend, Senor Coronado, was kind enough to send your message, but it never went through. Senor Coronado was a good friend of mine, too. I'll be attending his funeral tomorrow."

As the young man left, he snapped his fingers. The others went to work on Harris. They took turns pushing him from one to another, each time piercing and slashing his torso with non-lethal cuts from their knives, painfully reducing him to a gory mass. The process lasted about thirty minutes until Harris lost consciousness and bleed out. On the mirror, in Spanish, with his blood, they wrote a warning—*Gringos, no cuelamos nuestros senoritas! Senoritas, no estamos cuelar Gringos.*

# CHAPTER
# TWENTY-THREE

GETTING BACK TO THE PHILADELPHIA AIRPORT FILLED DERRICK AND Savannah with a deep appreciation for everything American. They never experienced commingled emotions involving the joy of accomplishment and fear of death that played havoc upon their sensitivities. They knew, if not for the twists of fate that worked to their advantage, they would have been doomed. They were grateful to be home.

Burdened by overwhelming fatigue, the specter of international plots threatening the nation's security seemed more surrealistic than fact. Exhaustion plagued their stores of energy. The need to survive became the driving force toward their respective residences. Saving the world would have to wait.

A less than appreciated, talkative military driver drove them home. It was one AM locally, and a schedule that often disrupted his sleep ruled his life. His job bored him, so he used discourse as the glue to keep his sanity intact. Being amiable, he managed to engage his fares in small talk until they dozed off to the rattled drone coming from the rickety van, a vehicle driven more miles than for which it had been engineered.

"Best time to travel. That's right, no better time to ride the roads. No one else around. I'd take this night shift any day."

He continued to speak in short sentences and fragments for much of the ride. Too spent to engage, Derrick and Savannah dozed intermittently. After an hour's travel, Savannah left the van for her apartment.

Now, Derrick was the lone company for this soul, so desperate to connect. Derrick's eyes fluttered on the verge of sleep when the driver made a turn faster than forces of gravity could resist. Derrick slid in his seat until he rested against the door. Now, fully alert, the driver's drivel accosted him along with bright lights coming from a strip center housing a large gas station at the corner.

"These all-night food marts are the best idea. This kind of idea keeps America one-step ahead of the rest of the world. That's right, no siestas in this here country."

Derick resisted responding, knowing it would draw him deeper into a banal conversation. The van traveled along gradually darker roads as they headed deeper into the suburban environs. Soon, they came upon the cemetery near Derrick's home. Beams of light from the mysterious tanker danced upon the tombstones as it approached its destination. Once in position, the truck stopped, and the headlights went dark. At this moment, the van began its struggle up the steep incline of Byberry Road. The engine strained, and the clatter escalated. Derrick had to speak up for the driver to hear him.

"Look . . . there. Do you see that truck?"

Oblivious to the peripheral borders of the road, the driver turned too late. In the shadows of the murky cemetery, the truck now hid from view.

"What truck you talking about?" he asked.

"It's too late. We passed it. It's the strangest thing, like clock-work. Just about every night, that damn tanker is in there."

"Why the hell would there be a tanker in a cemetery at night?" asked the driver, not expecting an answer. "I remember years ago there was this tanker unloading waste from a chemical plant in the woods near my house. That's something you should want to check out. Your drinking water, you'll want to check on that."

"Have you noticed all the roadkill this time of the year?" asked Derrick, changing the subject.

"I can't say I have. But that don't mean it ain't there. I drive a lot, so much so the road becomes pretty much a blur. You know, you can't remember everything you see."

They drove on for another mile to Derrick's house. As he unloaded his luggage, the driver continued his banter.

"That truck, the one you see all the time in the cemetery. You should look into that. I remember years ago there was this tanker unloading waste from a chemical plant in the woods near my house. That's something you should want to check out. Your drinking water."

The odd cadence of speech and the repetition of content seemed strange to Derrick, but lots of people are peculiar, many are forgetful, and many exist from day to day he thought. Derrick entered his house and closed the door behind him.

# CHAPTER
# TWENTY-FOUR

Field trips for Justice lawyers didn't hold much drama since they played out in and around the Philadelphia or Washington D.C. vicinity. Debriefings following a field trip were not much of an event either. All of the lawyers assigned to the team involved in forthcoming litigation had to attended. However, this meeting garnered unprecedented attention since it involved foreign travel with attendant complications.

The principals of the mission, Derrick and Savannah, attended, along with their immediate superior, Mason, and a stenographer who recorded the proceedings. Two special agents from the CIA joined them, making this meeting of special concern since they came onboard in matters involving the security of the United States.

Mason wore an uneasy face. He fidgeted with a paper clip as the stenographer set up her equipment. It was clear to Derrick, his boss felt intimidated by the presence of the outside agents. The stenographer motioned readiness and Mason began the meeting.

"This outing had problems we never faced in the past. Before we begin the debriefing, I am sad to report we have two missing in action. Karl Armstrong and Harris Morganstern have yet to check in. This is most unusual. As you are all aware, the "four d's" set into motion when operations hit a roadblock. You know, complications and the difficulties."

Savannah turned visibly upset and asked, "What the hell are the four d's?"

"Please Miss. Ambrose. This is a professional meeting, and I want to keep the language professional."

Before he continued, Mason looked at Savannah sternly. He pointed to the stenographer and shook his head "no" to emphasize they were being recorded and required propriety.

"The four d's. Delayed, distressed, detained, or dead," Mason responded. "When you are delayed or distressed, you have the access code that notifies our operatives anywhere in the world. They will get assistance to you. When we don't get a contact after your designated late date, we have to assume you are being detained or dead. Standard operating policy. Why do you act as if you never heard about this?"

"Because we haven't," said Derrick with a tone of anger. "And I want to know why we weren't privy to such a basic instrument for our survival. We damn near died out there," said Derrick, ignoring the admonition about using professional language.

"I don't know," said Mason with an air of mocking confusion. "I thought all of your team received briefing on the overseas protocol. At Justice, a situation like this is so rare, it's possible we just took for granted you knew the rules. It's all on your itinerary, plain as day. Look here."

Losing patience, Mason tossed a copy of Derrick and Savannah's traveling papers upon the table.

"What the hell did you think that means where it says, *late date* and *access code* and all of the fancy numbers next to that?"

"That's ridiculous," countered Derrick. "We don't read that crap. That's like reading all the notations on airline tickets. We just look for the flight details. And if we didn't know how to contact you, what makes you believe the others did?"

"You're correct. But that doesn't change the fact they never got on their flights to get back home, and their whereabouts are unknown. We have to assume there has been some sort of foul play. Having two Justice attorneys missing from a mission during a relatively peaceful history points to a big problem according to these gentlemen at the CIA. Rather than speaking for them, let me introduce Agent Randall Catcher and Agent Michael Roberts."

Agent Mike Roberts was in charge of domestic concerns at the Pennsylvania regional office of the CIA. Nearing sixty-years of age, he was well beyond a time when most agents recognized they passed their prime. Content to shuffle papers, a desk assignment wasn't beneath him when the orders came down ten years earlier. Age brought him the midriff expansion consistent with a sedentary life of beer and televised ballgames. His thin wire-rimmed glasses gave the appearance of frailty while they also functioned to hold in place temple hairs that grew too long. As an active agent belonging to the elite CIA, he did not look the part.

Agent Randall Catcher, by contrast, presented as an All-American male. Heading up CIA investigations concerning the welfare of all government agents networked throughout the world placed him into the upper echelon of one of the most elite clubs. Though tall, his broad shoulders gave the appearance of lesser height. A shadow of facial hair, already emergent this early in the morning, accentuated a sharply angled jaw line. When he stood to speak, his fluid motion and baritone voice commanded attention.

"We have suspicions that Karl Armstrong and Harris Morganstern are dead," he announced.

The blunt statement darkened the worlds of all in the room. While the CIA dealt with missing and dead issues daily, Justice Lawyers felt insulated from these assaults on matters of mortality. At first, no one said a word. They did not know how to respond to such a horrid circumstance.

"What makes you so sure?" Derrick challenged.

Embarrassed that one of his own doubted the beliefs of an agent from the Company, Mason jumped out of his chair and shouted in an unexpected and unprofessional manner.

"They have ways of knowing. Where do you come off questioning this man?"

Derrick backed away. He had no desire to get into a no-win pissing match with his superiors. The Company men were, by definition, his superiors, along with Mason, an indelible fixture at Justice.

Agent Catcher cleared his throat in the usual manner to indicate he was about to continue. He looked at Derrick with contempt.

"Sir," he started confidently, "we don't guess. When we say we have suspicions, it's as good as fact. You see, we have double agents on the inside of most crime organizations and subversive groups in this country and within the governments of every country where our interests reside.

"It's been reported that a group of jealous Colombians killed Morganstern. It appears he picked up the wrong hooker. From a reliable source, we learned they cut him up rather bad. We aren't even claiming the body. An investigation there won't get us anywhere. The whole thing will just hurt his family. They're better off thinking of him as a hero missing in action."

"This means what he just told you stays in this room. You never heard this story," said Mason, eager to interrupt so as to affirm his authority.

"Normally we keep facts like this to ourselves," said Catcher, "but we need to learn as much information as possible. If we gave you half the story, you might leave pieces of the puzzle out when you think back on your travels. We can't take chances here. Any detail you give us could be the clue we need to help crack this case. When answering, please try your best to remember all details, no matter how insignificant it may seem to you.

"Let's begin with Miss Ambrose."

Savannah nodded in affirmation.

"Were you having an affair with Mr. Morganstern or Mr. Armstrong?"

Blood drained from her head at the suggestion she had relations with either man. She found the question to be rude and intrusive.

Had they interviewed her alone, she would have taken the question in stride, but in a room full of men, she felt violated.

From the moment the interrogation began, Catcher's partner avidly observed and wrote in his notebook—a team effort. The process of group interrogation often had more substance than the questions. Catcher preferred to use this method in breaking white-collar criminals when he worked domestic corporate crimes. As a student of psychology, he knew secrets are much harder to stay veiled when the body language of involved parties is available for observation. The reactions of accomplices often trip up the best liars. The innuendoes cast by the interrogator had Derrick and Savannah questioning his motives.

"Where are you going with this?" demanded Derrick in defense of Savannah.

"Please, Mr. Daniels, please don't try to second-guess me. I have a job to do. I wouldn't think of telling you how to conduct your business, and I would expect the same courtesy."

"This is ridiculous. I wasn't even on the same side of the world as him. You're acting as if I had something to do with Harris' murder," said Savannah.

"Please don't take this personally, but in all murder investigations, everyone involved in the victim's life is a suspect. As hard and cruel as that sounds to the bereaved, it's a fact of police work. Now, if you don't mind, I will continue.

"Was there any sexual relation between you and either of the missing agents?"

"Certainly not," Savannah stated indignantly.

"Were you involved in any business relationship outside your work at the Justice Department with either of the missing agents?"

"No," she replied tersely.

"Mr. Daniels, I have to ask you the same questions."

Derrick blushed at the thought of them suspecting him of homosexual union. He felt blood rush to his head, and knew red covered his face. From the corner of his eye, he saw Agent Roberts taking notes. Unable to control bodily responses, his heart pounded. Feelings of self-consciousness grew within him.

"This is ridiculous," shouted Derrick.

"Ridiculous! Sir, I can't begin to tell you how serious this is. A scorned lover, one who could reveal embarrassing information about one's preferences, has been motive more than once in murders. So, I ask again, have you been involved in sexual or personal business relationship with either of these two men?"

"No," said Derrick.

"Please understand, everything about you and your lives leaves a trace that can be discovered when the need to search is deemed important enough.

"What did you find out about the Sheik?" asked Catcher directing his question to Savannah who was in charge of that mission.

"He has a well-guarded compound. We infiltrated the grounds after hearing a generic lecture that provided nothing. We found out he's performing experiments that cause animals to act out of character."

"Out of character?" asked Catcher.

"Sheep aren't supposed to be aggressors. We saw him inject an animal with something that produced aggressive behavior. It was like nothing I have ever seen."

"Miss Ambrose, that could have been as simple as oxygen deprivation," reasoned Catcher. "You haven't seen cyanide poisoning either, I suppose. The victim gasps for air, kicking and flailing about. It's gruesome. That may be all you saw. We will not jump to conclusions. We need hard facts."

A silence followed. The brand of silence that statements of reason undercut further response. Catcher looked at his notes.

"In the desert, we provided you with a guide. Her name is Nicola Petronov. Did she prove to be satisfactory?" asked Catcher, as his partner continued to write incessantly. It seemed odd to Derrick that Agent Roberts took notes when no one yet responded. He felt intimidated by the pair. The questions seemed to be formalities, tricks or tests, the motives of which were to probe their minds. Derrick wondered if the agents already knew what happened. It seemed possible they suspected Derrick and Savannah of wrongdoing. Derrick remained silent while trying to analyze the design of their query when Savannah responded.

"Yes, she was very good, but she never made it back."

"What do you mean?" queried Catcher.

"She was attacked by one of the guards at the compound," explained Savannah.

"Did they find out about you and Mr. Daniels?"

"No, we made it out. It was when she went back for the ..." Tears pooled within Savannah's eyes.

"It was my fault," interrupted Derrick. "I left my attaché in the lecture hall. It contained our visas and personal notes on the assignment. If discovered, it may have jeopardized the operation and put us in immediate danger. She went back to protect us."

Savannah looked confused, but she knew she had to go along with Derrick's version of the tale. Now fearful of answering anything that could conflict with his story, she let him continue.

"She had us wait at the SUV for what seemed like . . . like forever. She came upon us half-dead, my briefcase in hand, but incoherent. She seemed drugged or something. I don't know."

Savannah placed her head into her hands recalling the horrible end to the young woman's life.

"Miss Ambrose, you were sent there to work up a case for the Justice Department. Did you find evidence that could relate the prions to terrorism?"

"According to your view on what I saw back there, it could have been nothing more than studies on cyanide poisoning. I don't believe that warrants a Justice Department action in the international courts. But if I'm right, Alimet is working on prions, and that changes the issue to one of a major domestic security risk."

"That's why we sent you over there," said Catcher. "It's the prions we're concerned about. But we need proof they're planning to use them as a biological agent against us. We know Alimet is the authority on prions. We know he has his research facility but unlocking the secrets behind the prions . . . if he can harness them, that's the key to world domination. We need to know how far he has come, and his motivation to use them as a weapon of mass destruction."

"I've told you all I can," said Savannah. "As far as I'm concerned, they are evil men doing evil things. Just like we can't put the bad guys away until we have evidence of their criminal conduct, we'll have to wait on this, but you had better be ready. When they launch this plague against us, there will be little to stop their assault."

"Miss Ambrose, you can leave that up to us. And rest assured we will be ready for any attack, foreign or domestic. We have a network extensive in scope and resources."

A dull vibrating sound saw Catcher reaching for the cell phone attached to his belt. He answered and spoke softly into the receiver to muffle words. After a moment, he placed his phone against his chest and turned his attention back to the meeting.

"Mr. Daniels, I want to move on to your findings, but first we can break for ten minutes. Why don't you get some coffee, or relieve yourselves, if needed? I have to take this call."

Derrick stood and exited the room. Savannah followed, caught up to him and tugged at his suit coat.

"What are you trying to do in there? Why didn't you want me to tell them about the lab book?"

"I don't know. I just felt uncomfortable in there, as if they are the enemy, or we are the enemy. I know it sounds crazy, but I feel the two pages from the lab book may be our key to safety."

Savannah looked confused, and she responded, "Aren't you forgetting something? They're the good guys. Once they interpret the pages, it can confirm our suspicions. I'm dying to know what they say."

"You think they're going to keep us in the loop? Once they get those pages, they will dismiss us. The next time we'll hear anything will be when they need our services in the courtroom, or maybe never. You can count on it."

"You're right," she conceded. "We can always get the information to them once we know what it's all about."

"That's true, so just be careful what you tell them."

Catcher finished his call and summoned the parties back into the room.

"Mr. Daniels, what did you learn about the union of the Colombians and the Pakistanis?"

"It looks like the rumors are true. It appears the two groups have united, and the Colombians are the more powerful of the two. They had this higher up, Alexander Durante, working out the deal. Captured by the Pakistanis, he confessed to a plot to spike all of the drugs entering the US."

"Spiking them with what?" asked Catcher.

"I don't know. He never got that far. He said they are using additives that have profound effects on behavior, negative effects such as suicide, civil disorder and lapses in morality. It sounded a bit preposterous, but that's what he told us."

"Who told you, Durante?" Catcher asked skeptically.

"No. It was the man in the shadows," said Derrick.

"What man in the shadows?" demanded Catcher.

Without answering, Derrick continued. "He told us. Isn't that what he said?" He looked to Savannah to confirm his story.

"Yes," she replied. "The man behind the bright light. He told us. But first, this Durante character said their goal was to take over the United States. He kept saying take over, take over, then he was gone. He died right there in front of us."

"We have no file on this Durante fellow," said Catcher. "I find it hard to believe you met with a high-level operative in the Colombian cartel, and we have no knowledge of him. That doesn't compute."

"Are you kidding me?" said Derrick angrily. "You have no file on this guy? According to the Pakistani agent we met, this Durante was a kingpin in the Colombian cartel."

"The agent with no name? The one behind the bright light so you couldn't see him? That's who's giving you your information?" said Catcher sarcastically.

Derrick indignantly arose from his seat. "You have to know the agent in Pakistan. For Christ's sake, your people set up the meeting."

"Calm yourself, Mr. Daniels. There's no need to get riled. Yes, we did set up a meeting for you, but it appears you didn't make it to that meeting. Colonel Bashkar waited, but he reported that you never showed up. That's when we thought you and Mrs. Daniels may have met with foul play just like your colleagues."

"That's not Mrs. Daniels," protested Derrick. "You mean Miss Ambrose."

"I'm sorry. Miss Ambrose. That's when we thought you and Miss Ambrose might have met with foul play."

"Then who did we meet in Pakistan, if it wasn't your Colonel Bashkar?"

"At the moment, we have no idea. When the Colonel's people contacted us, we feared for your lives. This whole experience you've described seems to have been contrived. For what reason, I do not know, though it's not unusual for these people to go to such elaborate efforts to feed us misinformation."

The fax machine next to Mason's desk rang. Catcher retrieved the transmission, making it clear to all he expected its arrival. He read for a moment and handed the page to Mason.

"I don't suppose you received a reply from the e-mail you sent to Harris in Colombia," said Catcher directing his comment to Derrick.

"As a matter of fact, I haven't."

"When Mason is done with it, you can read the reply yourself. We intercepted it from an unknown encrypted server. Basically, he went on to tell you there isn't any Durante there in Colombia. This entire story is fabrication as far as I can tell. To be quite honest, I don't know what the real story is at present, but we will figure it out in the due course of time.

"We have many enemies, and they want to see us disappear from the face of the earth. Fortunately for us, none of them have the means to carry out their wishes."

The meeting ended after going over each detail for several hours. It was an interrogator's way of searching for cracks in the wall of truth. By the time the session finished, Derrick and Savannah felt like pawns in a dangerous game and didn't know whom to believe.

It was late, and everyone wanted to go home. Derrick wanted to drive past the cemetery that preyed on his mind. The convoluted mystery he reluctantly became part of seemed to touch every aspect of his life, causing more bizarre thoughts.

# CHAPTER
# TWENTY-FIVE

Traveling west along Byberry Road, Derrick came upon the cemetery he feared, and yet now it so intrigued him. Approaching one AM, the road along this secluded strip felt dark, long and lonely. It would have surprised him if the fuel tanker wasn't there.

Like a fixture, the truck silhouetted against the dark background of great weeping trees cradled in the darkness of night. Had Derrick not known of its existence, it would have been missed.

The late hour, the stresses of the interrogation and duty affected Derrick's sensibilities, causing within him a compulsion to act.

*I have to do something. If not now, when? If not now, perhaps never. This is the strangest thing. Every time I go by, he's here.*

Derrick pulled to the side of the road and watched. The operator steadied a hose that provided payload from the tanker. It appeared he was pumping his fill into an opening in the ground. Derrick parked too far away to see clearly.

As much as he didn't wish to get involved, as much as he bore a fear of cemeteries, the bizarre nature of this setting seemed a harbinger of danger for the community requiring action. A toxic dump under the cemetery fed by these night deliveries generating little notice or concern seemed the plausible explanation. The likelihood of busybodies investigating at night in the home of the dead was slim. Derrick removed his cell phone from his belt and made the call.

"Southampton Police Emergency."

"Yes, I want to report a tanker truck being emptied onto the grounds here at the Mt. Royal Cemetery."

"Can I have your name and exact location?"

Derrick hesitated. The question reminded him why he never wished to get involved. The intrusion into his life for the sake of being a "Good Samaritan" didn't seem to merit the risks.

"I'm sorry. I'm just a guy who wanted to report this to someone. If you don't care, then I'll be on my way," he said coolly.

"I'm trying to assist you, sir. If you wish to remain anonymous, that's your choice, but I must have a location."

"Byberry and Philmont, the cemetery right on the corner. Almost every night, there is a truck dumping something onto those grounds. You should check this out," he stated boldly.

"Is there anyone at immediate risk, sir?" the dispatcher asked.

"No. I just think someone should check this out before he drives away. This could be a toxic waste site," he said, and then hung up, no longer wishing to risk consequences of valor for peace of mind.

Knowing how quiet this suburban neighborhood remained late at night, the chance was good a patrol car would be upon the scene in short order. Derrick decided to wait for just a moment. To avoid discovery, Derrick extinguished the headlights. Exhaustion caused his eyes to flutter. The heat from the air vents warmed his face making his conscious state more precarious. He could easily have been lulled to sleep if nothing happened soon. Turning off the engine and cracking the window allowed the crisp, cold of the night to keep him alert.

To his surprise, a patrol car arrived in record time. Oddly, the car was an unmarked vehicle with the bar of emergency lights attached to the roof as evidence of some type of authority status.

A tall man dressed in a black leather bomber jacket stepped out of the patrol car and approached the truck. He wore some style of police cap, which delineated one man from the other at the distance separating them from Derrick. They appeared to speak for a moment, after which time the officer went to his patrol car and pulled out a scope of sorts. He scanned the landscape and came upon Derrick's car, whereupon he stopped his rotation. This frightened Derrick and he froze, wishfully hoping his lack of motion made him invisible. Together, the men started briskly pacing toward Derrick. Frantically, and with hands trembling, he turned the ignition key with difficulty.

Once started, Derrick jammed the car into drive. With the lights off, he sped away, hoping to keep the assailants from identifying him.

*That's the last time I'm the good guy. Who knows what they would have done if they caught up to me? It has to be illicit. Who the hell delivers oil in the middle of the night every day of the year? They'd kill me if they got hold of me.*

Sweating profusely in spite of the cold night air, Derrick pulled into his driveway and rushed into the house. As usual, inside everything was clean and neat. Adrienne, a stickler for order, didn't permit the kitchen table to collect plates, the day's mail, or any objects other than the one vase bought for display. The radiance of a dozen vibrant, long-stemmed red roses attracted Derrick's eye upon entering the room.

From the protection of his personal dwelling, Derrick allowed a glass of bourbon to calm his frazzled nerves. Adrienne had long since gone to sleep. He didn't want to wake her, though the need for discourse on the experience he encountered was strong. Savannah would still be up. He could call her, but upon further thought, his imagination made much too much out of the situation.

Though the alcohol leveled Derrick's thoughts, his heart raced on. This prompted him to take another shot of bourbon. He rarely drank, but whenever he had this feeling in the past, alcohol seemed to help. After a half-hour lying in bed, it had no effect. His prayers, an informal ritual, usually sent him spiraling toward a deep sleep. To no avail, his heart continued to race, speeding up beyond reason. He reached for his cell phone and went back to the kitchen deciding he had to make the call to Savannah.

A startled, "Hello," greeted him. He offered a deep regret for reaching out.

"It's Derrick. I woke you. I'm sorry."

Clearing her voice and sitting up in bed she responded, "That's okay. What's wrong?"

"I can't seem to get all the things we experienced out of my head. I think I'm having an anxiety attack or something. I just couldn't sleep."

"Where's Adrienne?"

"She's sleeping."

He wanted to tell Savannah about the truck and the men he encountered. At least he thought that was the reason he called her. As the conversation released his mind from the clutch of menacing thoughts, he decided to keep the cemetery experience to himself for now. How silly he felt, calling out in the night over nothing tangible. They spoke for about fifteen minutes when he realized he recovered. His heart no longer pounded, and the alcohol and late hour made him groggy. Unable to sustain much thought on the conspiracies on which they conjectured, he apologized for his intrusion and bid her goodnight. To Savannah, it was a joy that he felt close enough to bare his sensitivities.

Much tossing and turning kept Derrick from sleeping well that night. Episodes of odd dreams invaded light sleep though forgotten by morning.

As the rays of daylight worked their way into his consciousness, Derrick awoke. While Adrienne remained sleeping, he reached over to give her a kiss on the forehead. She responded by giving a cursory peck on his cheek and turned away to resume her early morning slumber.

Derrick sat up and thought about the previous night. Adrenaline spent, and time having worked its curative effect, allowed him to reach a more credible level of interpretation concerning his experiences. Still, unexplained events unfolded all about, but he now had some clarity of thought.

Derrick went to the kitchen, where he poured dry cereal into a paper cup to nibble on between sips from his coffee mug. His thoughts took him back through every detail of the trip. In another hour Adrienne joined him wearing her robe and slippers.

"You got in late last night," she said with little concern in her voice.

"They kept us there for hours going over the same damn things. It's like you don't know who to trust. I don't think I was made for this."

"You're damn right. You were made for private practice where the real money waits for us. One more year, darling, and you'll be a hot property. Every law firm that matters in Philadelphia will want you. I can't wait," she said excitedly.

"Where'd the flowers come from?" asked Derrick.

"Jim Young. Aren't they fabulous?"

"Who?" asked Derrick with an exaggerated look of confusion contorting his brow.

"Jimmy Young, the head of City Council. I introduced you to him at the gala ball. Don't you remember? He's the most influential guy in the politics of this city, not counting the Mayor."

"And why might this busy man buy my wife flowers?" asked Derrick with a hint of jealousy in his voice.

"Don't be silly. I've been helping on his campaign. He's running for Mayor in two years. He asked me to head a committee for him. This is the kind of connection we need. You know, once you finish at Justice. The timing is perfect. He'll be at the top, and you'll have his ear whenever you need it if I play my cards right. I don't have to tell you what that's worth."

"I don't know who's worse, the thieves we go after for Justice, or the thieves running this city," said Derrick with disgust.

"Oh, you're just jealous because you didn't think of the flowers first."

"I don't have to be in until one. How about we go out to a nice brunch?" asked Derrick.

"Oh, I wish you would have told me yesterday. I have to be in town to set up the mailing lists for Jimmy."

"You know, we aren't getting to spend much time together," said Derrick as he stood close to Adrienne. "I miss you," he said as he pulled her near. He untied the belt to her robe, placed his hands upon her naked back and stroked her body tenderly. They kissed a kiss filled with the passion of one. Adrienne pulled away.

"Not now. I haven't showered. When you get home tonight," she promised.

# CHAPTER
# TWENTY-SIX

Lunchtime at Justice, once a joyfully anticipated break in the tedium of morning routine, turned hollow. Of the five who argued over the trials and tribulations of life, Mercedes didn't get drawn into the foreign intrigue that resulted in the death of Karl and Harris and the spooking of Derrick and Savannah. The now solemn lunch table reminded them of the fragility and uncertainty life could present to those who just the other day seemed so vital. Circumstance altered their lunchtime team in ways they could have never imagined.

Though Mercedes never became directly involved in the suffering that struck her friends, she was no stranger to violence. Violence felt all too common to her, being the chief investigator for all cases involving government workers who had gone berserk. Between dainty bites of her lunch, she sat busy at work on last minute questions for her next appointment. Following several weeks of research, she had to set out on another dreaded field trip to interview the family of a deranged government employee as part of her investigation.

Derrick and Savannah went to the lunchroom together and joined Mercedes. She continued scrawling her notes. Neither

Derrick nor Savannah interrupted her. Following a few moments of silence, affording them time to begin their lunch, Mercedes raised her head and said, "It's spooky when you lose people you know, people you see every day."

"I never lost anyone close," replied Savannah.

"No one, ever?" asked Mercedes surprised.

"I know it sounds odd, but I guess I've been lucky. My parents and grandparents are still around, and all of my aunts and uncles are, too. Good genes, I guess."

"There's got to be someone you've known who's died," said Derrick.

"No, never," countered Savannah. "This whole thing is freaking me out. That Russian woman dying in my lap, and then Harris and Karl, this made up for my inexperience in matters of death."

To change the subject, Derrick glanced toward Mercedes' papers and asked, "So, what great project do they have you on now?"

"The usual; interviewing the family of some loony. This guy went into work and shot ten co-workers before he killed himself. All sorts of sad cases, and I have to work them up for the defense. You know, every victim and their families sue Uncle Sam like he should know when a loose cannon's about to fire."

"What can you find out that would help the defense?" asked Savannah.

"Not much. I'm there to limit the damages. I have to see if a pattern to their behavior existed. The plaintiff will claim we should have discovered these things in the hiring process. You know, the Monday morning quarterback play the plaintiffs' attorneys love to use.

"Tell me more about your ordeal. What did you find out from the Arabs?"

"You wouldn't believe it if I told you," said Savannah. "There's something threatening going on in the Third World, and we got close to it all."

"Aren't you being a bit dramatic?" asked Mercedes.

"We may have uncovered something involving behavior modification the Iranians are working on," countered Derrick. "And independent of that, the drug cartels may have started a campaign to smuggle spiked drugs."

"Spiked with what?" asked Mercedes.

"We don't know yet," said Derrick.

"Did you tell Anderson and the Company guys?" asked Mercedes.

"They discounted our story. They can rationalize a reason for everything," Derrick replied.

"We should compare notes," said Mercedes. "Maybe there's some connection. I'm seeing too many nutcases out there . . . Oh, my God, I'm late. Gotta run. Yeah, we should do that. Gotta run."

Mercedes ran late for everything. She rushed everywhere, and this was no exception. Looking for the Devlin home, she drove along narrow streets crisscrossing the working-class neighborhood of Frankford. Over the years, this region produced two other rampage killers, but no one made an association between them.

Her Audi looked out of place, parked along the rows of American-made economy cars proudly decorating the streets. In this neighborhood, the hard-working people had strong affiliations with their churches, parochial schools and trade unions. In recent years, the scourge of drugs and crime infiltrated this once stable community, causing flight from the city to the suburbs by those who could afford to make the move. It was the best way to escape the personal violence that grew as a plague on the streets and in the homes. Everyone knew law enforcement could not guarantee protection.

While of limited means, the homes remained well-kept by the long-established residents. The newcomers, the federally subsidized, often let their houses deteriorate. Many areas passed through various stages of decline as evidenced by graffiti growing like a cancer upon the homes, businesses and even upon houses of worship. Sacrilege and disrespect flourished and usurped traditional values.

Mercedes knocked on the screen door. She saw the veiled

shadow of an elderly woman rise from a chair in the living room and walk to greet her. The old lady experienced much pain with each step. She lost the battle with an arthritis that nearly fused every articulation of her frail skeleton.

"Mrs. Devlin, I'm Miss Carpenter. We have an appointment today, two o'clock."

"Yes, yes, come right in," she said as she unlocked the latch on the door and guided Mercedes into the parlor. She spoke in a kind manner with a trace of sadness.

"Please, have a seat. Let me offer you some tea."

A plain porcelain tea set sat before them. Cracks fixed into the glaze spoke of its age, as it belonged in this woman's family for generations. With an endowed pleasure, she poured two cups of heated water. She remained steady in her task even though her fingers grew gnarled and exhibited the perceptible tremors from early stages of Parkinson's disease. She motioned for Mercedes to partake the offering of cubed sugar and plain black tea.

"I want to thank you for agreeing to meet with me. I'm sure this is very difficult."

Tears pooled in the old woman's eyes. This response always made Mercedes uncomfortable. The routine was so predictable and sad she knew her days at Justice were numbered. She could not keep enduring so much heartache, and opening the wounds of others, while necessary, seemed heartless.

"I'll try to be brief, Mrs. Devlin, and again, I'm sorry," she said with delicacy. "Is Mr. Devlin home?"

"He won't speak to you. No one, for that matter," said the old woman. "After it happened, he had to go to the hospital. They say it wasn't his heart, but I know it was. It's a matter of time until . . . he can't bring himself to speak of it, not even with me."

Without prodding, the old woman continued, having a desire, perhaps a need, to speak with someone who might understand.

"Billy was never a problem. All throughout school, he didn't give us a lick of trouble. He was a good boy. I don't know what happened. Something at work, but he never discussed it with me."

"Was he using any drugs, prescription or street drugs?"

"Not at all. He was always the outcast in that respect. When all the other kids experimented with drugs, he stayed in his room."

"I guess he didn't have many friends," said Mercedes, trying to prompt an elaboration that might indicate some type of behavioral dysfunction. Mercedes had special training for her job with forensic psychologists who taught her how to probe during an interview.

The old woman thought for a moment and then responded, "Matter of fact, no. Billy didn't have much in the way of friends. In grade school there were a couple of neighborhood boys he played with, but like I said, when they all took to drugs, he stayed home a lot."

"Did he have friends at work?"

"I can't say he spoke of anybody at work. He went in and came home same time every day. Then he would go to his room after dinner and watch the television, I guess. He bought his own television."

"Did you have conversations at dinner?"

"No. Not much. It was always, just all right. I'd ask him about his day, and it was always all right. He never much talked about his work."

"So, he didn't mention or discussed the people he killed. Did he say they did anything to him?"

The old woman shook her head remorsefully. Ignoring the question, she commented, as if to herself, "It's a pity, what those families went through. If I could get them relief for their pain, I'd do anything."

The old woman blankly gazed into space, with her thoughts fixated on the past. Mercedes heard a chair from the next room squeal against the hardwood floor. She looked up to see a large figure coming toward her with beastly scorn in his eyes. It was Mr. Devlin, a hefty Irishman with a big gut. Years of outdoor labor planted deep wrinkles on his weathered face. Muscles in his arms remained large and still somewhat defined, but now wrapped in skin too large. Mercedes stood in fearful retreat. He got close and backed her to the wall.

"I'll tell you why he went berserk," he shouted. "Incompetent supervisors passed him over for jobs. That's what did it to him."

Mercedes felt threatened by the hostility and proximity of the messenger, however, this was her opportunity to hear a version of the story that never made it into the reports she reviewed.

"Mr. Devlin," she inquired, hesitatingly, "did he speak with you about this?"

"I know," he hollered.

"Dear, please don't raise your voice to this young lady," said Mrs. Devlin. "She's trying to help. She's defending Billy from the lawyers who filed suits against him and us."

The old man retreated from his hostile posture but could not control the rage that exposed itself in a reddened face and bulging veins throbbing at his temples.

"Please, sir, anything you can tell me might shed light on this tragic incident," pleaded Mercedes.

"Those fucking fairies down there wouldn't give him a chance. Every time he was up for promotion, it went to a favored type. It was a disgrace. Half the people at his station were deadweight, screw-ups. They couldn't even do simple things."

"Like what?" asked Mercedes.

"You know, simple things. They couldn't get a message right. They forgot what they were doing in the middle of doing things. They're all pathetic. About the only place people can get away with shoddy work is in a government job. That's the place they tolerate them and let them survive. On top of that, they use the system. It ate him up alive. He started to get like the rest of them. You know. He'd forget things and mess up on his work. That wasn't like him. He was a smart kid. They just rubbed off on him, I'm telling you. Then when they passed him over, the supervisors showed him all his screw-ups. It ate him up. I have all of the rejections. I saved them as a reminder. I know how he felt. The feelings just came from nowhere after a while."

"From nowhere?" asked Mercedes.

He didn't answer. A trance bound him within painful thoughts. Following an awkward moment, he broke away from the depth of his hurt and continued. "Some nights I can feel the rage building inside of me. It's uncontrollable. It's always at night. Terrible feelings, just like my Billy got. Used to wake him, too, and he'd come downstairs here, and we'd talk."

The old woman interrupted. "Why didn't you tell me about this?"

Again, he ignored a question. "I'm having a hard time fighting it. I didn't want to discuss it. When I heard you talking about the pain of those other families . . . I couldn't hold it in any longer. They don't know pain."

The old man placed his hands to his face as if to hide from the shame of his inability to resolve his fears. He stumbled over to a chair and practically fell into a seated position. Shallow breathing forced the red color to fade from his face, replaced by an ashen gray hue.

The old woman stood with difficulty and made way to her fallen mate. She rocked his head in her bosom. Without another word, Mercedes rose and made her exit.

On the way to her car, she heard the sounds of children cheering. When she got closer to the crowd, the bloodied faces of two teen combatants bobbed about for a moment before one pounced upon the other and delivered a hail of blows to the head of his foe. Mercedes hastened her pace as the days of respect or fear of an adult figure had long since passed. Relief came when she locked out the hostilities from this underclass world at the securing of her car door.

# CHAPTER
# TWENTY-SEVEN

The confrontation with Dr. Alimet, the Sheik, intrigued and frightened Savannah to the point of obsession. She had to speak with the one person who, perhaps, knew more about prions than Alimet. The day to meet with Dr. Mendelssohn, the University of Pennsylvania professor, was long overdue.

The discoveries they made intrigued as much as frightened Derrick. By now, involved in all of the conspiracies Savannah conjured in her imagination, he, too, held concern over the possibility of an assault on the mainland of a magnitude incomprehensible to all. It was not going to be easy convincing the authorities of the danger lurking in the crusade of an ill-defined enemy. Minus sufficient evidence, they would be ignored. Without substantive proof, they feared being labeled lunatics, just as history branded oracles and those who spoke with God. Personal investigation seemed the best way to expose a believable plot.

Parking on the streets around the University Hospital proved futile as expected at any major big-city facility. They drove into the parking tower. These structures had become the storage unit for urban travelers in all places where commercial real estate values exceeded the value of the life residing in the surrounding neighborhoods. Pollution from diesel buses, made ever more noxious by the dense humidity, filled the air with choking vapors. The walk to the hospital, made longer by a maze of interconnected buildings, streets and corridors, seemed borne of defective planning and poor design. On the ground floor entrance, Derrick approached the reception desk.

"We are here to see Dr. David Mendelssohn."

The smartly dressed receptionist interrupted from her activities, and without looking up to face Derrick, she typed the name *Mendelssohn* into her desk station terminal.

"I'm sorry, sir, I don't see your name on his appointment list," said the unenthusiastic gatekeeper.

"That's rather odd," responded Derrick. "I didn't give you my name, so how would you know I don't have an appointment?"

"The one with an appointment to see Dr. Mendelssohn today is a Ms. Savannah Ambrose."

"That's me," said Savannah, now moving up close to the reception desk next to Derrick.

"There's a note here directing you to Dr. Affelbaum's office. That's room 350."

They exchanged amenities, and the duo walked to the gang of elevators hoisting visitors and other parties of the hospital to their destinations.

"I thought we were meeting with Mendelssohn," Derrick said.

"We are, but he must be very busy and eccentric."

"What do you mean?"

"Well, he was hard to contact. I could speak with this Dr. Affelbaum, and he gave me the third degree. I suppose not just anybody can see this guy. I had to get clearance from the top brass at Justice."

"Who, Bernie?"

"I said the top. I mean the Attorney General's office had to open the door for me, or I would never have gotten this meeting. Believe it or not, I had to get special permission to get you to tag along."

"Me, a tag along?" said Derrick lightheartedly.

The elevator stopped at the third floor. Derrick and Savannah walked the long corridor that brought them to room 350. The glass door displayed, in black lettering, *Peter Affelbaum PhD., Chairman Neuropsychiatry*. Beyond the door sat a clone of the ground floor receptionist. She wore a headset and typed into her terminal. Without looking up, she greeted the pair with the conventional, "May I help you?"

"Hi, I'm Savannah Ambrose, and we're here to meet with Dr. Mendelssohn. We were told we had to see Dr. Affelbaum first."

The young woman now looked up and said dryly, "That's correct. Won't you please have a seat? I'll announce your arrival."

There were not too many options considering the small waiting room had two seats. Trying not to let the receptionist hear, Derrick leaned into Savannah and spoke in a whisper, "Neuropsychiatry? Have you heard of that?"

"No, but I haven't heard of dozens of specialties out there. I remember when they had to take my brother to a pediatric neuro-ophthalmologist for migraines when he was eight-years-old. So, I guess they can combine two or more fields of study together and make up a new specialty anytime they need it."

"I don't suppose he sees too many patients with two chairs in his waiting room."

"Dr. Affelbaum will see you now. Go right through those doors," announced the detached secretary.

The inner sanctum, much smaller than the waiting room, had one seat for patients. The desk and the bookshelves spoke of complete disarray, similar to the appearance of Dr. Affelbaum. He looked several years beyond the age of retirement, perhaps early seventies. His mind, much sharper than his appearance would suggest, was vastly more organized than the texts and journals strewn about.

Savannah took the seat, while Derrick stood at her side.

"Ah, yes. It is, I am told, the lovely Ms. Ambrose and her cohort, the notorious Mr. Daniels, who greet me today in their desire to meet with the renowned Professor Mendelssohn," he said in a soft, slow manner. He sang his words in a peculiar fashion as if speaking with children. The character of his speech influenced Savannah's response to that of an equally juvenile cadence.

"It seems Dr. Mendelssohn is a highly regarded national treasure. I had to jump through hoops to get this meeting today," said Savannah.

"Life is filled with obstacles," said a smiling Dr. Affelbaum. "Before you can have your audience with the professor, you must prove the meeting will be mutually beneficial. It is my understanding from the Justice Department you had an opportunity to hear Sheik Alimet, the Arabian counterpart to our Dr. Mendelssohn."

"That's correct," said Savannah.

"Does he experiment upon camels with one hump or two?"

Savannah looked to Derrick with confusion on her face, not knowing the relevance of the question.

Derrick answered, "Sheep. They experimented on sheep," he said confidently.

"Very good," said Dr. Affelbaum. "If you weren't there, you would have not known sheep are the model, not the dromedary, that isn't amenable to the experiments with which we are concerned. Dr. Mendelssohn, too, may have some questions for you if he is up to it.

"Once you have the opportunity to hear Dr. Mendelssohn speak, you will better understand the secrecy and precautions we take here at the hospital. Come now. Let us not make waste of precious time. As we speak, so does he. You can go ahead to the Bahrn's lecture hall. It's room 559. Here, take these passes, and present them to the attendant at the door. He will let you enter. Just take a seat in the back and listen. You learn that way. We all learn, by listening. I have his every word recorded as he speaks. That way, I miss nothing. With Dr. Mendelssohn, you don't want to miss a word. We never know when one of his resounding theories might come forth. He is in possession of an amazing mind. You'll see for yourself. At the conclusion of his lecture, we have arranged a private meeting for you. Go now. I will join you in just a few moments."

An orderly sat at the door to the Bahrn's lecture hall. He couldn't care less about the proceedings as evidenced by his *Daily News* sports section that owned him and the thorough perusal of city sports fans. He neither looked up nor acknowledged the presence of Savannah and Derrick. After an awkward moment, Savannah initiated the dialogue.

"Excuse me, is this the Bahrn's lecture hall?" she asked.

Without effort to inspect the guests, he held out his hand and said, "Tickets, please."

Derrick handed their passes to the attendant and pulled Savannah toward the door. The lack of civility in so many affairs of the day disgusted him.

"Let's just get in there before we miss the whole show," said Derrick leading the way.

They needed a moment for their eyes to adjust to the dark space. An overhead projector offered the illumination as it cast scribbled, arcane notations upon the screen at the front of the room. The strong halo of light surrounding the projector illuminated the professor. He looked mid-fifties. Outfitted in standard hospital issued scrubs, his telltale mask dangled around his neck. It seemed to indicate he either just left or expected to go to surgery. Strong and dignified features contrasted oddly with his long and wild growing gray hair. It hung over his ears and was even longer in front. The silky texture allowed for motion when he tossed his head back to clear it from his eyes. He was clean-shaven except for a pencil-thin mustache worn in an age long-gone.

Derrick and Savannah stopped in the center of the last row where they sat to listen to the wisdom of the master. The lecture room was sparsely filled with a few scattered attendees seen from the upper tier as the light reflected from their heads. The video recorder Dr. Affelbaum mentioned sat on the edge of the desk unobtrusively recording the entire lecture.

"As we progress in our understanding of the structure of DNA and its relation to the essence of life, we have uncovered some of the mysteries of life itself. My recent research has tremendous implications for the health and well-being of every man, woman, and child who inhabits this planet."

Derrick leaned close to Savannah and whispered, "Sounds important. I believe we got here just in time." He intended to amuse.

"Shhhush," she chided. "Keep quiet, and maybe you'll learn something."

"The response to injury and infection is inflammation." After each sentence, Dr. Mendelssohn had to clear his throat in an obvious habituation. "For years, we have discovered many of the chemical mediators of this fascinating process. We know that when we experience a wound by an injury or an attack by an infection, our cells release at least two-hundred chemicals, called cytokines, into the blood stream. These chemicals, in addition to our specialized cells capable of digesting invaders, become our defense against assault. These cellular and humoral elements swarm and attack. They destroy the invader, carrying the infection and injured tissue away."

He spoke each word emphatically in an almost theatrical manner.

"We have always known inflammation, or shall we say the immune response, is a double-edged sword, destroying the host's good cells in the process of eliminating the invaders. And it is for that sake we have over the years tried to control the response."

"I think I'm ready to split," said Derrick with indifference. "This is going nowhere."

"Please," begged Savannah, "if you pay attention you'll learn something."

"You mean to tell me you understand all this mumbo jumbo?"

"Quiet, he's going to hear you, and we'll be thrown out."

"And for that sake," Mendelssohn stated loudly, almost as if he wanted to make sure the guests from the back of the room would hear him, "we have over the years strived to control inflammation. Thus, the advent of the anti-inflammatory agents arrived."

Unexpectedly, Dr. Mendelssohn slapped his hands to the desk. He began swallowing and tried to cough. Once the harsh episode of stridor seemed uncontrollable, an orderly from the front row jumped up to help the professor. Dr. Mendelssohn motioned him back, and again he tried to expel the air from his lungs. A shrill wheezing sound, at its height, turned into a productive cough extracting content from deep within his lungs. All of the little nervous coughs now seemed justified as the prelude to a bolus of phlegm expelled and landing upon the bell jar housing a brain specimen.

Never skipping a beat, and without the least bit of embarrassment, the professor continued, "Zinc is our salvation. A salvation not found in the anti-inflammatory agents, neither the nonsteroidals, or in the steroids. It is the zinc that will stop the processes that have wreaked havoc upon the human race."

Derrick and Savannah turned to one another, both with brows raised. The complexity of the information, combined with the profound desperation of the delivery confounded them.

"You can see from this relationship," Dr. Mendelssohn pointed to scribbling on the overhead projector, "the use of these agents is letting the invaders into our bodies, deep within our cells to become our masters." A murmur filled the room that he then seemed to address. "That's right, every time we swallow an aspirin, an ibuprofen or other over-the-counter formulas, they relieve our symptoms by cutting off some of the critical elements of the immune response we desperately need to fight off the invaders. The invaders are the viruses, the prions, and the countless, yet unknown, groupings of atoms that can control our cells for their purposes.

"I do not profess these simple structures, I cannot call them lifeforms, have a mind of their own. However, they can and do cause all of the scourges of humankind, with no motive as I can see it. It is almost as if they have been put upon the earth to modify life, as we know it. It is almost as if they are the engine for evolution. They select out the physical as well as the behavioral traits they so desire."

The exaggerated swallowing began once more. This time, it distorted the professor's face and caused him to double over in pain. Again, the orderly approached. Dr. Mendelssohn straightened himself against the desk and motioned for the attendant to back away. With much effort, he projected another bolus of phlegm, this time, onto the floor.

A gasping for breath to fill depleted lungs roared loud from the echo resonating in the silent room. The aura of professionalism changed into a sentiment of theatrical doom.

"We had the answers all along. It was right here," he cried out as he produced a black book from the desk. He waved the book over his head and ranted on. "All the time, right under our eyes, but we were too blind to see it. Oh, Lord, what I have tried to do in the laboratory was not required had I heeded the words."

He bent over the desk, laid his head down and began to sob softly. The lights turned on, and two orderlies stood to help the professor, who no longer made protest. Clearly, the lecture ended. The door at the front of the room opened. In walked Dr. Affelbaum with three nurses.

From their vantage point, Savannah and Derrick could now see the audience. Seven men wore hospital robes and slippers. Some had been using crayons to make childish drawings upon sheets of paper placed before them. Some resided in another world, holding the crayons, while their heads bobbed aimlessly, and their hands made the repetitive motions of the insane. They sat with blank sheets of paper.

"Where the hell are we?" Derrick asked quietly.

"I don't know," responded Savannah, dumbfounded.

Avoiding further discussion, the pair walked down to the

lectern and approached Dr. Affelbaum. When they got close enough for him to notice their advance, he motioned for them to go back.

"Wait there, please," he commanded. "You will be summoned when Dr. Mendelssohn is able to see you."

# CHAPTER
# TWENTY-EIGHT

THE NURSES AND ORDERLIES CLEARED THE PATIENTS FROM THE ROOM.
They curiously collected the phlegm expectorated during the
lecture into a broad-based Erlenmeyer flask. The way they handled
the phlegm gave the impression it held some importance.

Derrick and Savannah sat patiently, waiting to learn the story
behind this enigmatic scientist and the odd circumstance of the
lecture and the attendees. Following a long fifteen minutes, Dr.
Affelbaum returned to the lecture hall.

"Please, come with me," he ordered. "I'm sorry for the delay. He
usually recovers much faster."

They walked down a long corridor leading to locked doors
where a guard sat quiet and still. Upon seeing Dr. Affelbaum, he
typed a code into a security panel. The sound of an electronic lock
resonated, signaling they could pass. Their path continued through
a protected hospital ward dedicated to the insane. Patients were
confined to beds, six to a room. While many slept, several lay upon
their beds staring into oblivion. Others wandered around the ward
unimpeded. None seemed hostile; rather one would guess heavy
medication controlled unwanted behaviors.

Dr. Affelbaum led Derrick and Savannah to the rear of the ward where they stood before two offices. On the door to the left, it read, *Dr. Peter Affelbaum, Assistant Director Department of Psychiatry*. On the door to the right it read, *Dr. David Mendelssohn, Chairman Department of Psychiatry*. Dr. Affelbaum ushered them into his office whereupon he motioned for them to sit.

"What I'm about to tell you folks is highly classified. The reason you received permission to have this meeting with Professor Mendelssohn is because our government needs certain information in the security interests of our country. I will tell you now, not a word is to leave this hospital without the sole purpose of use in your assignment. That means you do not discuss this with your friends, family, or spouses. Certain national interests could be jeopardized if we are not careful. Is that understood?"

Stunned by the peculiar situation, they did not respond. "Is that understood?" Dr. Affelbaum repeated sternly. They nodded heads in unison, like puppets but didn't grasp anything going on about them. They had many questions but no idea where to start. They remained silent and let Dr. Affelbaum guide them.

"Professor Mendelssohn was brilliant beyond your wildest imagination. When you speak with him, you may find him a bit eccentric, perhaps even a bit disoriented, but you would never guess he suffers from advanced Alzheimer's disease."

"What?" exclaimed Derrick.

"You would never guess a person so afflicted could be so incredibly lucent at times. Most everyone afflicted by Alzheimer's disease disconnects from their surroundings. They make absolutely no sense in anything they say. His intellect was so incredibly vast that even with the loss of sixty percent of his brain to disease he is smarter than anyone I know. This is testament to the incredible genius he possessed in his prime.

"Two years ago, he noticed he could not function at the level to which he was accustomed. The changes were subtle. No one here at the hospital noticed a thing. We thought he was just being hypercritical about his performance. You see, even while his brain is eaten alive, he remains beyond our level of comprehension.

"Like everything about him, he took his theories and experimentation to the extreme. For the life of me, and anyone else here at the hospital, we couldn't understand what he was doing. His notes were not clear, and at times he would lecture us at a level beyond our grasp."

In the corner of the office stood a flat screen monitor attached to a computer. Dr. Affelbaum turned away to set up the device. With purpose, he selected a file from a folder containing at least fifty others, all lectures of the Professor, as indicated by labels on the display.

"Let me play select footage from the professor's lectures before we meet with him in his office next door. This review should prove helpful. You may have noticed we keep his title on the door. Even though he lives here as a patient now, in order to get this continuous flow of brilliance, we have tried to maintain his comfortable and familiar environment."

Poorly edited videos made the transition from lecture to lecture rather obvious. Each section was short but filled with sufficient information to characterize a specific thought or concept. The first section of recorded tape had a date superimposed on the screen—October 14, 1997.

"Viruses, being the simplest of microbes, are made up of the simplest units of life, as we know it, DNA or RNA. It is through the virus, inserting its DNA or RNA into the cell of its host, that it commandeers the cellular machinery of the host to replicate itself in an endless fashion. Thus, the common cold, the most common of the viruses the lay public understands, would continue to reproduce itself until it destroys the host, were it not for the immune system mounting a formidable attack. The cells of inflammation and the humoral elements in the bloodstream, known as cytokines, clear the virus from the body before it can grow uncontrollably."

The video fluttered, indicating a transition to the next lecture. The date superimposed on the screen read March 15, 2002.

"When I initially became interested in viruses, it was quite obvious to me and everyone else they included a whole bunch of different animals. The latency for infection was a factor that had, and still has, been overlooked. I have classified four types of viruses based upon their incubation periods. I call them fast, regular, slow and ultra-slow viruses.

"The common cold virus would best be described as belonging to the fast incubation period. These I call the fast viruses. Within days of infection, the symptoms surface, as the host is attacking the virus. The host's protective inflammatory response, in fact, causes the symptoms. You know, runny nose, sore throat . . . miserable.

"The viruses causing childhood diseases, with which everyone is familiar, have a defined incubation period. Measles, mumps, chicken pox—the list goes on to include many more obscure diseases. The common factor in these is, again, the incubation period, two-to-five weeks. These I call the regular viruses.

"The slow viruses, due to their rather long incubation period, eluded all of us researching the cause of AIDS. Two-to-ten years is a remarkably long time for the infectious agent to lie dormant within the tissues of the host before it can mount an observable response, thus ending with the discernable disease. Two-to-ten years, it's absolutely a miracle of life, that is, to the scientific mind.

"If that wasn't remarkable enough, God saw fit to trick us again with the ultra-slow onset virus, cancer."

Derrick and Savannah cast simultaneous looks of dismay toward Dr. Affelbaum. He used his hand to motion silence, so they could hear the explanation forthcoming from Dr. Mendelssohn on the video.

"That's right, cancer is a viral disease. Now, I know my respected colleagues have disputed me on this statement, but I say here now, and I say it emphatically, cancer is a virus.

"The naysayers can deny it all they want, but the evidence comes in yearly. I would suspect in ten years, maybe twenty, the medical establishment will be in agreement with me.

"Just look to the studies out of Japan. One form of leukemia traced back to blood transfusions forty years before the disease surfaced. We have confirmed the viral etiology of most cases of cervical cancer, oral cancer is next and even some forms of breast cancer. These are what I call the ultra-slow viruses. They can remain dormant for decades before they surface. Mark my words. It is only a matter of time. What I say here today will be in the medical textbooks of tomorrow."

The video fluttered once again. The date superimposed on the monitor read July 11, 2004. The professor appeared somewhat older than the dated progression of tape recordings would predict. His face had more wrinkles in areas where stresses take their toll. A prominent deep vertical line of stress made its impression between his eyebrows and traveled up to the middle of his forehead. He emerged ponderous with his step dampened.

"For several years I have had trouble formulating my theories about viruses. No, no, I still maintain that cancer is a viral disease. What troubles me now, is I have not been able to find a virus model to fit many of the degenerative diseases of the central nervous system. I thought, for sure, viruses were the culprits behind such diseases as Kuru, scrapie, and bovine spongiform encephalopathy, often referred to as *mad cow disease.*

"I admit now that I held onto the dogma that transmissible diseases require genetic material, the DNA or RNA, to establish an infection in a host. To my dismay, I now believe the proteinaceous infectious particles described by a brilliant colleague at another University, who will at this time go unnamed, are the cause of diseases we didn't know were transmissible in this manner. He termed these particles prions, a portmanteau, where pro is for protein, and ion is for infection. After realizing these may be the elusive critters I have been searching for, I dove head-on into the research."

The video fluttered again. The date superimposed on the screen read September 26, 2007. The professor looked much older than on the previous tape. His appearance matched the way he looked in the lecture hall that morning. Gray hair drifted wild and hung over his ears. Unattended beard stubble produced a grubby appearance as he had not shaven for several days. His speech and movements displayed more agitation than the morning's live performance.

"I can now say, for a fact, prions are the cause of many diseases in animals and humans. The known prion diseases are all fatal, except one I will discuss shortly. They have a common trait in that they are all spongiform encephalopathies. The name comes from the way the disease attacks. The brain becomes riddled with holes, giving the appearance of a sponge when examined by the pathologist at autopsy. The process can take years to surface in animals, and even longer, perhaps decades, in humans. You can see similarities to my viral theories based on incubation periods. The ultra-long incubation periods of prions are what make the study of these diseases so elusive.

"The most common of these diseases is scrapie, found in sheep and goats. The animals lose coordination, slowly at first, but gradually, they become so incapacitated they cannot stand. Irritability sets in, along with an intense itch causing them to rub and scrape off their wool or hair. Thus, the farmers, who first noticed this disease years ago, derived the name scrapie. Of course, they had no understanding of the cause back in 1732, and neither did we, until now.

"Mad cow disease, traced to feed consisting of the meat and bone meal from infected dead sheep, decimated the beef industry in England. The scrapie agent entered the cattle and resulted in the tragedy. While there have been no confirmed cases transmitted to humans, there is still much fear people who ate the tainted beef could eventually become infected. As we discussed how long latency periods made the detection of AIDS so difficult, these people have good reason to fear an epidemic of spongiform encephalopathies in the future."

The video fluttered again. The date superimposed on the screen read November 5, 2007.

"The prion disease I find most amusing, if you can indulge my relegation of a disease to the world of humor, is Kuru. This was God's perfect retribution for a people lacking in the spirit of brotherly love. First described in 1957 by Gajdusek of the National Institute of Health, and seen among the Fore Highlanders of Papua New Guinea. They called it the *laughing death*. They became afflicted with this strange fatal disease characterized by a loss of coordination followed by dementia. They acquired this disease by eating the brains of the dead, a ritual of the cannibalism practiced by this not-so-brotherly tribe. Since this practice of cannibalism stopped, Kuru has virtually disappeared.

"Creutzfeldt-Jakob disease, another prion infection, this time striking humans, in contrast, appears worldwide. It results in dementia and strikes one in one million at around the age of sixty.

"Fatal familial insomnia, where dementia follows difficulty sleeping, is rather new, and I will not discuss it here."

Dr. Affelbaum stopped the video, and he spoke.

"We are coming to a rather interesting part. Please, pay close attention."

Both Derrick and Savannah having just heard what seemed to border on breakthroughs of medical science felt perplexed. Even without medical training, they knew the statements made by Dr. Mendelssohn were trailblazing, if at all believable.

"Let us continue," urged Dr. Affelbaum, as he pressed the button to start the video.

"My recent findings suggest implicating prions in an epidemic that has grown beyond anyone's expectations. I believe the National Institute of Health keeps the statistics under wraps to prevent panic among the populace."

A dreaded feeling fell over Derrick as he thought about his conversation with Mercedes concerning government reports having conflicting data on suicide. He shifted anxiously in his seat. Sensing an uneasiness, Savannah turned to Derrick who waved her back to the content of the recording.

"It is my opinion that Alzheimer's disease is the result of a prion infection with an ultra-slow incubation. It's not that the disease is lying dormant. To the contrary, it is actively doing its destruction, but it is just a slow process. It can take years to destroy enough cells to become clinically noticeable. If I am correct in my theory, then Alzheimer's disease is so slow growing it will become the only prion disease we know of that cannot be classified as fatal until it reaches final stages following decades of destruction. It is my hypothesis the disease is present in millions upon millions of children and young adolescents right now, destroying their brains slowly and methodically until it results in a life of oblivion. Before it becomes what we know of as Alzheimer's disease, the brain pathology, I fear, can result in mental changes bringing a tidal wave of aberrant behaviors including psychosis."

Savannah shuddered upon the mention of a flood of aberrant behaviors. She reached for Derrick's arm and he grabbed her hand in full understanding of the implications.

"My biggest fear is this prion disease, which is nothing more than a protein that induces the normal proteins of our brains to alter shape and thus clog neural pathways. It will, in due time, speed up its activity. The result will be that the symptoms appear in a much shorter period. This phenomenon is threatening our existence as the dominant lifeform on the planet."

A murmur surfaced, coming from the audience in attendance. Dr. Mendelssohn paused to let the implications of his notion set upon the minds of his colleagues.

"Now, I am happy to say, my investigation has taken me beyond all other research facilities on the globe, save one, perhaps, in a third world region where they could be conducting human research since they don't have a governing body to control such activities. Here, in America, and all of the free world, we must follow ethical guidelines that slow our research, though for good cause. To overcome that obstacle, that disadvantage, I announce here, today, I have begun human research . . ."

Another murmur arose amongst the audience. This time, more animated, as evidenced by the rustling of chairs and generalized rattling of notebooks and papers.

". . . I did not break any rules," he stated as if answering the collective voice before him, "in that I have started taking prion infusions myself."

The murmur of the audience in the video grew louder. Focused and listening intently, Derrick and Savannah heard the comment from one of the spectators asking, "What's he, crazy?"

To answer the ill-mannered comment, the professor continued, "I'll let you know. I do believe all of you who know of my work realize I would not cause myself harm. To the contrary, I am close to breaking the secrets behind this unusual disease and finding a cure. The one thing stopping me now is the clinical trial. My work is so far advanced that few understand the concepts. My hypotheses, though yet unproven will alter the way we think about disease. No governing body would give me approval for human trials. Yet, I believe so strongly about my work that when the future of a world without disease beckons, I cannot refuse the call.

"Let me state this clearly. It is all right here."

The professor held up what appeared to be the same black book he hailed as the gospel earlier that morning. The refined musculature of his face contorted. His professional delivery of scientific theory changed to that of an apocalyptic warning.

"I had the answers all along," he stated emphatically. "It was right here. All the time, right before my eyes, but I remained too blind to see it. Oh, Lord, what I tried to do in the laboratory . . . I did not need to do. Temptation to play your role lured me. I was never fit to ascend to your throne."

Dr. Mendelssohn collapsed upon the lab table, just as Derrick and Savannah witnessed earlier. This time, rather than orderlies, several distinguished looking members of the lecture audience came to the professor's aide.

Dr. Affelbaum stopped the video.

"Following this pronouncement that he infected himself with the prions, he went into mental decline. In his periods of lucidity, he directed, or shall I say convinced us to biopsy his brain. While this is not done in living Alzheimer patients due to the risks, the board decided since he was an experimental subject by his own design, the benefits of his research outweighed the risks of brain biopsy."

"Alzheimer patients are not biopsied? How do you confirm diagnosis?" asked Savannah.

"On autopsy. That's the way we know. Well, there is a PET scan, but it's not definitive as originally thought. Dr. Mendelssohn's work opened up a vast new view of prion diseases. Sad to say, we never understood his experimental protocol. In his compromised condition, he can't tell us the secrets that convinced him to infect himself. It's very sad. Come, now. You can see for yourself."

# CHAPTER
# TWENTY-NINE

"Good morning, David," said Dr. Affelbaum with delicacy, as he greeted his colleague. "You have guests. I told you about them earlier. They wish to ask you some questions. Would that be alright with you?"

The professor rocked in his chair, clutching the black book to his chest with the authority of one possessed. He appeared exhausted from the lecture hall episode. Dark patches beneath his eyes told a sleep deprivation story of long duration.

"Any help to the Department of Justice will be my pleasure," he stated amicably.

Dr. Affelbaum motioned with a friendly nod. Savannah could now begin her interview

"Dr. Mendelssohn, I met with Dr. Alimet a few weeks ago . . ."

Savannah's pronouncement elicited a discernible expression of distress from the professor. He interrupted her before she finished her sentence.

"That villain. You had the audacity to listen to him. Lies, they're all lies, I tell you."

"David, please, David, calm yourself," pleaded Dr. Affelbaum.

"They went there to investigate his activities. They're on our side, David. Let her continue."

As suddenly as the professor's demeanor transformed to that of hostility, he returned to the kindly old gentleman. The volatility of his conduct shook Savannah. She didn't know where to go with the questioning and chose caution and placation to guide her.

"I'm sure he is a villain. That's why we have to investigate him. It's our goal to bring him and his supporters down. What we need to know is whether it is possible for him to control behavior with prions. Can he use them to control rage? And even more important, how much can he speed up the incubation time that you described?"

"It's all right here in this book." Dr. Mendelssohn began rocking back and forth in his chair in a manner that seemed to offer him comfort like a child embracing a favorite toy. "You need not look farther. Right here in this book, everything you can want or need to know."

"But Dr. Mendelssohn," continued Savannah, "that's your lab book, and I'm sure you would have to explain the contents to me. I'm a Justice Department attorney. My science background is limited. We need your help."

A smile took form on the professor's face, and he stopped the rocking. He looked at ease, and he asked, "Do you eat the scavengers?"

Savannah looked to Dr. Affelbaum for assistance. He remained silent without changing his expressionless face. She turned to Derrick who looked even more confused.

"I'll ask you again. Do you partake in the scavengers?" queried the professor.

The room remained eerily silent.

"How about the flesh of the forbidden? Do you lay down with your mother's brother? If you can answer me that in the negative, you will be a step closer in finding the answers to your questions."

His peculiar questions left Savannah devoid of any response.

She felt helpless, realizing he spoke in riddles. They could be the riddles of the brilliant scientist or those of the man whose brain was being replaced by malformed proteins. In either case, they were beyond her comprehension. As a last effort to come away with some sort of useful information, she attempted a final request.

"Could I make a copy of your lab book?"

The professor looked at her coldly. He clutched his book even tighter.

Derrick stepped in front of the professor. From his trousers, he produced the pages from Dr. Alimet's lab book. He held them out for the professor to see.

"These might interest you. We took these pages from Dr. Alimet's lab book."

Excitedly, the professor leaped for the pages. Derrick pulled them away and motioned that he would be willing to make a trade. Following a tense moment of hesitation, an eager Dr. Mendelssohn initiated the simultaneous trade of documents.

"Hurry," said Derrick handing the black book to Dr. Affelbaum, "make me a copy of this before he loses interest."

"I don't think that will be necessary, Mr. Daniels," said Dr. Affelbaum. He handed the book back to Derrick. Upon opening the book, he recognized it as a handwritten copy of the Old Testament. Turning page after page confirmed the content as biblical and without commentary.

"What's this? The premiere scientific mind in the country, the world, and he's clutching a copy of the Bible? Am I missing something here. Are there hidden notations in cryptic form?" asked Derrick.

"Follow me," said Dr. Affelbaum. "Let him peruse your papers. They seem to have excited him more than anything in the last year."

Retreating to the confines of his office, Dr. Affelbaum offered explanation. "After Dr. Mendelssohn infected himself, he exhibited changes in his behavior. One thing we found rather odd was his devotion to the Bible. He read it day and night. By hand, he copied every word of the Old Testament into this lab book. No notes, no commentary, nothing, just each and every word of the bible. He can quote the entire scripture, verbatim. What is so peculiar is the theme of his lectures always comes back to the same thing."

"And what is that?" asked Savannah inquisitively.

"That all of the answers are in that book, in particular, Leviticus. I can't believe it myself. This scientist was an agnostic. No, I'd have to say atheist best described his belief. After the prions affected his brain, he changed. He turned into a religious zealot around the time he became infected with hepatitis A, a virus found in shellfish. He began observing the Hebrew laws governing food. The types of food and the preparation of everything he eats are strictly based on the Bible. He hasn't come out and said it, but many of his rants seem to indicate he believes viruses inhabit the scavengers of the land and sea. It appears he believes these are the source of much of the suffering of humanity. His prion infection set off a light bulb in his head. He started to read the Bible. I stand corrected. He began *consuming* the Bible. He seemed to unlock a secret that has since guided his life. That's the best I can tell you. We're not going to get a straight answer from him at this point."

"What about the zinc? What was that all about earlier today; the salvation thing?" asked Savannah.

"We don't know. Great ideas fill his mind. He has the ability to synthesize data and then interpolate and utilize the material in ways all great minds have done throughout history. These are people with a gift. In Dr. Mendelssohn's case, a short-circuit lets some things through in a lucid manner, while other times, it's as if we are speaking with a child or the Riddler.

"I know this sounds rather simplistic, in terms of extrapolation, but my best guess is that it has to do with the anti-viral attributes of zinc that's claimed by the makers of throat lozenges."

"What?" exclaimed Derrick, at a complete loss.

"The throat lozenges that claim to prevent or lessen the duration of the common cold. You can buy them in pharmacies and food markets everywhere. I know it's a stretch, but that was the best I could make out of it. He goes back to that statement rather often, but there is nothing in his notes about zinc."

"One more question, doctor," said Derrick, "what do you do with that mucous your staff collected from his cough? What was that all about?"

"Very, very odd. He insists we save that phlegm. I have no idea why. When we go back to his room, look to the bookshelf on the right side. Perhaps it represents his vital forces in some way. Whatever the reason, it is hidden in his mind. We do not argue with genius. Even one with Alzheimer's disease."

The three of them returned to Dr. Mendelssohn's office. As described, the wall to the right side of the room had a shelf that housed over a hundred flasks of mucous. Derrick and Savannah made eye contact and simultaneously raised their eyebrows acknowledging the bizarre nature of their experience. Dr. Mendelssohn finished reviewing the papers from Dr. Alimet. He sat with a cocky grin plastered across his face. Without exchanging a word, he handed Savannah the papers aggressively.

The brusqueness of his action, and the awkward silence that followed, hung heavily in the room.

"So, what did you make of the Sheik's notations?" asked Derrick as he returned the Bible.

Dr. Mendelssohn grabbed the sacred book and exaggeratingly turned his head up and to the left like a defiant child.

"Go on, David, tell them what it said. Give them your take on the papers," coaxed Dr. Affelbaum.

Dr. Mendelssohn did not wish to cooperate, and it was soon evident they were not going to inspire him out of his stubbornness.

"Well, it was nice meeting with you, Dr. Mendelssohn," Savannah said, extending her hand.

He placed his book in lap, shook her hand and held it between both of his for a moment.

"Your hands, they are lovely, the skin of a princess. Don't forget to wash them before meals," he said kindly. Abruptly, he turned and stared at the blank wall. With collective disappointment, the group exited the confines of Dr. Mendelssohn's quarters. He called out, "The papers you showed me . . . he can do it. He can control rage, modify behavior, and even speed up the incubation period as you suspect."

# CHAPTER
# THIRTY

"So, what brings my itinerant patient here today, if it isn't the bi-annual sinus infection?" asked the clean-cut, fifty-something doctor. He wore a smart shirt and tie covered by a bright, white, starched lab coat. The iconic stethoscope around his neck topped off a look that defined the epitome of professionalism.

Derrick saw Dr. Klein twice a year for the effects of seasonal changes on his sinuses. It seemed a year could not go by without two episodes of sickness. These regular visits assured Derrick a doctor-patient relationship usually reserved for the more infirmed. The rest of the year, he had no problems requiring medical attention. Here he sat, sporting the skimpy patient gown, ready for Dr. Klein who suspected something different bothered Derrick.

"I figured it was time for a checkup."

"Most of my patients don't begin to think of the yearly routine physical until at least forty. What problem brings you here?"

"I was out of the country, and I thought it might be a good time to get blood work to make sure all the systems are in order."

"I see there hasn't been a change in your weight. Your bowels, are they normal? Any dark or loose stools?"

"None. I'm fine. Just wanted the blood worked up . . . maybe a little problem peeing when I wake up. And ..." Derrick hesitated out of embarrassment, long enough for Dr. Klein to help him along.

"Come on, Derrick, what's the problem?"

"I wanted to ask you some questions, but I felt funny about just calling. I know you're busy, and I figured during the exam, I could ask . . ." Derrick stammered but found the words. "You're Jewish, right?" he asked.

"You're about to submit yourself to a prostate exam just to find out my religion?" He motioned for Derrick to lay back and turn on his side as he donned a pair of rubber gloves. "Knees to your chest."

"No, seriously, you're Jewish? Ouch."

"Derrick, it's just a finger. The name, Abraham Klein? I'd worry if you didn't figure that one out, but to answer your question, yes.

"Your prostate is doing fine. Too much sex can do that to you."

"I can assure you that's not the problem."

"Not enough can do that as well. Working too hard. Too much stress. You have to slow down. So, what's with the Jewish thing?"

"Are you versed in the Bible, the dietary laws of the old testament?"

"I'm aware of them, but like many Jews, I don't practice them anymore. When I was a kid, my parents did, so I did, but that was long ago. Are you having an eating problem, Derrick? You can sit up."

"No, Dr. Klein, I can't explain too much. It's something I'm involved with at work. I need information about the dietary laws, and the Internet didn't help relate the laws to medicine. What I need to know . . . I know this sounds foolish, but can you get viruses from scavenger fish, the forbidden fish in the Bible?"

Derrick expected a look of confusion on Dr. Klein's face. He was surprised when the response came without hesitation.

"Sure, hepatitis A. It's a common finding in undercooked shell-fish. However, it's not that serious, not like hepatitis B, or worse yet C, and they don't come from shellfish. Those viruses are blood-borne; dirty needles, contact with blood from an infected person.

You don't have to worry. Before you went on your travels, you came in and Angie gave you the hepatitis A vaccine. Uncle Sam wouldn't let you go without it. Did you forget?"

"Now that you mention it, I do remember. Justice told me I needed those inoculations before I could get my visa, and I did get them, but that's not why I'm asking. Can other viruses be transmitted by eating the various things forbidden in the Bible?"

"I never thought about it, but if hepatitis A can, I'd have to guess others could as well. There are so many viruses out there we haven't discovered. I would have to say they could transmit in the same way. It's funny you brought this up. A friend of mine, who keeps kosher, told me the act of salting meats to remove the blood is a healthy practice the Jews knew about thousands of years ago. That's part of the koshering process. At first, I argued with him, but the more I thought about it, most of the bad viruses we know of are in the blood of the host, so it makes sense to try to remove as much as you can and to purify the blood. The salt helps do both. I guess he was right, but of course we aren't getting diseases from our foods that we don't know about."

"How can you be so sure?" asked Derrick.

"That's where the science of epidemiology comes in. If, for example, people were getting hepatitis B from meat, it would show up in large numbers, and we could trace it back to the source. You see it all the time. In the news, they mention an outbreak of E. coli or some other food poisoning. In a matter of days, they find the source and that's the end of it."

"Dr. Klein, I know you're busy but one more thought. If the incubation time was years, two or ten or even twenty, would the epidemiologists still be able to match the diseases to their source?"

"In that case . . . yes . . . well, maybe. It was hard enough to figure out the source of AIDS, but they did. Same with Legionnaire's disease. Of course, that was because lots of people were dying off rather fast. When you get an epidemic of a transmissible disease, it is always traceable. It just takes time to find the link and then to find the organism responsible."

"Is cancer a virus, Dr. Klein?"

"Some cancers have been shown to be viral, but most aren't. That's an interesting question. Thirty years ago, we didn't think viruses caused any cancers, and now we know some of the leukemia's were transmitted by blood transfusions given up to forty years ago, and some other cancers have been linked to viruses. For example, now we know that a wart virus called HPV causes cervical cancer and probably mouth cancers. Who knows what they'll know twenty years from now?"

"Is cancer considered to be at epidemic proportions? How prevalent is it?" asked Derrick.

"Cancer is not described as an epidemic or pandemic. We use those terms to describe infectious diseases. But in the loose meaning of the term, yes, it is pandemic, because it's worldwide. It affects an unbelievable number of people. You can't imagine how many people in my practice have, or had, one type of cancer or another. It wasn't always like this either. Sure, cancer has been around since the beginning of time, I'd guess. But even in my small perspective of twenty-two years in practice, I can't believe the increases I've seen."

"Could a hostile country have infected us with an epidemic of cancer?"

"I just told you, cancer isn't contagious ..."

"I thought you just said some cancers are viral, that certain leukemia's were transmitted through the blood. That defines contagious."

"You're trying to understand medicine, and it's extremely complex," responded a frustrated Dr. Klein. "Let's look at this logically. If a hostile country wanted to kill us with biological warfare, they would use anthrax, or nerve gas. If they wanted to get sophisticated, they would try Ebola or the Hantavirus. They wouldn't waste time with something that wasn't quick and effective."

"If they wanted to take us out without our knowing, they wouldn't use a known, and obvious disease, would they?" reasoned Derrick.

"Derrick, you don't have cancer. Just try to forget about all of these silly notions. You're going to live a long time; it's in your genes. You're lucky you're not Jewish. We have all of this guilt because we have to follow all these rules, and when we don't, we die from guilt. Trust me; you are better off not dealing with all of this.

"If you're so interested in the Bible and the laws, go speak to the Rabbi Barbar. Avrom Barbar, he's the fellow to ask these things. He may not be able to relate all of your concerns with cancer, but he knows the Law better than anyone else."

Dr. Klein jotted the name and number of the Rabbi on a prescription pad and handed it to Derrick. Not satisfied, but realizing that Dr. Klein wasn't about to, nor did he have the time to have a deep discussion on Biblical Laws and the way they relate to medicine, he took the prescription and went on his way.

In Derrick's chart, Dr. Klein made a notation: *Cancer-phobic? He displays the type of anal-inquisitiveness that can lead to paranoid reaction. Recent visit to Asia seems to be the precipitating factor. Perhaps work-related stress. Monitor prostate.*

# CHAPTER
# THIRTY-ONE

SHEIK ALIMET DEVOTED HIS LIFE TO SCIENCE AND RELIGION. HE planned and plotted his entire professional life looking for ways to use his gift toward the destruction of all enemies of Islam. Raised with a fundamentalist philosophy, he viewed the West as a derivative of the devil.

Having reached a respected station, it gave him pride to represent his people in the halls of science and technology. For too long, the world looked at his brethren as primitive desert dwellers. The Sheik's accomplishments gave credence to the superiority he believed existed in the bloodline of his people had they the opportunities so bountiful in the West.

In the Sheik's private chambers, he met with two adherents for their final briefing. Their mission would define his life's work. Aminur and Bitar were the means to accomplish that which no military might could imagine. The disciples were well trained and eager to carry out all wishes from their superiors. The opportunity to meet with one so elevated in the hierarchy of the movement was an honor they cherished.

"You know your task and have trained long and hard for this mission. Do you have any regrets?" asked the Sheik.

In a trance-like manner, they spoke in unison, "No regrets, Holy One." By design, they chose identical words. To respond to all possible scenarios, they sat through meticulously briefings. They answered alike, acted alike and thought alike.

"You must understand your lives are second to the cause. You cannot fail."

"Failure is not an option, Holy One," the duo responded.

"These are your travel documents. You will enter America with these visas issued by Saudi Arabia. I wish you the speed and safety of Allah."

"Allah Akbar!" thrice shouted the devotees.

Aids escorted both foot soldiers from the chambers and the Sheik made notes in his workbook: *The time has arrived for all people to be free from the vice of occupation and depravity. While it will not come fast, it will come, and our victory will be complete. The infidel will never defend that which he cannot see.*

Aminur and Bitar made the long journey to America and settled into their motel room next to Highway 59, 45 miles outside Omaha, Nebraska. In a world of massive immigration, diversity, tolerance and international travel, people did not see them as foreign in a land more frequented by foreigners than in eras past. In a country with leaking borders, the door was wide open, and their plan took distinct advantage of this flaw.

The stated goal was to combine the contents of twenty pills into fresh beef and incorporate the mixture into the feed trough at the nation's largest cattle breeding ranch. Pills in prescription bottles brought on no suspicion when carried between borders. The necessity and innocent nature of medicines assured that authorities would not confiscate them. The pills contained altered proteins, the plague that would unleash its fury upon the infidels of the West.

To Aminur, the plan was simple and rather straightforward. Following the ceremonial consumption of an elixir used to calm the nerves of all devotees on missions of stealth, they would depart on the road to accomplish their goal. With miles and miles of fence bordering the cattle farm, unseen infiltration would be easy to accomplish. They would intermingle with the workers and deposit the tainted mixture in a vast bin used to feed hundreds of prize cattle. These cattle were not fated for slaughter; rather buyers from cattle ranches throughout the country would purchase them as breeders. The Sheik's prion-infested brew would find a home in millions of unsuspecting victims should the plot succeed as planned.

"Bitar, the room spins, and I do not know how I will be able to travel. Give me a moment to rest," said Aminur.

Bitar was privy to information Aminur never knew. Unlike the plans described to Aminur, Bitar had a different set of instructions. He knew the altered prions manufactured at the Sheik's farm could not remain potent in the form of a pill. The infectious agent stayed viable in the brain tissue of a living host in order to infect others. They could not bring livestock into the county without serious oversight. Instead, the Sheik transported his menacing formula within Aminur's living brain. While all faithful swore an oath to die for the cause, some, on occasion, would want to renege on their commitment. In this most important mission, neither apostate nor deserter would spoil the destiny of destruction.

"My brother, I am saddened to say our mission is not what you expected."

"Not what I expected?"

"The pills, they contain no toxin. It is in the living brain that we can fulfill our mission. It is our destiny to defeat the infidel. You are the chosen one. You, Aminur, are the martyr."

"What do you mean?" screamed Aminur now knowing precisely what he meant.

He tried to rise from his chair and tumbled to the ground. Crawling towards the door in a feeble and useless attempt to escape his fate, Bitar rushed to his side to comfort him.

"My brother, you now go to Allah and may the virgins give you joy and pleasure unlike any joy we find here on earth."

"No!" screamed Aminur. "You can't do this to me. This was not a mission to die. I must live. My true love waits for my return."

Those were his last words. As much as Aminur struggled, the sedative fully engaged. He could neither speak nor move. As he lay incapacitated upon the floor, Bitar slit his throat to end the struggle that would ensue without complete anesthesia the sedative could not offer.

Using a hacksaw secured from the local hardware store, Bitar meticulously removed the skullcap as he did a hundred times before on sheep back at the Sheik's farm. Using a spoon, compliments of the motel, he skillfully scooped the brain from its casing and severed the attachment from the brainstem to the spinal cord. He prepared the lethal blend by chopping and mixing the brain matter with the fresh ground beef purchased that morning at the local grocery store.

The ride to the ranch, an anxious excursion now that he traveled alone and had no discourse to keep his mind from wandering, was fraught with fear of detection. However, Bitar trained hard for this mission, and it wasn't long before he shed his guilt and hid all worries allowing him to infiltrate the breeding farm in an unassuming manner. Emptying the package of tainted meat was simple, and once he confirmed the feeding time had begun, he started his journey home to give his report.

One of the hundreds of bizarre news stories that passed through Mercedes' database on her Justice Department computer involved the story of a body found at a motel with the brain removed in a cult-like murder. She never read this particular violence-laden story because just too many macabre and violent incidences occurred every day.

# CHAPTER
# THIRTY-TWO

Adrienne awakened earlier than Derrick in recent weeks. She had to leave the house before the morning rush-hour to meet with Jim Young's affluent campaign donors before they started hours. A pretty face with a resounding personality helped loosen the pockets of these wealthy donors. Their egos coughed up thousands of dollars as a means of impressing that pretty face. Jim Young counted on this happening when he recruited Adrienne.

"Gotta run, honey. I'm late." Adrienne bent down to kiss Derrick on the cheek in a cursory manner. The sound of her voice and the physical contact assaulted his faculties as he attempted to hold onto precious minutes of slumber. The minutes he so cherished diminished with each glance at the clock. Almost instinctually, he kissed her and offered words of love and devotion in exchange for the chance to drift back to an interrupted dream.

The dream was odd, and it was odd Derrick dreamt at all. He knew everyone is supposed to dream every night and often forget those dreams by morning. However, Derrick swore he didn't dream. He based this notion on the fact he didn't remember any dream for the last five years.

This rare dream placed him in the desert. Crawling through a sand storm, he could barely see. Shallow, forced breaths of arid, hot air burned his throat and parched his lungs. The discomfort took form in his actual sleep, where he labored to inhale and exhaled in an agitated manner. His tightly clenched eyes, revealed distressed, rapid movements beneath his lids.

A few hundred feet ahead, the vision of a person appeared. As the image drew closer, he saw it was Savannah. From a distance, he saw another figure approaching. Soon, he recognized Sheik Mohamed Alimet. From beneath his cloak the Sheik pulled out a shotgun, took aim upon Savannah and fired. The blast resonated, propelling Derrick from the grip of his dream state. He jumped up in bed, and at that moment, realized the gun blast from his dream occurred simultaneously with an explosion outside his home.

Derrick ran to the bedroom window, pulled back the curtains and saw a plume of smoke rising skyward, not more than ten feet from where he stood. A sense of panic overwhelmed him. He knew something terrible happened and ran outside to investigate. Neighbors from all directions came running. There on the driveway, his automobile stood smoldering. The interior, demolished, contained a charred residue.

Derrick reassessed, with relief, that it was his car that exploded. In his bewilderment, he turned to see Adrienne's car untouched, expecting to find her at the wheel hiding from the blast.

"She's dead! She's dead!" screamed a neighbor sobbing uncontrollably.

"That's impossible," cried Derrick. "That's *my* car. That's *my* car," he cried out frantically pointing to the charred wreck.

"She got into that car and it exploded. I saw it all," shouted the neighbor.

The feeling of undeniable doom overpowered Derrick's limbs. He tried to move but found himself paralyzed by numbness invading his extremities. Losing his balance, he fell to his knees, and cradled his head in his hands.

"Oh, my God! Oh, my God!" he called out when he realized Adrienne had taken his car, and she was now dead.

All present in the crowd turned speechless. No one approached Derrick to comfort him. Sirens drew near.

The first on the scene, an unmarked car, belonged to the Chief of Police, Joe Thompson. Unmarked first responders became common practice in the suburbs, where the closest law enforcement official scouted out calls to ascertain the needs for their limited emergency personnel.

Derrick, still on the driveway, now stood with a disorientated expression on his face next to the incinerated car, the interior charred beyond description.

"Is this your car, sir?" Thompson inquired.

Still stunned, and unable to grasp the reality of the moment, Derrick did not respond.

"Sir, is this your vehicle?"

"Yes, yes, it is," said Derrick, eyes rolling to the back of his head. He steadied himself on the vehicle to regain his balance.

Thompson strolled around the car several times, scratching his chin and shaking his head while observing the scene. His deputy arrived, and he followed Thompson around the car observing in silence, waiting for him to say something.

"This is the damnedest explosion I ever did see," he exclaimed. "The windows are gone, but not a bit of broken glass, no piece of the car missing. I never seen anything like it. Almost looks as if you could be standing right next to it when it went off, and you would be fine. Was anyone inside?"

"I saw it all," declared the witness. "She got into the car, and it turned red. I mean red. It started to glow, and there was a flash, and the sound, and a cloud of smoke."

Once Thompson had a basic understanding of the situation, he ordered his deputy to get written statements from the neighbors who had something to contribute. He then escorted Derrick into the house to take his statement.

"Mr. Daniels, I know you're in shock from what took place. If you'd like, I can run you over to the hospital. That may be the best thing for right now."

"No, no, I can't leave her," said Derrick referring to Adrienne as if she was somewhere nearby.

Knowing the severity of the experience, Thompson didn't wish to start the intensive investigation that always follows a murder case. He was not particularly versed in these matters, as specialization for cases involving homicides does not exist in the small police forces of the suburbs. He had to do it all. Because of the unusual nature of the explosive device used, Thompson directed one of his officers to notify the FBI. A first response team arrived, did a preliminary investigation, conveyed their findings to the Chief who turned his attention to Derrick.

"I can come back later. You need time to be alone."

"No. We have to find out who did this, and the longer we wait the more difficult it will become," said Derrick in an insightful manner.

"Did your wife have a job that could have brought on enemies?" asked Thompson.

"No, you don't understand. They meant this for me. They were trying to kill me."

"Kill you?"

"That was my car she got into. I was supposed to be in that car. I don't understand why she got into my car."

"My deputy tells me your wife's car was just about out of gas," explained Thompson.

"That's it. She was running late. She took my car. That should be me out there. They were after me."

"Who was after you, Mr. Daniels? Who did this?" asked Chief Thompson.

Realizing he didn't know who committed the crime, Derrick became tacit in his responses. The image of the unmarked police car in the cemetery flashed in his mind. The unmarked police car now parked in front of his house flashed into his mind. A sinister revelation entered Derrick's thoughts. He feared the bombing might be related to the deliveries at the cemetery. He glanced around looking for answers nowhere to be found. His thoughts, and suddenly timid actions, bred a self-conscious fear of exposing his innermost belief that Thompson could somehow be involved. Derrick had to speak with caution to avoid revealing the suspicions he now fostered about the man interrogating him.

"I don't know who, but someone wanted me dead. Can't you see that?"

"Who would want to kill you, Mr. Daniels?"

"I'm an attorney at the Justice Department. I'm involved with drug prosecutions on an international level. There are people all over the world who would want me and my department out of the picture. Then the dozen or so dealers I've prosecuted locally. They could want to get even with me."

The chime of the doorbell interrupted the conversation. Derrick sat motionless, ignoring the call.

"I'll get it for you," offered Thompson. Derrick did not respond, suggesting he needed the offer. He could hear the conversation coming from the entranceway.

"Joe, looks like a professional job, wouldn't you say?" said the friendly voice belonging to Alex Hawkins, FBI special agent in charge of the affairs of this particular Pennsylvania County. His friendship with Thompson went beyond the casual relationship that might be associated with their jobs.

At fifty-five, Hawkins was not the prime example of a government agent. The younger members dressed well and groomed themselves with pride. Hawkins grew heavy and out of shape. Clothing did not make it onto his list of priorities. His shirt, tucked unevenly into his trousers, looked wrinkled and appeared to be what he slept in the previous night.

"They woke you up for this one," joked Thompson. "Mr. Daniels, the victim's husband, is in the other room." Hawkins' smile faded at the announcement. "I'm doing preliminary questioning, but he's pretty shaken. I don't think we're going to get too much from him now," added Thompson.

Hawkins introduced himself to Derrick as the official now in charge, and he explained his initial impression. "It appears somebody rigged your car with an advanced incendiary device that has come on the scene. Unlike most explosives that cause a lot of collateral damage and risk to those in the vicinity, this device causes a flash of incredible heat. If you examine the car, you'll find the glass from the windows became fused by the intensity of the heat. It became molten before it vaporized. I can assure you your wife didn't know what happened, and she didn't suffer."

The sterile explanation offered no comfort. The thought of Adrienne scorched to ash caused a wave of nausea to surface. Derrick stood abruptly and demanded, "That's enough. You were right earlier. I want you to stop back at another time. I need time alone. I hope you can understand."

"Sure, sure thing, Mr. Daniels," said Thompson. "You get some rest. We'll be back sometime tomorrow to continue our talk. I'm sorry . . . truly sorry," he said with a genuine sense of regret.

Hawkins also extended his condolences, and the men left Derrick to himself. Outside, they continued to talk as the team of federal investigators continued to comb the scene for clues. They roped off the driveway and ordered the crowd, that had now become substantial, to disperse. News cameras finished their shots for the evening report, and the crews left once they realized their requests for an interview fell upon deaf ears.

# CHAPTER
# THIRTY-THREE

Breaking the news to Adrienne's family would be fraught with difficulty, compounded by a relationship already non-existent. They didn't get along with Derrick who showed no interest in their material ambitions. Derrick had no family to notify. His parents died, and he had no siblings. The few cousins who remained drifted from his life, leaving him all alone.

Night came, and Derrick's house appeared dark except for the light in his study. He sat staring beyond the blank wall, recalling his life with Adrienne. Their years together were few, and he regretted not making time to live for the present. His dreams and aspirations nurtured a future that now would never happen.

The phone rang several times. Each time, he let the answering machine respond so he could screen the calls. They were summarily ignored, all but one.

"Derrick, I hope you are alright. I'm here for you, please call me as . . ."

"Oh God, I'm so glad it's you," interrupted Derrick grabbing the phone from the hook when he recognized Savannah's voice.

"I saw it on the news. I'm so sorry," she said mournfully.

"This is a nightmare. I can't believe what's happened. They're out to get me," he said ominously.

"Who? Who's out to get you?"

"I don't know who, but they were after me. Adrienne took my car this morning. That bomb was meant for me."

"I'll come over," offered Savannah.

"No," said Derrick, whose voice filled with agitation. "You can't. If they're after me, they could want you, too."

"Do you think this is related to the prions?" she asked.

"Anything's possible, but it may be the drug cartel, or the cemetery. I can't help but think the cemetery could be the connection, and you aren't involved with that. You can't come here. It's too dangerous."

"Cemetery? What cemetery?"

"I'm telling you, it's too dangerous to discuss this by phone," demanded Derrick.

"I've got to come over. You can't stay alone at a time like this. I'm leaving now."

"No!" he shouted. The piercing sound of his unintentionally rude response awakened him to the validity of her plea. He calmed down and said, "You're right. I don't want to be alone, but I will come to you. I can't risk your safety. I couldn't bear to see anyone else hurt because of me."

The drive into town was mechanical. He passed traffic lights with unconscious oblivion. Derrick's thoughts were distant, entertaining the meaning of life, the frailties of existence, and the need to see a beacon of hope in the future. He could not understand how he came to such a dark place. His assumption of virtue in the world blocked out the risks that he thought were negligible. For the first time in his life, he had no direction. His material and professional goals were shattered, yet he ran not knowing the destination.

Savannah embraced Derrick when he entered. Words were not necessary as all of the condolences were conveyed through the warmth of the contact. Derrick wanted to speak, but he found his throat choked with sorrow. The grief-laden emotions building within made him feel naked, vulnerable. Savannah sensed his weakness. She understood and continued to hold him tight, letting him know she was there for him.

He wanted to run and hide from the world, but a force stronger than his ego would not permit him to release his grip.

"Follow me," prodded Savannah. She took him by the arm and guided him to the bedroom. She sat him down and placed his head upon the pillow.

"You need to sleep. Close your eyes."

Night passed into day, and when he awoke, Savannah was lying next to him. She looked angelic in slumber. Her presence provided a security of spiritual connection foreign to Derrick in his marriage. The moment brought him peace in the wake of chaos. A serene harmony grew from this time with Savannah by his side, and it made him feel good.

# THIRTY-FOUR

DERRICK HAD NO TIME FOR MOURNING AND FELT TROUBLED BY HIS short-lived sorrow. He knew he loved Adrienne, but their love, looking back, seemed like an empty shell, the result of harried lives. Derrick blamed himself for the hollowness of their union. He could do nothing about the past, short of living haunted by regrets. Instead, his goal focused on maintaining the momentum of the investigation. Derrick, now lived eager to find the killers and felt pressed to get back to the office. Having the investigative might of the government on the case offered some comfort. The authorities at Justice would dissect the incident and determine how it related to Derrick's work activities.

At their next meeting, Mason wore the face a person visibly upset. The assurances of safety he had made to Derrick before he left on his mission proved false. Two agents went missing, one dead, the other presumed dead, and the life of a third, Derrick, in jeopardy. Fear that Savannah, too, was a target couldn't be ruled out.

"The guys from the Company are going to have to speak with you," Mason told Derrick. "There's got to be a connection to your work here. I'm so sorry and . . . Adrienne . . ." Mason could not bring himself to speak of Adrienne's death. His voice faltered. "I can't believe what's happening. The one thing I'm sure about is the Colombians aren't behind this."

"What makes you so certain?" asked Derrick. "They have more power than we'd like to admit. And talk about motive; our mission is a threat to their existence. Put yourself in their shoes. What the hell do they have to lose?"

"After you talk to these guys, you'll feel better," said Mason. "This is the agency that brings them all down. They have unlimited resources. After you talk to them, you'll feel better."

"That idiot, Catcher, thinks I had something to do with Harris' murder, for Christ's sake."

"That's the nature of his job. You have to trust them. They can protect you. They are the only ones who can protect you."

"Where were they when my car blew up?" countered Derrick.

"That's because there's something they don't know. There is something missing. They are working on all the details, and they are going to break this case. Now let's go upstairs and see what they've got so far."

An air of hostility left over from Derrick's previous encounter with Catcher set the tone of the meeting. In attendance were Mason, Derrick, Catcher and his silent partner, Agent Roberts. Instead of a stenographer, a recorder sat on the table. In Derrick's mind, this offered another element of suspicion and mistrust to the proceedings.

As much as Catcher tried to introduce a compassionate quality to the interrogation, his investigative nature always surfaced. He stood to begin the meeting. Part of his style when he worked included achieving a position of physical dominance.

"Mr. Daniels, from recent conversations with Mr. Mason, I understand you have expressed concern over the possibility the Colombians had a hand at your attempted assassination." Derrick glared with indignation before nodding in affirmation. "While I can appreciate your concerns following the death of your partner, Mr. Morganstern, I must assure you there is no connection."

Mason smiled. He believed every word the men from the Company told him. He held uncompromising faith in the agency.

Derrick, not convinced, countered, "How can you say that? Do you have any idea what we are in the process of doing to those people?" asked Derrick with scorn and contempt in his voice. "We're planning to use international tribunals to close them down for good. By the time we're done, you can send in the troops and take them out with a World Court sanctioned military operation. How can you think they won't put up a fight?"

Catcher looked deep into Derrick's eyes with a cold austerity doing nothing to soften his style. "Mr. Daniels, please, let's not be naïve, here. Do you believe we need your help to get rid of these vermin? Over the years, we've taken out their biggest players. I don't care how big and bad they think they are, we can go into their own backyard and annihilate them. It may take time, but we get the job done. Your work just gives us the respectability needed when planning a big operation. We need you for world opinion, and nothing more."

"World opinion? Respectability?" Derrick responded in dismay.

"That's right. You serve to legitimize our activities. The last thing they want to do is mess with our prosecutors. They know we don't tolerate that shit. They know that kind of activity will bring us on like a ton of bricks."

"Then why are you in on this investigation? Why not leave it to the FBI if you think the killer was a local dealer? They've already been out to investigate."

"Mr. Daniels, we have to investigate all threats to any Justice agents involved with international activities. We have to rule out the possibility of foreign influences. But besides that, the FBI contacted my office before Mason."

"What do you mean?"

"It seems most criminals don't know anything about the incendiary device detonated in your car. It's the product of rather high-tech engineering. They call us in for this type of investigation. It becomes a joint effort until we determine who has jurisdiction. For example, if it was a plastic explosive traced to the military, the case belongs to the FBI. If it were a Russian-derived plastic device, CIA would handle the case. In this situation, the materials were experimental . . . something out of the labs at Los Alamos. We believe we are dealing with a security leak to a foreign country now with access to the device. The odds of a criminal enterprise, local or foreign, having the ability to make this device are slim. As noted, if it's foreign, it becomes our case. Either way, we need a motive. You have to tell us something we *don't* know. I have a list of the dozen prosecutions you have handled successfully. The people at the FBI are checking them out.

"Is there anyone else you can think of who would want you dead?"

Derrick felt reluctant to speak. He thought for a moment, all the while Agent Roberts continued to write relentlessly in his notebook. It unnerved Derrick that this agent continued his documentation even with nothing said. Derrick had doubts about Catcher, but he was his best hope of learning if the cemetery incident might be related to the attempt on his life.

"This is probably not an issue, but near my home there's a cemetery where a tanker dumps its load just about every night."

Agent Roberts stopped his incessant note taking and looked up at Derrick, for the first time showing change in his activities. It seemed rather odd to Derrick his unrelated incident seemed of interest. It appeared Catcher thought the same.

"What does that have to do with you?" Catcher asked, breaking his composed stride. "A lot of people live in your area. Why would this event threaten *your* life?"

"I reported the dumping to the police. Maybe they found out it was me. I don't know. A cop, or someone who looked like a cop, showed up when I reported the incident. He seemed to know the driver of the tanker. I think there's toxic dumping going on, and maybe a cop is in on it. That could make the stakes big enough to want a snoop out of the picture," explained Derrick thirsting for an explanation.

"Interesting," said Catcher. "Pretty soon, you'll think the waitress at lunch is out to get you because you didn't leave a big enough tip."

The agents, along with Mason, laughed at the paranoia reference, that being the first sign of levity since the meeting began. Derrick mustered a nervous smile.

"I'll have Agent Roberts, here, check out your story. We can't be too careful."

Agent Roberts nodded to confirm he would investigate.

"We've been focusing on you all along," said Catcher, "but did your wife have enemies?"

"Adrienne? You have to be kidding. She got along with everyone. Besides, they targeted my car. She never takes my car. No one could have known she was going to take my car."

"Actually, someone could have," added Catcher.

"What's that supposed to mean?"

"Please try to understand, in this kind of investigation we have to be meticulous. Sometimes, we uncover rather disturbing things."

Angered, Derrick asked again, "What do you mean?"

"The night before your wife died, she called James Young, the president of City Council."

"She worked for him. There's nothing unusual about that."

"She could have told him she was going to take your car because hers was low on gas. It could have come up in conversation."

"So what? Why would he want her dead? Where are you going with this?"

"Mr. Daniels, I don't like the job of messenger, but your wife was having an affair with Mr. Young."

Derrick's face turned red, revealing uncontrolled embarrassment. He didn't know what to say. The natural response was to deny the allegation, but he believed the Company men did not make baseless accusations.

"You're sure about this?" he said in a faltering voice.

"I'm sorry, but we are sure. This raises the possibility he could have viewed your wife as a liability in his bid for higher office. We have no proof yet, but he is a suspect."

"I can't believe it. This doesn't make sense. We loved each other," said Derrick.

"When did you last *make* love to her?" asked Catcher.

Derrick flushed red once again. For him, the crimson radiating from his face became a blazing realization and admission of shame and inadequacy. He had just declared his love and affection for his dear wife, and he could not remember the last time they made love. Hesitation in his answer would have looked suspect. Worse yet, he could not respond at all.

"It's not a complicated question, Mr. Daniels. Was it the night before she died, or the week before?"

"I know this sounds ridiculous, but it's been some time. We are both so busy. She's always there working with him on his campaign . . ."

Derrick stopped speaking. No need to go on. He realized his own words afforded legitimacy to Catcher's pronouncement, unthinkable moments before.

"Mr. Daniels, where did you sleep the night following your wife's murder?"

The choice of the word *murder*, used in context to Adrienne's death, took on an ominous tone. Derrick realized his answer would elevate him one rung higher on the ladder of suspicion. The husband is always a suspect when the wife is murdered. His decision to stay with Savannah that night served to cement his guilt as a cheating husband. He knew he could not lie. It was readily apparent Catcher owned many of the answers sought.

"I stayed with a friend," he said calmly.

"Who was that friend?"

"I'd rather not say. I don't want to involve anyone else. The risk is too great."

"Mr. Daniels, you're an attorney, so I don't have to tell you your rights, but your cooperation in this investigation will help find who killed your wife. If you have nothing to hide, it will be in your best interest and safety to tell me what I need to know."

"Okay, I have nothing to hide. I went to see Savannah Ambrose that night. I was in shock, and she called. She wanted to comfort me. She wanted to come over. I told her I feared for her life and didn't want her to come to my place. She wouldn't listen, so I went there. That's all that happened."

"Did you have sexual relations with her?" Catcher's face turned rigid as he played the stoic interrogator.

"Of course not. How can you even think such a thing? I just lost my wife, for Christ's sake!"

The futility of his pleading showed on the faces of all in the room. Mason seemed shocked most of all. He never suspected any union between Derrick and Savannah. The line of questioning now made him wonder if he was blind to the daily activities in his charge. Derrick himself realized from an observer's perspective, his pleading appeared preposterous.

"I know whatever I say looks bad, based on the circumstances, but as you noted, I am an attorney, and unless you came here to charge me based on concrete evidence, I want to go."

"I'm sorry, Mr. Daniels. Right now, everyone is a suspect. I'll be speaking with you soon," said Catcher, ending the interrogation.

Derrick went late to the commissary for lunch, as the morning passed much too fast. Savannah began eating in her usual seat. Derrick lost his appetite since Adrienne's death. To maintain his health and energy, he forced himself to eat. His tray held the basics of nourishment, a bland salad with a few morsels of chicken and a cup of coffee.

"How did your meeting go?" asked Savannah.

"This whole thing is getting more and more complicated," said Derrick, looking down and picking at his food.

"We have to talk, but I'm being watched, so I'll let you know where and when."

"If you're being watched, you should let Mason know,

shouldn't you?" offered Savannah. "He can get you protection from the CIA if necessary."

"They're the ones watching me."

"How's that?" she asked.

"Suddenly, I've become a suspect in Adrienne's death."

"Come on Derrick, you're a lawyer, for Christ's sake. They always suspect the spouse. They wouldn't be doing their job if they ignored you," added Savannah.

"Maybe you're right, but I feel like they are onto something that could implicate me. I want to talk, but not here, not now. I will give you a call later. Will you be home?"

"Sure."

It was time to go back to work. Derrick had several briefs to review. Rather than stay late, by five o'clock he went Savannah's office. She was finishing her work. Being so engrossed, it startled her when Derrick entered.

"Oh, hi," she said cheerfully.

Derrick looked over his shoulder, furtively glancing all around to make sure no one watched them. He approached and secretly handed her a note. Without saying a word, Derrick left.

The scribbled message read: *I am sorry for the cloak and dagger. We must talk. I'll lose my tail and be at your place by 7:30. Burn this note when you get home.*

# THIRTY-FIVE

DERRICK ELUDED THE AGENT STATIONED OUTSIDE HIS HOME. AFTER THE attempted assassination, traveling the streets and highways proved to be fraught with suspicion. Every vehicle behind him seemed another imagined assassin. His heart beat heavy and his mind raced in too many directions to be of benefit in resolving his plight. By seven-thirty, he pulled up to Savannah's apartment and rang the bell.

"What's going on?" asked Savannah worriedly upon seeing Derrick distraught and looking over his shoulder as he entered.

"I've never seen you like this. What's going on?" she demanded again.

"At the meeting today, that Agent Catcher placed me under the gun."

"They have to treat you as a suspect," Savannah said sympathetically. "You can't take this personally. The husband is always a suspect. You know they have nothing to implicate you. It always works this way. Everything's going to be alright," she said with confidence.

"You don't understand. Catcher told me Adrienne was having

an affair. I cannot believe it. I keep thinking he just made it up to trap me."

"An affair? With who?" asked Savannah.

"The asshole she worked for, Jim Young, the guy running for Mayor. That makes him a suspect. Worse, they think you and I have been screwing around, too. How's that for motive? I can't fucking believe this is happening to me."

"So that's the reason for all the secrecy?" She paused, "They don't have a thing," said Savannah.

"They do. The night they killed Adrienne I was here. Remember?"

"Oh, my God. You were. That looks terrible. But I'll testify for you. Everyone knows you are straight as an arrow. They'll all testify for you."

"Who, Harris, Morganstern, you? Haven't you put it together yet? They are preparing to interrogate you next. You're a suspect, too."

Savannah didn't digest, nor did she respond to her status as a suspect. Her mind raced toward other matters. "What about the cemetery you mentioned on the phone? You never explained that to me."

"It's just another thing in my life that may have put me in jeopardy. I don't want you to get involved. The less you know the better. Anyway, I'm sure it's the Colombians. They have the most compelling motive. They want me out of their hair. It's how they send a message to discourage adversaries, and that was their first attempt. It's all related to our trip abroad. It has to be, and we'll have to wait until another attempt on one of us plays out before our people give up on their suspicion we had anything to do with Adrienne's murder."

"I sure hope you're wrong," said Savannah somberly.

She could not hold back any longer. Her long lashes, drowning in tears, forced her to turn away. Her head fell to the arm of the sofa, and she began to sob. The sight of her crying broke Derrick's already shattered heart. Hesitatingly, he leaned over to comfort her. Willingly, she turned to him and buried her head into his chest.

At first, Derrick felt uncomfortable holding Savannah in his arms. He was passionate once ignited, but had difficulty displaying affection or emotion. The tears she shed were cathartic, and he, too, began to weep in a muffled manner. Derrick had not cried at Adrienne's funeral, and his soul turned hollow since she died. Upon learning the truth about her infidelity, the hollow turned to hurt.

Loneliness seeking sanctuary explained the gentle kiss Derrick placed upon Savannah's forehead and the passionate connection that followed.

"We can't," she said without conviction. "We can't," she repeated as she pulled Derrick's hand away from her breast, hoping he would ignore her plea.

"I'm sorry," he stated with a deep sense of regret for his actions. He released from the embrace and turned away shamefully. "I don't know what's come over me. I feel being here is a betrayal to Adrienne. It's ridiculous; she cheated on me. Is it revenge? It should be, but I can't use you to get back at her. For Christ's sake, she's dead. You are the one thing in my life that's good. I want to be with you more than anything right now. I know this is going to look bad, but I can't go on without something good in my life."

Derrick turned back to face Savannah and pulled her to a reclining position. Eyeing with desire, her mouth appeared warm and inviting. He kissed her again, ever more passionately. His hand, now unencumbered, explored the soft skin beneath her blouse. Her body quaked in excited anticipation of having what she desired since she met him. She let Derrick remove her clothing, and while he kissed and caressed her with increasing possession, she tore at his shirt, ripping it from his chest. They lay naked, baring body and soul. The invitation to join completed, they gave themselves to each other. At the moment of rapture, Savannah called out, "I love you. I always loved you. God, I know I was wrong, but I couldn't help myself." Again, she began to sob. Derrick kissed away the tears rolling down her cheeks.

As much as he wanted to express his feelings through words of love and devotion, he remained silent. Too much guilt, hurt, and loneliness flowed through his veins. This caldron of mixed emotions was about to boil over. He didn't know how it would happen, but once he could clear himself, he would be with Savannah.

Though he remained silent, the way he held her so very close filled Savannah's heart with joy. She smiled, knowing the tears of sorrow, now coming steadily, were tears of happiness.

Once enough time had passed to cool their collective passion, Savannah stated, "If they're trailing you, coming here will make things worse."

"I almost don't care what they think," said Derrick defiantly. "They don't have anything on me, but you're right. We can't meet this way until something breaks. I still want to look into the cemetery incident. It's a long shot, but I have this feeling the attempt on my life is somehow related. If I can prove that, we'll be fine."

Derrick slipped out of Savannah's apartment into the darkness. He found comfort in believing he avoided the surveillance. It was a cold night. The air breathed fresh and clean. The sky, unusually clear, served as backdrop for countless points of light. To Derrick, these lights defined the precision of design that hosts all of existence. Derrick smiled while looking up at the glory of the heavens. He had a new feeling of purpose in his life. On the ride back from Savannah's a sense of euphoria resided within. The feeling faded when as he approached Byberry Road.

Derrick's wristwatch read two AM. From a distance, he saw the menacing unmarked truck making delivery. Derrick hoped Agent Roberts might have acted upon Catcher's request to investigate the report of nocturnal dumping. In the dark, a mysterious driver stood alone. Derrick rode on toward his house. He was much too tired. Playing detective would have to wait until another night.

Derrick and Savannah had to keep their communications limited in order to maintain a proper appearance during the ongoing investigation. Trying to keep a respectable distance to their public relationship, they avoided one another as much as possible. Until Derrick could clear his name, he wanted to nix the potentially maligned efforts of the various agencies that might be investigating him. This strategy made the desire for union surge to levels of grandeur the few times they found ways to get together.

In order to stay connected, Derrick purchased two disposable cell phones. This gave them a way to call each other with no trace on the part of the surveillance team. It worked well. When leads on the cases they worked on by day seemed connected to their plight, they spoke at length in the night trying to figure how they might relate to the attempt on Derrick's life.

For three nights, Derrick slipped out of his house and hiked to a nearby garage he rented. There he kept his old Cougar, the car he restored from his youth. This provided the transportation necessary to elude the agent who had his home under surveillance.

Each night, he positioned himself out of sight on the road near the cemetery. In the time he spent observing, he discovered there were three deliveries every night—at eleven PM, at one AM and two AM. Other people drove by oblivious to the sight. It seemed odd not a soul noticed or had the concern to inquire into this unusual occurrence. Everyone remained in their own little world caring for their own affairs and had no time for community interests.

The morning following the third night of sleuthing, Savannah stepped into Derrick's office. "What's been going on?" she asked.

"Why do you ask?"

"I tried to call you, and there was no answer for the past three nights."

Derrick looked at his cell phone and declared, "That's impossible. I have it with me all the time. Something must have gone wrong. Tonight, I'll call you, late."

"Don't forget," she said.

That night Derrick, again, slipped out of his house without detection. He made his way to the cemetery. This attraction to nightly sentry duty seemed bizarre and inexplicable. He didn't know what he was supposed to learn, but an instinctual need prevailed. Each night he waited and let his mind wander, trance-like, to places of importance and concern though later he could not recall those thoughts.

As he waited for the clandestine truck to make its appearance, he decided to contact Savannah. After dialing her number, he heard the familiar busy signal indicating no connection due to cellular problems rather than a true busy line. He tried again with the same result. Looking at the phone's signal indicator, he realized a weak cell prevented any calls.

By eleven forty-five the truck had not appeared. This was incon-sistent with the observations he made over the last three days. He did not have enough sample days to say this was an anomaly, but it surprised him.

To defuse the thoughts of conspiracy taxing his mind over the past two months, he turned to the pleasures of discourse offered by talk-radio any hour of the night. Surprisingly, when he pressed the channel selector of his favorite station, the static of an un-tuned radio filled his ears. He pressed the button to pick another station, but static seemed to be the order of the night. Button after button met with the same findings.

*This is crazy. The AM stations better get their acts together. If they don't upgrade, they'll become the dinosaurs. Everyone will be listening to FM or streaming stations.*

To Derrick, his thoughts were not odd in the least. For years, he noticed the clarity of AM stations remained crudely behind the times. Derrick was not a techno-wizard, so he did not have an explanation available to him. He just knew that at times he couldn't receive the stations he liked on the AM dial.

Resigning himself to relaxing music on the FM dial, a better therapy for his psyche, he pressed the button again. Nothing. Not a sound.

*How can that be? Do all the radio stations go off the air by midnight? Was there a new directive I missed? This is ridiculous. Maybe the world ended, and I'm the last survivor, waiting here in a cemetery for an unmarked truck to deliver whatever.*

The absurdity of his thoughts and constructions of conspiracy made him realize his ability to think rationally took a blow. Recognizing the futility of this quest, he started his engine to return home. After traveling five-hundred feet from where he parked, he noticed the flicker of his radio, letting the sound of music through. He stopped, turned the car around and drove toward the cemetery. At a particular point, the radio faded and morphed into silence once again. To determine the range of this effect, he drove in the opposite direction and noticed a repeat of the phenomenon at about five hundred feet, now east of the cemetery. Derrick repeated the drive in all directions until he mapped out a perimeter beyond which he could get clear reception. He tried his experiment while listening to AM stations that replaced silence with static and repeated it as he monitored his cell phone signal meter. He found a clear demarcation within which he could neither send nor receive radio or cellular signals.

# CHAPTER
# THIRTY-SIX

DERRICK DIDN'T KNOW ANYONE WITH A STRONG TECHNOLOGICAL background. All of his friends and acquaintances studied law. To the contrary, they didn't know a tube from a transistor. In his constant replay of the events encountered since the trip abroad, the name of Joel Davis surfaced.

*Sure, Joel Davis, Karl's friend. He can help. He's an expert on wireless and radios and all of that stuff. I think he's on the tenth floor, in ATF. Those guys are always making things for investigative use. Christ, he invented that cosmic phone for Karl. He's got to be able to help. I don't want anybody else to get hurt. And I don't want Catcher to know what I'm doing. I don't know why. It's just this feeling I have.*

The Alcohol, Tobacco and Firearms Division of the Justice Department held operations on the tenth floor of the Federal Building. An armed guard greeted Derrick when he stepped out of the elevator. Once he scanned Derrick's security tag worn around his neck, he let him pass.

At the reception desk, an elderly woman directed Derrick to room 1014. He walked along a sterile corridor, past private offices, followed by laboratories and two soundproof firing ranges. The muted ping of gunfire rang in Derrick's ears as he passed by.

Shadows filled the translucent window of the door to room 1014. Derrick rapped on the pane, more as a neurotic gesture than as an expectation of a response. He was about to try the door handle when, to his surprise, a voice called out.

"It's not locked. Come on in."

There, in the dark, Joel Davis sat at a lab bench working on some type of electronic device. A screen radiating a curious green glow illuminated his distinctive silhouette. It was the silhouette of an unusually large, hairless head, providing the clue it was Joel.

"I was expecting you."

Surprised by Joel's words, Derrick stopped abruptly, and he asked, "What do you mean?"

"I knew you'd be here sooner or later. It was going to be you or the Company boys. I figured it would be you first."

"You knew I'd be here?" asked Derrick, repulsed by the lack of explanation offered by so many characters invading his life.

"Only you, Savannah, Karl, and I know about the cosmic phone conversation. I figured, I don't know why, being I don't know you well, but I figured you weren't going to tell the story to the Company, so you'd have to stop here to find out what it was about."

Still tinkering in the dark, he waited for Derrick to respond.

"You got that call, too?" asked Derrick.

"Who the hell else would he be calling when they killed him?"

"What? Who killed who?"

"Those Jap bastards, they fucked him up something awful."

"If we got the same call, how in the hell did you come up with your conclusion? I can assure you, he didn't speak to us. The entire call was gibberish"

"That's where you're wrong. He spoke to us, but in the form of a puzzle. Here, let me show you."

Joel flipped a switch at his bench to turn on the overhead lights. At his computer, he opened one of the audio files showing on the screen and attached an oscilloscope. It took him a few moments to hook up several other devices. He played the file, and they heard the exact static filled call Derrick and Savannah heard when on their way to Kuwait. Through a loud clatter, he recognized occasional words. Derrick's face revealed an obvious level of familiarity.

"Heard this before, didn't you?" Joel said confidently.

"That's the call. That's exactly what we heard. We couldn't make anything out of it, just a few words . . . Cyclops and old woman. I think we even heard his name once."

"You did good but wait until you hear this."

Joel pressed buttons, rewound the audio, and played it again without the static.

"I was hoping it would not come to this, Mr. Armstrong. Are you ready to tell me what you know?"

"God help me; I have no idea what you are talking about."

It was Karl's voice and the voice of a stranger.

"This is the government's main means of feeding the poor," explained the unrecognized voice.

"You can't be serious," Karl responded.

"You can't comprehend this kind of world. How do you think we keep a city of so many poor in line? There is essentially no crime here. As far as the outside world sees it, our prisons are respectable. They house our petty thieves. Moreover, we have no death penalty, as it would appear to the sniveling critics of world injustice. Those who commit capital crimes end up here. They pay their debt to society in a rather novel way. You see, they come back to feed the poor.

"Living in a world of wealth and corruption, it's hard to imagine some people must resort to an institutionalized cannibalism." The old man paused as if waiting for an answer he knew would never come. "It is hard to imagine. There are many things your people can't imagine. The way my people suffered at the hands of your bomb. People had to resort to despicable acts of barbarism just to survive."

"When our backs press against the wall, we are all capable of doing things the civilized side of us suppresses. Perhaps you will be able to shed light on my questions now that your back presses flat against the wall. So, my good friend, does this room help you remember any more about the relationship of the Japanese and the Thai government you may have forgot to mention?"

A whining shrill sound briefly obliterated further conversation. More dialogue followed.

"Tell me what you know about Cyclops. I'm more interested in Cyclops."

"Cyclops is the code name of the actual project."

"Tell me more."

"That's all I know, I swear."

The shrill sound returned, and Joel forwarded the audio. He flipped a switch on the oscilloscope producing a split screen with two flat lines waiting to display the waveform of the input from the audio file. He then pressed play to continue the recording. Each screen displayed the images of sound waves matching the audible wailing coming from the recorder.

"This took me awhile, but I figured it out with filters," said Joel. "On the right, you're looking at the sound of a bandsaw, probably a Japanese version of a Powermatic 1791260 model 2415. That's my best guess, based on wave analysis. That was the noise drowning out so much of Karl's call. I identified the sound, quantified it, and cut most of it out. I used filters," Joel stated again, with the redundant annoyance of a scientist explaining things to a layman who just wants the simple explanation.

"That's why you can hear so much more now. Listen to what we are left with when I filter out the bandsaw." As Joel turned the filter dial, the wave on the right screen disappeared along with the noise from the saw. The wave on the screen toward the left leaped wildly and represented the grotesque howling of a person suffering intractable pain.

"That there is Karl screaming for his life as those cock-suckers cut him up. The similarity of the sound waves masked his screams. That's my take on it."

Derrick felt the blood drain from his face. He imagined the terror going through Karl's mind at the time. It was a gruesome way to die. An upsurge of revulsion mixed with a profound feeling of hopelessness caused Derrick to grab for the bench lest he fall.

"You've got to have this all wrong. Tell me this is just *your* guess," begged Derrick.

"I wish I was wrong. I'm an expert on wave theory. You know, sound waves, light waves. I have my PhD in this shit. As much as I regret to say it, I'm right on the money."

"What's it all mean? Do you have any idea what all the talk was about?" asked Derrick.

"That's what I thought you'd be able to put together. Weren't you over there to investigate an auto dumping scheme?" countered Joel.

"No. Karl was on that project. We were there for other matters. Savannah Ambrose did research on terrorist activities, and I was there on drug interdiction affairs. Does this make sense to you?" asked Derrick.

"The Cyclops thing, that's been troubling me. You see, about five years ago, while driving at night on a dark road, I looked down when stopped at a red traffic signal. I saw this dim flashing light coming from under the dashboard. It kept flashing and the beam landed on my left foot. I didn't make much of it, but when I got home, I dragged out a few of my meters and measured the light source."

There was a long pause. Joel wanted Derrick to coax him to continue.

"Yeah," said Derrick in an annoyed, yet nervous voice. "So, what did you find?"

"Nothing."

Another pause. Derrick hated to play games. He decided to let Joel hang. Eager to tell his story, but unhappy Derrick wasn't acting as interested as he would like, Joel nevertheless continued.

"Did you hear me? I said nothing. Not a goddamn thing registered. I have all the equipment you can imagine at my place. Here I was, trying to measure light, that according to my instruments, does not exist. It freaked me out. To make it more insane, this light beam is flashing . . . pulsating on the footrest. It's hitting my fucking foot and I had no idea this existed."

Another pause. Now, Derrick started to put it all together, and he wanted to hear the conclusion.

"Could it be dangerous?"

"Initially, I figured no. It wasn't emitting enough energy to show up on my meters. How dangerous could it be, I figured. Then I went over to a friend's house and asked to borrow his car. I didn't want him to know what I was doing. You know how people start thinking you're a quack or something? So, I checked out his car, and nothing."

"The flashing light didn't register on his either?" asked Derrick showing interest.

"No. This time, nothing there, no flashing light. I guess I would have forgotten all about it if my brother-in-law didn't have to use my SUV, and he left his little sports car for me to use. I figured what the heck, so I checked his out, too, and nothing."

"So, two out of three didn't have this light thing," Derrick said, struggling to follow the story.

"Wrong. This time the light was there, but as I said, on the meters, nothing. Now I really want to know what's going on. I borrow everybody's car I know. I can't do this sort of research fast, you know. I didn't want to let on to what I was doing, so it took a couple of weekends. I found this flashing light only in cars from Japan, but not all of them, just the higher end ones. Not one American car had this shit in it."

"Okay, so where did this get you?" asked Derrick starving for a conclusion.

"When I realized how pervasive and selective this was and the position of the beam on the footrest, I decided to take it to the next level. I start focusing the beam through different lenses, prisms, all this shit I have to work with.

"Then I shoot it onto different isotopes of different elements. That's where this gets freaky. After all of my calculations, I find, all along, I'm not looking at nothing."

Joel turned around and listened for a moment to make sure no one would hear him in the empty lab. He lowered his voice. "I was looking at an energy source so strong my meters can't even measure it. This beam is so powerful it's beyond anything I ever studied in terms of wavelength. This is in a spectrum I didn't know exists. What they do, is form harmless radio waves and split them. These half-waves modulate at a frequency that has a whole new spectrum."

"Try to stay away from terms like *modulate*. I'm just about following you. Keep it simple, for my sake," pleaded Derrick.

"Modulate, you know, it's the frequency at which electromagnetic waves travel, the amplitude. Here, look at this."

Joel drew a wave on a note pad.

"You see; this wave is large; this one here is small. These are simple sine waves, up and down. Simple, huh? What they have done is to somehow cut these in half and modulate them. Sorry . . . they send them out looking like this instead of like these here," he explained while pointing to his primitive diagram that failed to give Derrick a better understanding.

"Oh my God, that must be the split waves mentioned on the tape."

"Exactly, and that's how they go undetected. No equipment out there can measure them . . . until now. This is my new baby. Now, I can read them like all other waves."

"If it's so strong, how come you're still here to tell me about it?" asked Derrick.

"When I say strong, we can be talking about all sorts of waves. You can have radio waves that are harmless. They are in the air, all around us all the time, but you do not hear a thing until you turn on a radio. Then there are microwaves . . . the strong ones. They'll boil your blood if you could fit in one of those ovens. We have strong x-rays that in small doses are relatively safe, but in higher doses cause cancer, yet higher they kill cancer and we even have strong waves that could destroy the world, like if we had a nuclear fallout or EMP."

"EMP?"

"Electromagnetic pulse."

"Okay, okay, enough with the science lesson. What type of waves are these?" asked Derrick.

"I don't know what these are, or what they are doing to us. I thought you could help me on that front. I'm still trying to understand these suckers. Look here."

Joel stepped over to a small cylindrical device he wired to a complex contraption, the likes of which Derrick had never seen.

"This is the condensing coil I pulled out of a junked, new Lexus that was totaled. They mount these under the dash, and they wire them to engage the alarm systems in these cars. You know that little clicker you have to arm and disarm the alarm in your car? This coil sets the alarm, as far as we are supposed to think, but it's also the source of this energy beam. This contraption is how I study it. What blew me away, while listening to the tape with Karl, was when they mentioned Cyclops."

Joel had the look of joy plastered upon his face. He hoped for Derrick to see the association as he did.

"I don't get it," said Derrick.

"Cyclops! Cyclops!" shouted Joel. "The one-eyed monster. This beam, it's the eye of the Cyclops."

Derrick stared at the pulsating beam flashing upon the surface of the lab table like a blinking eye. It all fell into place. The people in Thailand were involved in the dumping of Japanese cars into the United States. The Cyclops that Joel inadvertently uncovered was the subject of Karl's interrogation and untimely death. If Joel guessed right, Cyclops had to be the code name for this device. The stranger on the tape wanted to know if Karl uncovered the Thai link and the connection to the Cyclops. With the scheme in jeopardy, he had no other choice than to terminate Karl.

"There are just a few things I want to know now," added Joel. "I want to know how this Cyclops beam affects us. Why it's not in all of the Japanese cars? Why is it in the high-end cars? And who the hell is responsible for Karl's death?"

Being the lawyer and taking up the task of devil's advocate, Derrick tried to find a flaw in Joel's assumptions.

"I can tell you why the high-end cars have them. They are the ones with the alarm systems. They don't steal the Corollas. And maybe, just maybe, that coil happens to be legitimate, and the split waves are an unforeseen consequence of the technology. Maybe they don't even know about it."

"Nice try, but no way. I checked it out. Even the cheap cars can be equipped with factory alarms, and they have these coils, too, but they are missing the specialized circuitry to produce the split waves. Only in Japanese cars, and expensive ones at that, Derrick. Don't you see it? This is the perfect device for warfare, the Trojan Horse, for the love of Pete's sake. We have no idea it's happening, and soon we'll all be . . ."

He paused again, but this time not to lead Derrick to inquiry. A look of bewilderment dressed his face.

"We'll all be what?" asked Derrick.

"I don't know. I know it sounds crazy, but I don't know what effect it has. Don't worry though. I'm working on it. I was hoping you came here to give me something I could go on. Why did you come up here if it wasn't to tell me about this Cyclops thing?"

"I need your help," said Derrick. "What I'm going to tell you is between us. Also, I have to tell you up front, I think what I need your help with is somehow related to my wife's death. I don't want anyone else to get hurt, but there could be risk involved."

"Hey, I'm sorry about your wife. That freaky explosive was something else. I'm no expert on explosives. If that's what you need help with, I know a guy who can help, but that's not my game. If this is a matter for the police, let them run with it."

"I don't know if I can trust the police," said Derrick. "For the last year, I noticed this tanker truck making deliveries to a cemetery in the middle of the night. At first, I didn't think much of it, but after some time, I figured what are the odds the few times I happen by, this truck is always there making a delivery?"

"So, you figured this is illegal dumping going on in your back-yard, another Love Canal," offered Joel.

"Exactly. So, one night, I report it to the local police. Then I wait. In minutes, a cruiser comes by, and the cop, or whoever, gets out and starts talking with the truck driver. It seemed odd, as if they knew each other. A few days later, someone makes an attempt on my life. They get my wife instead."

"In your line of work, a lot of people want to see you dead. It probably had nothing to do with this cemetery incident," said Joel.

"Initially, I thought that was the case. I'm involved with other things just like Karl, and they are more likely the story behind the attempt on my life. However, I went back to investigate the cemetery thing. For the last few nights, the truck made three deliveries each night. This is where you come in. I find out my cell phone doesn't work when I'm near this cemetery and . . ."

"Derrick, you don't need me. Any cell guy will tell you when you are between cells you can't make or receive calls. There's no mystery there."

"I know that. I'm not very good at this science thing, but I do know that much. At first, I made little of it. Then, I couldn't get my car radio to work."

"AM?" asked Joel.

"It didn't matter. Nothing but static on AM and nothing on FM Anywhere within five hundred feet of this cemetery, all I got was static or silence."

"Now, that could interest me," Joel replied with uplifted brow.

"This could be a dangerous . . ." Derrick tried to explain, but Joel interrupted.

"If it has to do with waves, that's my thing. And I can handle myself. I'm ATF you know."

# CHAPTER
# THIRTY-SEVEN

With his usual level of caution, Derrick exited the rear of his home at eight P.M., figuring he would have enough time to get to Joel's by nine P.M., as agreed. Approaching the back edge of his property, not more than twenty feet from where he stood Derrick heard the electrostatic sound of a communications device. In the stillness of country living, he easily heard the message. "The subject is approaching the posterior perimeter."

He heard more static, and from the other end of the line a voice responded, "Don't approach. Stay with him."

Derrick made an innocent looking intentional inspection of bushes and trees at the border of his property and then went back inside. His CIA guardians heightened their level of surveillance. Derrick reasoned they must be on to his nighttime ventures. The added manpower would help keep him under scrutiny at all times.

Derrick picked up his unlisted cell phone and dialed 911. It took but a second for a response in this township where excitement or need for emergency services rarely occurred.

"Yes, I want to report two or three men with guns approaching my neighbor's house. It looks like some sort of mob related activity."

After giving the address, he waited anxiously. In minutes, two patrol cars sped up to the surveillance car stationed in front of Derrick's house. Guns drawn, two novice deputies approached the unmarked car that stood sentry each night.

"Put your hands on your head," demanded one of the officers.

Knowing the volatility of police operations, the Federal Agent complied immediately. The officer opened the door to the car and continued his commands.

"Step out of the car. Keep your hands on your head."

Before being frisked and causing undo concern regarding the holstered weapon beneath his coat jacket, the agent identified himself.

"I'm Agent Sills, with the CIA. My ID is in my left jacket pocket."

The officer withdrew the agent's I.D., and following a careful examination, called off his partner, who nervously trained his gun at the heart of the perceived threat.

"A call came in tagging you as a one of a group of prowlers. It came over to us as a mob hit going down. Who else is with you?"

The agent called for his backup to join the party in front of Derrick's house. He explained all things necessary to account for their being there. The police officers rang Derrick's bell to make sure he was still there and explained that a neighbor must have mistook the security team as prowlers. From the street, Agent Sills observed, and felt satisfied Derrick remained in his home.

Being a perceptive judge of human behavior, Derrick watched for a moment as the agents conversed with the police officers. This scheme gave him the opportunity, and the alibi necessary, to make his exit through the rear of his house with no one the wiser for his plan.

Derrick reached Joel's at nine P.M. Joel insisted on driving his SUV, a Japanese luxury model, loaded with electronic devices and sophisticated surveillance equipment. Since the government covered the tab, he spared no expense.

"Do you seriously believe we are going to need all of this?" asked Derrick.

"You can never be too ready for trouble. Like you said, could be some risk here."

Joel pulled back his jacket to reveal a rather large caliber handgun holstered in an unusual breakaway device. The sight of guns bothered Derrick. In this case, he felt more secure knowing an ATF agent, armed, licensed and trained in the use of firearms accompanied him.

They arrived at the cemetery by nine-thirty P.M. Derrick directed Joel to the spot he used for his nights of observation. The choice troubled Joel, and he drove around for another fifteen minutes casing the terrain.

"What was wrong with where I suggested we wait?" asked Derrick.

"Trust me. This is what I do. When I do a stakeout, I look for things you might overlook, elevation, lighting, escape route. That kind of stuff."

Joel positioned his vehicle in an area of underbrush where Derrick's car could have not entered nor exited. The brushwood, thick like jungle twine, ensnarled the ground and hung upon the trees that grew thick. Joel took another half-hour to set up his collection of meters and scopes.

"What the hell is all of this shit?"

"Like I told you, this is my bag. Just leave me alone for another five minutes."

Derrick waited patiently, and in a matter of minutes, Joel called him over.

"Nothing," said Joel in his now familiar statement known to reveal what he announced or some fact he wanted pried from his closed lips.

"Nothing what?" asked Derrick.

"I don't know why your cell phone or car radio wasn't working. There's no interference here. Not one bit."

"That's impossible," said Derrick. "Your meters must not be working right."

Joel reached towards Derrick's waist-mounted cell phone and pulled it off his belt. He opened it, looked at it for a moment, and dialed. In ten seconds, they heard a ring coming from Joel's phone he kept in his pocket. He answered it and handed it to Derrick. "It's for you."

Derrick put Joel's phone to his ear.

"Hi there, Derrick. I told you, this is my field of expertise. You don't have to second guess me."

Feeling foolish, Derrick exchanged phones.

"I can't understand it," he said dejectedly. "Now you think I'm a paranoid schizophrenic."

"No, I don't. I just think you need a different cell phone provider. This is a weak area for your particular company. It could have been sunspots or a strange celestial phenomenon that affected the radio waves. Those things happen all the time. Sometimes you get a signal, other times you don't. Let's pack it up."

"No, wait. You came all the way here. At least see this truck."

"Derrick, according to your notes, he won't be here for another half-hour, and that's if he's not late."

"How come you're still driving this car if that beam is constantly hitting your foot?" asked Derrick, hoping to distract Joel long enough to have him stay until the truck arrived.

Joel reached under the dashboard just below the handbrake release. He removed a thick piece of lead he taped over an opening that housed the pulsating light. This provided protection from what Joel believed was the Cyclops beam spoken about on the call from Karl.

"There, look. It's hard to see, but if you look close, it's dark enough here to make it out."

Derrick's eyes needed a moment to adjust, but soon, he saw, with difficulty, the light Joel described. The subtle white light beat at a rate of one flash per second. Like a nurturing heart, it sustained each succeeding pulse with a remnant glow that never completely faded. For a long moment, the two stared in silence.

Joel wanted to get back to his work on the Cyclops beam. He knew Derrick was desperate for the semblance of affirmation he could provide by waiting a little longer to see the tanker. By two minutes after eleven, Joel made his announcement.

"I got to get going. We waited 'till eleven, and you said it yourself, one night he came 45 minutes late. Let's cut out."

"No," insisted Derrick, "your watch is fast. I have five of."

"That's ridiculous. I set my watch by radio-control to the atomic clock in Boulder. I'm never fast."

Joel pressed the button on his dashboard to hear the time on the radio. Static, they heard nothing but static, just as Derrick described. Rapidly, Joel pressed each button, AM, then FM. It did not matter. He reached for his cell phone and saw the signal strength meter showed no bars, unlike moments before when it indicated a strong signal. That was enough for him to change his mind.

"Holy Jesus, you were right. Look here. Look at my meters. They are going ape-shit off the dials."

The timing could have not been more convincing, for at that moment, the tanker turned the corner. Derrick's eyes lit up.

"Here he is," Derrick proclaimed.

The big truck made its way through the grounds of the cemetery until it reached the designated spot for delivery. The driver stepped out of the cab and began pumping the contents of the truck into the hatch on the ground. Joel pulled out two pairs of night vision scopes and handed one to Derrick. They saw the stranger performing his task. He looked at his watch and glanced about furtively in the manner of one doing something illicit.

"Give me your phone," commanded Joel. Derrick responded without hesitation.

"You told me this is an unregistered phone, right?"

Derrick nodded, and Joel placed the phone in a Faraday cage to shield it from the strong waves and made a call to 911 to report the mysterious delivery. He avoided giving his name, same as Derrick, when he made his call weeks earlier.

"Now, take this phone to the clearing over there, about fifty yards. Drop it on the ground, and then come back."

When Derrick returned, he was astonished to see all of the preparation made by Joel in the short time he was away. A dark camouflage drape covered the SUV. Swatches of the same material covered each of the electronic meters set up behind the SUV.

"Get down here. Get under this blanket. Pull this hood over your head, and put these on."

Joel handed Derrick a pair of headphones attached to a black parabolic reflector. Derrick positioned himself beneath his camouflage, scope in hand, and headphones mounted, waiting for a transmission.

"We should get action any minute based on your previous experience," said Joel with excitement in his voice.

It didn't take long for a response. The police cruiser drove into the cemetery. It followed the path and pulled behind the tanker.

Out of the car stepped Joe Thompson, the Southampton Chief of Police. Derrick could hardly believe what he saw. Though he had suspicions, the reality of the moment terrified him. Now Derrick observed the culprits and heard their conversation thanks to a most experienced government-trained sleuth.

"Good evening, Joe," said the burly driver. "Nice and clear tonight. What brings you around?"

"I told you last time, when you see me, it's because there's some trouble," said Chief Thompson.

"I thought you told me and Claire there wouldn't be problems with this job. Now, I see you twice in a month. Maybe we should get out of this deal while we can."

"When I recruited you, I told Claire I wouldn't put you in harm's way. She's my sister, for Christ's sake. You know I wouldn't let you get in trouble. Don't start getting spooked. I'll tell you when we ditch this deal. In the meantime, some poke around is out there bitching again. I got the call just now."

The Chief went back to his cruiser and returned with his night vision scope. He scanned the area in a haphazard fashion.

"Anything out there, Joe?"

"Nothing."

Another cruiser pulled up. A man in futuristic, spandex garb stepped from the car. He greeted them in a formal manner and proceeded to engage in his duties that involved scanning the area with a hand-held device.

Joel tapped Derrick on the shoulder and whispered, "He's looking for your phone. He'll find it in less than a minute."

Just as Joel predicted, the man jogged over to the spot where Derrick left the phone. He returned and went back to Chief Thompson.

"Let me have your night scope," commanded the stranger.

In a methodical manner, he searched every section of the perimeter.

"He's a pro," whispered Joel as he pulled his cover tight over his head and motioned for Derrick to follow. Gradually, Joel made the slightest slit in his cover to observe.

"We have more than a nosey snoop at work here. You cannot afford to get caught. It will be at least twenty years in prison and forget about your nice cushy job protecting the suburbanites from their errant burglar alarms," warned the stranger.

"I'm doing everything you told me," Chief Thompson responded obediently.

"After you leave, run a patrol through here every hour," demanded the stranger. "If you see anything suspicious, I want a call."

The stranger and Chief Thompson drove away in their respective vehicles. The brother-in-law left once the he completed the delivery. Joel got up and instructed Derrick to help him pack up the SUV. They loaded the equipment in a harried manner with little respect for delicacy and expense related to damage.

"I want to get over to where he dumped the load," exclaimed Joel. "We don't have much time. They'll be back in about an hour."

At the delivery site, Joel took measurements on one of his sophisticated meters. A thick gelatinous slime covered the ground next to the pipefitting used to receive the contents of the truck. Joel removed a lead vial from his coat and collected a sample of the material they assumed was toxic waste.

"I'll run this by my buddy in the chemistry lab over at the ATF."

"Be careful with that. Maybe it's radioactive," cautioned Derrick.

"What do you think I'm doing with all of this equipment? I already tested for radioactivity. Besides, the three of them were next to it, so it can't be harmful to just be near it," reasoned Joel.

After Joel took more readings all around the delivery site, they left. On the way back, Derrick felt confounded by his lack of technical training. He had many questions but could not conceptualize where to begin. He composed a generic query.

"What do you make of all this?"

"I'm so glad you got me involved," Joel stated excitedly. "There's high-tech shit going on there. First, I have never seen electromagnetic forces that strong. You know what an MRI is?"

"Sure," said Derrick, not wishing to elaborate on his answer due to his limited knowledge.

"The area around there is radiating astronomic levels of magnetic energy. It's the same energy produced by an MRI, just thousands of times stronger," explained Joel. "The odd thing is this energy hasn't affected my watch. I haven't figured that out yet, but this energy should have ruined it. The waves from an MRI aren't harmful to living things, but they don't come close to this amount of energy. At this level, I can't imagine it's good for your health over the long haul unless, somehow, our bodies are immune to the effects like the watch. And there's no way any phone or radio could work in that field."

"Then how did you make the call to 911?"

"I figured that one out when I took readings back where we parked. This field of energy wasn't activated earlier. When the tanker pulled up, my meters went nuts. So, I put the phone in that cage, thing. It's a Faraday cage and it bocks out all electrostatic interference. That's when I made the call. Then, the energy field seemed to shut down again. I confirmed the readings back at the pad. It all fits."

"I'm not following you on this. It doesn't make sense to me. It sounds like bunch of contradictions."

"Look, when it's on, the energy is so strong you can't send out anything. Your calls can't go out. In addition, all waves coming in, waves from your radio or cell phone, are sucked into this black hole. Whatever is going on underground, it's sophisticated. When I dialed 911, my call was intercepted into this force field and filtered to a receiver that took the message underground."

"You mean I wasn't talking to the police department when I originally called?" asked Derrick.

"Something like that. I don't know exactly what, but if that wall of energy was on when you made your call, it channeled down under that site to someone other than the police department. I can tell you, when I made my call to 911, it went to some close receiver. It didn't make it to a cellular tower anywhere near here. It's almost as if they want to intercept all calls that might implicate them. It's all very sophisticated," said Joel, mildly out of breath from the excitement.

"So, you're going to help me? You'll try to figure this out?"

"Let me tell you something, Derrick. I am on this, like flies on shit. Even if you didn't want me here, I'm onboard. This is my life. This kind of opportunity is unheard of. I'm with you."

Derrick dropped Joel off and returned home by one AM. He felt good about enlisting Joel's help and expertise. No way Derrick would have known what to do. He could never get so far, so fast, without such sophisticated efforts at staking out the cemetery. He was glad he did not have to jeopardize Savannah in this venture. Her own investigations brought enough peril to her life.

# CHAPTER
# THIRTY-EIGHT

"Hi, this is Derrick Daniels over at Justice."

"What can I do for you, Mr. Daniels?" replied Agent Catcher. He used formality as his calling card. He got close to almost no one professionally or personally. Even having met with Derrick numerous times, it was always Mr. Daniels. The distance offered him a perspective often lost as the level of familiarity rises. While detachment denied him meaningful relationships, he accepted this failure as a price for his commitment to profession.

"I was wondering if you heard anything about the cemetery incident I mentioned to you. I believe Agent Roberts was going to check it out."

The awkwardly enduring pause at the other end of the phone line troubled Derrick. Though he knew Catcher had other things on his mind, the slow response appeared calculated rather than a lack of recall regarding information garnered since they last spoke. If he relegated the cemetery anecdote to a position of unimportance, a simple yes or no would have prompted less suspicion from an already edgy Derrick.

"He did report back to me," Catcher responded. "Let's see. His preliminary findings indicate the tanker delivers heating oil to the funeral home facility situated on the property. He didn't make much more out of it. I don't believe you have anything to worry about."

"Heating oil deliveries at night?"

"It does seem rather odd, but it doesn't appear to be anything illegal."

Agent Catcher didn't elaborate, and Derrick didn't expect to get any more from his inquiry.

"I'm sure by now you've noticed I have you under protective watch. After my men were mistaken for prowlers by your local police department the other night, they lost their cover. But don't you worry. If anyone is coming for you, we will be there. Keep me informed if you have the slightest suspicions regarding anything that seems threatening to you. Just like the cemetery incident you reported, most of these things are nothing, but I want a call if you have concerns."

When they hung up, Derrick stared blankly through the wall ahead of him. He felt confused, threatened, and defiled by the revelations of the past weeks. A puzzle appeared before him, but he could not yet envision the whole of the parts.

*He seemed sincere enough, but I just don't know what to make of him.*

*How can an elite CIA operative make the assumption that heating oil is being delivered to a cemetery three times a night, every night? It isn't logical. How can I trust him? He suspects me of murdering my wife, yet he places me under protective surveillance. This must be a cover to get me to let down my guard. That has to be it, or maybe this is their way of getting me off the trail of the cemetery issue.*

After processing his day's work, Derrick hurried to meet with Joel on the tenth floor. Joel was talking on the phone when Derrick knocked on the door to the lab.

"Come on in," he shouted above the drone of a motor laboring on the bench where he worked.

"Yeah, yeah, we'll be right over," he said, and hung up the phone.

"Let's go. The Bird has some important findings. This is beyond what I could have imagined," Joel said as he removed his lab coat.

"Who's the Bird?"

"Cornelius Birdsworth. He heads the Biological Sciences Department here at ATF. The guy is brilliant. He's the chemistry expert—the guy who analyzed the specimen we picked up. He's *The Bird*, or just plain *Bird*. Whatever you do, do not call him Cornelius, or Birdsworth. He hates those names. He's also a bit . . . odd. I can't define it other than he's just a little peculiar."

Bird's department resided on the sixteenth floor in a space designed identical to the tenth floor, with long corridors leading past many laboratories. The Bird's office stood at the far end of the hall. On the glass door, his full name, and a string of titles and academic pedigree filled the pane—M.S., M.B.A., PhD., MD, Chief of Biologic Sciences, Director of Federal Emergency Management, Director of Experimental Chemical Development.

"Bird, this is Derrick. He's from downstairs, one of the litigating crew. The guy who turned me on to this whole thing."

Lacking in social graces, Bird hesitated in extending his hand to meet Derrick's, who stood waiting to consummate the introduction. His handshake was fragile, limp and sweaty, and he spoke to his shoes rather than look at faces.

Bird's mind could erratically travel to another place, far from the present. His eyes blinked incessantly from habit. Tilting his head to the left rather often syncopated with his blinking. He wore oversized plastic-framed glasses and clothing at least twenty years out of style. His knit pants, the type not worn since the sixties, draped too short for his long legs. The one-inch collar of his oxford shirt could not harness the bulky tie that screamed out in bright colors.

"Look here," he said excitedly. His voice sounded hoarse and scratchy, almost annoying. "You've got to see this. I have not seen anything like this in my life, in my life. This is the most unusual molecular structure you can imagine, you can imagine. Here, look at this, this." The repetition of words, the later grouping having a bizarre emphasis, added to the strange nature of this most curious being. Joel gave Derrick a look that spoke of the odd character he mentioned earlier.

Bird directed them to a hooded laboratory bench where a sample of the slime collected from the cemetery sat in a cement crucible. With his hands donned in gloves allowing him to work safely under the hood, Bird lifted a drop of the material on to a nichrome wire and placed it into the flame of a Bunsen burner. There was a deep red glow, nothing more.

"As you can see, this material isn't flammable at this temperature. Not at this temperature. I want you to trust me, you can trust me when I tell you this isn't flammable at any temperature I can produce in the lab, yet this harbors an energy source on par with nuclear energy . . . nuclear energy."

"What's its composition?" asked Joel.

"I haven't finished the spectrographic analysis yet, not yet, but there's a good amount of strontium. That's what accounts for the red glow. Wait, it gets better, much better. That device you gave me to study, the one you called the Cyclops. Cyclops."

"Yeah," said Joel, shaking his head sarcastically, acknowledging that, of course, he knew what he gave him.

"I ran tests on that device when I notice this gel, this slime, started to bubble, started to bubble. The stopper on the bottle pops off. It startled me. The closer I brought the Cyclops to the hood over here, the more reactive it became. Naturally, I turned it off. Naturally. I was concerned there could be an explosion. I was concerned. Looking back on my concern, it's a good thing I didn't leave the room. After analyzing the potential for this material, we might not be in this building if it ignited. Not here if it ignited."

"So, you're saying this slime detonates from high frequency waves," said Joel who followed the story much better than Derrick.

"Precisely right. But wait, just wait, that's just half the story." Bird covered the bottle of gel with a thick lead shield and removed his hands from the gloves attached to the protective hood. "Come over here, right over here."

Impatiently, he walked them to another lab table housing numerous crates of laboratory mice. There was a large flat box with an elaborate maze built inside. He lifted one of the mice by its tail from a crate marked, *AB-124* and placed it into the maze. As if programed, the mouse scampered through the maze to receive a reward, a small piece of peanut butter coated grain.

"That's rather impressive," said Derrick, amazed by the skills of this lower lifeform.

"That's nothing unusual, not unusual," responded Bird. "This whole crate of mice was trained to run this exact maze. All AB-124 mice can do this. We buy them from a company that raises and trains mice for all sorts of experiments. Now watch this. Watch."

He lifted another mouse by its tail from a crate marked *Cyclops* and dropped it into the maze just as he did before. The mouse moved down a blind alley. It came back and followed another blind alley. It hesitated and bumped into walls. Within a matter of sixty seconds, it came to a halt. It licked its hands and seemed content to sit still.

"That one seems to need training," said Derrick.

"This one had the same training. Same training. It's an AB-124; at least it was before I exposed it to the beam from the Cyclops."

Derrick, didn't understand the science behind the experiment, but he did know enough to sense an extreme fear of the secrets revealed each moment. The severity of the effect on the mouse terrified him. He could not understand how Joel and all of the millions of people exposed to this hidden beam were not dead by now. Joel read the look of confusion and dread on Derrick's face.

"Don't worry, Derrick. Anytime we do studies on mice, we have to realize the effects are exponentially different when we try to relate them to humans. It takes a hell of a lot of a chemical to cause cancer in a human while in a rat it takes a fraction of a dose. These rat studies give us a speeded-up view of possible effects. Remember, these are *possible* effects. What I don't understand, Bird, is how did you know to test for behavioral effects? When I gave you the

Cyclops, I thought you were going to analyze the light beam for cellular effects and toxicity."

"That's how it all started. I exposed various tissues to the Cyclops beam to see how it affected them. I exposed the cornea, the skin on the underbelly, and the oral mucosa. That's the way I like to start. Best to start that way. Later, I go for effects on internal organs.

"It turns out I was upset with my assistant because he used the AB-124 mice for the tissue studies. They're expensive; the AB-124s, they're expensive. On tissue studies, I sure don't need a trained mouse. I was furious. I yelled at him. I don't yell, not usually. He kept telling me he used the plain mice. I showed him the identifying markers to prove he used the wrong mice.

"To get my point across vividly, I tossed one of the little suckers into the maze, you know, one of the AB-124s. It should have run through like a pro. I couldn't believe it. I couldn't believe what I saw. It just stood there same as the cheap mice. I had to check again. Same thing. It was labeled AB-124, and again it just stood there, right there.

"Now, I felt bad for yelling at my assistant. I figured they were just mislabeled. As it turned out, after careful inspection, they were the AB-124s just like I said, but the beam made them forget the maze. So, I was justified in yelling at my assistant. He did use the AB-124s. Yelling was justified. Quite often, great discoveries come by accident. You know, serendipity, by accident, whatever."

"There's an apparent effect on memory," remarked Joel. "I never saw waves giving off so much energy. I figured it was just going to show some level of toxicity, or DNA damage. This is incredible."

"Wait, it gets more incredible. You probably don't remember, but a year ago you gave me a wave amplifier for a study you wanted me to do where we varied the amplitude of the waves."

"Oh, yeah, I remember. I thought you gave it back to me," said Joel.

"So did I. I did. Turns out it's been up here all along. You won't believe this."

Bird removed the lid from a crate of mice confined to cubicles so small they had no space for the least bit of movement. He picked up one of the immobilized mice and placed it into an empty open crate. The mouse ran toward the wall of the crate, slamming its head violently. Dazed by the trauma, the mouse needed a moment before it made another run toward the wall at the opposite side of the crate. Derrick cringed as he heard the cracking sound of fragile bones shattering. The second blow resulted in the death of the small rodent.

"Holy shit!" yelled Joel. "What do you make of that?" he asked.

"I don't know. I don't know," Bird shrieked, while the pace of his blinking increased with concurrent double twitches of his neck. "This group here, I exposed to the beam with the greater amplitude. I know biological sciences, but I'm weak on physical sciences. I'm going to have to pick your brain to figure out why these waves are having these effects on the animals. Like I told you, I've never seen anything like this in my life, not in my life. What I can't figure, is why you and Derrick and the truck driver from the cemetery aren't dead," said Bird.

"I wasn't exposed to that beam. I drive a German car," Derrick responded.

"That's not what he's talking about," said Joel. "He means when the slime is delivered, it should blow sky-high from the electromagnetic waves generated at the cemetery."

Joel pointed to the hooded lab bench where the gel sat under the protection of the lead shield.

"This is all too unreal. We have to report this to the authorities," said Derrick.

"Which authorities?" countered Joel.

"I'd say this is a domestic matter. Let's talk to the FBI," offered Bird. "I'm tight with these guys. Half the time they have me investigate for them. I can get those guys to check on this. They'll check it out. This all sounds subversive to me."

"I don't know," said Derrick. "I got the brush-off from the Company guys."

"You reported it to the CIA?" asked Bird.

"It's a long story. They are investigating an attempt on my life, and being that I reported this dumping, I thought there could be a relationship. Now I'm sorry I got involved. I'm beginning to not trust any of them."

"Bird's right," said Joel. "If there's subversive activity going on, it's more dangerous if we don't get the authorities involved. They can't all be in collusion over this. Bird, why don't you run it by someone from the FBI? Don't give them the details for the moment. Just tell them you suspect dumping of interstate waste. That should be enough to interest them. See what they come back with."

"That's fine with me. Fine with me. I want to go out to the site. I have to see this first-hand. I need to see why the gel doesn't detonate out there with the energy readings you described."

Bird picked up the dead rodent by the tail, removed the cover from a bin that read *Biohazard*, and banked the small creature off the wall into the container.

# CHAPTER
# THIRTY-NINE

THE OLD MAN SAT IN A PLUSH LEATHER CHAIR NEXT TO A BLAZING fireplace. Unseasoned wood consumed in the flames bore embers that danced to crackling syncopation. His face wore wrinkles etched over a lifetime of worry and wear. The common lines of experience drew patterns in all of the usual places. He had a deeply carved vertical line of stress running between his bushy brows. A thick, untamed beard sprouted from his cheeks and rested upon his chest. The skullcap he wore corralled a mere fraction of frizzy hair growing uncontrollably on his head. The aroma of good food filled the home, giving added warmth to an already comfortable setting.

"Tell me, my son, what matters trouble you?" asked Rabbi Barbar.

"That's odd, you called me, *Son*," said Derrick. "I thought priests used that term."

"Are we not one another's brothers and sisters? Do we not teach one another as the parent teaches the child? We are all one big family with many roles, that of child, parent, teacher and friend. Titles change as we move through life. They change as we move through relationships. We can hold many at any one time. Tonight, you come for answers so that makes me the father and you the son."

Already, Derrick had a good feeling about this learned man who expressed kindness shrouded in wisdom.

"Thank you for meeting with me. As I mentioned, Dr. Klein told me you were the guy to see. I have questions. I'm sure some of them have no answers, but . . ."

Rabbi Barbar nodded and raised his brow demonstrating his agreement.

"I want to learn about the laws of the Bible, and how they might relate to health." Derrick paused, not knowing where to go from his opening statement. The Rabbi seized the moment.

"Your interest is universal," he said. "Throughout the ages, people from all backgrounds have been intrigued by our Laws. I speak of our Laws with a reverence that you may misunderstand as proselytizing. Please understand that is not the intended purpose of the passion with which I speak."

"Certainly," Derrick replied in an understanding manner.

"If you study the history of my people, we have been persecuted in many lands by many people. Our oppressors were often the most advanced cultures in their day. We have been endowed with the strength of the mind and the laws that have kept us alive, the laws of the Torah."

"Please forgive me, I'm not familiar with the Torah," said Derrick. "I'm not a religious man, and I don't remember much of what I learned as a child. I didn't understand whatever I learned then anyway."

"There are simple examples I can give you, and you will understand why my people survived, when so many others perished. Some of our commandments are all too simple, but the implications of their practice have been profound.

"We have laws governing sexual behavior, food preparation and prohibitions, laws regarding sanitary life practices, and others, all designed to keep my people safe from the scourges of antiquity. While the *Black Death* devastated whole populations all across

Europe during the Middle Ages, my people survived in greater numbers than most.

"The plague began over six hundred years ago at Caffa on the Crimean Peninsula. Within two years, it spread throughout Europe. It destroyed a quarter of the population.

"The plague spread from filth and poor practices of hygiene. People reared pigs and goats in the streets. Throwing refuse out of the windows was common practice. Had people followed simple biblical laws of hygiene, they could have avoided suffering and many deaths.

"Deuteronomy commanded us to deposit human waste outside of our living areas and to bury it at a time well before the discovery of bacteria. People laughed at us. They ridiculed us as outsiders. Many still do. Today, my own people do not know the Bible contains rules regarding excrement. Not until centuries passed did science confirm the benefits of such uncomplicated acts the Bible commands us to follow.

"The simple act of washing one's hands before a meal may have helped slow the spread of the plague as well as other diseases. For us, washing was a commandment, for others a social grace, and for the masses a neglected burden."

"That can't be right," said Derrick. "I thought rats spread the plague."

"In the midst of the filth, rats thrived," explained the Rabbi. "The vector was the flea traveling on the skin of the rat, but once bitten, the person-to-person transmission turned airborne. The coughs and sneezes allowed sputum to spread near and far. For those who practiced proper hygiene, they merely washed away disease from their hands during the course of the day, and they didn't get sick.

"Sadly, the people from that dark time noticed our relative immunity as they looked for a scapegoat to explain the Black Death. Instead of embracing our ways, they killed many of my people, blaming them for their suffering. It is out of the same ignorance many of my own people today ignore the laws so graciously given to them by God.

"One of the greatest assets we have are our food laws. Woefully, most of my people cast them off as outdated, primitive tradition. Very sad indeed," said the Rabbi shaking his head woefully as he gazed trance-like into the fire.

"Today, scientific scrutiny declares the practices handed down from the Torah are good practice. We must butcher our meat promptly. The blood must drain, and the flesh salted to kill off the parasites, many that are probably yet unknown. Ask any health official if these practices make sense. They cannot deny it. The practices make sense to anyone who analyzes them, but because there is no known specific disease prevented by these practices, universal acceptance never took place. That was not the case years ago, before your time.

"The pig is a forbidden meat for my people. Long ago, this prohibition meant my people weren't afflicted with the trichinosis parasite found in pork, if they observed the law. Not until modern times did the world realize the meat from the pig could be harmful. To resolve that concern, they learned how to kill the parasite by cooking the meat well. Mind you, they still eat the worms, but instead of rare worms, now they are well done."

Derrick chuckled and added, "I guess they figured out all of those health concerns by now. So, it's tradition guiding your observance."

The Rabbi's face turned crimson red. Derrick struck a sensitive note yielding the first sign of emotion in an otherwise sedate persona.

"It is *faith* that guides my observance. It is the faith in *Hashem*, who has commanded us to abide by the laws. How impudent would it be if I were to say all forms of disease related to our food sources were conquered? Though I am not a man of medicine or science, I would guess there are untold numbers of diseases yet discovered.

"Who's to say *Hashem* gave us commandments to be followed

until the twenty-first century, and then it would be fine to castoff His word? If I lived in the Dark Ages, I could have made the same argument to reject His word then. I could have paid the ultimate price by denying Him then as many do today. To relegate one's beliefs to tradition and deny faith is an insult to the pious."

"I'm sorry," said Derrick regretfully. A moment of silence passed. By now intrigued, Derrick needed to continue. Unfortunately, he felt lost in matters of the spirit, much as he felt lost conferring with men of science. Derrick realized how he had limited expertise in the scheme of all things. Willing to learn and willing to ask to formulate and expand his philosophy of life, he proceeded, "Who is *Hashem*?"

"The omnipotent Creator is called *Hashem*, the Force that dictates all natural laws."

"I didn't mean to make light of your laws," said Derrick apologetically, "but laws are created to control behaviors a society deems unacceptable. People practice them neither from tradition nor from a belief. Governments write them to dictate behaviors, and people follow them to avoid punishment. It seems your laws should follow the same order, but they don't according to the Bible, or do they?"

"If you mean, do they prescribe a punishment for each infraction, they do. The Bible contains laws that prescribe punishment, but they are the ones that speak to civil and criminal matters. The laws that don't concern legal matters we follow because they are from *Hashem*. It is not for us to question His ways in the interpretation of His Law, any more than it is for us to question His ways that determine our number of numbered days."

"You gave me the example of washing before meals and the food restriction of the pig. Aren't there many other restricted foods?" asked Derrick.

"Take this book," said the Rabbi. He lifted a leather bound, gilded Bible from the table and handed it to Derrick. "It is my gift to you. Read Leviticus and you will find all of the restrictions spelled out."

"Thank you for your generosity. I must confess, I read Leviticus before I came to see you, hoping I would have better insight for my questions. It seemed the laws were rather simple, almost primitive. I still couldn't relate them to health concerns of the modern day until you pointed out some of the basic hygiene rules. This is all so new to me."

"Not true. You have had exposure to these laws for many years. Leviticus is, after all, one of the first five books of the New Testament you had exposure to as a child. Sadly, people do not read that which has been so eloquently spelled out for them."

"I know it's getting late, but can I ask you one more question?"

"You can ask all you need to unearth your answers, but even then, you will find there are more questions."

"One of your restrictions is for shellfish and scavengers in general. Any thoughts on the possibility of diseases related to these scavengers? I know this sounds ridiculous, but is cancer mentioned in your laws?"

"It is interesting you mention cancer, the scourge of mankind for the millennium. The disease is of epidemic proportion. It often results in death, the end of life, as we understand it as humans. If you study the Bible, you will know God saw fit to destroy humankind by way of a flood. When man left the image of his Creator to pervert his very existence, the Creator destroyed him. If you don't interpret the Bible literally, and even if you believe men of ancient wisdom and observation compiled it, you learn, in time, that the Bible is a prescription for living a wholesome life.

"There are six-hundred and thirteen commandments in the Bible. They engage all aspects of living. When you see how far our society has come in perverting those laws, it is easy to understand how man can, in time, be the source of his own destruction. Even if you believe the tale of Noah is nothing more than a fable or metaphor, it makes a weighty point. In time, given the freewill bestowed upon us, combined with no boundaries for behavior, the world becomes violent and wicked.

"Do we not see evidence of that now? Sex, cherished as a sacred bond between man and woman, has become a personal gratification devoid of spirituality and beauty. Sexually transmitted diseases abound. Sure, we defeated some of the plagues that have existed since ancient days, like syphilis and gonorrhea, but a host of new illnesses arose along with new strains of the old ones that become resistant.

"Your concern is with cancer. Ancient man's understanding of bacterial disease was where our understanding of cancer is today, inexplicable. How are we to know whether the cancers that have become epidemic in recent years are not the result of a transmission that we do not yet understand? It is my contention that for every disease we conquer, another shall evolve in response to unclean practices. This is just as much a law of biology as it is a law of *Hashem*. He guides us, since the earliest of days. Those who cast off the Law have found solace and cure in the secular world of science. This is good, but how about those who have suffered waiting for the answers? Perhaps the Lord, who vowed to never destroy mankind by flood, chose cancer or other diseases to rid the world of those who pervert his law, the laws of Nature."

"Are you saying that everyone with cancer is unclean or evil?"

"I am not. I am saying that we cannot understand the ways of Hashem. Just postulating possibilities clouded by his wisdom. If life was as simple as do this to prevent that, there would be no need for faith. There would be no freewill. That is not what Hashem has given us. We all make choices."

Derrick had difficulty absorbing the complexity of the Rabbi's words in their brief conversation. In his earlier years, Derrick discounted the level of faith exhibited by the pious. Now, the concept of faith had new meaning for him. He wasn't sure how it fit into his life, but with the specter of death perched upon his consciousness, he hoped something existed bigger than the individual ego. Derrick realized, for the first time in his life, that which philosophers have known throughout the ages. Matters more profound than he could imagine eluded all of humankind. Moreover, he realized as incomprehensible as matters of existence might be, there comes a time in everyone's life to search for those answers.

Derrick could not accept a God who destroys the innocent, let alone all of humankind. Yet the model of a people who are guided by, but fall from the grace of this God, made for a reasonable argument. "Doesn't the parent teach the child?" he thought. "And doesn't the wayward child pay, at times dearly, for not listening?"

It was all too complex to arrive at conclusions, but Derrick wanted to make another point borne of his confusion.

"Haven't men destroyed one another throughout the ages? How can one of faith accept the cruelty of mankind?" asked Derrick.

"There are answers for every concern, my son, found in discourse throughout the ages. Scholars who study the true essence of life by devotion to the Talmud, the commentaries on the Torah, deliberate, argue, and refine the meaning of all matters. That is where spirituality reaches the more cerebral level. These studies have occupied the lifetimes of our most knowledgeable people in the hope of gaining a higher level of understanding.

"I cannot, in an evening, answer your questions on the nature of evil. I can tell you there is an answer for all, depending on how far you wish to travel.

"There is a simple theory I formulated over the years. It relates to our perception of knowledge. Every child reaches a point in his early development where he thinks he knows it all. For some, it comes early and for others, it comes later. Then, as the child gets older, new problems teach him he, in fact, didn't know it all. Of course, now he thinks he does.

"It is a natural inclination to think we are right in our beliefs and actions. We go through life reaching plateaus of "knowing it all." Those who trend more intellectual, they run the biggest risk of believing they know it all. It is often at that point they abandon the spiritual, as there is nothing left for their inquiry. They even laugh at those who, with blind faith, follow the word of their God. Long ago, my father told me when people believe in nothing; fear them for they are shallow.

"As an observer, we often see the fools who think they know it all. We laugh or feel sorry for these fools, because they pay the price for their actions."

"They deserve what they get, because they act foolishly," added Derrick trying to show he understood.

"Don't we all deserve what we get?" asked the Rabbi. "Are we not all fools at various points along the road of life? Do we not often think we know it all?

"The most brilliant man to grace this earth to date was Albert Einstein. As I said, the intellectual is often the guiltiest of believing he knows it all. To the contrary, Einstein respected the sanctity of *Hashem*. With all of his understanding of the physical universe, he revered the power of the Creator and the structure He provided for the world.

"Our animal soul has a macabre attraction and interest in evil. Religious and societal taboos suppress this impulse. It has been long recognized by all cultures that evil, when unchecked, results in depravities at the core of a spiral into oblivion."

It was late. The Rabbi stood, signaling the meeting ended. He accompanied Derrick to the door and bid him goodnight. The Rabbi's last words, *spiral into oblivion*, reverberated in Derrick's mind. The words ignited feelings of grief. He felt tired, almost intoxicated, and his body ached. The intensity of the conversation drained him. Beyond the physical exhaustion, Derrick felt lonely and helpless. Hoping to find answers to the growing mystery Derrick left feeling an emptiness that cut deep into the heart and soul of a near defeated warrior.

# CHAPTER
# FORTY

In the car ride, on the way back from the Rabbi's home, Derrick pulled out a new unregistered cell phone. Before he could press the buttons to make his call, the sound of the ringer surprised him. It was twelve-thirty AM. The thought of Savannah reaching out melted his gloom.

"Savannah," he said affectionately.

"Derrick, it's me, Joel." The unexpected voice of the one other person who had his phone number ruined his expectations. "We're here at the cemetery. The tanker just left."

"I thought you can't make calls there, with the tanker just leaving and, and the magnetic field," Derrick stammered, not sure of his facts.

"We figured it out. It's incredible," Joel continued. "On the delivery pad itself, there is no energy field whatsoever. There are certain grave markers that form a perimeter. It's a protected area. That's why the gel is stable here. That's why I can get through to you with no problem. We're going to look around a little more before the next delivery."

"Maybe you should get out of there now. I don't like this," cautioned Derrick.

"Are you kidding me? The Bird is having an orgasm. He's never seen anything like this. While I'm going ape-shit over the wave strengths, he's picking up samples of vegetation he says show evidence of an unheard of cellular alteration. He's ready to set up camp here. I'm . . ."

The phone went dead.

"Hello. Hello." shouted Derrick.

No answer. He shook the phone, hoping it had a loose connection.

"Hello."

It was late, and Derrick had no way to reach Joel. Tomorrow would have to tell the story.

The next morning, Derrick arrived behind his desk by eight AM, early enough to begin clearing away his Justice Department projects for the day. Mason was not a tyrant, but he did expect his staff to get their work completed. Joel would arrive by nine-thirty, and Derrick wanted to breakaway and speak with him as soon as possible.

By half-past nine, Derrick became so intensely absorbed in a case, for the moment, he forgot about Joel and didn't notice Mason enter his quarters. Mason watched Derrick in silence, as it was his habit to observe people when he came upon them unannounced.

After a solid minute, Derrick, feeling the stare, glanced up, and with a startled expression he asked, "How long have you been standing there?"

"Oh, about ten minutes," answered Mason. "I bet they could use me on surveillance over at the ATF. I'm pretty good, you know," bragged Mason.

The comment should have been innocuous, but the mention of surveillance and ATF together concerned Derrick.

*He's onto us. Catcher must have caught on to my slipping past his men. He must know all about the cemetery. God, could he be behind it somehow? Could Mason? I have to be careful and play along.*

"They sure could use you over there at ATF. You are a real sleuth, Mr. Mason. Your folks should have named you Perry."

Derrick paused, waiting for acknowledgement that his dated joke scored. It never came.

So, what's up?" he asked.

"I guess you haven't heard. Joel Davis from the ATF, he's in the hospital."

Derrick scented danger and felt the blood drain from his head. A queasy feeling made his stomach drop. He wasn't sure if his face turned pale, but he knew his appearance changed enough to reveal he had more than a passing interest in Davis.

"Are you alright?" asked Mason.

"I find that news unsettling. I've just become friendly with him. He was a good friend of Karl's, you know. What happened?"

"We don't know yet. They admitted him last night or early this morning. They say he's in stable condition. The officer on the scene found him wandering along a country road up in the northern suburbs. Out your way, I believe."

"What hospital is he in?" asked Derrick.

"They shipped him to the University of Pennsylvania Hospital. The people from ATF are in touch with the FBI. They call them in whenever there's an incident with government employees. You know the story."

"If you don't mind, sir, I want to go over there to see how he is this morning."

"Sure thing. Why don't you go over now? You can let me know what it's all about this afternoon."

Before going to the hospital, Derrick needed to see if Bird could tell him what happened to Joel. He went to the laboratory on the sixteenth floor where Bird conducted his experiments. The room was dark. Derrick knocked, hoping he was in the back working on one of his projects. No answer. He knocked again.

"Hasn't been in today," announced a voice coming from the door at the opposite side of the hallway. The unexpectedness of the declaration, and the haunting baritone delivery startled Derrick. "I suppose you're looking for Birdsworth," said a frail woman who owned the deep voice, wore dark rimmed glasses covering much of her face, and dressed in an oversized lab coat.

Derrick responded cautiously, "Yeah . . . yes. Do you know where he might be?"

"Not really. He hasn't missed a day since I've worked here, and that's going on fifteen years. The man is never sick."

# CHAPTER
# FORTY-ONE

THE RIDE TO UNIVERSITY OF PENNSYLVANIA HOSPITAL TROUBLED Derrick. He had no desire to go there again. The pathetic souls wandering aimlessly about in the mental ward entered into Derrick's dreams often since he first met with Dr. Affelbaum.

Derrick arrived at the ground floor and went to the receptionist's desk. She ignored him as if she had no peripheral awareness. After a moment, Derrick realized she had to be intentionally disengaged from her computer screen before she would voluntarily offer help.

"Can you tell me in what room will I find Joel Davis?"

Once she typed the name into her terminal, she responded with a scowl indicating she did not appreciate the interruption.

"Mr. Davis was transferred to room 584 in the white building. Use the second bank of elevators."

When Derrick stepped out of the elevator, onto the fifth floor, he experienced a déjà vu. Finding himself in the same corridor that led to the Bahrn's lecture hall, where he originally met Professor Mendelssohn, triggered the feeling of familiarity.

Outside the door to room 584, Derrick paused. He entered, expecting to see Joel in traction, or hooked up to assisted ventilation, the result of an accident. To his surprise, Joel lay curled into a fetal position with his back to the door. As Derrick got closer, he noticed an unusual patch of ulcerated skin at the nape of Joel's neck. From the raw flesh grew two white hairs. Otherwise, he appeared normal and rested or somewhat sedated. He no longer had the look of inquisitiveness that jumped out upon first meeting him. His eyes were open, and he stared expressionlessly toward the window.

"Am I glad to see they didn't hurt you? What happened?" Derrick asked.

Joel didn't turn his head; rather, he moved his eyes to stare at Derrick, and said, "The girl saw that she wasn't there. I know. I know. It doesn't matter."

"What girl? What doesn't matter?" asked Derrick.

"We can't expect that to happen. Only if I go would they wait. It's okay, though. It's okay if I go. We can eat. That's all right. Yes. Yes. Sure. Sure I can."

Derrick panicked. He went to the counter next to the bed to see if the chart, mistakenly left there, had mention of a diagnosis. He tried to read the chicken scratched jottings of a physician whose penmanship held little to be desired.

"It says *psychotic reaction-tentative diagnosis*. Does that help, Mr. Daniels?"

Derrick jumped at the sound of the voice tackling him from behind. He turned to see Agent Alex Hawkins of the FBI.

"So, we meet again, Mr. Daniels. I was there the day your wife was murdered." He spoke without compassion. He was on duty, and it showed. To him, everyone remained suspect. "As you know, the CIA took over that investigation," he said with a hint of jealousy. "What brings you here?"

"I was friendly with Joel . . . here. He and I were friends," said Derrick, with the redundancy so often a product of guilt or hidden motive. Being unable to handle unexpected confrontation with confident retort bothered Derrick. He felt warm and certain his face revealed the flush associated with false testimony.

"I guess you had to be close friends to get here so fast," said Agent Hawkins.

Derrick had to watch his every word. He didn't want to slip up and give Hawkins reason to trap him. He didn't want Hawkins to find something he could interpret as a connection to Joel's condition.

"Not really. We just started to get friendly. Common interests, you know how it is. Then my boss told me about this and suggested I come over to see what happened."

"A couple days ago, Cornelius Birdsworth contacted me. He calls himself Bird. Do you know Birdsworth?" asked Hawkins.

*How do I answer this without being caught in a lie?*

"I don't know him well. Met him once. I believe he's a friend of Joel's."

"He wanted me to investigate a toxic waste site in your area. Does that ring a bell?" asked Hawkins.

"I told you, I don't know this Bird fellow."

"Well, if you see him, you can let him know I checked it out, and it's heating oil deliveries. The owners of the cemetery don't want the deliveries coming when people might be visiting the graves, or if a burial ceremony is taking place."

"Yeah, I'll tell him if I see him," said Derrick who had trouble digesting the story.

*It's odd he volunteered that information. I just told him I don't know The Bird.*

Hawkins made his way out of the room. He didn't leave the floor. Instead, he positioned himself near the nurses' station, like a vulture waiting for the next suspect to descend upon the scene.

Derrick walked along the corridor toward the bank of elevators at the opposite end of the building. His peripheral vision told him Hawkins watched as he entered the elevator. On the third floor, he exited and made his way to room 350, Dr. Affelbaum's office. The lights were off at the reception area, and the young woman was away from her desk. A glimmer of light from the back office offered

Derrick the hope he needed. He rapped on the glass door. No response. He tapped harder, getting the attention of a passing nurse. He waved to the interior of the closed office to create the appearance his party was coming for him. To his delight, he did see movement from the backroom. It was Dr. Affelbaum coming to let him in.

"Why, Mr. Kramer, it's so nice to see you. What can I do to help you?"

The friendly greeting made Derrick wonder just how confused Dr. Affelbaum was regarding their acquaintance. Though not long since they met, a renowned doctor would not recall everyone he meets over the course of a busy professional life by their correct name.

"It's Daniels, Derrick Daniels. I met you for an interview with Professor Mendelssohn. Do you remember?"

"Of course, I remember. How can I help you today?"

"There was an admission early this morning or last night, a Joel Davis. He's a friend of mine. Could tell me something about his condition. Maybe you could call upstairs to get the report."

"There's no need for that. I examined Mr. Davis. He's been admitted with a tentative diagnosis of psychotic reaction. How well do you know this Davis?"

"We work together."

"Is there any family?" asked Dr. Affelbaum.

"I can't say. I know he lives alone. He's not married, but I don't know about other family. Why do you ask?"

"This patient isn't getting better. I don't know if you had a chance to see him, but that's as good as it gets, and it's going to get a lot worse," said Dr. Affelbaum shaking his head mournfully.

"What do you mean?" asked Derrick. "I thought psychotics are treatable today with all of the new medicines."

"He isn't psychotic, Mr. Kramer. I just wrote that into his medical record for internal reasons."

"Internal reasons? What's that supposed to mean?"

"The NIH, they sponsor much of our research and they have

concerns about some occurrences. They prefer that we don't advertise our findings at this time."

"What concerns?"

"I'm sorry; I can't get into that now. I can tell you, your friend has an advanced case of Alzheimer's disease. He's lucky if he has fifty percent of his brain left."

"The last time we were here, you told us you can't make the Alzheimer diagnosis until you biopsy the brain of the dead patient."

"That's correct. We can't make the definitive diagnosis. However, when you have seen enough of them, you can make a good determination of what you're dealing with. This man exhibits the kind of the disease we see in an unprecedented number of younger people. Men and women in their forties with this early onset, rapidly progressive disease are the latest population to become so afflicted. We have an expert here at the institute who specializes in these disorders."

"You mean Professor Mendelssohn?" asked Derrick.

"You've heard of him. A genius who taught me all I know about the disorder."

The obvious confusion on the part of Dr. Affelbaum troubled Derrick. He couldn't expect him to remember everyone he met, but no more than two minutes before, Derrick reminded Dr. Affelbaum he already met Dr. Mendelssohn. Now, he acted as if he had no recollection. Though troubling, it didn't matter to Derrick, as long as the doctor would feed him the answers he needed.

"Do you have any idea how a person, seeming to be in perfect health, could become so afflicted?" asked Derrick.

"Sadly, these are the mysteries we're trying to uncover here at the Institute."

"What about that sore on the back of his neck? Did you see that?"

"I did."

"What's that all about?"

"Take heed concerning the plague of *Tzaraas*," replied Dr. Affelbaum.

"What?" said Derrick confused.

"I'm sorry. It's a biblical reference, Leviticus 13:2. It's not something most people heard mention. Rather arcane, you know. A skin disorder of ancient times."

"You mean leprosy?" added Derrick trying to appear worldly.

"No, not that. Some other disorder afflicting the Hebrews as they wandered the desert four-thousand years ago."

"Yeah?" was all Derrick could muster. Somehow, he felt as if every new revelation he came upon had a connection to the bizarre puzzle he now called his life, but he could not put the pieces together.

"It was described in the Bible. I don't know much about it, just that the lesion on Mr. Davis looks just like the Biblical description. An old professor I had as a student in medical school told us about it."

"And that's all?" asked Derrick.

"Well, I've seen that lesion on several of the early onset cases of Alzheimer's disease we see here at the Institute. Hmm, very odd finding. We haven't figured it out . . . yet."

"Could I go see this old professor?" asked Derrick.

"I'm sorry, he's long since gone," replied Dr. Affelbaum.

# FORTY-TWO

"I suppose you knew it was inevitable we would have to meet." The words coming from Jim Young garnered deep feelings of repulsion and contempt. Young presented his outstretched hand of greeting, but Derrick simply stared at him with scorn.

*How could he have the nerve to come to my home? How can he meet me face-to-face? Even a reasonable man would shoot him dead. I have to maintain myself. I must see why he's here. I'm just thinking of myself. This has to be hard for him, too.*

The unwelcome guest lowered his hand after the awkward moment indicated a friendly introduction denied.

"I'm sorry, but my coming here is important to both of us."

Jim Young's appetite for power and lust came full circle. Now, forced to supplicate himself before one of the victims of his devices, he felt vulnerable, a feeling he rarely encountered. The meeting was painful yet necessary for both men, but in different ways and for different reasons. Young wanted to save his name and sudden threat of lost freedom, while Derrick needed to understand why his wife betrayed him.

"I don't know how much you know about the details of Adrienne's murder investigation, but they've turned up the heat on me at the worst time in my career," confessed Young.

"I'm aware we are both suspects, but I know I didn't do it," said Derrick. "As far as I'm concerned, you could be the killer, and you deserve anything they throw at you. I don't think we have any more to discuss."

Though Derrick wanted to know more, the loathing he felt forced him to close the door. Jim placed his foot at the base to keep it from shutting him out.

"You don't understand. I need your help. I know what you think of me. Sure, I'm a real asshole. However, if you didn't do it, and I didn't do it, we have to work together, or one of us may take the heat. I cannot afford bad press. So far, because of my position, I have been able to keep my name out of the papers. I don't know how much longer I can hold them off."

"You son-of-a-bitch. You don't give a shit about who killed Adrienne. All you care about is your ass and your future. You're a prick."

Derrick went to force the door shut, when he realized Jim Young had connections. He had contacts that might prove useful in the investigation. Since Joel was out of the picture, Derrick needed all the help he could get, even from the man who defiled his relationship with his wife.

Derrick doubted that Young killed Adrienne. The killers were after him. According to all of the reports, whoever tried to kill Derrick was more sophisticated than any local politician. Of course, he could now question Young to see if he, perhaps, did have links to agencies capable of using the type of bomb that killed Adrienne.

"Come in, and speak your piece," Derrick stated reluctantly as he released his grip on the door. "But I can tell you, your first mistake was coming here. That car across the street, it's CIA. Now, they know you contacted me. That will look bad for both of us. If you have to speak with me in the future, call here."

Derrick wrote the number of his unregistered cell phone on a paper and handed it to Young.

"I have to get this situation cleared up," explained Young. "If the story breaks that I was involved with Adrienne, I'm ruined. From what I can tell, it was an attempt on your life, and had nothing to do with her. However, what some theorize is that I knew Adrienne was taking your car that day, and I wanted to get her out of the way. On the other hand, their motive for you is the spurned husband who want to get rid of his cheating wife."

"They got it all wrong," interrupted Derrick. "If I found out about the affair, and I was going to kill my wife, don't they think I'd take you out, too, if I had a connection to get an experimental incendiary device to do it? Anyone with that much creativity and hate would not have let you live to take office."

"I guess you're right, but the prosecutors don't think that way. They search for any motive and any scenario they can. They live and die by convictions. Look, I know I'm innocent. They can't find anything on me other than we were having an affair. But that's all it takes. If this gets out, I'm ruined. My future, my career, I'm finished. What am I supposed to do then?"

"I don't understand how people who think like you can live with themselves. All you're concerned about is power. Integrity means nothing to you."

"We live in different worlds," Young replied. "My world has different standards that many people find repulsive. Like it or not, if we don't play by our rules, we can't govern. Did you, for a second, believe the political process has no corruption? You can say you'll change the world when you get into the black hole of politics, but in time, everyone involved learns they have to play the game. That's the way it works."

"Why don't you just make your case? What do you want from me?" asked Derrick.

"My people tell me the investigating agencies believe the attempt was on your life. That means you aren't a suspect. It doesn't help me, because I could still have motive. They have phone records showing I spoke with Adrienne the night before she was killed. My investigators also tell me there is a host of people on the list of suspects wanting to see you dead; drug dealers, drug lords, even industrialists involved in shady dealings. The problem is they have not been able to implicate anyone with certainty.

"They tell me you've been on record making claims about a possible suspect involving a toxic dumpsite that you reported. My people aren't privy to the details. I need to know how much you know, so I can get the investigation headed toward that possibility. If we can prove they killed your wife, and they get a conviction, they will let me off the hook. It's *quid pro quo*. My people break the story to the press, and they leave me alone. It's my best chance."

"And why the hell should I care to get you off the hook? As far as I'm concerned, you can rot in hell."

"Let's be reasonable," said Young. "You want to know who wants to get you, and who killed Adrienne. Don't you?"

Derrick thought for a moment. He knew his options to break the case dried up. If the people involved at the cemetery wanted him, he had few resources to combat their assault. Young's friends in high places seemed to have more information than Derrick suspected. As much as he detested making a deal, he felt he had no other choice. Perhaps the ways of the political process were more complicated than he wanted to admit. Derrick used this rationalization to justify cooperating with Jim Young. Derrick thought the same compromise he now entered into might help him understand his wife's infidelity.

"If I tell you what I know, how can you help?" said Derrick.

"I can go all the way to the Senate if I have to. I have friends in both Houses of Congress. Every investigative body in the nation has to answer to these people. That's how I can help."

Derrick explained as little as necessary to get a good return on his investment. He told Young about the dumping. He directed him to the location. He described the arrival of the crooked cop. He noted how just days after he reported the incident, someone made the attempt on his life. He left out all of the important details regarding the nature of what he learned along with Joel and Bird.

Young agreed to use his contacts to uncover corruption in the investigation. He assured Derrick while one agency could be bought, no way anyone could buy them all. He knew the buying game as good as anyone.

It took weeks before Derrick heard from Young. He contacted him on the cell phone as instructed.

"I thought you forgot about me," said Derrick.

He assumed he would never again hear from Young if nothing positive developed. He read Young well, as the type of person who seldom went out of his way if there wasn't something in it for him.

"Nothing gets done fast in Washington," explained Young. "I went to the top. My friend in the Senate, I can't use names, you understand, but he placed me in touch with the head of the committees funding the CIA and the FBI. I wasn't wasting my time with a crooked, piss-ant local sheriff."

"So, what did you find out?"

"I wish I had good news. Nothing, not a thing to get me off. That's why I called. I need a favor."

"Wait, what do you mean *nothing*?"

"Both the FBI and CIA did a comprehensive investigation. It doesn't get more thorough than that. It came back that it's heating oil deliveries. I know that's not what you wanted to hear. Neither did I, for Christ's sake. I heard it from their top people. The heads of both agencies looked into the matter and reported to my contacts. This was a joint investigation by two independent agencies. They do not fuck up. Sometimes you can buy an agent here and there, but not from both elite agencies. Conspiracies like that just don't happen.

"As I was saying, I need a favor."

"What's that?" Derrick asked with dismay.

"If you could sign an affidavit saying Adrienne didn't know which car she was taking until the morning, it would make my story go better. Could you do that for me?"

"What?" exclaimed Derrick.

"I know. I'm the asshole who corrupted your wife. You have no reason to want to help me. However, if you do this for me, I can make your career. I can get you a partnership in the most powerful law firm in the City the day I'm put in office. No working your way up the ladder. No more ass kissing at Justice. What do you think?"

Derrick felt intense pressure build within his head lending fear of a stroke. The pressure eased and turned into primal rage, a feeling he never experienced. If Young stood in front of him, he would have realized the capacity to kill him. Such thoughts made Derrick sick. He had difficulty getting his words to flow.

"You . . . you dumb-fuck! You think you can buy anybody, don't you? You would have me perjure myself for you. You would have me sign away on a fact that could help you while implicating me. Are you crazy? Do you think through any of your depraved behavior?"

Realizing he no longer had a chance at benefiting from anything Derrick could offer, Young decided to end the relationship, but not without a barb. "Let me tell you something, Mr. Self-Righteous," he shouted. "All I got back on your cemetery story was everyone believes you're a paranoid nutcase. So, Daniels, good luck with the rest of your life, you loser. And always remember, when I was poking your wife, she loved every minute of it . . . the kinky bitch."

Derrick slammed the phone to the floor. He stood trembling, unable to stop the rage and contempt that took over his faculties. His temples pounded, and a high-pitched sound clogged his ears. His throat felt parched, having trouble finding the saliva to afford a swallow. He felt used and cheap. The sadistic comments and the vile nature of the author broke him, and he began to sob.

The phone rang. He reached for it, but then hesitated. He reached again, deciding he would put the fear of God into this base creature.

"You mother fucking . . ."

"Derrick, what's wrong?" was the alarmed response from the other end.

"Oh, my God, it's you. I'm so sorry, Savannah. I thought it was . . ." He hesitated.

"I need to see you, right now," she begged.

Savannah's request defused his rage.

This time, he didn't hesitate to exit his home through the front door. Gallantly, he stepped into his car and cavalierly waved to the steward of his every move. Both cars sped away on a ride to Savannah's place.

When he entered, Savannah met him with an embrace filled with desperation. She trembled in his arms. He knew that for the moment, words were not necessary. The physical touch provided a comforting connection, the potion of revival for which they both were wanting.

"What's happening to me? Everything scares me," Savannah said with tears in her eyes. "I was never this way before. I don't know what's real and what's my imagination."

"Tell me what's going on." said Derrick.

"Every day, something happens to make me think I'm destined to die violently. It's a premonition. Just today, when I left work, I notice this Asian guy following me as I pulled out of the Federal Building."

"He just passed by when you were leaving," suggested Derrick. "It was a coincidence, I'm sure."

"No, it was more than that. I got nervous because I noticed him the day before, and the day before that. When I leave, it's as if he's waiting for me. It's more than coincidence. I know it sounds crazy, but I believe the people who got Karl sent him. I know I don't have proof, but what else could it be? And that's not all. I have been getting hang-ups. Since we got back, I'm getting hang-ups. I never got them before, never. My number is unlisted, and only a handful of people have it. How do you explain that?"

Derrick motioned for her to follow him. He went to the window where he pointed to the street at a black sedan parked at the curb.

"Is that the car he was driving?" Derrick asked confidently.

"Oh, my God." She shuddered. "Is he in there?"

"Probably," responded Derrick, and then he laughed.

"What's so funny?" she demanded.

"That's a Company car, you paranoid screwball. Look over

there." He pointed across the street to another cloned black sedan. "That's my tail. I let him follow me here. Now, we are doubly protected, all at the expense of the taxpayers of this great country."

"Are you kidding me?" she asked, now feeling ridiculous.

"No, I'm not."

"Okay, explain the hang-ups," she demanded.

"That's may be harder, but it could just be your detective down there making sure you didn't leave the house. It's just a guess, mind you, but I've been getting hang-ups, too. The difference is I was out. My guy had to assume I wasn't taking calls, because he stayed there each night until he was relieved in the early morning. Those hang up calls are standard operating procedure for these guys."

"I feel so stupid," said Savannah.

"Don't. We have been through a lot. I have good reason to believe someone wants me dead, and possibly you, too, if the Arab connection or the Pakistani drug lords or the Colombians are involved. It's enough to make anyone jumpy. I'll tell you this right now; I'm not leaving you alone anymore. That's if you want a boarder."

Her eyes lit up at his declaration, but she realized the problems that lay ahead.

"It'll look bad for you with the investigation and all."

"Screw them. They have nothing on me. I need a life, and I'm here to claim it. And you deserve better than a protective shadow scaring the hell out of you. I can't believe they didn't even have the decency to mention you were being tailed."

Savannah's heart swelled with joy. They embraced.

# CHAPTER
# FORTY-THREE

Since the Justice Department foreign travel debacle, Mercedes kept to herself. While she joined Derrick and Savannah for some of their lunchtime meetings, her demeanor and accessibility changed. The good old days gone, she felt more hardened than her job duties already made her feel. It surprised Savannah when Mercedes came to her office with a request to meet her for coffee across from their building. When Savannah arrived, she watched as Mercedes fumbled with a stack of folders.

"Well, well, well if it isn't the ever-hard worker bee. Don't you want to take a little downtime from this job?" Savannah asked kindly.

"I've been busier than ever. Things are crazy in my department, or should I say all around the world," she said as tears blotched her cheeks dark with mascara.

"Here's a tissue; your eyes. What's happening?"

"Before you went abroad with the others, Derrick stopped by my office and he found a file on my desk labeled confidential. I explained that they were on my computer one day and taken off the next. When I inquired about the content, my boss's boss came to see me, and he showed an odd level of concern regarding my inquiry. He told me to just forget about what showed up on my screen. He said my computer errored. I got the vibe to keep quiet."

"That's odd. Did anything come of it?"

"Well not until just now."

"How's that?"

"I've been concerned with the amount and type of violence taking place, so I started doing searches on our government server. I got odd results that seem tied together."

"Why didn't you tell Derrick about this?"

"I know this sounds crazy, but I don't know who to trust other than you. I found him snooping around my office when he first learned about this whole thing. It seemed innocent enough. He said he just stopped by to say hi, but he was snooping. Now I'm paranoid."

"Oh, come on, Derrick is the least person in Justice to get involved in a spy game for the higher ups. He and I are feeling the same way you are, and we are trying to do some of our own investigating."

"I know. I felt the same about Derrick. However, back when I initially brought all this workplace violence stuff up at lunch, you were the one who showed concern. The others just laughed."

"So, what's up now?'

Mercedes removed a pile of papers from her attaché and handed them to Savannah.

"I received these confidential statistics that show a much higher rate of violence and suicide on my terminal. When I did more research, a series of other confidential material came up."

"It's like they primed your terminal for a higher-level security clearance and forgot to shut it down."

"Exactly. There's serious shit taking place. I don't know what it's all about, but I remember at lunch you mentioned something about mind control and behavior modifying drugs. What more did you find out?"

"There was speculation that drugs coming from somewhere may be tainted, but that's just a guess. We were counting on Harris to report on that, but as you know, he's not coming back. The bigger concern that I worry about is these prions."

"That's it. You mentioned them at lunch."

"Right. I think they are being smuggled into America in order to infect us."

"What do they do?"

"I don't know, but it seems they make us forget things."

"Everyone forgets things."

"No. I'm talking about forget things—Alzheimer's forgetting things."

"That's so insidious. Everyone would blame it on normal aging at first, and we'd never see it coming until it too late."

"Wait. It gets worse. It seems they can modify prions and use them to make animals violent . . . unbelievably violent. If they could do the same to people, it might be why you see so much crazy stuff happening."

"Do you know if they started with this scheme?"

"No. We have no proof, and Derrick and I are trying to get more information, but it's not easy. Just like you, we don't know who to trust."

"One last question. Do you know what Cyclops means?" asked Mercedes.

"What do you know about Cyclops?"

"Not much, but I received one of those strictly confidential memos that wasn't for my eyes. It mentioned a Japanese device developed to affect memory and violent behavior as well. They didn't seem to have proof, and it was mentioned with little explanation."

"That has something to do with the people Karl met in Thailand."

"And?"

"And nothing. I don't know how it ties in, but this is serious. I'll have to run this by Derrick and see what he thinks we can do. I'll get back to you."

# CHAPTER
# FORTY-FOUR

The silence of rural winter seemed absolute. Freshly fallen snow covered the terrain in a sterile robe of splendor. City dwellers seldom experienced this pristine beauty of the wild outdoors. The cabin, located in the Poconos, just west of Allentown, hosted weekend warriors journeyed to these parts in their quest to leave the stresses of city life behind.

"This is not good. I didn't put in all these years to see everything disappear. The hell if I want to spend my retirement in the slammer," complained Agent Alex Hawkins.

"Hey, Alex, no one is going to the slammer, not if you follow the rules," said Agent Michael Roberts. "Of all of us, you have the least to worry about. Big deal, you did a preliminary investigation, and nothing showed up. That's your story, pure and simple."

"He's right. I'm the one who can go down hard," said Joe Thompson. "They won't think too kindly of their police chief being on the take to let a polluter dump in their backyard. But the way I see it, there ain't no harm done. If there was, I wouldn't have got involved," explained the Chief. "The new laws have become so restrictive I feel we're doing the right thing. You should have been there. They explained it all. They make these deliveries of this industrial waste product. It goes underground in special tanks they say have been there since the war. Nobody gets hurt. They assured me there ain't any underground lakes or streams. I know they're right. I checked into the underground waterways and there's no problem. We're just helping them get past this bureaucracy shit."

Agent Roberts opened another beer and took a long swig before he spoke. "As long as we are consistent there'll be no problems. As far as your superiors are concerned, you checked it out, and it was a heating oil company making their deliveries. Joe's brother-in-law has the documentation. We all made copies for our files. We are home free. And the money, holy crap. I can't believe how generous they were. I don't know about you guys, but I'm retiring early . . . by next year. This gig helped me out big-time."

"I don't know. I feel like that shit, Daniels, knows something. He can be the spoiler," said Agent Hawkins.

"Don't worry about it. We're okay," replied Agent Roberts. "If anyone should be concerned, it's me. I have that prick, Catcher, to answer to. I told him our story, but he's the kind of guy who can see through you."

"Seriously? He bought into it. If he didn't, you'd know. You have the same instinct he has," said Chief Thompson. "Look here. We've been friends for twenty years. We've towed the line, been straight arrows and put up with all the bullshit. So, some sophisticated industrialists find out about our unique relationship, and they need our help. It's karma. They needed an ironclad cover, and because we represent every investigative agency with jurisdiction, we delivered. That is why they have to pay the big bucks. No need to feel guilty or worried. No one can touch us unless one of us falls. We just got to be there for each other. Without one, they can't get the others. You just have to . . ."

Hawkins interrupted, "I know you guys are right, but I get the creeps when the higher-ups get involved. That corrupt piece of shit running for mayor in Philly, he opened up locked doors. That gets me nervous. I don't like the heat when my boss comes to me for a special report because a senator or congressman is on his ass. You know how it is. Everyone is on everyone's ass."

"Hey, you don't think I had the same drill with my boss?" said Agent Roberts. "I had to give an oral report to the Director, himself. It doesn't get gutsier than that.

"Well, boys, that about sums it up. Now, let's get out there and find us some game. The weekend's a wasting."

The three friends dressed warm in their gamesman's best and grabbed their shotguns, off to another hunt in the wild, to live their dream of leisure.

# CHAPTER
# FORTY-FIVE

Derrick struggled to put all tragic events into hidden recesses. Living with Savannah the last several weeks helped him dissociate from his tumultuous thoughts. In spite of the mystery shrouding his life, he felt happier than ever.

The underlying and often surfacing guilt over having lost Adrienne to the arms of another persisted. He could not sleep for more than a few hours before frightful awakenings. He tossed even more when recurring dreams of Adrienne's death visited almost nightly, feeding his despondent feelings. He didn't give her the time and attention required of a sacred relationship, he reasoned, and she left him.

After much soul searching, he came to recognize that his relationship with Adrienne grew from shallow values and incompatible interests denying any chance of a viable future. With Savannah, he seized upon shared happiness, companionship built upon common goals, respect and desire, but the final verdict would have to wait. Unsettled matters pushed good omens to the bottom of his conscious thought.

At work, Derrick completed the briefs to be served upon illicit drug operatives in Colombia. A task force was supposed to be in place, but communications with his South American counterparts seemed suspicious. It would require a visit to the prosecutor's office in Colombia before he could determine the chance of success in the International Courts. Derrick did not relish the task, and anything he could do to avoid such a mission was paramount.

Agent Catcher arrived at Derrick's office unexpectedly and not any friendlier than at earlier meetings. This time, he entered without an invitation and shut the door behind him. His physical brusqueness matched the out of character, sharp, verbal attack. He pounded his fist onto the desk in cadence with his words.

"Daniels, you're making my job harder than I prefer. Moving in with Miss Ambrose was a bad idea."

The subject, more than the hostile tone, riled Derrick, and he fired back.

"You may find this hard to believe, Catcher, but my life has been turned upside-down in service to my country. I am not claiming to be a patriot, but I need a life just about now, and you and your whole fucking organization will not deprive me. Do you understand what I'm saying here?"

Catcher showed a semblance of compassion for the first time since they met. He retreated from his aggressive posture and took a seat.

"You don't understand what's going on, and I don't want to see you in more danger than you are already. When you two were apart, we had the opportunity to follow several sets of enemy operatives, and I could tell which one of you they were after. It was easy. If they followed you, they were the drug cartel people. If they followed Miss Ambrose, the Sheik's people had her in their sights. Now, it's a nightmare.

"You don't know how they maneuver. They send out waves of operatives who move into cells located throughout the city. From these shelters, they do their research to determine just when and how to make their move. Sometimes, all we see is what appears to be an unrelated petty theft or burglary where they take your notes or steal your computers. Other times, their mission is to get rid of you.

"We have to protect you and Miss Ambrose. It's hard enough not knowing when they will strike. Now we have the complication of two, possibly three, investigations going on together involving principals, you two, living together. It makes our efforts much less effective.

"Look at these pictures," Catcher said as he handed Derrick a package of official-looking photographs used in police work. The first photo pictured a young Hispanic man in a mug shot, holding up numbers under his chin. In the next photo, the identical man lay in a pool of blood inside a cheap motel room. The next three sets of photos displayed the same sequence depicting the demise of three other young Hispanic men.

"You see those guys? They were on their way to eliminate you. We intercepted them in South Carolina, coming from their landing in Miami. The drug lords sent them as a team to stop your collaboration with the Colombian prosecutor's office. We have intelligence feeding us this information. As you can see, we have no time to fool around. We have to axe these assassins as they come."

"Mason told me about your methods, but he heard it second-hand. How do you pull off that kind of operation without the wrath of the ACLU?" asked Derrick.

"Technically, we don't do anything illegal. Let's just say my men know how to provoke an incident."

"An incident?"

"Yeah. Once started, we don't take prisoners. Don't let our ways trouble you. It's for your protection. If not for our methods, we wouldn't be talking right now. You'd be dead."

Agent Catcher spoke with pride. He knew more about the world of espionage and crime than most people in the game. He based his experience on a lifetime of incidences with the most elite enforcement agencies in the world.

"Protective custody is a terrible option, but with you and Miss Ambrose living together, you are placing yourselves in jeopardy."

"How long can this go on?" asked Derrick.

"This goes on until you achieve your objectives and those at the highest level are put away, or until they've terminated you. It's not win-win. It's one winner takes all.

"The best case we have, at present, is a group of Thai nationals deployed to the States. We believe they seek information concerning the ongoing Japanese automobile dumping investigation. That's the one conducted by the State Department in conjunction with Justice. For a long time, we have tolerated the practice, but now we have to protect the American workers. They can't compete on an uneven field. Somehow, the Thai government is involved in this. We believe the Thai were responsible for Armstrong's death. We haven't been able to confirm it yet, but they are the most probable suspects."

"It happened in Thailand, but the Japanese killed him, and I can confirm it for you," said Derrick.

"How's that?" said Catcher, with eyebrows perked.

"I can't tell you my source right now. Don't push me on how I know. When I'm ready, I'll tell you. Just make sure your men follow the leads that take them to the Japanese being Armstrong's killer."

Feeling good about Catcher, for the first time since meeting, now Derrick wanted more from him.

"Help me out. What about me being a suspect in my wife's murder?"

"That's a bunch of crap. It was a case of mistaken identity. We know you had nothing to do with your wife's untimely end. They were coming for you, and it got messed up."

"Who are they?"

"We don't know. That's what I'm trying to tell you. That's why we need to continue this investigation with all the help we can get."

"What about Jim Young?" asked Derrick.

"He's a small-time crook trying to march up the political ladder. The FBI has an investigation concerning his malfeasance as we speak. He's going down. They're going to make an example of him.

You watch the papers. It will break soon . . . any day now. But he didn't kill your wife."

"I'm glad you came here," said Derrick. "I still don't know who to trust, but your explanation helped to clarify things."

"So, you'll split from Miss. Ambrose? You'll help my men do their job?"

"I'm sorry. I am very sorry, but I can't do that. She needs me. She's fragile and I can't leave her right now."

"I can't force you to leave her, but I just want you to know, if she gets hurt, it's your fault. You're tying my hands."

Catcher did not wait for a response. He stood and walked out, shutting the door aggressively in frustration. Derrick felt relieved to have some insight as to the direction of the investigation. He could now tell Savannah with confidence her fears were not imaginary. They must maintain their vigilance and guard against potential enemies.

Derrick felt certain he could find answers to mysteries surrounding the events threatening them. He believed there was a relation between disparate parts. Somehow, he felt Rabbi Barbar had the answers to solve the puzzle.

# CHAPTER
# FORTY-SIX



"You are so kind to entertain my inquisitiveness, Rabbi Barbar. I do hope I won't wear out my welcome."

The old man's eyes peered out above bifocals perched upon the farthest tip of his nose. "Learning is a lifelong-adventure. It is our responsibility to study. With that obligation comes the task of teaching as well. For if there were no teachers, how could we learn? It is my job, pleasure, and duty to entertain your query. What brings you here tonight? You look troubled."

Derrick had been staying up late every night scouring the Bible for clues. Though his search had no actual direction, a peculiar premonition told him answers resided in the pages of the ancient manuscript. He became so confused he did not know why he returned to the learned man. He hoped the Rabbi held the answer to the reminder he jotted on a scrap of paper—*See Rabbi Barbar regarding the Plague of Tzaraas—Take heed concerning the plague of Tzaraas*. If the old man could tie the arcane reference to something tangible, perhaps Derrick would get closer to understanding his fate.

"I work for the Department of Justice, and my work led to some dangers. I'm trying to find out what happened to a friend of mine.

He's in the hospital, afflicted by Alzheimer's disease. When I saw him, he had this strange rash or sore on the back of his neck. I asked the doctor what it was. He didn't seem to know. His words to me were, *take heed concerning the plague of Tzaraas*. He told me there was an ancient rash described in the Bible called *Tzaraas*. I've looked in the medical texts books and found nothing, and then I went to the bible. *Tzaraas* is mentioned in Leviticus, chapter thirteen, but I don't understand anything."

Rabbi Barbar smiled and sucked deep upon his pipe causing it to glow warm and friendly. Following a long exhalation he spoke. "*Tzaraas* is a rather obscure notation in the literature. It has to do with commandments my people follow. There are six-hundred and thirteen commandments in the Bible . . . the Torah. They can be separated into two types, the performative and the prohibitive, those that command us to do or *not* to do particular acts."

Derrick looked puzzled. The perceptive teacher stopped to give an example.

"It sounds confusing, but you're familiar with many of these commandments. The most well-known ones are the Ten Commandments. Thou shall not kill is prohibitive. Thou shall honor the Sabbath day and keep it holy performative; a directive to do something versus to not do something."

Derrick understood and nodded.

"Of the performative commandments, there are two-hundred and forty-eight. There are three-hundred and sixty-five prohibitive commandments corresponding to each day of the year. This reminds one, on a daily basis, concerning the transgression of the commandments. These make up the six-hundred and thirteen mitzvahs, commandments, transmitted to the ancients through the Torah.

"Numbers play a significant role in the teaching of my people. Each letter of the Hebrew language has a number value, and we find relationships between the spoken word and the numbers they represent.

"Today, no one follows all of the laws, as many no longer apply following the destruction of the Temple."

"The Temple?"

"Yes. Long ago, the Romans destroyed the Temple where my people protected their holy laws, the Torah, the Bible. Some of the commandments are looked upon as outdated in the world in which we live. You could describe the one of which you inquire as archaic. *Take heed concerning the plague of Tzaraas.* It is commandment number 584, and more precisely, prohibitive commandment number 350."

The numbers the Rabbi named flashed upon Derrick's memory. For a moment, his mind's eye took him back to the University of Pennsylvania Hospital where, peculiarly, 584 was the room number in the hospital where Joel lay as a mental defective. He then pictured the door to Dr. Affelbaum's office, 350. The look of dismay on Derrick's face concerned the Rabbi.

"What I said seems to cause distress. Are you all right? Shall I continue?"

"No, I'm fine, Rabbi. Just an odd coincidence, I'm sure," he said hesitatingly. "Please continue."

"What, in essence, the commandment says, it is forbidden to remove the sign of *Tzaraas* infection, or to burn it away. The commandment concerning *Tzaraas* then references commandment 169. This states, *When a man should have in the skin of his flesh, the sign of Tzaraas, then he shall be brought to Aaron, the Kohen, or to one of his sons.'* You see, the Kohens, they were the priestly sect. The man so afflicted was obligated here, in performative commandment 169, to go to the priests who would determine if he was ritually impure. If he was so determined to be impure, he must then conform to the laws of the Torah.

"This person they termed a *metzora.* The priest would search for three signs—the presence of two white hairs on the affected area, raw flesh, and the degree of its spread. Once declared contaminated, they quarantined the person. The condition of the *metzora* was of huge concern to the ancients. They considered it more severe than any other ritual impurity, even more so than the *zovim*, those who had contact with a human corpse.

"When Jews wandered in the wilderness, in their exodus from Egypt, they expelled the *metzora* from all three camps. A zov, the *zovim*, were permitted to inhabit the outer-most camp, farthest from the sacred Torah. When in Israel, the *metzora* was expelled from the walled Old City of Jerusalem altogether."

"What does all of this mean?" asked Derrick. "Why isn't there any modern reference to this disorder in the medical literature?"

"I suppose, because it's no longer a plague that afflicts humans. Many diseases have disappeared over the millennia, just as cultures have perished. Whatever it was, it put the fear of God in the ancient people. Some say it was an affliction assigned to those who slander. It was a sign of an obscure meaning. I am sorry I cannot tell you more. Like many of the ancient laws, perhaps there is a profound meaning, even today, that we do not yet understand. It could be much like the things we discussed the last time we met."

"One more question, if I may?" asked Derrick.

"Certainly," replied the Rabbi.

"How is it you know so much about such an obscure law that has had no relevance for so long?"

"How is it, you as a lawyer can, I suppose, quote laws and legal decisions constructed years ago, some still useful and others ancient?"

The question created sufficient reason to end the inquiry, but it was not adequate to quench the appetite for the mysterious connections that captured Derrick's interest. It appeared the same disease or process afflicting the ancients infected Joel and, perhaps, others. Whatever the significance, it tendered enough importance to be included in learned scrolls handed down throughout the millennia. Just as new significances derive from study of ancient writings, there had to be a deeper meaning to the plague of Tzaraas.

# CHAPTER
# FORTY-SEVEN

Savannah eagerly awaited Derrick's return late on the evening he visited with Rabbi Barbar. She worried about everything. Behind each corner lurked a dreadful event. She knew her fears were irrational, but she could not control them.

Under constant surveillance by the CIA meant all threats would result in immediate assistance. Even this assurance did not remedy her apprehension. She could go to work but avoided leisure events. A simple trip to the supermarket became an anxiety-ridden adventure. Her worries only disappeared when she spent time with Derrick.

"I'm so glad you're back," she said as she jumped into his arms.

He held her tight to show his support and love. She returned the notion with her embrace.

"Why are you so late?" she asked.

"I told you, I don't want to get you involved. Let's just say it has nothing to do with the villains already after us. The last thing you need is another worry. How was your appointment with Dr. Klein?"

"He's great. I'm so glad you told me to see him. He takes his time, a real saint. I felt like he didn't have anyone else to see but me."

"Yeah, he's great that way. There can be a whole waiting room full of patients, and he will answer all your questions without making you feel rushed. So, what did he say?"

"He told me it was perfectly normal that I'm having these anxiety attacks living with a paranoid like you."

"Come on, he didn't say that?"

"He did, but he laughed. He was just joking. He said it's normal to have these feelings when there's a known threat. For many of his patients, he said the peril is imagined, but real in their minds. Knowing we are under protective surveillance by the CIA, he was much more comfortable recognizing an actual threat basis for my anxiety. He gave me these." She held up two bottles of pills. "Let's see, Klonopin, and this one is to help me sleep, Ambien. He said I would feel like a new woman in about two weeks.

"It was interesting, what he said about panic attacks. They didn't exist twenty years ago. He said now it's the psychological disorder of the decade."

"That's because there is so much more stress in the world today," explained Derrick. "Years ago, life was simple. You had three television stations, and you put out your trash in a can. Now, for Christ's sake, we have five hundred television stations and you need a PhD to figure out which day for recyclables, and which bin takes aluminum, and which takes glass, and what type of glass. It's enough to make anyone have an anxiety attack."

"You're right. But how do you explain all the other conditions he mentioned?"

"What conditions?"

"Fibromyalgia, Epstein-Barr, AIDS and slew of other diseases he said weren't in the textbooks when he went to medical school."

"I'm telling you, it's stress. Modern life is taking its toll on us," said Derrick, not convinced he had the answer.

"What happened when you spoke to Mercedes about those concerns of hers?"

"We never had that conversation. Something strange going on. She hasn't been in work for the past week, and when I tried her at home, there was no answer."

"What do you make of that?"

"I don't know. She's always been accessible and never misses a day, so I don't know what to make of it."

"She told me she felt antsy. Paranoid, that's how she described it."

"Yeah. With what she works on all day it would make anyone paranoid."

# CHAPTER
# FORTY-EIGHT

Mason barreled his way into Derrick's office. He appeared distraught more than mad. He shut the door to keep the impromptu meeting private.

"Daniels, we have a serious problem."

"Wouldn't you say we have had a serious problem for some time now with two dead attorneys?"

"You can make that three."

Derrick jumped out of his chair.

"What? How's that possible?"

"I don't know. I just got word from Agent Catcher. He told me that they found Mercedes dead in her apartment. Apparent suicide."

Derrick's knees buckled, and he lost balance. Mason rushed to his side and helped settle him back into his desk chair.

"I'm sorry about this Derrick. I know you were more than coworkers. I mean you were friends . . . all of you."

As Derrick regained his composure, he held his head in his hands to cover his face. He didn't want Mason to see the tears welling up in his eyes.

"I just can't believe this. She was the most grounded person I know. I guess all the pressure of the world she lived in got to her."

"I guess so. In any case, Catcher will want to interview you and Ms. Ambrose."

Derrick wiped his eyes with the palms of his hands and looked up at Mason.

"Oh no, he can't do that."

"And why not?"

"She's falling apart. We can't tell her, at least not now. I'll talk to Catcher."

"Okay, I won't say anything to Savannah. See what you can do to convince him to leave her out of the investigation for now, but he also wants to discuss Birdsworth with you. You know him from Joel is my understanding."

"And what's that all about?"

"He's gone missing and somehow they believe you were the last to speak with him."

At that moment, Agent Catcher entered the room unannounced.

"Mason, when you told me Daniels would be in his office, I didn't expect you to run down the hall to sound the warning."

"Catcher, my attorneys have been through the mill, and I wanted to give him a heads up. As it is, Daniels didn't take the news well."

Ignoring the death of Mercedes as a courtesy, Catcher began his inquiry elsewhere.

"Daniels, we believe you were the last to speak with Birdsworth. Is that so?"

"He preferred Bird. I don't know if I spoke with him last. I don't know who he knows or where he goes. The last one I spoke with was Joel, and now he's in the hospital like a vegetable. Mercedes is dead at her own hand. Of course, that is assuming no one from government did her in for knowing too much. If you want to get clues as to what's going on, I'd suggest a brain biopsy on Mercedes. If I'm right, you will find that she has a deteriorating brain. This is not a case of depression. I say something we discovered back in Iran infected her. You heard about it when we were debriefed. Go check your notes."

Catcher looked visible upset by the pronouncement, and without saying another word, he left Mason and Derrick alone.

# CHAPTER
# FORTY-NINE

The love Derrick felt for Savannah brought to life his elusive dream of unity in a relationship. They had the same values, wants, needs and desires. Every passing moment together found happiness. With this perfect relationship came an unwanted complication. The more his love grew, the more vexed he became knowing it could end at the hands of evil.

The medications Dr. Klein prescribed for Savannah worked well. She seemed much more relaxed and less consumed by daily prophecies of presumed violence toward her and Derrick. Before, any sound of a passing car required a trip to the window to investigate. Now she could let it be.

Each night deep and uninterrupted sleep helped to renew her psyche. As an unwanted side effect of the prescriptions, her affect seemed dulled. Though her fear tempered, so did her vitality and appreciation of life. Once Derrick eliminated the threats from their lives, he was certain she could stop the medications and be back to herself.

The mysterious activities at the cemetery appeared to have no explanation. Derrick had nowhere to turn. He would not get help from the local police, the FBI, or the CIA by reason of design, incompetence or malfeasance. The longer the mystery broiled within his mind, the more certain he knew he had to take action. Having lost his advantage with the technological challenges of the task when events incapacitated Joel, and with The Bird missing in action, Derrick formulated his attack on pure instinct.

He designed a plan in simplicity. He decided to use the uncommon powers of the superior technology to his favor. If his understanding of the high-powered gel and the strength of the half-waves generated at the delivery site were correct, he could sabotage the very people producing the waves. This would either destroy the site or gain the type of attention needed to force the authorities to intervene. The people involved in this toxic waste site had to have powerful connections to remain in business and avoid prosecution. They seemed willing to protect their franchise at all costs, even if it meant the murder of an informer, and who knows what they did to Joel and Bird.

Slipping away from the surveillance team assigned to Derrick and Savannah became more difficult. Derrick no longer lived near the rented garage where he had his extra car stored. Savannah's apartment building had two easy-to-watch entrances, front and rear. He decided to try the direct approach.

Leaving through the front door, Derrick walked to the surveillance car housing the weary second shift of government agents. They were due to go off-duty once their replacements arrived at midnight. Derrick approached at twenty minutes before twelve.

"I need sweets, you know, a couple of candy bars. Can I get you guys coffee?" he said in a friendly manner. Derrick always acknowledged their presence, and they responded in a courteous way. It had since been established that their duty was more protective than restrictive. Should Derrick ran off, their jobs would be in jeopardy if the enemies who had him marked for assassination succeeded. Derrick relied on complacency to make his break.

"Sure, why not? Decaf no cream, just double sugar."

"And how about you?"

"Decaf, cream and sugar, please."

"You got it."

Derrick walked across the street and disappeared into the bustling convenience store. Out of the view of his protectors, he exited through the back door into the alley. Getting a cab in Center City was not a problem. From there, he drove to the suburban garage, got into his Cougar, and went back to the cemetery. He arrived at twelve-thirty AM, between deliveries. He had to make his move before the arrival of the truck.

With a spoon he took from his home, Derrick scooped the gel residue lying on the pad and filled a two-ounce ointment jar with the material.

He remembered what Joel told him the night before authorities found him mindlessly wandering the streets. He described a perimeter within the delivery pad devoid of electromagnetic waves, an energy-free zone, delineated by grave markers.

Without the proper metrics, Derrick had to guess which markers defined the safe area. He left the bottle of gel at the center of the pad and placed the smallest dollop of the material on the head of a pin. Walking to the edge of what he guessed was the end of the safe zone, he wiped the drop of gel onto the ground. Nothing happened. He went back to the bottle, retrieved another drop and repeated his task a little farther away from the pad. Again, no response.

The energy field did not yet activate, or he would have seen a sign of combustion. Just like the first night he brought Joel to the site, a ghostly silence persisted. At any moment the electromagnetic field could activate, making Derrick's task most dangerous. He could not waste more time. Beyond what he perceived to be the perimeter of the safe zone, he placed minuscule amounts of accelerant gel every few feet.

The gel began to sizzle right before he finished the placement of the last bit of material. It appeared that Derrick would now expose his infernal nemesis.

Hard and fast, he ran to escape the explosion sure to follow. He underestimated the intensity of the blast. Once the sizzle stopped, a brief silence preceded the force that slammed Derrick to the ground. The wave of air compression from the explosion, the force of which was enormous, knocked the wind from his lungs. In a state of shock, he turned around to see an astonishing sight. There, in the backdrop of a darkened sky, the forest of trees appeared to burn in the conflagration without being consumed.

The adrenalin flowing within Derrick's veins fed his pounding heart. He wanted to cry out in desperation for a breath of air, but his lungs remained locked tight. He tried to stand, but a weakness of limbs pulled him to the ground. Once on his back, it took but a moment for his diaphragm to ease, allowing a gush of air to reflate his lungs.

With renewed energy, Derrick came to his senses and stood to flee. Men clad in spandex uniforms came from all directions and swarmed him. He tried to fight them off, but they overpowered his efforts. As he continued his struggle, they carried him, no more than a hundred yards, to the building that housed a funeral home set upon the grounds of the cemetery.

Still somewhat stunned, he noticed the Chief of Police arrive at the site. As chaos ensued, he heard the Chief ask the other men if he they needed him, to which they replied all was under control. When they brought Derrick into the building, another team exited with fire-fighting equipment.

Inside the funeral home, modest furnishings providing for the comfort of mourners and their guests filled a small parlor. They marched Derrick behind the elaborate front, along a short corridor lined with caskets to a waiting elevator. They bound his hands and handed him over to three other men in almost identical spandex garb except for an infinity sign attached to the left chest panel of their tight shirts.

"We'll take him from here. Make certain you assure anyone who might report this incident that it was a heating oil explosion now under control. Have the grounds freshened and remain on alert," were the orders to the grounds crew.

Once inside the elevator, Derrick noticed buttons to three floors, two leading up, and one down. They pressed the down button, and the descent began. The elevator emitted a whirling sound as it traveled. Derrick experienced an odd feeling of lightheadedness, the type produced when traveling fast in a vertical direction. In spite of the apparent speed, it took an inordinate amount of time to get to their destination, well over ten minutes.

Following exit from the elevator, the men marched Derrick down a long winding passageway into a room designed like a NASA space control center. A main command console built into a curved wall filled three-quarters of the room. It extended at least fifteen feet high to the ceiling. Rows and rows of lights flashed in random patterns of white and blue. At the center of the console, a high-backed, titanium chair sat anchored in place by heavy cables attached to the floor.

They seated Derrick onto a stool. One of the men flipped a switch resulting in a crackling noise followed by repeated zapping that sounded like the discharging of a high-energy electrostatic generator. From above, in the ceiling, a red beam of light shined upon Derrick. It made him feel warm and relaxed in spite of the hostile abduction. The men systematically walked to assigned corners of the room and waited patiently.

# CHAPTER
# FIFTY

After fifteen minutes passed, an eternity of dread for Derrick who feared he would soon be dead, the door at the front of the chamber opened. In walked an elderly man with long, wavy, silver-gray hair. He sported the body of a much younger fellow than his weathered face revealed. While all of the others wore black, he sported a white spandex outfit. Muscles bulged from beneath his garb, that did not match hands that looked worn and of the same vintage as the skin on his face. His neck, wrinkled and loose, offered the best gauge of his many years.

"Let us begin," he commanded with poise.

The men waiting at the corners of the room approached Derrick. The two larger men stood on either side of Derrick and restrained his arms. The third attendant carried an adhesive-backed patch from which protruded two hair-thin white wires on one side and two thin needles on the reverse. He walked behind Derrick and placed the patch upon the nape of his neck, producing an intense sting as the needles penetrated his skin. Then a jolting electric shock stunned Derrick, for but an instant, as the needles acted as electrodes that entered his spinal cord. The technician pulled the adhesive patch from Derrick's neck. It resulted in a sharp burn as it tore a thin layer of flesh, leaving the wires protruding from a raw base. Derrick now better imagined the fate Joel faced days before.

With military precision, the three assistants marched out of the room at the completion of their task. The elderly man turned a dial on the sophisticated control board producing a high-pitched noise that gradually became more and more perceptible. At first, it seemed far off and muted, but as the sound grew more intense, Derrick felt a profound ache in the back of his neck and ears. With each increase in volume and frequency, it became more painful, bringing on an overwhelming feeling of nausea and light-headedness.

At the brink of unconsciousness, Derrick became aware he lost his freewill. He could neither move nor speak. The numbing of tactual senses over his entire body made him feel as if suspended in mid-air. The muscles in his jaw froze. His mouth remained open. He could not produce the slightest sound. Unable to swallow, a sudden and heavy flow of saliva dripped from the corners of his mouth.

"Your inquisitiveness and perseverance act as a thorn in our side, Mr. Daniels." The old man spoke slowly and methodically. He adjusted three dials for several moments before he uttered another word.

"What's real, what's imagined? Can one know for sure? A blur exists taking you from consciousness to dream state every night. Sometimes this dream state is filled with darkness, and other times it brings feelings of serenity. Yet other times there will be no recollection. Who's to say, once captured by the fancy of the imagination, what is real and what is the construct of the mind? The mind contains one form of reality, but is it the reality of others?

"Your actions have become disruptive to our cause . . . *your* cause."

As he continued to fine-tune the dials, the frequency of the high-pitch sound changed to a deep register, and with it, Derrick felt his mouth freed from the paralyzing grip controlling him. He realized he could speak.

"My cause?" asked Derrick.

"You are basically a good man. We have the same goals and aspirations. The difference between us is I have a more direct control on the path of the humankind. While you toil in the courts, I am involved with a more unfailing approach to make the world," he paused, "a better place."

Indignant, and seething over his abduction, and with complete disregard for his own wellbeing, Derrick mockingly shot back, "So, you're playing God."

"Yes." The reply was terse and unexpected.

"And the assassins you sent for me, I guess they were the archangels?"

"We never sent anyone to harm you. You have us confused with one of your own enemies. Your assassins were sent from Colombia."

"How do you know about that?" asked Derrick, perplexed by the information this man possessed.

"There is little we do not know, nor have the ability to discover."

"The police chief and his men, they didn't have anything to do with my wife's death?"

"That is correct. They did not kill your wife. They are but pawns. We use their greed to predict their behavior for our benefit. They are paid to protect what they think is a toxic dumpsite. We convinced them our activities cause no true harm, and they complied. Aside from their greed, they are generally good men, too. They stand on the front lines helping to combat crime. They try their best, but temptation overwhelmed their character.

"We do not wish to interact with the humankind, but the need arises from time to time, more often in the early years of a new millennium."

"You make it sound as if you've been around to see more than one," stated Derrick. He decided to use his lawyer interrogation skills to learn more about this place, the man and his plot.

"You can say that, but not literally. What I represent has been around since the beginning of time. Our unit has been in charge for the last six-thousand years, our task to guide the humankind, to see to it that he fulfills his destiny. Sadly, we have come upon failure again. The humankind, that is, has failed."

Derrick had no idea of what or whom he encountered.

*If this is an illegal dumpsite, is it their goal to kill me? That would have been easy enough. Perhaps they wanted to know who else knows about their activities. This is a large operation needing extreme stealth and security.*

Derrick figured this grilling was for the purpose of frightening him or tricking him into telling all he knew. He decided to play along, not that he had other options.

"You make it sound as if you are God. Isn't that a bit impudent on your part?" inquired Derrick.

"No one here professes to be the Omnipotent One. We do His work. You could say we are the archangels if analogy offers you comfort."

"If that isn't toxic . . . that blue gel, then why all of the secrecy?"

"The gel is the fuel that gives life to our very purpose. It is the one fuel powerful enough to run our wave generators. Each of four industrial chemical companies has a proprietary formula that, when combined, makes up our unique fuel. This way, no one knows the actual formula of our energy source. I do not expect you to understand all I am telling you. Your friend, Mr. Davis, he understood much more."

"How could you do that to him?" exclaimed Derrick.

"Let me continue. When creatures first came out of the jungle to be the humankind, they needed certain traits to survive. Some of the very traits needed to survive had the potential for evil. Jealousy, hate, gluttony, greed, and lust have a protective mechanism needed for the species to survive."

Bewildered by the comments, Derrick interrupted, "How can hate be anything but bad?"

"Your question is well-based. The answer is not obvious. However, without the ability to hate, one tribe could devour another. Hate is the most primal protective mechanism for self-preservation. It makes an otherwise peaceful man capable of killing his enemy."

The man paused. He waited for Derrick to grasp the meaning of his words. It made sense in an odd sort of way, but he continued his challenge.

"What about lust?" asked Derrick. "How can you make a case for that?"

"Humans have been endowed with a diverse set of traits meant to govern behavior and provide a host of vital needs. Without the capacity for lust, we cannot assure the propagation of the species. Lust is the ultimate expression of the sexuality needed to procreate. Yes, it is an extremely strong drive. Over the history of the humankind, it has worked its underlying good in the shadow of abomination.

"These traits have the curse of a double-edged sword. When they become excessive—out of balance—the system breaks down. This failure destroys the species.

"There is much to be said regarding the duality of man's nature. There is good and evil in the composition of all men. There is capacity for each trait we consider sinful in every man. While it is held in check rather well for most, even the capacity to kill is a part of the essence of man, if hate roils within the soul."

*Everything he says seems so logical. He has some kind of physical control over me. He probably controls my mind as well. This has to be a force of evil. Why is he explaining all of this to me?*

The old man continued his exposition. "Periodically, the dual-edged traits tilt toward the blade of evil. They get out of balance, and the future of humanity is at risk. Look around you, Mr. Daniels. Men raping children is but one example of lust out of control. Sexual perversions have ventured well beyond the biblical restraints we put upon the masses."

"What?" exclaimed Derrick. "You wrote the Bible?"

"No. God handed The Word to us, if you will, to guide the assembly. You are educated, Mr. Daniels, so I am sure you will understand what I am telling you. Even though on the surface it may appear evil, to the contrary, everything we represent is for the good. Not unlike the child's perception of parental punishment as a force of evil, it is, through the child's eyes, misunderstood.

"Much in life seems barbaric. One species thrives off another. It is the very essence of the food chain. It is the nature of existence. There are countless ways in which the masses are child to God and do not understand His plan. It is our charge to maintain the balance, inconspicuously as possible, with the least amount of meddling. To make ourselves, our missions known is an assault on freewill. Even though we must intervene, at times, to balance the negative outcomes of freewill, that freedom is what the Creator wants.

"Unfortunately, every few millennium, we are forced to heighten our involvement in the subtlest ways. You see, much of the controlling nature of the lives of the humankind has been in place since the beginning of man's existence. With the advancement of technologies and the attitudes of the intellectual elite, modern humanity is now in jeopardy. It is the leaders of the New World Order who have put you at risk toward total destruction."

"I don't understand how you can say we used technology to harm ourselves," said Derrick. "The world is a better place through the advancements we've made. We've staved off world wars through the balance of power generated by the threat of nuclear annihilation. We've conquered diseases and plagues that filled the world with suffering. How can I believe what you are saying? What New World Order?"

"You will see what appears to be simple is in actuality very complex. Aggressive and homicidal behaviors have been genetically part of humanity since the beginning. This aggression is a recessive trait that surfaces in ten of every thousand births. As populations grow, the aggressive homicidal types can mutate into psychopaths, allowing these killers to become more and more numerous. Based on Darwin's laws of survival, you can think of these individuals as Guardians. That is what we call them. They protect their tribes. Wars keep their numbers in balance. as they die in large numbers defending their nations. We cannot expect you to understand the concept yet, but wars are good, as they purge the overabundance of Guardians from the tribes."

"Everything you're saying goes against all I ever learned. None of this makes sense," said Derrick.

"Soon you will understand. Many things in life are not as they appear. The Guardians are the souls you knew as the bullies in your youth. Today, they are defined as toxin men not realizing their importance. They were the young men who were a little bit crazy, ready to attack anyone with the slightest provocation. When a society needs these types, they are molded into what can best be understood as, soldiers . . . infantrymen. They are on the frontlines in wars, ready to kill or be killed. They are what you call first responders, there to fight for a cause. Without Guardians, cultures give way to the aggressors.

"To appreciate this concept, you must compare two worlds that co-exist on the planet—the Third World and the First World as you know them. Today, only in the Third World can wars easily exist. Look to the African continent, the Middle East and other hot spots where wars and genocide have raged, at times, throughout all of eternity. War is the nature of man. These wars were once part of the natural order of things.

"As man became more, shall we say, civilized, he was denied the process of war in many instances. The convention of diplomacy became the means for dealing with disputes. War, which appears to be a disaster of the human condition, is the means to cleanse societies from the overgrowth of Guardians. After war, what is left are the weak, who, in fact, do inherit the earth. Those who survive are the ones spared from the field of battle. The survivors are the intellectuals, the scientists, the architects, engineers and craftsmen. Natural selection spares them to rebuild their cultures. This process takes civilization to new heights.

"The physically and mentally stronger societies survive. The embedded Guardian gene, the recessive trait, then has a chance to proliferate over the years to provide a protective shield against future aggressors that threaten the existence of their people. In times of peace and calm, the numbers of Guardians swell. The effect is that of increased violence and crime. When the natural order of things is in place, a war comes upon nations, and the problem is neatly self-limited. Unfortunately, in the First World, the paradigm no longer works."

"How can that be?" interrupted Derrick. "For thousands of years you say this pattern has been in effect. How can you blame man for the changes that have taken place?"

"It is not that man is to blame. It is a consequence of his freewill, which is the moral imperative. While the Maker expected great advances in technology, he never anticipated certain events would collide, producing a disastrous outcome.

"It was the unexpected end product of nuclear proliferation that became the deterrent force, preventing high-mortality wars in the First World for the past many decades. For the last eighty years, there has not been a purge of the Guardians in the First World. It takes a conflict with lost life that goes into the millions to accomplish a true purge as seen in the World Wars. This lack of a major war has put a severe toll on humanity as it coupled with democracy."

"Now you're going to tell me democracy is evil?" Derrick asked.

"You see the same duality in good systems as well as bad ones. Do not be so naive as to think good things taken to excess cannot lend towards perversion. The very freedoms and rights offered by democracy destroyed the deterrent effects used to keep Guardians under control as they live within society. Criminal justice has become so diluted the Guardian is no longer kept at bay. Without deterrents, Guardians become menacing operatives within a society that allows them to flourish."

"You can't be serious. We have more people behind bars than at any time in history. There are more people in American jails than all other nations on earth. We have the death penalty while other First

World countries have abandoned it. We have deterrents every-where you turn," argued Derrick.

"Your lack of understanding surprises me, Mr. Daniels. Don't you see it everywhere you turn? Are you blind, or have you become numbed and thus oblivious to all that goes on around you?

"You are an intellectual, so for you, incarceration is a deterrent. You don't think like a Guardian. You can't. You don't have the capacity. Jail is no deterrent. As you would not volunteer for the infantry, your type could never understand the violence of prison life is sanctuary to the Guardian. Prison pampers Guardians in a system affording them more rights than their victims. They have good food, clean healthy surroundings, recreation, sex and drugs.

"The two things your prisons offer as a disincentive are the loss of freedom and the fear of physical harm by the hands of another inmate, never by the guards. These supposed deterrents are an environment where the Guardian thrives. In this environment, they rule. To the Guardian, this is like charging onto the beachhead against a blaze of enemy fire. This excites the psychopath. This puts fury into his heart.

"You cannot prevent behavior you do not understand. Your death penalty is ineffective. As a man of the bench, you should know how many murders are committed each year, and that the number increases yearly.

"The Guardian is homicidal, but he is neither suicidal nor stupid. It becomes rather clear to him the numbers are in his favor. You have to find him, after he kills, rapes or maims. Then you have to find him guilty against all of the protections that keep evidence sequestered. Then you have to show his behavior warrants the ulti-mate penalty of death when weighed against mitigating circum-stances that put the blame of his behavior on anyone but him. After all of these hurdles, it still takes years of appeals before he is executed. During those years, he can explore all depths of depravity from within his cage. If all goes against him, he receives a painless, humane death after decades of living on death row.

"Compare the number of murders in your country against the

number of executions, and you can see you have no death penalty that rids your world of the predator Guardian any more effectively than lightning strikes by chance. You fool yourselves.

"Years ago, when rape, kidnapping and murder were capital crimes, and sentences were carried out swiftly, the Guardians remained deterred. They had to suppress some of their urges toward violence knowing they would otherwise die.

"Times have changed, and the Guardian no longer fears society has the will to take his life. You combine this with the inability of the First World to engage in a meaningful war to reduce the population of Guardians, and you have death and destruction in the streets. That would be your destiny if it were not for our intervention."

"So how do you work into this equation?" asked Derrick.

"I am your Savior."

"Oh, like Jesus Christ, I suppose," stated Derrick with an air of sarcasm.

"Not in the literal sense, but understanding he was a man who wanted a world of righteousness, so are we charged to see it come to pass. To overcome the societal and technological forces resulting in this unstable state, we must change the mindset or the minds of the intellectual elite. The mindset is impossible to change in short order as it develops over an extended time. The older one gets, the more set the mind becomes."

"Then you plan on controlling the mind?" Derrick asked cautiously.

"Correct, Mr. Daniels. As we speak, there are several, simultaneous, high-technology wars going on. Your people are unaware of them. These wars have become so sophisticated we have to intervene.

"America holds the largest brain trust accumulated in the history of the world. This resulted from vast emigration during the World Wars, Korean War, Vietnamese War, the Cold War against communism, and the various genocides occurring in so many lands. The most brilliant people from all corners of the earth came here looking for refuge, opportunity, and freedom from persecution while the Guardians died on the fields of battle. These advanced minds flourished under your protections.

"Right now, following years of peace in the First World, this brain trust is in jeopardy of annihilation. If we refrain from taking action, human civilization will succumb to the overgrowth of Guardians. The humankind will revert to the days when the barbarians ruled. The gene pool of the intellectuals will be lost once they perish. Then, the humankind ends up in a world of utter chaos and turmoil. For the first time the Guardian could become the dominant life-form. It is exceedingly difficult for a recessive genotype to make the shift to the dominant form unless the environment selects for it, or if there is a technological manipulation of the gene pool. This has been discovered by your enemies."

"I'm confused," said Derrick.

The man ignored Derrick's comment. He seemed to know all of his words registered sufficiently to explain the plight he described.

"Regardless of amassing a magnificent brain trust through emigration, America also made formidable enemies. If you think back to World War II, the atomic bomb decimated the Japanese. This was like no other war. In one day, a bomb brought the Japanese to their knees. It humbled and humiliated their valiant warriors. Though they were the aggressors, some of them never forgot that dishonor. Vengeance bred in the minds of a small group of industrialists and scientists who still had access to power. They joined forces to exact their revenge.

"As it played out, World War II provided for the best purging of Guardians the world ever experienced. The weapons of war came a long way from swords and spears with the advent of black powder, nuclear power and aviation. The purge of Guardians advanced so effectively we feared the balance of human existence was at risk. Just as we can't allow the annihilation of intellectuals, we cannot allow extinction of the Guardians without dire consequences."

A feeling of mental acuity stirred within Derrick. His concerns and objections seemed to consolidate within his mind like pieces of a puzzle falling into place. He felt able to post a sensible challenge.

"If you got rid of all the aggressors, the Guardians as you call them, then the desire for war would cease to exist. Having a society of intellectuals would be best for all. There would be a new era of world peace."

"The essence of the humankind is not that simple, Mr. Daniels. The intellectuals still have survival instincts and the duality each holds true. You see, even the intellectuals have the capacity to hate and to kill, though very much suppressed. The most effective control on the intellectual's capacity toward aggression is fear of personal harm. They cannot thrive in an environment devoid of Guardians. There would be no one there to fight their wars, to protect their possessions. If the Guardians disappeared, the intellectuals would self-destruct. Suffice it to say the order of the Maker requires a defined balance of forces.

"In our fear that the Guardians would be annihilated by the highly effective conventional weapons developed over the years, we offered humankind the breakthrough discovery of nuclear energy and the mutually assured destruction that comes with it as a means to stop wars, and thus stop the complete destruction of all Guardians.

"The atomic bomb worked beautifully, or so we thought. It even had the effect of eliminating some of the intellectuals in the Japanese population which we thought would further the balance of forces. The effect, so profound, got rid of too many Guardians, causing another major imbalance. This one event in history, the atomic bomb, slowed the ascent of the Asian people. Had they not entered the war and become the victims of the bomb, they were on the path to becoming the dominant culture in the world. Some of the finest intellectual genes cultivated over thousands of years were lost forever. Some of the Japanese didn't forget, and now they are striking back with a vengeance.

"The Japanese are our friends, our trading partners," argued Derrick. "How can you make these accusations?"

"We don't make accusations. We speak in fact. You cannot see your enemies, and they are many. They became bold and sophisticated while you became blind and vulnerable.

"Your enemies currently annihilate the American brain trust by invading your country with cars, computers and video games. The process is rather ingenious. They learned how to generate high-frequency radio waves that destroy brain cells at a controlled methodical rate.

"They embedded a few small microchips in most all consumer devices. Cunningly, and with careful preparation, they came to provide these components. Their goal is the permanent destruction of all cognitive function of your people. They studied classic literature, and they emulate the stealth of the Trojan Horse.

"All of your enemies realize the futility of engaging you on the field of battle. They have to attack in the dark, striking their foe, blinded by complacency, into oblivion.

"In your cars, they installed the device they call Cyclops. They target different groups for various effects. By using Cyclops in the luxury cars, they attack the intellectual elite, who own these vehicles. There, the waves deplete the capacity to function. It is on a minuscule level, making the effect unnoticeable initially. Gradually, victims see the little changes of memory lapse they attribute to normal aging. It is so perfect. No one suspects an agent destroying intellectual capacity.

"Cyclops reduces the capacity of the leaders of society. Without the intellectuals, your society will tumble out of First World status into decline. This brain drain has the same effect emigration had on all countries that persecuted their great thinkers, causing them to flee. Emigration of the intellectual elite resulted in the decline of societies and the emergence of new powers throughout history. The difference between the First and Third World nations is the number of intellectual elite and entrepreneurs able to thrive within their populations.

"The Japanese vengeance seekers' attack on the youth is even more insidious. Children play video games for hours on end, exposing themselves to the effects of these dangerous radio waves. This process destroys centers in the brain that produce chemical mediators needed for the feeling of well-being. With a depletion of these chemicals, the youth are experiencing an unprecedented amount of depression, resulting in serious effects, including an inability to learn and epidemic rates of dysfunction and suicidal behavior."

"There's no way you can be right about this. It's too huge, too complex for them to pull off," countered Derrick.

"That's why it's working so well. No one suspects it's happening. These people let their deranged desire for revenge drive them. They are from the same culture that advanced Kamikaze suicide raids. Honor is the core of their lives. To save face is vital to these people. You will have to trust me when I tell you they developed this plan and are enacting it with extreme precision. Only the most elite of their cult know about their mission. Remember, this isn't a government-sanctioned attack on the American people. It is well orchestrated and financed by a small group of powerful industrialists. The underlings, the people of Japan, are mere pawns in the project. They are building and exporting to America these stealth weapons of mass destruction with no idea they are participating."

"If you are right about this, why don't you let us defend ourselves by giving us the information we need? We could fight back," demanded Derrick.

"We cannot interfere in that fashion. There are too many events that interlink, and interference with anyone can result in untold catastrophe."

"What events are you referring to?" asked Derrick.

"I trust you know America is perceived as the devil in many countries of the Middle East. You and Miss Ambrose have knowledge of the prion studies conducted under the auspices of governments hostile to America. They already unleashed their infectious agents on your people in limited trials. The inordinate amount of violence you see in America is the result of this infection entering your population. It, too, spreads insidiously. In the unsuspecting, it could go undiscovered for decades. When authorities diagnose the problem, they will blame the natural forces of prions, mad-cow disease, with no knowledge that intentional inoculation destroyed them. That is, if your scientists still have the capacity to detect anything relevant after being diminished by the concurrent assault of the radio waves and the prion attack on their cognitive abilities."

During the last several minutes of the dissertation, Derrick experienced a noticeable loss of his ability to articulate his thoughts. Now, he needed tremendous effort to keep his intellectual competence whole. His speech slurred, and his vision became clouded. While he had no power over his ability to stand or move, he felt in control of his mental faculties until this moment.

"Why am I here? My specialty is drug prosecutions. If you expect information from me, you have the wrong person."

"Mr. Daniels, we are not here to get information from you. Your position now is to listen and learn.

"The drug smugglers your team tried to bring to justice are after you. They made the failed attempt on your life."

"How can that be? The CIA, they told me the type of incendiary bomb used was too advanced to be available to just anyone. They said it had to be . . . There's no way the drug dealers could have access to that technology," Derrick argued.

"Your agencies have gaps in their intelligence. The Colombian drug lords had one supreme goal over the last number of years. When they saw how effectively your agencies foiled their efforts at smuggling their drugs into America, they made a commitment to combat your interdiction at all cost. Their money did what they could never do alone. It bought them the incendiary technology needed to defeat you. Your recent attempt to thwart them in the International Courts would effectively shut them down. They couldn't let that happen, and you were one of the links in the chain they had to break. They are still looking for you. They are waiting for the right moment, and they will strike again.

"Their goal is total world domination, and while that sounds rather ambitious for a criminal enterprise, the very essence of drugs makes their goal obtainable. They want to create a world of slaves who do their bidding for access to their drugs. The addictive nature of drugs is the perfect vehicle to feed the users with anything from deadly poisons to agents of control. They have chosen to dominate by contaminating their drugs with various agents that cause loss of will. Their plan is brilliant. The victims are blind to the plot. Certain drugs induce a desire to do no more than exist bent over in a stupor. When they spike the drugs with a concentrated pharmaco-active agent producing the desired effect, only ten times stronger, they create zombies whose sole purpose is to get more drugs. No one expects the addict to do much more, so there is no investigation, just an inexplicable increase in the use of drugs blamed on unsolved social issues."

There was no specific threat spelled out for Derrick's welfare, but he felt agitated by an awareness he would not get his life back after hearing this tale. He began a violent struggle to free himself. The man adjusted the dials at his control panel, and within seconds Derrick had neither desire nor ability to craft the slightest attempt toward resistance.

Almost as if the old man read Derrick's mind, he addressed the very concerns causing the agitation.

"We have no reason to destroy you. To the contrary, we want you alive. It is not in our authority to intervene on an individual basis. Our protocol has always been to change things, but our means are protracted. Our way of controlling your evolution physiologically and behaviorally is through the genetic manipulation of your DNA. We use viral inoculants to insert the desired changes into your chemistry."

Derrick thought back to his conversations with the Rabbi and Dr. Kline. He remembered how they explained that viruses can cause cancer. He did not understand how anything he learned now fit into his puzzle, but the confused blocks of information seemed to build an interrelated template for life.

"The cancers, you cause them? It's you who feeds them to us?" asked Derrick.

"We put them in place, and it is you who feed them to your-selves. The dreaded diseases you call cancer are our way of selecting for various physical, intellectual, and behavioral traits. We gave you directions for working your way through the minefield of life, and yet people ignored the Law. There are reasons we need to modify and redirect your very essence, and that is one of the ways it is done. It is not instant, but it is effective to bring about the needed changes."

"You're talking about the Bible, aren't you? That's not fair. Everyone isn't a believer. How could you put so many at risk?"

"That is the purpose of The Chosen. The opportunity is there for all, but we explained it to the few who we directed to obey the laws, and to pass them on to others.

"Too many forgot or ignored the Laws. That's when we had to intervene. He used various means to repopulate isolated people from Gomorrah and other such places, but total annihilation of civilization came four times. The diluvian became the last time in your recorded history where the Maker had to start over. That is what you call the Big Flood. Several cultures that had the interest and capacity to make chronological note documented this event in their historical records. Geological excavation confirmed it to warn future generations.

"Plagues and fires and natural disasters today are never associated with the Creator as they were by primitive cultures. Now, everyone turns to science for explanations. However, there is a Supreme order to the Universe. It can never be understood my mortal men.

"As for your purpose, you have been chosen. You will lead your people back to repopulate the earth once His will is done."

"I believe you have the wrong guy. I'm not religious. I'm not a pious man. There is little I could do to help," argued Derrick.

"The mere fact you don't beg for the chance to survive, and you do not recognize your ability makes you one of the chosen. You will go back. You will wait until we complete our task, and then we will call upon your service.

"The waves generated here, and at centers all over the world, spread out to affect all of the humankind. These high-frequency magnetic waves produced by our gel fuel generators will destroy minds of the humankind everywhere.

"The lower animals in the path of our waves undergo suicidal transformation. Their minds, being primal, cannot survive the forces of our electromagnetic waves."

Derrick thought back to the roadkill he encountered along the road next to the cemetery. Everything the man told him seemed to explain occurrences that took place in his recent life.

"The most intelligent humankind shall be reduced to the capacity of the lower forms of life, where the ability to reason and understand mortality do not exist. The humankind of lower intelligence shall become utterly violent and destroy themselves and others in their paths."

"It sounds like you plan on turning us all into obedient pets," said Derrick.

"That's an excellent analogy. We will destroy all but the elemental IQ needed to function in the wild. *There will be lions and lambs among you. You will walk naked and have no shame.*"

Derrick saw that quote before in a religious book, but he could not remember where. The old man continued.

"The process you now call Alzheimer's disease will protect those like you. Your minds will lie dormant and become immune to the effects of destruction."

"What about all of the good people in the world? Certainly, you'll spare them?" pleaded Derrick.

"The Creator makes all determinations. He is the Supreme Judge, and we do not question His word. If He sees their worth, He will spare them, but He will destroy most.

"We have been forced to act sooner than planned because of the effect of the split waves and prions developed by your enemies. As a side effect of their assault, a number of your people are getting Alzheimer's who have not been chosen. As such, when we call upon you to repopulate the earth, you will find the new world will have those who do not belong. They will contaminate the purity of the new civilization. You must be vigilant in obeying the Laws and not let them subvert your efforts. They will be the non-believers found in every age. They will be as the snake of Eden, corruptor to Adam. Their influence must be crushed within the bounds of the Law."

"How will I know the corrupted ones?" asked Derrick.

"You cannot tell the quality of the individual by outside appearance. By their actions, you can tell. It will take time, but you will learn. You will be of the priestly sect. You will work with the other priests to lead. Then you will know. They are the Priests of Tzaraas. They are the marked ones. They will join with you to lead."

"I was told those so marked were afflicted," noted Derrick remembering Rabbi Barbar's description of the ancient plague.

"The ancients didn't understand. The marked ones were the true leaders who survived the last destruction. Just as you shall know your destiny, this knowledge is not to go beyond the priestly sect. There are things the masses should not know. Some things require faith.

"I pray your descendants will be fruitful and multiply."

Those were the last words Derrick heard before the spine-numbing jolt of pain passed throughout his body. He hoped to remember everything in his life that made sense after listening to this old man.

As his consciousness swooned, in the distance he saw a black hole. He began hurling toward the source of the darkness at tremendous speed.

# CHAPTER
# FIFTY-ONE

As rays of daylight elevated Derrick to consciousness, his eyelids fluttered. Not yet clear minded, the arousal caused a sense of confusion. Too weak to lift his head from the pillow, he blinked several times to sharpen his sight. Radiant sunlight peeked through the blinds and particles of dust, usually not noticed, danced about in clear view. Derrick felt secure. Goodness embraced his spirit. Nostalgic feelings associated with the simplicity of youth comforted him. He remembered how protected he felt waking up to a sunny day with the warmth of family present in the home. Days filled with love and adoration lived in his past.

Voices occupied the background, but initially, they went unnoticed as detached chatter. Once he regained waking faculties, a sudden realization interrupted his moment of refuge. The cemetery and his terrifying ordeal came to focus. He broke into a cold sweat as fear traded places with the sacred moment of serenity. Still under the remnant influence of slumber, he could not yet rise to see who sat in the room with him, though his thoughts emerged.

*My God! The old man, he told me . . . Davis, I have to find Joel! I have to warn them all. Poor Savannah, what will happen to her? They're doomed, all of them! I have to do something!*

"Yes, Dr. Klein. He has been sleeping much better than when they first found him. No longer restless. I'm so grateful you were able to stop by to check on his progress. They told me he might not be able to stay here if he didn't respond."

"You know I'm here for the two of you, anytime," replied Dr. Klein.

Derrick's mind cleared. His eyes focused, and he saw Savannah and Dr. Klein sitting by his side. He smiled, but was not yet ready to speak, though his thoughts continued to drift.

*Of course. It was all a dream. I can't believe how real it seemed, yet so outrageous. Thank you, God, for bringing me back from wherever my mind took me.*

Still too weak to get up from the bed, he lifted himself just enough to face Savannah and Dr. Klein. He blinked a few times to clear more film from his eyes.

"Look, Savannah, we have a visitor," said Dr. Klein in a friendly, childish way.

"I'm back. I'm back," said Derrick," lifting his voice calamitously in a shrill tone as he turned side to side waiting for acknowledgment .

Ignoring his outburst, Savannah spoke to him in a calm manner.

"Oh, darling, you're up. Dr. Klein came to see you."

"What's going on? Savannah, tell him what we have been through." Derrick spoke with desperation bordering on panic.

Looking weak and bewildered Derrick examined both visitors peculiarly. He remained silent while breathing heavy. Savannah looked at Dr. Klein and went on to explain.

"You can see what I was telling you. Gibberish. I can't understand a word he says. Before the tragedy overseas, he seemed fine. When we came back, everything changed. Having lost two attorneys on a foreign mission . . . that is just not supposed to happen. They assured our safety before we went. The whole thing sent him into a darkness of sorts. I don't know."

Derrick, now more agitated, sat up and swallowed repeatedly as he tried to speak. Dryness in his throat produced a grotesque stridor, but no words.

"Is he okay?" asked Dr. Klein.

"That passes and soon he'll settle down."

"Well, I do remember reading about those Justice Department disappearances. Did he know the others well?" asked Dr. Klein.

"Two were office friends. They consulted with one another about their cases, but he didn't spend time with them socially."

Derrick gulped one more swallow to find his voice and yelled at them.

"What do you mean? They died in the field. They are now after both of us. Did you forget? Are you out of your mind? Why are you acting like we didn't know the others?"

Exhausted from this outburst, Derrick fell back to a supine position and panted.

"He gets this way. It passes. See, he's quiet now," said Savannah.

"How about the coworker found on the street the place they found Derrick, were they close?" Dr. Kline offered a look that warranted explanation.

"Derrick's odd behavior started when we became targets. I can't speak to that other than saying Derrick was being hunted and the pressure got to him," Savannah offered reluctantly

"He became somewhat despondent. I told him to see you, but he refused. Instead, he kept obsessing about the plots and these people out to get us. He kept referring to the cemetery down the road. The one where they found his friend half-dead and Derrick wander along the roadside."

Dr. Kline pursed his lips, and his brow frowned in contemplation. "It sounds like Derick experienced a form of psychotic reaction. These things can take you to another dimension that seems so real. He may have entered into this foreign world and got stuck there. Now the psychosis could have left him in this condition," Dr. Kline explained.

Animated once again, Derrick spoke, but in spite of a vain attempt to be clear, his words remained nonsense to the others.

"You won't believe the experience I had," said Derrick, seeming to have forgotten his previous outburst . "It was terrible. I uncovered a plot to destroy all of humanity by an advanced underground culture. They told me all about our enemies and their plots against us."

Not able to connect with the reality of the situation, Derrick directed his words to Savannah.

"It seemed so real. If I can just remember it all. I have to tell you. Maybe if I write it down. Everything . . . he explained everything. Maybe it was a dream. It doesn't matter. Now I know . . . all of the mystery behind our investigations. Maybe it was a premonition, but now I understand everything. The information can save us."

"That's about it," said Savannah turning to Dr. Klein. "When he's not in a fetal position sleeping, he talks a little here and a little there, but it's all gibberish. He has these outbursts and then calms down. All a bunch of gibberish."

"Gibberish?" Derrick protested.

Ignoring Derrick's incoherence, Dr. Klein spoke.

"It's such a pity to see a brilliant mind fail. He came in and asked these questions that, at first, had me thinking he was a paranoid cancer phobic. After some thought, I couldn't believe the depth of the issues he raised. I've come to look at medicine and my own personal spirituality in a new light. He had a brilliant mind."

"Is there any chance he'll get some of it back?" asked Savannah as tears blurred her eyes.

"What are you two talking about?' clamored Derrick. "My mind is *perfect*. I'm fine. Besides, I now know things that make my earlier questions pale in comparison. Savannah, we were in this together. Dr. Klein, I have answers. You just have to listen to me. I can explain."

They heard him speak, but his words remained unintelligible.

"That's not how this disease works, Savannah. Even if we came up with a cure today, the destruction already done is likely irreversible," explained Dr. Klein.

"No, you're wrong," Derrick challenged. "It *is* reversible. He *told* me it's reversible. When they call upon us to lead, that's when you'll understand me."

"Does he go on like this all day?" asked Dr. Klein, referring to Derrick's incessant attempt to communicate his thoughts.

"This is the first day since they found him that he's spoken so much. In the beginning, he just slept a lot. Then a few words here and there. At Penn, the doctor examined him and said his brain is gradually being destroyed. He told me, in time, I would find it too burdensome to care for Derrick. He said in time I'd have to have him institutionalized," whispered Savannah as if Derrick would perhaps understand.

"Who was that?" asked Dr. Klein.

"A Dr. Affelbaum, I can't remember his first name."

"Peter. I believe it's Peter," suggested Dr. Klein.

"I believe you're right," said Savannah. "He was a very nice fellow. He offered to take Derrick anytime I felt the need. He said the clinic there is a wonderful facility. They are doing some of the world's leading research on this terrible disease. Maybe there is hope for the future."

# ABOUT THE AUTHOR

Dr. Robert M. Fleisher holds a BA in psychology and DMD with a specialty in endodontics. Engaged in writing for the past forty-five years, he has written for professional journals as well as having produced several non-fiction books. *The Divine Affliction* is his first novel and seventh published book. Dr. Fleisher looks forward to telling his stories to an audience interested in difficult subjects. He is an active member of International Thriller Writers.

facebook.com/robert.fleisher.908
x.com/DoctorRobert5
instagram.com/robertmfleisher

www.ingramcontent.com/pod-product-compliance
Lightning Source LLC
Chambersburg PA
CBHW030521120726

47904CB00005B/1566